The Honor of Peter Kramer

Augusto Ferrera

The Honor of Peter Kramer

BART

NEW YORK

Reprinted by arrangement with Dodd, Mead & Co., Inc.

ISBN: 1-55785-047-X

First Bart Books edition: 1988

Bart Books
155 E. 34th Street
New York, New York 10016

Manufactured in the United States of America

Out of Hitler's war of nihilism names emerged that have since been placed in the honor rolls of history—Raoul Wallenberg, Oskar Schindler, and more.

Yet, there were others who also acted in the name of decency. All over Nazi-occupied Europe, they were there, those nameless heroes. Even in Germany—especially in Germany—that most dangerous of secret arenas of courage, these anonymous men and women risked their lives upholding the dignity of life.

It is these, the unnamed, unheralded ones, the Righteous Gentiles, to whom I dedicate this book.

The Honor of Peter Kramer

PROLOGUE

MONTAFON VALLEY, WESTERN AUSTRIA

THE PRESENT

The fat man looks out the window of the chalet and gazes up at a sky that has turned sullen. Clouds have blocked out the late-summer wash of warming sunshine, and soon the entire valley and the tiny villages nestled within it will be erased from view. The fat man clucks in grim foreboding, not at the sudden inclemency of weather, but at the problem at hand.

The fat man is Heinz Langfeldt, doctor of economics and king-pin of Swiss banking. Of more import, he heads an association that controls the world's wealth, its politics, indeed its destiny. It could be called a cartel; its members know it as the Montafon Group, named after the place in which they meet periodically, and, as now, in emergency. The nature of the emergency is a set of circumstances that may shift the delicate political axis of the globe, bringing it to the brink of destruction.

Langfeldt's troubled eyes drift down from the moody sky to the black strip of roadway below and a mile away. A car appears for a moment as it glides up the narrow road, then it disappears from view. It will be the last of the participants to the meeting he has called; the other six are there already, by the fire, some of them, drinking tea with rum, impatient for the extraordinary meeting to begin.

Extraordinary. Yes, he concludes, that says it well.

They will meet today not to discuss the Vatican portfolio one of them controls, not to talk about the Texas pipelines and Saudi Arabian oil revenues two others are responsible for, not the multinational marine insurance assets another has a grip on, not Latin American banking conglomerates, not even covert Mafia investments. No, they will review the options of only one problem—the unbalanced mind of Simon Bolivar Jensen, President of the United States.

WASHINGTON, D.C.

THE PRESENT

Peter Kramer thought of the lower jaw of Martin Bormann for the thousandth time since its discovery. He stood alone on the terrace of the British Embassy sipping champagne, oblivious to the strains of a popular song being played by a string quartet and the din of hundreds of voices in dozens of languages. That jaw was occupying his waking moments—and sometimes his sleeping ones—more and more of late, especially because of the constant, almost nagging reminders by Erika. Erika the worrier, Erika the paranoid. Erika his beloved.

He lifted the glass to his lips and again visualized a German laborer in blue trousers and jacket, heavy shoes, and a blue peaked cap, boredly digging in that field of rubble in Berlin once known as the Invalidenstrasse, striking with his spade what he thought was a stone and then, to his gruesome amazement, discovering that it was a jawbone. They said it was Bormann's. But was it? He had argued time and again with Erika that it *was* Borman's. And yet, his instincts told him, maybe it was not.

A high-pitched rapsy voice with a trace of an accent broke his spell. "Are you that bored with all this, Peter, or are you scheming your next strategy for the Cairo meeting?"

Kramer turned and saw the cheery face of Aleksandr Korsakov, the Soviet ambassador. He smiled at the Russian, a smile that came from an open, honest face that most people liked immediately. "Hello, Aleksandr Sergeievitch. No, no strategy planning; my part in the treaty is over. I'd like to get back to my work at the university, which, by the way, is what I was thinking of. All those theses I've got to grade—I can't put it off any longer."

Korsakov grinned wryly. "From the ridiculous back to the sublime, eh, Peter? I would be willing to bet you a case of the best Russian vodka against one bottle of Scotch whiskey that your days as a university professor are a thing of the past, at least with Jensen in the White House. They won't let you go, my friend. There is no one else who can make the peace accord a reality, and that includes Jackson Hetherington *and* Simon Bolivar Jensen. That is what the diplomatic community says, and I happen to agree."

"Well, the diplomatic community is wrong, as usual. This President is committed to peace. Hetherington and his people are superbly qualified." Kramer took a cigarette offered by Korsakov and reached for his lighter.

The Russian blew smoke. "Thank you. Just between you and me, Peter, I hate Russian tobacco, but for appearances I have to smoke it at the embassy. Moscow expects me to set a good example!" He inhaled the Winston deeply and smiled in satisfaction. He turned serious. "No, Peter, you will get the call once more. You'll see, my friend."

"Yes, well, we'll see," Kramer said, looking back out toward the wooded gardens. "Besides, Aleksandr, why should you care? I should think the Kremlin would love to see me fall on my face. I don't think you people are very anxious for an Arab-Israeli peace, are you?"

Korsakov moved closer and looked around them. "Peter, I tell you this from the heart," he said, placing his hand on his breast. "For my part, I want you to succeed. Frankly, I like it here in America. I like your cigarettes, your liquor, your thick steaks, your women! I'd be a hypocrite if I said I didn't like my job. But that job depends on a cold war, not a hot one. However, if you don't make peace in the Middle East, that madman in Libya will do something to make the United States step in. If that happens, maybe we'll have to step in, too, and then we'll have a hot war that will end my splendid job here—and the rest of the world as well."

"You reduce it all to such simple terms," Kramer said. "Is this your own view of things, or does the Kremlin see it that way, too?"

"I don't blame you for being cynical, Peter. The fact is, there are cliques of hotheads and nuclear theorists in the Kremlin—such as you have in your own Pentagon—who want to hit the button before Jensen hits it, no matter what the consequences. But we also have men of reason, thank God, who know that the world can go on as it has for the past few decades despite all the inflammatory rhetoric and name-calling and saber-rattling. The cold war, my friend, it must go on. It's healthy. Like in a lightning storm, if you can hear the thunder, you're okay. In the cold war, if you can hear the sabers rattling, you're okay. It's the silence that is deadly. That's why you must make peace in the Middle East." Korsakov, who had spent more years in the United States than in his own country, first as a journalist, then as a diplomat, smiled at Kramer as he inhaled his American cigarette smoke, pleased with his own assessment.

Kramer drained his glass silently. If only he could be sure of that jaw, he thought. Erika was right—the stakes were too high to take further chances with the ghosts of the past. Korsakov was right, too, in everything he said—and those stakes would be the highest of all.

"Ah, Peter, there you are!" It was Jackson Hetherington, looking the complete diplomat in his white tie and tails, a small line of miniature medals adorning his silk lapel.

"Watch out for these Russians," the secretary of state said, glancing at Korsakov. "They get more clever with age, especially this one. He and I go back to Yalta, don't we, Aleksandr Sergeievitch?"

"Ah, the bad old days, Jack. Did you know I was on Stalin's shit list? I managed to hide under Molotov's skirt, and that saved me from the purge. I'm a survivor, as I was telling Peter."

"Thank God for Molotov," Hetherington said.

"Please, Jack, we Communists do not acknowledge the existence of God."

"But Alex," Kramer said, smiling, "a minute ago you said, 'Thank God we have men of reason in the Kremlin,' didn't you?"

"Yes, but that was unofficially!"

Korsakov walked away to the sound of laughter, exhaling smoke from yet another Winston.

Hetherington turned to Kramer. "Peter, the reason I'm late here is due to good news. I just heard from Leslie Pyle in Damascus. The Syrians have agreed to your five points. Leslie tells me they're ready to be nailed down. Naturally, I passed on the news to the President. He wants a meeting with you and me right away, so let's bid our *adieu*s quickly and get over to the White House." The secretary was beaming with enthusiasm. The Syrian delegation had been an obstacle all along, beginning with President Haddad.

Kramer sighed inwardly. He wondered how he could have been so naive as to think that it was over for him. "That's wonderful news, Mr. Secretary."

A few minutes later Secretary of State Hetherington and Special Ambassador Peter Kramer were being escorted through the Treaty Room in the executive wing of the White House. An aide opened the sliding doors to the President's study, the Oval Office. The overwhelming blue carpet and its huge presidential seal dominated the room. Seated behind his massive desk, with the national and presidential standards behind him, was Simon Bolivar Jensen—lean, virile, handsome. With athletic smoothness he rose and indicated a suite of upholstered chairs around a coffee table.

"Thanks for coming, fellows," Jensen said. "I hated to pull you away from your party, but now that the Syrians are playing ball, it's important that we maintain game control. We've got to get over there now."

"I couldn't agree with you more, Mr. President," the secretary said, taking the cup of coffee offered from the three Jensen poured from a silver service. "The Syrians tend to be prima donnas in this. They change their minds over the slightest issue."

"Yeah, that's my feeling," Jensen said. He looked at Kramer. "Do you see it that way, too, Pete?"

"I agree that Haddad is a bit capricious," Kramer said, "but we mustn't lose sight that he is a Sunnite Ba'thist. He will not want to disappoint his fellow Sunnite and Ba'thist Party supporter, Kämil. Especially in view of the political risks Kämil has taken for Haddad with the Copts and the Circassians in Egypt. Kämil is in full accord with the necessity of a treaty. He'll keep Haddad in line. There should be no problems with him, as I see it."

Hetherington wagged his finger. "Astute analysis! That certainly validates your insistence, Mr. President, that Peter Kramer, and no one else, carry the ball, as you put it, sir." Turning to Kramer, he said, "Can you leave in the morning for Cairo, Peter?"

Kramer bit his lip. "That would be most difficult, Mr. Secretary. I've neglected my work at the university far longer than I originally expected. That, and other reasons. As I understood it, aside from occasional consultations, my work with the treaty would be terminated by now." He looked at the President's stony face.

"What other reasons?" asked the President coolly.

"Personal ones, Mr. President."

"Come now, Peter," Hetherington said. "The university will surely understand the import—"

Jensen cut off the secretary with a wave of his hand. "Ambassador Kramer," he said in measured tones, "as you know, this administration is committed to two major goals, goals that got me elected. First, a sound economy, and second, global peace. In the three years and eight months that I've been in office, the first of these two promises, these two goals, is well on its way. But I still can't deliver a balanced budget; for that I need another four years in this place."

"Yes, sir," Kramer said, looking at the handsome and youthful President. He was right; he *was* well on his way. With the help of a cooperative Congress, the charismatic Jensen had put through some sweeping and revolutionary economic legislation. Jensen's policies had also changed the image of the United States around the world. Ambassadors, normally wealthy appointees under political patronage, were now taken from the rolls of lifetime foreign service officers, men and women who not only spoke the language of the country of assignment but were sensitive to the customs, culture, and needs of those countries. Gone were the flashy limousines for the high echelon of the foreign service that did nothing but provoke ill will toward the United States. Gone too were the uniformed and armed Marine guards at the missions abroad; security personnel were now inconspicuous in their civilian clothes. Jensen's idea was to promote diplomacy overseas, not militarism. Underdeveloped nations were beginning to progress through the help of the Jensen-revitalized Peace Corps, in which nations helped themselves while maintaining their dignity. Global peace was another matter; the Arab-Israeli peace accord was a giant step, however.

"The most important of these goals," Jensen continued, "is world peace. Oh, I don't mean we're going to stop every little war that erupts here and there. I mean peace between the big powers, nuclear peace. And that means disarmament. But first, we must defuse that powder keg, the Middle East, and more important, keep it

5

defused. The only way to do that is with me in the White House for another four years. That fellow they're running against me in November isn't going to do it, that's for sure. Not the way he looks at the Russian thing. My relations with the Russians are the best of any president since FDR. Maybe better, 'cause Joe Stalin walked all over Roosevelt. Anyway, I need those four years, and the peace treaty will get them for me. We've got to get those fellows to Geneva and sign the damned thing before November." Simon Jensen looked directly at Kramer. "Well, Ambassador Kramer, now that I've told you where I place my priorities, where do you place yours?"

The question was forceful, the tone sharp. Under the circumstances, Kramer didn't blame Jensen for using such words. What he didn't understand, however, was the President's cold demeanor ever since the start of the meeting. It wasn't like him; something had changed in their normally warm relationship.

"Mr. President, please be assured that I am totally committed to the goals of this administration, especially as regards the peace accord. As to my . . . reluctance, perhaps I should have been somewhat more candid with you. Aside from my excuses about getting back to my work, I should have told you that I feel, well, inadequate in these stages of the treaty. I recognize the susceptibilities of the accord, and because I consider myself more a theorist than a diplomat, I felt it would be best handled by the vast experience of the secretary of state. I hope you understand, sir."

"With your permission, Mr. President, I should like to respond to that," Hetherington said, turning to Kramer. "It's very kind of you to say that, Peter. However, the assessment of your capabilities, while modest and even humble, is inaccurate. All along, you have adroitly handled the trickiest issues with these most difficult participants in the peace process. You have wisely and judiciously negotiated provisions that had been judged impossible, given the history of both sides. That is true diplomacy. Your book is recognized as the objective viewpoint of one of the most emotional issues of this century, a viewpoint with which few can argue, and that includes the combatants about whom you write, all of whom read and respect your book. No, Peter, I judge you are by far the best qualified to successfully conclude the treaty."

The book Hetherington referred to was Kramer's thesis, *Abraham/Ibrahim—Semite vs. Semite*, a study of the crises in which the

Arabs and Jews had been embroiled for most of the twentieth century, with an in-depth historical and political view of those two peoples; the denouement of the work showed the ethnic and religious parallels. It was the book that had brought Kramer to the attention of the State Department and, ultimately, to Simon Jensen.

"All right, I agree with Jack," the President said with a touch of impatience. "Are you with me, Pete?" The tone, the look in his eyes, the tenseness of his body said the unspoken words: *If you're not with me, you're against me.*

So. In effect, it was a presidential order. Erika would understand. She would have to understand.

"I'm with you, Mr. President."

"Splendid!" Jackson Hetherington said.

Jensen said, "Okay, let's close this now and get on to other things. Let's look at the game plan once more."

Details relative to the U.S. position in the United Nations peace-keeping forces were gone over, together with other items of importance to American interests. Finally, close to midnight, Kramer was dismissed.

Simon Jensen sat looking at the door through which Kramer had left. "What's his game, Jack?" he asked.

The secretary smiled his confusion at the question. "I'm afraid I don't understand, Mr. President."

"Kramer. What's he after? Anyone else would've offered his balls on a platter for the chance he's getting, and he's playing hard to get. What's he after?"

Hetherington frowned deeply. "The question perplexes me, sir. I don't know that he's after anything other than trying to do the best job possible for us—and for you."

"I know that's what it looks like, Jack, but there's something that bothers me right here," Jensen said, patting his belly. "It's as if by downplaying his ability, we'll tell him how good he really is, and then we'll tell the world how good he is, and suddenly the whole thing'll be his ball game, not ours. See what I mean?"

Hetherington rose wearily from his chair. Deep in thought, he paced near the President's desk. He stopped squarely atop the large presidential seal woven into the carpet, as if to gain insight by its very symbol. He straightened his bow tie, which did not need straightening, and looked at Jensen.

"Mr. President," he began, "I don't know what to say other than to express in the strongest manner that I disagree with your statements. I have the utmost confidence in Peter Kramer, in his character, in his honor, and above all in his loyalty to you. Further, I would ask you—with due respect, of course—why, if you have even the slightest doubt about Kramer, sir, do you entrust him with this most delicate mission? Delicate to world peace and to you?"

"I'm doubting only his motives, Jack, not him," Jensen said dryly. "Besides, the Israelis like him, especially Ben-David. But you can bet I'll watch him."

Hetherington shook his balding, freckled head.

"You're also a little naive, Jack," the President said sharply. Then, in softer words, "Your problem is that you're too much of a gentleman. I'm a street fighter. You've got to be suspicious with these Krauts. I know what they are. Remember, I fought them in the war."

The secretary looked up slowly. "Did you say Kraut? Peter Kramer is Swiss, Mr. President!"

"Yeah, I know. Swiss, Austrian, German—they all have the same Teutonic mentality. When you come down to it, Jack, they're all Krauts."

Jackson Hetherington, in overcoat, scarf, and hat, walked to his waiting limousine. His shoulders slumped more than normal that evening. He thought of this President and of other presidents whom he had served since his days as a whiz kid in the Roosevelt Administration. He knew that this President had done more, had been more effective at home and abroad, than any other since Roosevelt. Yet this President was the most enigmatic of all. As he settled into the back seat of the car, he remembered Winston Churchill's words describing the Soviet Union: "a riddle wrapped in a mystery inside an enigma." That too described this President. This President worried him, and he didn't know why.

Simon Jensen worried Peter Kramer, too. And like the secretary of state, he didn't know why. That, and having to face Erika, accounted for his moroseness and anxiety as he gently closed the garage door and walked into the kitchen of their Georgetown house.

"Hello," he said softly to Erika, who was preparing hot chocolate.

8

"Hello," she said. "How did everything go?"

"Boring, as usual. It's just as well you didn't come." He tried to measure her mood. "Also, Hetherington came and got me out of there for a meeting with Jensen. I've just come from the White House. The President sends regards."

Erika looked at her husband for a moment. Then she asked, "Did you eat? Would you like something? Some hot chocolate?"

He knew it was her way of putting off what she didn't want to hear. "No, thank you," he said.

She sipped chocolate and said to the window, "They want you to go to Cairo." She spoke calmly, quietly.

"Yes," he whispered.

"And of course you're going."

"I must."

Erika crashed her cup down on the counter, chocolate spilling from it. "You promised!" she said in German.

"I promised to resist, which I did. Believe me, I did. But it was no use. Jensen, Hetherington—they explained the gravity of it—it's critical. It means so much—I can't back out now. Please try to understand."

"Oh, but I do understand, Hans-Dieter! You're telling me it's your duty, but I say it's your ego! All along it's been that—your monumental ego—hasn't it? They gave you impressive titles—what are you called? Special Assistant to the President, with offices in the White House and your own staff? Special Ambassador?"

"Please, Erika." She had called him Hans-Dieter. She never called him by his assumed name when passions were high. Hans-Dieter was the name by which she loved him—and by which she hated him.

"Oh, yes," she went on with even more irony in her voice, "let's not forget that what was once known as the Jensen Initiative is now called the Kramer Plan. Well, my dear, you can't say that these wonderful things deflated your ego!"

"The press came up with that. You know their penchant for the dramatic." Yet he knew she was right. He *did* enjoy the attention, the admiration.

"Exactly!" Erika said. "The press is interested in everything you do, and yet you keep tempting fate!"

He was about to argue his case in anger. But instead he looked at her with eyes filled with love. She must have felt the wave of affection, for her eyes softened, too. He put his hands on her shoulders. "Erika," he said tenderly, "first, I want you to know that I love you more than ever. Second, I ask you not to worry. Nothing will happen."

"But your picture, it was in that magazine!" Her anger was now transformed to simple worry.

"That was more than three months ago. We would've heard by now if anything . . . Besides, they're all dead."

"But what if—"

"What if! What if!" he chided her gently. "We can't play the 'what if' game all our lives. We can't change what happened; we can only try to make it right." He put his arms around her and held her closely.

"*Hans-Dieter,*" she whispered, "*ich ängstige mich so!*"

"*Ja,*" he said, "*und ich liebe dich so!*"

EN ROUTE TO PARIS

THE PRESENT

The President of Egypt, Abderrahim Kämil, kissed Peter Kramer on each cheek, black bristles slightly stinging his face. They gripped each other's hands tightly, each man aware of the momentous event that was on the verge of becoming a reality. Kramer shook hands quickly with the foreign minister and the others and just as quickly boarded the State Department Boeing 707 that would take him to Paris.

Minutes later, Kramer gazed at the Mediterranean as the plane climbed. The sea shimmered in tones of blue and green in the bright sun of history. Here and there he saw the unique sails of a xebec or some other ancient fishing boat, its occupants oblivious to everything but their harvest. For a moment, he envied the fishermen below the simplicity of their lives.

The tinkle of ice in a glass placed in front of him brought him back to the reality of the trip to Cairo. He sipped the gin and tonic, thinking that things had gone quite well this time and that the road to Geneva was paved with optimism. Or as the President had put it that morning on the phone, it was "first and goal on the one-yard line." Kramer still hadn't learned many of the sports-oriented analogies that President Jensen was so fond of using, but that one was clear—it *was* first and goal. And he, Peter Kramer, had quarterbacked the drive.

The protocols had been drawn; minor points had been renegotiated, rewritten; in phone calls with Shaban in Jerusalem the foreign minister had approved some issues. Then, barring unforeseen hitches, and with the advice and consent of the President of the United States and the Chairman of the Presidium of the Supreme Soviet, an accord would be signed and ratified by the heads of state of Egypt, Jordan, Syria, Lebanon, Qatar, Saudi Arabia, and the State of Israel.

The Palestine Liberation Organization had agreed to attend the signing as a Most Interested Spectator, although not enthusiastically. Kramer had agreed that its leader, Shaffir Mahamet, would address the assembly in Geneva for the benefit of Mahamet's image with the Palestinians. It would be a speech not condemning the accord, but not fully approving it, either, because of the impasse of the Left Bank. It was a compromise. It was in such compromises that Peter Kramer excelled and with which his star had risen so high. He was cornered once at a diplomatic reception by Korsakov. "Peter, I don't know what you are doing exactly," he had said in admiration, "but it must be right." To which Kramer had responded, "Aleksandr Sergeievitch, I simply recognize that every coin, whether shekel or dinar, has two sides."

Kramer sipped the drink; it tasted like lemonade. He rang for the steward and ordered more gin. He felt a wave of general discomfort, but he dismissed it as a slight hangover from the previous night's banquet, in which Kämil had presented him with a medal, the Grand Order of the Nile, for his "indefatigable and unswerving friendship to Egypt and the cause of peace."

But Peter Kramer knew, deep inside, that the discomfort, now in the form of a swarm of butterflies in his lower intestine, was for another reason: the prospect of being once again in Paris.

He massaged his abdomen and tried to think of his meeting there with Jackson Hetherington, for that was the purpose of this leg of the trip. The butterflies were now a blizzard as he tried not to think of another Paris. Paris, and the beautiful memories . . . Paris, and the horrible memories. He had not been back since then. The pain in the recollections was too great.

Kramer looked absently at the Cyclades below, interrupting the sea of Phoenicia and Hellas. He removed a velvet box from his pocket and opened it. The elaborate medal nestled in silk. He fingered it, staring bemusedly at the Mediterranean, and remembered another medal. . . .

The Knights Cross—a cross that, in its simple and unrelenting lines, had at one time symbolized heroism. He tried to remember the causes surrounding his being awarded that cross, but he had long ago allowed them to fade from his memory. Not even the sounds of the churning of tank treads and the thunderous clanking of the big gun of the Panther came through with fidelity. Then, as if waiting confidently for its chance, Kramer's olfactory memory went into service. Taste or smell something connected with certain events, and those happenings—and the players—come back clearly, even if it was decades ago, as if they had happened yesterday. Now, the memory brought back the smell of burnt powder, gunpowder, and with that everything else came back.

Fresh cement and paint and waxes. Those were the smells of the new Reich Chancellery as he walked down its long halls to receive the medal. It also smelled of power, he remembered now. Fresh cement, paint, and power. He felt uneasy with these sudden and easy rembrances. He thought briefly of turning it all off, but the wheels of memory were turning now, so he went on, allowing that day in April 1941, to live again within him for the first time in aeons. . . . Ah, yes, now he heard the sounds of the place, the sounds of polished boots on polished marble. Soon those sounds transformed themselves into words—Reichsminister This, Gauleiter That, Reichssecretär So-and-So. He could not recall conversations, not even bits of them, but what he did remember was a word—a phrase, in fact—but the words seemed to have run together so that they sounded as one, and it came out *derführer*. That appeared to be their common interest, these men of the polished boots and armbands: *derführer*.

He continued the powerful exercise, and he brought back the aroma of cedar, which he attributed to . . . yes, to Himmler. Heinrich Himmler smelled of cedar, and Peter at once felt the limp handshake, and he could see moths and other things dying around this Himmler. And then . . . oh, yes, the dill. At the thought of dill the face of Heydrich was suddenly there. But he was getting ahead of himself. That was later, at lunch. Reinhard Heydrich was the dill at lunch.

The others, however—the faceless ones with their armbands and leather belts and gold braid—they as a group might have had an odor if collective fear smelled. If fawning, groveling, cringing, and ass-licking smelled, they would clearly have smelled of these things. But he could not recall it, and for that he was grateful. No, he could only *see* their fear and the salty sweat under which the cloth frayed, the leather cracked, and the braid tarnished. And he could see even then, even though the awe-struck eyes of his youth, that their common terror was induced by their beloved *derführer* and that they did not deserve to wear the uniform, but they did.

Suddenly, the scene, so much alive an instant before, became nebulous and hazy. Everything lost definition. Everything except the gray-blue eyes of *him,* who stared balefully and with piercing, silent eyes as he draped the cross over his shoulders, and now, as much as he tried to recall a scent, an odor, there was none. He could smell the others and those days, those times, but he could not recall the scent of *him,* and he wondered if perhaps his olfactory plexus tried— kindly but naively—to erase all memories of him, as if without a scent, he had never existed, had never been. But he had existed, and the world was not the same for it. Nor would it ever be again.

He shook his head, trying to clear it of the images conjured up by the smells, but he still had one more to deal with: the dill. Actually, it had been boiled beef in dill sauce, a specialty of the Bristol Hotel, Berlin. And with that, he thought of the devil. Or, more correctly, of Reinhard Heydrich. Oh, Heydrich didn't smell of dill; he smelled of Havana cigars and Spanish brandy. But ever since that April day, every time he was near the stuff, he would remember the devil. It wasn't so much the taste of it, he remembered now, but when the devil ordered him—after cajoling ("Bergdorf, you'd be perfect for Paris, what with your title and your breeding. . . .") and bribing ("I'll promote you two ranks, Colonel Bergdorf, and you'll be the youngest general in the SS. . . .") and pressing (". . . and you'll find out who the consipirators are that want to murder the Führer!") and threatening ("You don't think, after I told you all this, that I'm going to let you go, do you? Damn you, Bergdorf, I'm ordering you to Paris!")—commanded him to go to Paris under the falsest of pretenses, the dill sauce came up in his throat and it tasted sour and he almost vomited.

Peter Kramer wiped his forehead. Now it was all coming back, but this time he was allowing it to come back and he thought of that beautiful spring day . . . when it all began.

VIENNA

SPRING 1941

Erika Schuler hurried down the gleaming corridors of the Maria Hilfer Allgemeine Krankenhaus, Vienna's general hospital. She was finished with her training, and she was anxious to get back home for a rest before starting her practice in the little mountain community in the Carpathians, not far from her hometown of Bistritz. The good-byes at her farewell tea party had been tearful, and she felt somewhat sad and let down. But when she walked out, the noon sun smiled on her.

She accepted the welcome of the sun like an old friend rediscovered, and as she queued up at the tram stop to wait for the trolley that would take her to the house of Professor Baumgartner, she felt better in its warmth.

Doktor-Medizin Erika Elisabeth Schuler. She silently mouthed the impressive title that she had worked so long and hard for. She owed it to Professor Baumgartner. He had done much for her in his role of sponsoring professor and surrogate father. He had been absent from her going-away tea—illness, they were told—so now, Erika would go to see him for their farewells. Doktor-Medizin Erika Schuler, she said again.

The sun, as though itself tired of waiting, suddenly left. The sky turned gray, and a fine mid-Continental drizzle started to fall. All at once Vienna became a sea of black umbrellas, and the *Gemütlichkeit* born by the sun gave way to to somberness. The fading pearl that was wartime Vienna lost a little more of its slowly fading luster.

The trolley came, and Erika was pushed into it with the crowd. That was normal; Viennese charm and chivalry disappeared quickly in the vicinity of a streetcar. She found a window seat; soon the unique smells of damp loden wool were present, together with the unseemly odor of wet newsprint as passengers opened the afternoon editions to read about the latest German advances. She looked out the window and noticed the shining wet nave of St. Stephan's and its sharp, angular designs, and she thought of Hans-Dieter. . . .

She remembered that lovely Sunday morning when her sister, Trudi, and Trudi's husband, Hans-Dieter, had visited her, and they had attended High Mass at St. Stephan's. She still heard the voices of the boy sopranos in the Bach Magnificat, and the thundering chords of the great organ still reverberated in her memory's ear. Those were safe remembrances for Erika Schuler; those memories she permitted. What she would not allow herself was the memory of Hans-Dieter's touch—his leg against hers in the pew, his scent, his look. Those things were not permitted into her consciousness, but they were there nonetheless, indelibly etched in her heart. There was another feeling, too, the most forbidden potential thought of all, the feeling that had been with her ever since she could remember having a heart. That emotion—a sensitivity that was as much her as the blue of her eyes—was that she was deeply in love with him.

Erika got off the tram at the Klempner Gasse and walked toward the Baumgartner house. She pictured Frau Baumgartner serving tea and Dobos torte. That scene vanished from her mind when she saw a large crowd of ordinary-looking citizens across the street from the professor's elegant three-story house. There were groups of two or three men in brown shirts and swastika armbands standing in the middle of the treelined cobblestone street, their brown boots spotted by the light rain.

Erika noticed a pleasant-looking hausfrau holding a child by one hand and a net shopping bag in the other. "What's going on?" she asked the woman.

"They're taking the Jews," the woman said flatly.

What did she mean, this hausfrau! Baumgartner is a professor!

One just doesn't "take" a professor of a major university!

She grabbed the woman's sleeve. "What do you mean, 'taking them'?" Her voice was demanding, as if the woman were responsible for the infamy she reported.

"Look, lady," the woman said, pulling away from Erika's grasp, "I don't know. I heard someone say they're being shipped to Palestine or somewhere in Africa." She paused. "Of course, there is also talk about the Wienerwald. You know, taken there and shot. I don't know. Why don't you ask them?" She motioned with her head in the direction of the SS men in the brown shirts and ski caps and swastikas and death's heads and truncheons and fists and snarls in the light rain . . . on the Klempner Gasse in Vienna.

Erika hurried wide-eyed across the street and rang Baumgartner's bell. She looked at the SS men, who stared back in a mixture of amusement and contempt. She tried the door; it was open.

"Professor Baumgartner," she called out uneasily, "it's me, Erika. Erika Schuler."

"Erika! Come up, my dear," Frau Baumgartner said.

Erika ran up the small flight of steps into the living room. The professor and his wife and daughter were frantically packing. He was wrapping a china figurine, looking out the window at the scene below.

"Herr Professor, they told me you were ill, so I—"

"Ah, Erika! How sweet you are, my child! I'm all right, as you can see. But we must hurry with the packing."

"Why? Where are you going?"

"They're letting us go, Erika. We must leave Austria. The Greater German Reich, is how they put it. We are Jews, you see. But don't worry, my dear, we're the lucky ones. We're going to Cuba, Erika!" He wrapped furiously. "I have a cousin in Cuba, Jacobo Grynspan," he said, pronouncing the name with a Spanish accent and a flourish of his arm, smiling proudly. "We're the lucky ones!"

"What will you do in Cuba?" Erika was close to tears.

"Work, what else? I'll find work, you'll see. And maybe someday, who knows? Perhaps I can teach again." The professor stopped wrapping for a few seconds, deep in thought, then quickly started packing again.

There was a pounding on the door below, then the sound of the door opening hard against the wall. Heavy boots were coming up the stairs. Two uniformed men entered; they had pistols in black holsters on their belts.

The shorter of the two, pasty-faced with steel-rimmed glasses on a puggish nose, shouted, "Why are you taking so long? You, Papa, what are you wrapping there? You are allowed only ten kilos each. Let me see." Pugnose tore off the tissue paper from the china figurine. "This is forbidden! You may not take these objects! Only used clothing and foodstuff!" He had a flat, high, nasal bark.

Baumgartner smiled nervously. "Please, Herr Offizier, these things, they've been in our family for so long, they're really worthless. Won't you let us take just this one?"

Erika watched at her teacher plead with the SS man. She had always known him as a rather stern, highly respected figure who wore the velvet collar of a full professor, whose writings on anatomy were known the medical world over. Suddenly he appeared vulnerable and pitiful, reduced to begging a little man in a sinister uniform who probably had completed sixth grade in school and no more but had been clever enough to join the gang when the joining was good. It sickened her. It also frightened her.

"You Jews are all alike," Pugnose offered. "Nothing you have is ever worth anything, according to you. 'Just this little diamond ring, Herr Offizier, just this tiny jade statue—it's so old anyway,' " he mimicked.

Both SS men laughed.

"Come on, hurry up," Pugnose prodded. "You've got only until eighteen hundred hours to get on the train." The SS men started for the door when Pugnose hesitated. He had noticed Rachel, the professor's seventeen-year-old daughter, blond, blue-eyed, and beautiful. "Of course, *you* can stay with us, Liebchen," he drawled in coarse Viennese, leering at Rachel. "You can pass for an Aryan, you know."

Rachel retreated into Erika's arms, a frightened look in her eyes. The other SS man walked over to them. "Who are you, please?" he asked Erika.

Erika lifted her head and spoke with authority. "I am Dr. Erika Schuler of the Maria Hilfer General Hospital."

"You're not a Jew, then. Excuse me, Frau Doktor, what is your business here?"

"I was a student of Professor Dr. Baumgartner, whom I love

and respect," she said, her anger showing, "and I protest this shameful behavior."

Pugnose stepped forward. "You protest? Well, Frau Doktor, I wouldn't protest to much if you really are their friend. They are the lucky ones, but that can change. Am I right, Papa?"

Baumgartner allowed himself the temporary luxury of contemptuous silence, which was not lost on Pugnose. He stepped up to Baumgartner and gave him a vicious backhand on the face, knocking his glasses off and bloodying his nose. "Speak up, Jew! I didn't hear you!"

The professor picked up his glasses and wiped blood from his nose. He looked at Erika. "Please, child, go now. Don't make things more difficult than they are. Please." He nodded assurance, smiling thinly.

Erika hesitated. "Times are difficult for everybody," he said softly. "Now, go, please. Go with God. We'll write you from Camagüey, where we'll be if God is willing." He took her hands. "Thank you for coming and for your concern. Now, let these gentlemen do their job." He kissed her cheek. "*Alles gute,* my dear, dear girl. And remember, *auf Wiedersehen!*"

Erika ran down the stairs and into the street, tears of anger and shame blending with the light rain. The crowd that had seemed to be only curious before had become boisterous and mean. Erika weaved her way through the throbbing mob of solid working-class Austrians. Groups of uniformed *Ordnungspolizei* stood around, seemingly oblivious to the explosiveness of the atmosphere. Black-clad SS men were escorting Jews into vans under the shouts of the mob. As she crossed the street she saw a man hurl a paving stone against a butcher shop window that had been painted with a crude white Star of David. At the sound of the breaking glass—as if that were the signal it had been waiting for—the throng began shouting in unison: "*Yoo-DEH! Yoo-DEH! Yoo-DEH!*"

Erika turned the corner. She leaned against a lamppost and vomited. Several people, attracted by the tumult on the Klempner Gasse, ran by without giving her a second glance.

She left for home the next day.

VIENNA

SPRING 1941

Hans-Dieter von Bergdorf walked out of the Franz-Josef Bahnhof carrying his suitcase. He hailed a taxi for the few blocks to Erika's flat on the Antoni Gasse. He had a little over two hours before his train left for Budapest, and he could have a quick meal with her and—well, see how things were going for her and what her plans were now that she had graduated. Besides, Trudi would expect him to visit her sister as long as he was going through Vienna, wouldn't she? And Erika was like his own little sister, wasn't she?

He sat back in the taxi and lit one of the Camels that Heydrich had given him, thinking of Erika as a young girl with a crown of blond braids on her head and skinny as a stork. *But now she's a woman—a doctor, just imagine!* A beautiful one at that.

His thoughts drifted to the time he and Trudi had attended mass with her at St. Stephan's. The choir was singing, and Erika's face seemed almost angelic, as though it belonged on a canvas depicting life in heaven. She was shy, he remembered, so unlike her sister. He wondered if today, when she saw him at her door, she would turn red as she usually did when he looked at her. He smiled at the prospect. He realized that she had been occupying a great deal of his thoughts of late, especially since he had been away. He knew the danger in those thoughts, but as usual, he dismissed his own warnings.

The landlady told him that Fräulein Erika had left for home sooner than anticipated, just that morning. He was quite welcome, she assured him, and it was her honor to be of help to the German army.

Bergdorf took his train to Budapest, where he would transfer to one bound for Sächsisch-Regen, then motor to his home, Bistritz.

His feelings were ambivalent. It wasn't so much the familial obligation of seeing Erika that had motivated him. He had wanted to see her, he knew now. He had even toyed with the idea of missing his train so that he would have to stay overnight. He didn't know why, and that alone made him uneasy. He looked out the window as the train made its way through the city on its way east, and he smiled thinking of how, after Berlin, he would have drunk her freshness and purity into his soul like a cleansing bath.

He was glad now that she had not been there. It would have been dangerous—and stupid. He closed his eyes, thinking of Trudi, as he should have all along. He thought of her dramatic beauty, her rounded hips, her ample bosom, her soft, velvety skin . . . the silkiness of her pubis . . . the moist warmth of her . . . her inexhaustible hunger. He felt a stirring in his crotch, and that made him feel better.

* * *

The earliest day for [Operation Sea Lion,] the sailing of the invasion fleet [on England,] has been fixed as 20th September. (*Oberkommando der Wehrmacht* directive from *Führer Conferences on Naval Affairs,* 1940.)

The weather situation as a whole does not permit us to expect a period of calm. . . . The Führer therefore decides to postpone Operation Sea Lion indefinitely. (*Führer Conferences on Naval Affairs,* 1940)

Hitler announced the most fateful decision of all: "The Beginning of [Operation Barbarossa] will have to be postponed up to four weeks." This postponement of the attack on Russia in order that [he] may vent his personal spite against [Yugoslavia] which had dared defy him was probably the most catastrophic single decision in Hitler's career. (William L. Shirer, *The Rise and Fall of the Third Reich*)

* * *

TRANSYLVANIA

SPRING 1941

The limits of the Bergdorf estate were just outside the township of Bistritz, starting at a narrow paved road at the edge of a densely wooded slope angling up to the castle. Perched on a high plateau overlooking the town and valleys was *Schloss* Falkenhorst, aptly named, for the mountain was called the Falkenberg.

The Opel went through the main gate of the castle proper and crunched to a stop on the circular gravel driveway. Waiting at the door were the Baroness Anna von Bergdorf and her daughter-in-law, Trudi. Hans-Dieter, Freiherr von Bergdorf, Major-General of the Waffen-SS, holder of the Knight's Cross of the Iron Cross, was home.

Later, he relaxed in the rumpled bed, his body still glistening with perspiration from the exertion of making love. He looked up at the carved beams of the ceiling, allowing his mind to drift into a blank, thoughtless world, luxuriating in the aftermath of the release of pent-up tension.

Trudi, conversely, was dry. Warm and dry. She was propped up on one elbow, playing with a strand of his chestnut hair, looking at him, studying his slightly crooked nose. She appraised his long, thin body, then traced his profile from the hairline down to his squar-ish jaw, feeling the stubble.

22

"You didn't shave," she said, chiding softly, feeling his chin. "I feel as though I slept in a bed of cactus."

It took him a moment to come back from the blankness. "What? Oh, did I scratch you?" he whispered. "I'm sorry."

He turned to face her. His fingers gently brushed her shoulder, then strolled leisurely down the velvety slope of her luxurious breasts, stopping at one of them. The nipple was pale puce, the color of veal, he noted. It stirred into light rigidity at the delicate touch. Its twin stood still, waiting for its own stimulus. She leaned forward and kissed his chin. "It's all right," she said, laughing softly. "I've never been scratched by a general's whiskers before." Her fingers went down his chest, across his flat belly to his pelvis. She whispered in his ear, her breath and lips warm against his skin, "It's a small price to pay. Just make sure the next time we make love like this, we'll be celebrating another promotion."

"By that time I'll be too old," he said, kissing her roughly, then more gently and deeply, lust again aroused, bodies once more as one, hunger once more gratified.

Later, as her husband slept, Trudi left the bed. She would bathe . . . and muse about their future.

She soaked in perfumed foam and thought of Paris. Paris! The idea excited her. He said she could join him soon, after he had established himself with his superior, Oberg. She wondered what kind of man he was, SS-Obergruppenführer Karl-Albrecht Oberg. Was he married? If so, was his wife beautiful? If so, was she with him in France? No matter; she was confident that she, Trudi von Bergdorf, would be the most beautiful of the German officers' wives in Paris. Yes, she decided, she would use her beauty and charm to help Hans-Dieter. She would flirt—not boldly, of course—with his superiors. Not that she would ever be unfaithful; just harmless flirtations now and then, those that could lead to further promotions for him. Maybe a posting in Berlin. *Berlin—now that is where the power is! What connections I could make there,* she thought. She had heard somewhere that the Führer was captivated by that scarecrow Magda Goebbels. Well, just wait—let him meet Trudi von Bergdorf! She'd have the Führer eating out of her hand. Yes, Berlin! She would work on that, starting with Karl-Albrecht Oberg.

The minuscule bubbles of her bath were bursting one by one, causing a microroar in the silence of her oversize marble tub. She smoothed the surviving foam onto her skin and scanned her body, inspecting, admiring. Yes, she had much to admire in that figure, which made men gasp in open lust and women sneer in undisguised envy. She lifted her legs above the surface of the water, placing them together at the ankles. Her knees, she noted for the millionth time, were small, as were her ankles, giving the upper and lower legs their shapely fullness. As she appraised, Trudi gave silent thanks to the designers of the high-heeled shoe and the knee-length skirt of the era. She shuddered at the thought of the long dresses of old.

Trudi von Bergdorf had a gymnasium built in her apartment in the *Schloss*. It was outfitted with the most modern German and American equipment. Every wall had floor-to-ceiling mirrors with banks of flattering lights. The drawers of her gym held powerful magnifying lenses with which she meticulously explored the exquisite topography of her body for the slightest anomaly. This preoccupation with her physical perfection kept Trudi busy and her husband curiously amused.

While Trudi was finishing her toilette, Bergdorf woke up from his light sleep. He lit a cigarette and thought for a moment of Heydrich, then consequently of Paris and the assignment Heydrich had thrust on him.

He hadn't been to Paris since his student days before the war. He remembered the sounds and smell of it. The walks he used to take from his little room on the Rue de Fleurus across the Jardin du Luxembourg to the Sorbonne, bereted Frenchmen sweeping the gravel paths with long-stemmed brooms in the early mornings. But that had been peacetime. Things would perhaps be different now, in his new assignment, whatever it might be.

He tried to picture where he might live, now, in 1941, as a conquering German. He tried to imagine what his life was going to be like. He tried to visualize his wife greeting him at the door of his house, whatever house it might be . . . but the picture of Trudi failed to materialize in his mind's eye. He saw another face, a veiled, undefined face, not Trudi's.

He angrily stubbed out the cigarette. He slipped on his robe and, still in the dark, walked to an open window and took a deep breath, hoping to chase away the guilt-provoking images. As he gazed out at the dark forms of the trees, the face at the door came back, delineating itself clearly now. It was pale, soft, and lovely;

blue eyes that were sad, blond hair—not black—and lips that were not so full, and a voice that should have had a crystal quality but was darker as it said things the crystal voice would not, could not say.

He gritted his teeth at his lack of mental control, but the image kept haunting him: Erika's face.

Bergdorf turned on all the lamps in the room. The dark brought the images. He needed light.

He knocked at the door of Trudi's bathroom and let himself in. "Hurry, darling." He smiled at his naked wife. "The guests will be arriving soon."

He stepped out of the bathroom, closing the door. He knew the face would be there that evening, the image of his daydreams—in person.

God, he said to himself, *what am I going to do*?

"What's he like, darling?" Trudi called out from her dressing room as she slipped on her gown for the dinner party that the baroness was holding in honor of her son's homecoming.

"What's who like?" Bergdorf said, selecting a black tie from his closet.

"Hitler-bacsi," she said. "You know, when he gave you the medal? What was he like?"

He smiled. Hitler-bacsi, she called him. It was the Hungarian title of respect for older persons, used primarily with the given name of the person. *BAH-chee*, it came out from her, who never spoke Hungarian unless it was to shout at the servants.

"What was Hitler-bacsi like? Oh, like any other man his age, I suppose," he said. "Like your father, or my father, before his stroke. Aren't you going to ask me how I won the medal?"

"I don't mean what he looked like. I mean, was he scary? Was he impressive? Oh, you know what I mean, Hans-Dieter!"

"Did he have a halo over his head? Well, I didn't see one. And he didn't walk on water, either. He's just a man, Trudi, just like anyone else, except more . . . intense. Don't you want to know how I won the medal?" he pressed.

"Oh, darling, you know I don't know anything about war and men things," she said, dissatisfied with his answers. "What are you wearing?"

He sighed. "Black tie."

"Hm. Géza will be disappointed at not seeing you in your uniform, you know."

"Géza can go fuck himself," he mumbled under his breath.

Trudi came out of her dressing room. His breath was taken away. She wore a strapless gown of a shimmering silk that clung tenaciously to her body. The deep emerald of the dress reflected her green eyes, eyes nestled in rows of lush black lashes. She wore no mascara or eye shadow; her heavy lids provided their own shade. Her dark eyebrows were sculpted into soft arches tapering to an end precisely at the temples. The line of her long neck was gracefully interrupted by a striking necklace of imperial jade set in diamonds, a necklace that had belonged to Bergdorf's noble grandmother, a lady-in-waiting to the Empress Elisabeth von Habsburg. Matching earrings hung from Trudi's earlobes. That evening, spellbound gazes from their guests would be cast at Trudi's eyes and ears as the candlelight frolicked with the green quartet of jewels.

She dabbed perfume behind her ears as the last detail of her toilette. Bergdorf caught the heady scent. *God, how beautiful she is!* he said to himself. He felt a slight stirring below his belt, which surprised him in view of the depleting episodes in bed just a short time before. But Trudi could do that to a man. At any time.

"I know why you're not wearing your uniform," she said as they left the bedroom suite. "It's because Géza will be here tonight, isn't it?"

Géza Szigeti was married to Hedwig, the oldest of the three Schuler sisters. He was a humorless bantam cock, seized by the small-man complex. He was a successful businessman dealing in ladies' shoes, a business financed by his mother-in-law shortly after his marriage to Hedi. There were those who still smiled with glee at the memory of Géza Szigeti's courtship, not of Hedi but of his future mother-in-law, Frau Schuler. Red roses and other flowers had come by the bushel to Frau Schuler. Bonbons, French perfume, Chantilly lace handkerchiefs, and other finery bombarded the lady until she fell in love with the notion of Géza becoming her first son-in-law, an event that took place in a splendid wedding a few months later. Soon after, Szigeti added the German *von* to his name on his calling card, despite the fact that he was Hungarian. The city of Bistritz enjoyed the joke, much to the pain of his wife, who insisted on being called simply Frau Szigeti.

Bergdorf raised his eyebrows in mock innocence. "How can you accuse me of such base behavior!"

He knew Szigeti would be greatly disappointed that his famous brother-in-law was not appearing in the uniform of an SS-general. Szigeti was a fanatical Nazi, one less concerned with the ideology of the party than with what its leader promised—the destruction of Russia and of European Jewry.

"Are you going to tell him you shook Hitler's hand?"

"No," Bergdorf said. "He'll slobber all over my hand trying to kiss it." He offered his arm. "Come, let's go down and have a look."

The couple descended an imposing staircase that ended elegantly in the large foyer. That, and the main reception room of the castle—the *Saal*, together with other key rooms—maintained their originality, except for the heating systems and other modernizations. Very old and very large tapestries graced the inner walls of *Schloss* Falkenhorst, and exquisite oriental carpets cloaked the highly polished floors, floors whose wear from the many generations of Bergdorfs showed in shallow valleys here and there on the almost-black parquet. Only a few traces of family heraldry were still shown in those rooms; pennants and shields, coats-of-arms and battle dress were displayed in the armory, which was now a small museum of the municipality, open to tourists during the summer.

Bergdorf and Trudi greeted guests and made small talk as the butler, Halloran, served apéritifs. Bergdorf was cornered by a guest asking him about the Balkan campaign. It was then that he saw who he was waiting for, who he was dreading—Erika.

He excused himself and went to greet her, putting on his most casual air. "Erika, I'm so pleased you could come tonight."

"Good evening, Hans-Dieter," Erika said, reddening slightly. "It was either supper here or in the kitchen with the servants. I live here, you know!" she said, laughing at Bergdorf's confused look.

"You live here?"

"I see Trudi has been too busy to bring you up to date on all the mundane things," she said with good humor. "The truth is, I'm staying as your guest until the equipment I need for the clinic in Maroshéviz arrives."

Bergdorf's brow knotted up. "Maroshéviz!"

"Yes, I'm opening a practice there."

"Good Lord, Erika, what in heaven's name made you choose that godforsaken place?"

"It's not godforsaken, Hans-Dieter. It's beautiful in those mountains, and peaceful. Besides, that has been my plan ever since

I first went to medical school. You remember, don't you? We talked about it before."

He smiled warmly at her. "Oh, yes, your Szeklers. Now I remember." He stared at her lovely face—young, innocent, idealistic, full of dreams and hopes. She would fulfill those dreams, he knew, and he admired her for having them. What was more, he envied her. She had aspirations and goals. He did not. He never had. All those schools, the universities—for what? To be a gentleman farmer? To speak in several languages about philosophy, history, religion? His was a future of dabbling in the arts, of charming his guests with his piano playing and his skill on a horse chasing a fox. A useless bonvivant.

But Erika had her Szeklers, her mountain people, sheep herders, woodsmen, peasants who would pay her with eggs and goat's cheese, with chickens and pigs—and gratitude. Her kind of medicine was often paid for with kindness and gratitude and love.

"Yes, my Szeklers," Erika said softly. Then her eyes took on a different look, a worried look. "Also, there is only one doctor for the entire region, Hans-Dieter, and that is Dr. Weissenberg, who happens to be Jewish. God only knows how long they'll let him remain."

"You make it sound so ominous, Erika. The Hungarians will leave him alone, I'm sure."

"It's not the Hungarians I'm worried about," she said urgently. "It's the SS. You know the pressure the SS is putting on Horthy regarding Jews—the so-called Jewish Resettlement Program." The scene in Vienna came back vividly. "Hans-Dieter, I saw some terrible things in Vienna. They're taking the Jews. They took my professor and his family. Where do they take them? What are they doing with them?" Her eyes searched his for an answer.

"I don't know exactly. Probably they send them to war production plants in Germany." He felt uncomfortable with the topic. "You know there's a shortage of skilled labor with which to carry on the war." He felt her anxiety. "But as far as your Dr. Weissenberg is concerned, I promise to speak to the SD chaps in Klausenburg. I'll see what can be done. Don't worry."

"They're killing the Jews, Hans-Dieter," she said softly, looking into his eyes for a reaction to the chilling words.

"No. Oh, no. I would've heard. That's just enemy propaganda. My God, Erika, we're not barbarians!"

Erika's eyes took on new hope. "Yes, I believe you would know," she said, "and you would tell me the truth."

"Of course I would." He smiled almost patronizingly. "By the way, Erika," he said, wishing to change the disagreeable subject, "I stopped by your flat in Vienna. I missed you by one day, your landlady told me."

"You did? Oh! I'm sorry, I—" She blushed slightly.

He caught her discomfort and quickly added, "Yes, I had a couple of hours before my train and I thought we might chat a little about your . . . studies over a good Sacher torte."

"That would've been nice," she murmured, looking down.

He looked at her silently, and the thought of being alone with her in Vienna came back to him. In the past, whenever he had wanted to get romantic with a woman, he had looked deeply into her eyes, imagining making love to her, and the look would make an eloquent statement. It never failed him. Now, however, as Bergdorf looked at his sister-in-law, another look, another expression was there—one of deep affection and even love. But it was not his old device; it was a true expression of his feelings.

She reddened peceptibly. And suddenly she knew his true feelings for the first time. And more, he knew she was acutely aware of those sentiments as she stared as deeply into his eyes.

Halloran made the dinner announcement, breaking the spell. Bergdorf and Erika parted wordlessly, each keenly aware of being suddenly thrust into a new world.

A dozen guests sat at the great table in the dining room. It was, as usual, a formal affair; the ladies in floor-length gowns, the gentlemen in black tie with their medals, badges, and ribbons from some past conflict of glory.

Local trout was the first course, eaten with a delicate Gray Friar from the Bergdorf vineyards. Wild boar from the East Carpathians made up the main meal, served with mounds of grated red cabbage and roast potatoes. A robust red Hungarian bull's-blood accompanied the pork. Afterward, iced mocca signaled the end of the banquet.

The Baroness Anna von Bergdorf spooned the last of her dessert into her mouth. "Yes, Paris," she told one of the guests. "It's wonderful, isn't it?" Turning to her son, she said, "You'll have to be careful, Hans-Dieter, or you'll get fat with all that marvelous French cooking."

The lean, hard Bergdorf nodded a smile at his mother.

"Tell me, my dear," she continued, "the war is over in France, isn't it? I mean, there is no more fighting?"

Géza Szigeti answered for Bergdorf. "No, there isn't, Frau Baronin. If French cooking is all he has to worry about, then a posting in Paris is the best thing that could have happened," he said, a hint of disapproval in his voice. Looking askance at Bergdorf, he added, "I congratulate you, Hans-Dieter. You made powerful friends in Berlin!"

A thick silence fell over the table. Bergdorf's jaw muscles twitched in silent anger. He could have pointed out to Szigeti that although there were no front lines in France and no field of battle between armies, and although the French had surrendered to the Germans, there was still a very active and very dangerous underground—the Maquis, the Armée Secrète, the FFI—all under the generic name: The Resistance. Their motto was "*Vivre libre ou mourir*." They were constantly supplied by the British with arms; they were fanatically patriotic, and in their large numbers life was cheap. Killing a German soldier was a worthy act; killing a high-ranking SS officer was high glory; and dying for it was the ultimate form of patriotism, with heroic immortality guaranteed. But Bergdorf chose not to say those things. Instead he said, "Save your congratulations for the day I get back my combat command, Géza, which will be soon, I hope. But to respond to your commentary, this is not, as you put it, a political job."

"Of course, I only meant—"

"Excuse me, please," Bergdorf interrupted, "allow me to continue so that you may be more enlightened as to my role."

"Naturally, but I want you to know—"

"It's an administrative assignment having to do with the fact that I speak French," Bergdorf said, ignoring Szigeti's attempts at correcting himself. "You see, the SS is actively involved in many industries related to the war effort in the occupied territories, and SS officers who speak the local languages and have management backgrounds are sorely needed. Because of my experience with the family businesses, I fit in those plans. I venture to say that if I spoke Polish, I should be sent to Warsaw.

"Oh, one more thing, Géza—and this will please you, I'm sure—when this post was given to me by my superiors, I protested.

I told them that I was a trained Panzer officer and that my place was in the field, not behind some desk. It was pointed out that in the SS we do not enjoy the luxury of choosing our jobs, that this assignment had the blessings of the Reichsführer-SS, and that further discussion would be fruitless. So you see"—Bergdorf smiled, arms extended in a gesture of helplessness—"I tried to be brave, but they wouldn't let me!"

Everyone laughed; Szigeti smiled through tight lips. "My dear General Bergdorf," Szigeti said formally, "the Knight's Cross from the Führer himself speaks for how brave you are. I meant only that we would all like to see you come home safe and sound after we win the war. Only that. My words were misunderstood, for which I am sorry." He struck his chest with a balled-up fist. "Mea culpa!"

More laughter dissolved the tension. Encouraged by it, Szigeti went on, "Which brings up another point. You all know that I have, shall we say, certain connections here in Siebenbürgen. I'm sure that a word or two in the right ear would find Berlin receptive to the idea that the Reich could be better served in its policies by posting Hans-Dieter in Klausenburg. That is, of course, if he wishes it."

Bergdorf laughed. "Whatever for?"

"As you rightly pointed out, the needs of the Reich supersede our own desires. Yours are a combat command, fighting the enemy. Well, the enemy is here, too."

"The enemy is here?" Bergdorf asked in mock seriousness.

"Yes," Szigeti said with passion. "Living among us. By that, of course, I mean the Jews. They are the enemy. The Jewish plague, the Bolshevik Jew, insidiously plotting and scheming to do away with our way of life. They are the enemy, I tell you, and they must be dealt with accordingly."

"You can't be serious, Géza," Bergdorf said. "Jews the enemy? Oh, they may be a little foreign for my taste, but to consider them dangerous? Please!"

"You may ridicule my words, and I am aware that it is a subject most of you would rather ignore, but for centuries the international Jew has been controlling us and our destiny. They've robbed us, they've caused wars, toppled legitimate governments with their Zionistic intrigues, and in doing so enslaved us. Hitler says it very clearly in *Mein Kampf*, and history is eloquent in this subject. History shows us that the Jew has been the curse of Europe. But now, thank to Hitler, we have a golden opportunity to make Europe free of this pestilence, provided, of course, we all do our duty. This is the Führer's mission, ladies and gentlemen. We must not forget that."

"And this is still Hungary, Géza," Bergdorf said coolly. "We must not forget *that*, either."

"No, I haven't forgotten. But we're fighting a common foe, all of us. Germans, Hungarians, the lot. And it won't be long before Horthy comes around. He will see that Hitler is right. If Horthy can't stomach the thought, then he should resign his offices!" Szigeti banged the table.

The Baroness Anna flinched at the clatter of her china. "I think the discussion of politics, Herr von Szigeti, would best be left in a forum other than this table, don't you agree? It's rather a gloomy subject in any case, and we have so much for which to be cheerful."

"Quite right, Mother," Bergdorf said, rising. "I suggest we adjourn to the salon for coffee and cordials."

Bergdorf struck up some lively Viennese songs on the Bechstein, with Trudi and some of the guests joining in. Even Géza Szigeti sang along. Halloran served cognac and other after-dinner drinks, artfully remembering preferences.

Halloran was very good at remembering details such as who drank what at social occasions. He was silently grateful that everyone in the room knew him—or more precisely, knew about him—so that there would be none of the usual raising of eyebrows at his slight but perceptible accent. Halloran was Irish.

Halloran had worked for an Austrian family in London and had learned excellent German during that time. While he was being trained for his profession in London, he came to hate that large and busy city, and he loathed the English with the passion of a son of Erin. Returning to his native County Tyrone in Northern Ireland was out of the question—the Protestant Irish were pro-British. But eventually he found a way out of his nationalistic miseries.

Halloran went into the service of the German chargé d'affaires in London. One night, as he was serving a guest of the German diplomat, a certain Baron von Bergdorf, he heard that a butler's post was available in the old baron's household. The tranquil life of a castle in faraway Translyvania seemed made to order for the frustrated Irishman, so he asked permission of his employer to apply. Soon after, in the late twenties, he came to *Schloss* Falkenhorst.

In little time Halloran earned the admiration and affection of the entire Bergdorf family. He was correct in his demeanor and efficient in his duties. By then his German was fluent, and despite the fact that most of the household staff were Hungarians, he insisted on using German exclusively. He couldn't help learning the Magyár language but avoided speaking it for fear of being laughed at. Romanian, the third language of the tricultural region, he emphatically refused to learn. In a letter to his sister he once termed the Romanian language "swarthy."

He was considered taciturn and spoke only when spoken to, but when hostilities broke out between Germany and England, he let his pro-German feelings be known. This, quite naturally, endeared him to the locals, including, later, SS-Sturmbannführer Dr. Huntziger, the Gestapo chief for Bistritz. It was Huntziger who supplied Halloran with the means for his only vice, Irish whiskey, of which he had a nip or two nightly before retiring. Flattered with the attention given him by an SS major, together with his sense of German patriotism, he accepted the role of *V-Mann* at *Schloss* Falkenhorst for Huntziger. *V-Mann* was the shortened version of *Vertrauensmann* in Gestapo jargon—informer.

Gradually the guests left. Bergdorf continued playing. In the middle of a tango by Albéniz, Géza Szigeti approached the piano. He offered his hand to Bergdorf, who smiled and wordlessly extended his right hand, the left continuing to play the accompaniment.

Szigeti said, "*Gute Nacht, Herr Brigadeführer.*" He took one step back and clicked his heels together, snapping his arm forward in the Nazi salute. "Heil Hitler!" he barked.

Bergdorf grimaced. "Géza, this is Albéniz, not Wagner. Good night." He continued playing and wondered why he didn't feel guilty of heresy.

As Hedi Szigeti said good night to her sister and the baroness, her husband studied Bergdorf with a mixture of puzzlement and contempt.

Halloran, meanwhile, observed.

Trudi kissed her husband as he played. "I'm going to bed, darling. I'm exhausted . . . and sore," she whispered. "I'll see you at breakfast."

Suddenly he was alone in the *Saal*. He stopped playing.

A voice said, "Please don't stop, Hans-Dietér. Play some more." It was Erika.

He felt warm and happy. Knowing they were alone, the feeling he had had in the taxi in Vienna, that of joyful anticipation, overcame him. He didn't look up but resumed playing a few arpeggios. "I thought you had left with the others," he said to the keyboard.

"I blend in the background," she said with a hint of irony. "Something I've always been able to do. But please play more; I truly love your playing."

"Yes? Then I shall. With such an incentive, I shall play as I never have before!" he said with mock solemnity, rumbling some minor chords in the bass. "But first let me pour us each a drink. Some cognac, perhaps." He stood up and poured two brandies.

They touched glasses and drank. Swirling the amber fluid around in his glass, he said, "So, you blend in the background?" It was obvious that she felt eclipsed by Trudi's extraordinary beauty. "Well, when you come out of the shadows, Erika, you are truly a beautiful woman. You really should come out more often." He looked at her and smiled. "At least when I'm around," he said softly.

Her eyes held his for a few long seconds. It was a questioning gaze that asked things she didn't dare even think, a gaze that held the intimacy of what his eyes had been saying to her earlier that evening. Suddenly he looked away, nervous and unsure of himself. He smiled uneasily and sat back down at the piano. He played an arpeggio to break the silence.

Erika perceived his nervousness, and she herself became apprehensive. She knew he had been flirting with her as she so often had seen him do with other women. It was his way, she knew—harmless, self-confident gallantries, coquettish displays of his overabundant charm. But now, seeing a side of him that was foreign to her, she became frightened. Frightened because it was the way she imagined it in her forbidden and wonderful dreams about him—about them—and she knew how those terrible dreams always turned out.

She broke the silence. "Play for me, Hans-Dieter," she whispered, knowing she was opening the door to the dream.

He looked up at her, now a different look in his eyes, a look she hadn't seen before. She became even more fearful, but not enough to stop whatever it was that was there to stop while she still had the wisdom.

"You like Chopin, I remember," he said. "I'll play a nocturne, one that should be played only on very special occasions . . . like now," he said softly.

She closed her eyes, sighing inwardly at his choice of words to her, thinking how the reality was even more than the dream.

He began the piece in a rocking, wide-stretched bass with deep resonances in the tender key of D-flat, the left hand setting the tone. A simple and optimistic melody completed the basic structure. Then, as if meant to be resavored, the melody was stated again with lacy filigrees, slowly, subtly weaving sensual fabrics, creating a spell-like effect. Then the voices of the piano began singing more and more urgently at her, his fingers producing passion in accelerating flows and bursts, and a rush of warmth struck her face, coursing down her body.

Now he too perceived the feeling, and he gave way fully to it. Now he kissed her with every delicate coloring of the nocturne and spoke to her of long-restrained love with every lush arabesque. Now he boldly caressed her with the fanciful ornamentation of the sensuous music, and he felt her swoon. Now his hands on the keyboard were aggressive as the nocturne became more assertive itself, more emphatic. Now with every thundering chromaticism he thrust deeply in her psyche, causing her to soar to heights of ecstatic pain, and together they were pushed into an untouching, unspeaking dream where souls intermingled in the most joyous of fantasies. Then in a series of agitated, stressful chords, the wondrous nightpiece reached its climax, as did Erika's soul, and tenderly, mercifully, the diminishing notes returned her. Gently the notes caressed and embraced her. Slowly the veiled harmonies of the night stole away, leaving an aura of magic. And in the fading echo of the magic, neither could speak or move.

Hans-Dieter looked at her. He went to her quickly and tried to find his voice. "Erika, now I know . . . I've always loved you!" He took her by the shoulders.

She put her hands on his chest, holding him back. "Oh, Hans-Dieter, please don't say that! You can't!" It was a bad beautiful sinful wonderful dream again.

He kissed her face, her neck and shoulders. "I love you! Erika, I love you. Don't you understand?"

She pleaded, pushing at him. "Stop! Oh, please don't do this!" *God, let me wake up from this wonderful dream!*

His mouth found hers. The muffled objections turned to groans as she kissed him back hungrily, years of want in that one, long, abandoning kiss. With mouths locked they slowly sat on a nearby divan and continued their embrace, kissing, touching, groaning, whimpering.

Suddenly she pulled away. "No!" she said in a vehement whisper. "It must stop here—and now! We can do nothing, don't you see? Nothing!" Tears welled up in her eyes.

"But Erika, I love you. I didn't know it before, but I do now. I've loved you for a long—"

"Don't say that," she said, tears falling down her cheeks. "It isn't fair, it isn't fair!"

"You're always in my thoughts, in my heart." He kissed her fingertips and she caressed his lips while she listened to the words she had wanted to hear for a lifetime.

He took her face in his hands and kissed her very gently. "Erika, my beloved Erika, our fate has been prescribed, and that fate is in the way of our happiness. I cannot accept that. I don't know how, but I will not let you go."

"Oh, you must, Hans-Dieter, you must!"

"I ask you now: Do you love me?"

"Yes, oh, yes! You know I do, more than anything."

"Then you must come with me to Paris," he said.

"Paris? But that's impossible." *Oh, God, why does he torture me!* The pain was more—a thousand times more—than she had imagined. And it was only the beginning.

"I want you to come. Trudi will—"

She put her hand over his mouth. "No! Don't even mention her name! I'm so ashamed!"

"I'm not ashamed that I love you, Erika. I'll tell her; I'll tell the—"

"You mustn't! She's your wife and my sister. No, you *can't* do that. Promise me you won't. Promise me!" she shouted in a whisper.

"Yes, yes. Very well, I promise. But—"

"Oh, Hans-Dieter, listen to me. It has to be this way, don't you see? Since I was fifteen my dream has been only you—that you would love me as I love you. But it's only a dream, my darling! The reality of our lives is that you are married to my sister! As much as I love and want you, I would die before dishonoring her and myself. I could never go through the nightmare of guilt, of shame, from the awful sin of adultery with my own sister as its victim."

"But Erika, I would tell her, and she would—"

"Please, no more. I can't stand anymore." Her eyes saddened

as she ran her fingers through his hair. "Believe me that the knowledge alone that you love me is enough for me. It will keep and comfort me, and it will be, in a way, the culmination of my dreams."

Bergdorf sought her lips again, but she turned her face, and he kissed a tear that ran down her cheek. "No more," she said. "Don't make it more difficult than it is. I think it best that we say good night now. In the morning we will see things more clearly . . . and bravely."

"In the morning," he said with a touch of bitterness, "in the morning. Tell me this—how can I face you again without my eyes, my soul, screaming 'I love you!'?"

Erika took his hand in hers. She shook her head, not finding the words to tell him that she would not be there in the morning because she too was afraid. She gathered up her shawl and left the room.

Bergdorf watched her go up the staircase. An emptiness gnawed at the pit of his stomach. He downed another cognac, but the sensation, the pain remained. He realized the cause of the pain and he asked, *My God, what have I done*?

From a cracked-open stained-glass window in the balcony overlooking the *Saal*, Halloran, Irish patriot, Gestapo informer, stood watching Bergdorf drink the cognac. He had been observing since the beginning; he had heard every word, every whisper that was spoken and sighed in the acoustically perfect room. His stonelike face betrayed no emotion, no approval or disapproval.

Halloran closed the window and went to his room. He had his nip of Irish whiskey and made his notes in a little book. He knelt at his bedside and prayed for his sister and Ireland. He got into bed and closed his eyes, imagining the scene with SS-Sturmbannführer Dr. Huntziger the next day.

At breakfast the next morning Bergdorf drank coffee and stared morosely from the terrace to a sea of roses. Trudi, her raven hair loosened over a white chiffon gown, prattled on to the Baroness Anna about the prior night's events. The baroness smiled in response, but she was more concerned about her son's cheerless mood. She intimately knew his disposition, and she sensed that something was wrong. She was too sensitive and discreet to ask.

Halloran brought an envelope on a tray. It was addressed to Trudi. She opened it.

"Oh, my! It's from Erika," she said between bites of a buttered roll. "She left early this morning for Maroshéviz. She says she wanted to get a head start before her equipment arrives. Says she didn't want to disturb us so early and that she'll write later. She thanks us for the hospitality and wishes us happiness. Oh, Hans-Dieter," she said, putting down her roll, "I *do* wish you had talked to her about Berlin! Goodness knows we have enough connections to get her into some society practice. What in the world is she going to do in those mountains with those peasants and those—those gypsies?"

Bergdorf wiped his lips with his napkin. "Apparently that's what she wants," he said coolly.

The Baroness Anna's eyes darted to her son's. In a microsecond of motherly instinct, the baroness knew. "Hans-Dieter is right, my dear. Erika knows what is best for her, and if anything, we should encourage her, don't you think?" That night she would pray for God to give her son the strength of the Bergdorf honor.

He rose from the table. "Yes. Well, if you'll excuse me, I'm going to saddle up for a ride in the woods. I'll join you later for lunch." He kissed his wife on the cheek.

"I still wish you had talked to her," Trudi said with petulance. "A lot you care!"

He pretended not to have heard the last words and walked toward the paddocks. The Baroness Anna von Bergdorf stared through troubled eyes at her son's back.

He galloped through the forest, and he felt the pain in his gut again, and the butterflies fluttered their wings.

He knew they would be with him from then on.

Trudi's last words echoed in his brain. He sighed. "Ah, Trudi," he said to the trees, "if you only knew how much I care!"

BISTRITZ

SPRING 1941

Halloran walked down the Miklós Horthy Strasse and halted in front of a dry-goods store, looking at the wares in the window and at the reflected images on the glass, which was his reason for stopping. Satisfied that the street was clear, he quickly went inside the adjoining building, on whose door a brass plaque read:

Sicherheitspolizeistelle—Bistritz
Geheime Staatspolizei u. Sicherheitsdienst

It was the two-story office of the Security Police, SD, and Gestapo for the city of Bistritz. Its head was SS-Sturmbannführer Dr. Huntziger, Halloran's part-time employer.

Things started off on the wrong foot that day for the two. Perhaps it was the way Huntziger behaved, which was well within his normal behavior: patronizing, arrogant, and aloof all at the same time. Or perhaps it was Halloran's mood. He had been pressured of late by Huntziger to produce something—anything—about *Schloss* Falkenhorst and its tenants. What was their attitude toward the German presence in Transylvania? How did they truly feel about Hitler? Did the old baroness exhibit fears about her son's involvement in the Waffen-SS, or was she proud of him serving the Reich? Was there any defeatist talk at the table, or isolationist ideas expounded, or did they blindly support Germany? What was their attitude toward Jews? Did they support the Reich's racial policies? Had they hired any Jews on the estate or at any of the family businesses since the German policy in regard to Jews was made known? These were the questions to which Huntziger expected answers from Halloran, and so far he hadn't given very much to the Gestapo.

Halloran sat across Huntziger's desk as the report was being perused. Without taking his eyes off the report the Gestapo chief tossed a packet of Chesterfields to Halloran, who withdrew one and lit it, pocketing the rest. He blew a plume of smoke toward the glossy ceiling and thought, *These bloody SS people, they have no manners*.

Still not looking up, Huntziger asked, "Did anyone see you come here?"

The question openly annoyed Halloran. "As usual, Major, I left my wagon to be loaded at Böhm's store and walked around. Nobody saw me. As always, I was careful."

Huntziger smiled patronizingly at the testy butler. "All right, don't be so touchy. It never hurts to be cautious."

Halloran blew another cloud of smoke. "You don't have to remind me. I'm always careful."

Huntziger winced at Halloran's accent. Although he spoke gramatically correct High German, he spoke it with a detectable foreign pronunciation. To a Berliner like Huntziger, with his clipped German, relatively free of dialectic idiom, the sound was especially irritating. "Herr Halloran, you'll have to do something about your German. You're sounding more like these Sächsischers every day."

"Major Huntziger, I do the best I can. After all, this is not my language, as you well know. Or perhaps you would prefer I report to you in English, in which case I should be more than pleased." *Bloody Jerry*, he thought, *he can fuck off, for all of that!*

Huntziger smiled a conciliatory smile. "You're right, of course. I beg your pardon, Herr Halloran."

Fuck off, Jerry! Halloran said in the silence.

"Now then, to your report," Huntziger said, breaking open a new packet of Chesterfields. "This exchange between Herr von Szigeti and Freiherr von Bergdorf—it strikes me as a rather disloyal bit of rubbish on the part of an SS general. What's your feeling, Herr

Halloran? I mean, you were there. Do you agree with my conclusion?"

Ordinarily, Halloran would have remained noncommittal, allowing the Gestapo official to draw his own conclusion based on the raw intelligence. But he was still irritated by Huntziger's manner, so he pulled back the carrot he offered, leaving little for Huntziger to chew on. "Freiherr von Bergdorf has always found his brother-in-law a rather insufferable little man. It seemed to me Bergdorf was playing a game only to irritate him. This Szigeti is quite a fanatical anti-Semite, you know. On top of that, he is a frightful bore, which is even less excusable. You yourself would have trouble refraining from challenging Szigeti's Jew-baiting lectures, if only because he is so pompous. Had Szigeti taken an opposite view, I assure you Bergdorf would have, too, just to provoke him."

Huntziger's eyes showed his disappointment. "In other words, it's nothing? Bergdorf seems loyal to the Reich?"

Bloody fool! thought Halloran. *Isn't it obvious?* "He wears the Knight's Cross to the Iron Cross, Major, put around his neck by Chancellor Hitler himself."

Huntziger looked up, eyes wide. "The Führer decorated him?"

Clearly Huntziger hadn't known, and it amused Halloran to think how little the Gestapo knew of other things. "Yes."

Huntziger busied himself writing in a folder. He did this calmly, but the veins in his temples were showing more than usual and his face was slightly flushed—in anger, thought Halloran.

"Very well, what about this other business, Halloran? This tender little love scene you mention in your report?"

"What about it? It's all there," Halloran said, pointing to the papers on the desk. He was sorry now that he had included it for Huntziger's eyes, eyes now grown cold with anger and frustration. He was proud of helping Germany win the war in whatever small way, but these Gestapo swine and their methods were not what he had intended.

"I know it's all here," the German said through clenched teeth, "but I want to know what you make of it."

Halloran stubbed out his cigarette. "Frankly, nothing. You told me to report anything and everything, no matter how minor it may seem or how unimportant it appears. You said that you would be the one to analyze the data. I have done precisely that, Major Huntziger.''

Huntziger slouched back in his swivel chair and brought his manicured fingers together, touching his lips. "Hm, so you have, Herr Halloran. Let's see: A man, an SS-general, makes love to his wife's sister under his own roof, and you make nothing of it. Correct?''

"Yes," Halloran said, lighting another Chesterfield. "When you consider that that man has a reputation for having an eye, shall we say, for beautiful women, and that the lady in question is a beautiful woman; that that man had several brandies that evening and they probably gave him the boldness for a little harmless flirtation; that considering that they both knew that she would be leaving the following morning for the Carpathians and that nothing further would come of the flirtation, yes, I make nothing of it, Herr Major.''

"I see. Now, what about this other item in which Frau Doktor Schuler makes remarks about the Reich's racial policies that raise some questions as to *her* loyalty? What do you make of that?'' Huntziger was beginning to pale.

"Again, Herr Major, you are asking for an opinion, in which case I shall tell you that those remarks were made by a newly graduated medical student, therefore still highly idealistic and motivated by a naive approach to the issue of Jews in Europe today. Her remarks were so lacking in political substance that she failed to pursue the issue, if there was one.''

"Yes, I'm sure," Huntziger replied irritably. "Then to sum up your report of, let me see"—he counted the sheets of paper—"two and a half pages, there were comments at dinner that on paper appear to be anti-Reich, but it was all *innocent* fun at Herr Szigeti's expense. Then Fräulein Schuler's comments vis-à-vis our Jewish policy were from the lips of an *innocent* child; and a love tryst between General von Bergdorf and Fräulein Schuler was merely the brandy encouraging the dashing Casanova, resulting in a harmless, *innocent* flirtation. Well, Herr Halloran, I've never seen so many innocents appearing in one single report. It makes one wonder, wouldn't you say?''

"You may wonder what you wish. You wanted anything and everything; you asked my opinion, which is what I gave, garnered from my observations.''

42

Huntziger sighed audibly. He wanted to finish the fruitless interview with the uncooperative butler. "Your opinion, Herr Halloran, is always of interest to the SD. By the way," he added as an afterthought, "our supplier in Lisbon had trouble getting your Irish whiskey, but it won't be too long, I assure you. In the meantime, I would like you to take some money for your efforts." He tossed an envelope across the desk.

"Thank you, no." Halloran pushed the envelope away like a side plate of cold turnips. "I don't accept money for my services to the German Reich. It would put me in the category of a paid informer, wouldn't it? I consider my involvement with the Gestapo as my duty, acknowledged from time to time by a bottle of Irish whiskey, which, under present circumstances, is impossible to acquire by my own devices. In lieu of the whiskey, Herr Major, a simple thank you will do."

Arrogant bastard! thought Huntziger. *Worse than a Britisher.* "Very well, as you wish. Was there anything else you wish to report?" he said, rising.

"Yes, as a matter of fact there is. Shortly after arriving home yesterday afternoon, General von Bergdorf *twice* visited his wife in the connubial bed in the space of an hour and a half. I believe that concludes my report, Major Huntziger." Halloran rose to leave.

"Hardly information for a dossier, is it?" the German said in bad humor. "In future, kindly confine yourself to pertinent facts, Halloran."

The butler ground out his cigarette. "As I said before, Herr Major, I only deliver the eggs—it's up to the Gestapo to make the omelet. I bid you good day."

SS-Sturmbannführer Dr. Otto Huntziger buzzed impatiently for his secretary, Fräulein Kessler, a buxom blond Valkyrie who did her best to serve her boss in ways other than with the stenographic pencil. That day Huntziger didn't look too hard at the extratight blouse and its resisting buttons, she noticed. She crossed her shapely legs efficiently, pad in hand, and in doing so she showed her boss a bit of thigh above her gartered stocking, which he also didn't seem to notice. *Well,* she thought, *maybe tonight he'll tell me why he is so upset about that* verdammter Irländer!

Huntziger dictated the following teletype message to the Gestapo section, Reichssicherheitshauptamt—the Reich Security Head Office—115/116 Kurfürstenstrasse, Berlin 6:

> V-Mann SiBi/Ha41 reports conversation of a disloyal and possible treasonable nature regarding Reich's Jewish policies attributable to SS-Brigadeführer u. General-Major der Waffen-SS Hans-Dieter, Freiherr von BERGDORF, and Doctor-Med. Erika SCHULER, both of Kreis Bistritz, Gau Siebenbürgen. Recommend classifying Code PURPLE. Further, recommend V-Mann SiBi/Ha41 reclassified Code PURPLE until further evaluation by Bistritz Sipo and Gestapo Amt.
>
> Dr. H U N T Z I G E R
> SS-Obersturmbannführer

Code Purple was "begin investigation of loyalty or defeatist attitude suspicion" in the Gestapo spectrum of the New Order, to be used only in cases of German subjects, whether Reich or ethnic. It didn't matter if there was no substantiation of charges; it was enough if an informer, reliable or not, made the charge. Huntziger's V-Mann, Halloran, had not made accusations that would be considered serious enough for a Code Purple, but he managed to anger the SD man into arbitrary action on Bergdorf and Erika Schuler. In Nazi Germany, that was tantamount to an indelible stain, capable of producing devastating consequences from then on.

The die was cast.

BERLIN

SPRING 1941

A day after the transmission of Huntziger's teletype, a fine, misty rain was glistening the paving stones of the streets of Germany's capital. The usual four o'clock tea-and-cakes crowd took their snacks indoors instead of at the sidewalk cafés of the Kurfürstendamm. And at number 115 Kurfürstenstrasse Reinhard Heydrich took his tea and cakes at his oversize mahogany desk as he packed his files for his upcoming move to Prague. Files—dossiers, really—of everyone who was anyone in the Third Reich; files of which only Heydrich had copies. Files in which even Adolf Hitler's name and private history appeared. Files that made Reinhard Heydrich the most feared man in Europe would now be going to Prague with their keeper. His appointment as prorector of Bohemia/Moravia, as dictated by Hitler himself, was in effect a consolidation of power because he had convinced Hitler that he should maintain leadership of the Reichssicherheitshauptamt, the RSHA, which was the National Security Service, the organ to which other powerful agencies were subordinate, including the Security Police and the Gestapo.

An assistant came in to take away the tea service and in doing so brought in some routine field report copies for Heydrich's in-basket. Heydrich halfheartedly glanced at them; then one of the flimsies made him stare hard and curse. It was a copy of Major Huntziger's report on Bergdorf. Heydrich paled as he read. "Holy bloody Christ!" he said under his breath. "That's all I need, to have those goons snooping around, mucking up the works! This will never do."

He buzzed on the intercom. "Get me Gruppenführer Müller at Gestapo headquarters." He thought better of it. "Never mind, I'll go there myself." If he told Müller that he wanted the Gestapo copies—all of them—Müller surely would consider them important and make copies of them for himself, just in case they might be of value later. Heydrich knew that that's what he himself would do if the tables were turned, and "Gestapo" Müller was just as devious as he.

He ran out of his office to his always-ready car, shouting at his driver to hurry. Two minutes later he was at Gestapo headquarters on the Prinz Albrecht Strasse.

"Is Gruppenführer Müller in?" he asked a secretary. He'd think of something convincing to tell him, an affair of the heart or some such thing. Müller would understand.

"He's not in, sir. He's with the Reichsführer-SS at the Ministry of the Interior, but he should be back shortly."

"Thank you," Heydrich said, "I'll wait in his office." He thanked his luck. He knew just where to look for the flimsies. He flashed the secretary a toothy grin.

The secretary closed the door behind her as Heydrich pretended interest in Heinrich Müller's photos on the walls. At the sound of the door closing Heydrich leaped to Müller's desk and the in box. There they were. Both copies. He folded them quickly and put them in his tunic pocket. He came back out to the reception office. "On second thought," he said, "I'll call him later. I just remembered an appointment."

Back at his office Heydrich opened a desk drawer and removed a telephone. He dialed a number. A voice said, "Yes, Reinhard?"

Heydrich told the voice about the Huntziger report and what he had done with it.

"What manner of fools do you have working for you, Heydrich?" the voice demanded.

"They're only doing their job, after all," Heyrich said, "and according to my instructions. How are they to know that you and I—and I mean *only* you and I—consider him special? But don't worry, I've handled it."

"If you have, then why call me? Do you want to make a change?" asked the voice, ever cautious.

"No, it would lead to too many explanations, explanations to the Reichsführer and all that. I called you for another reason."

"Yes? What other reason?"

"I occurs to me that when our friend gets to Paris, he may need more than his general's oak leaves. Especially in view of that damned report. He's going to involve himself in some rather, shall we say, precarious deeds, and the wolves will be snapping at his heels."

There was a pause at the other end of the line. "I see," the voice said finally. "Let me work on it. I'll let you know. There's my buzzer, Heydrich, my master calls. One last thought, my dear Reini. If you screw up, *your* hide will hang, you know, not mine.'

"I won't screw up. I can assure you."

"Better you should assure yourself. He's your man, remember?" There was a click as Martin Bormann hung up.

That evening, well after midnight, Martin Bormann knocked softly on the door of the Führer's study and gently let himself in. Adolf Hitler was poring over a large campaign map on a table. He held an oversize magnifying glass and was wearing spectacles, something few people ever saw him do. He was alone, but he still wore the simple gray uniform tunic, unadorned except for the National Socialist Party badge, and the Iron Cross, First Class, earned in World War I.

"Ah, Bormann! Come in, I'll be with you in a moment," Hitler said, going back to the map of Western Russia and the Ukraine. "You know, I do my best thinking when I'm alone and at this hour, a time when my generals are asleep."

Bormann was quite aware of the time—almost 2 A.M.—and he was further aware that Hitler in fact did *not* do his best thinking at that hour. He was too tired by then. That's why Bormann was there. At that hour. With the document.

"My Führer, excuse me for disturbing you during your work, but this must go out immediately. Please read and sign this document." He took a piece of typed paper out of a tooled leather folder and handed it to Hitler.

"Yes? What is this, Bormann? What am I signing?" Hitler trained the magnifying lens on the paper, frowning.

It was a *Führerbefehl*—a Führer order—which meant it carried with it the supreme authority of the state and was in no way challengeable.

The bearer, SS-Brigadeführer and Major-General of the Waffen-SS
Freiherr von B E R G D O R F, is under my personal command. I
thereby order that he receive unconditional and unquestioned cooperation from all military and civilian personnel having contact with
him in the execution of his duties. Failure to comply with this direction shall constitute insubordination to my orders and disobedience
of my commands, with the appropriate consequences.

Adolf Hitler looked at his secretary over the rim of his glasses.
"What is this about, Bormann?"

"My Führer, we need this authority to carry out Operation Nibelung. Bergdorf will be working for Heydrich in France. You may
remember Bergdorf; you presented him recently with the Knight's
Cross for heroism in Yugoslavia."

'Yes, yes, that young colonel from Siebenbürgen."

"That's correct, my Führer."

"And he now works for Heydrich?"

"Yes, he does. Excellent choice, I might add."

"Yes, now I remember," Hitler muttered as he sat down.
"Now, please, Herr Bormann, tell me once again about Operation
Nibelung. I'm tired and I don't quite remember it."

"Certainly, my Führer. It's a top-secret operation that was
brought to your attention by General Heydrich and me some weeks
ago and, I might add, of which you approved. Heydrich informed
you that the Reich was short of hard currencies—U.S. dollars, English pounds sterling, et cetera—which the Ausland-SD and in some
cases the Abwehr needed for operations abroad."

"Is this the counterfeiting scheme you fellows thought up to
break the Bank of England?" Hitler smiled in anticipation; he liked
that plot.

"No, my Führer, that's Admiral Canaris's operation. This one
is something new in that we are counting on Jews to subsidize the
plan." It was Bormann's turn to grin. "French Jews, my Führer."

"French Jews? How is that, Bormann?"

Bormann crossed his arms over his wide chest. "Well, I should
say relatives of French Jews, living abroad. Like the English Rothschilds and the American Morgenthaus and others." Two key names
to drop. "Heydrich has information that they will pay many millions
of U.S. dollars and other hard currency for these French Jews, and
we will have gotten rid of a lot of troublemakers."

"That's what I like about you, Bormann," Hitler said, reaching for the document and signing it. "You are clever and imaginative!"

"Thank you, my Führer, but it was really Heydrich's idea." Far from being modest or generous, Bormann was simply paving the way in case something went wrong.

The following morning the document was hand delivered to Heydrich. Operation Nibelung would continue without a hitch. Except for one small thing that both Bormann and Heyrich forgot about that would surface in Budapest three years later—Huntziger's own file copy of his report on Bergdorf and Erika Schuler.

Major Huntziger ended up getting killed by Russian artillery in the Battle of Lake Balaton, but his files, with typical German efficiency, were transferred to Budapest, in the building of the Hungarian Ministry of the Interior on the Andrássy Út number 60. In 1944 that address would serve as an office for the last-ditch effort to deport Hungarian Jews to Auschwitz. Heading that effort was an obscure SS-lieutenant-colonel named Adolf Eichmann.

OBERSALZBERG, ABOVE BERCHTESGADEN

SPRING 1941

The Sunday morning sky was a cloudless watercolor blue, and the rarefied air was crisp in Martin Bormann's lungs as he sucked in huge draughts of it. He paused for a few moments in his solitary walk through the woods and waited for a belch brought about by the German sausages he had consumed for breakfast. The satisfying belch resounded through the pines and he moved on, clad in his old reliable Lederhosen, heavy walking shoes, and woolen stockings that girdled burly calves.

He had come a long way from the plans of his youth, he mused. He had wanted to be a farmer; a scientific one, an agronomist, but still only a farmer. Ah, but that was then! Now, he told himself, even the high-and-mighty generals gave him wide berth and respect. Now he had reached that point of almost indispensability to the Führer that made the others look on him no longer as a shadowy figure in the background but as someone with whom they had to reckon. Yes, he was still the nominal subordinate of that lunatic Hess, but that too was changing. The Führer was fast running out of patience with that crackpot, and it was only a matter of time before Hess did something really crazy that would embarrass the Führer for the last time.

As things happened, Bormann didn't have long to wait. The

"something really crazy" had already occurred. Rudolf Hess, "the loon," had done it. And he had done it in style.

Bormann thought he heard someone calling from a distance. He looked over his shoulder and saw a man in uniform running down the hill from Haus Bormann, furiously waving his arms.

"Party Comrade Bormann! I'm so glad I found you!" the young man panted, catching up with him. "The Führer is asking for you. He wants you at once!"

"All right, let's go," Bormann said, almost running in the direction of the Berghof, Hitler's house. "Just what is going on?" he asked the young officer.

"Herr Pintsch, from Deputy Führer Hess's staff, brought the chief a letter," the lieutenant said, panting more out of excitement than from running. "It was from Deputy Führer Hess. The chief read it and—well, I never saw anything like it. He went into a kind of convulsion, you know, shaking all over and flailing his arms. It was very scary; we didn't know what to do. He had just read the letter when all of a sudden he shrieked. It was more like a howl of pain, and tears were running down his face, and—"

"All right, all right. You don't have to be so graphic. Did the chief say what was in the letter?" Bormann could hardly contain his excitement.

"No, Party Comrade. When Herr Pintsch handed him the letter, the chief put on his glasses—he was quite calm at the time—and then he read it, screamed, and immediately called for you. Field Marshal Keitel sent me to find you. Frau Bormann told me you went for a walk in the woods."

"Yes, well, Lieutenant," Bormann said, nodding to the SS guards stationed at the door of Hitler's villa, "we'll soon find out what the flap is all about."

Bormann went into a trot and flew into Hitler's study. "My Führer, I am here!"

"Ah, Bormann! Where have you been?" Hitler demanded. "Just look at this—the swine has gone stark raving mad! Look for yourself!" He skimmed the note across the desk to Bormann, who read:

Mein Führer! By the time you read this, I shall be in England. You can imagine that the decision to take this step has not been an easy

51

one for me, since a man of forty has other ties in life than one of twenty. . . .

The rest of the letter went on to say that he was going to do everything possible to force Britain to make peace with Germany by guaranteeing her dominions as long as she did not interfere with Germany's goals in Europe. He even offered to suggest that, if he failed, Hitler could always repudiate him as being mad.

"But my Führer," Bormann sputtered, "this is impossible! He *must* be mad, as you suggest. Of course, we'll have to issue a statement before the British have a chance for a propaganda coup." He was striking while the iron was hot.

"You're right, Bormann. Get Göring here, Ribbentrop, too. And Goebbels and Himmler. We've got to think of something. What will our allies think?" Hitler wailed. "They'll never believe I had nothing to do with it!"

"Yes, my Führer, at once." Bormann knew that as of that moment, nothing stood in his way to the power he envisioned for himself. Hess was through, and he, Bormann, was just beginning.

It was near midnight when they were all finally assembled in the large living room of Hitler's alpine retreat. Luftwaffe Chief Hermann Göring, bombastically outraged; Foreign Minister Joachim von Ribbentrop, aloof; Reichsführer-SS Heinrich Himmler, anxious and fidgety; Propaganda Minister Paul Josef Goebbels, sardonically glib; Wehrmacht Chief of Staff Wilhelm Keitel, stiffly military and distant; and Martin Bormann, in the shadows . . . waiting.

Adolf Hitler stood at the huge floor-to-ceiling window looking out at the snow-capped peaks of the Bavarian Alps; a bright moon bathed them in a silvery blue. He was in pain, due to the realization not that his old friend and trusted lieutenant was mad but that he was an embarrassment.

He turned to the ministers, who suddenly stopped talking. With a distant expression in his eyes and in a flat voice, Hitler stated, "If only he had fallen into the North Sea!"

After an appropriate and awkward silence, Goebbels said, "My Führer, we must give out a press release on this sad affair immediately, before the British make an announcement of their own to the world. I suggest something like this, to be read on the air: 'Party Comrade Hess, affected with hallucinations resulting from wounds in the Great War, believed he could bring about an understanding between Great Britain and Germany. He was a confused and deranged idealist, and his act will have no effect on the prosecution of the war, which was forced on the German people.' "

Hitler absently nodded his assent. Goebbels looked at the others in triumph, and they murmured their approval.

Hitler spoke again. "Herr Bormann, please take the following note: 'As Führer and Chancellor of the German Reich, I decree that Party Comrade Rudolf Hess be stripped of his ranks and all offices held by him, effective immediately. I further decree that, for his treachery to the German Reich and to me personally, he is to be found guilty of high treason and thereby sentenced to death in absentia. I further decree that Party Comrade Martin Bormann assume at once the offices of Party Minister, Chief of the Reich Chancellery, Reichsleiter, and Secretary to the Führer.' "

With those pronouncements, Adolf Hitler excused himself and went to bed. As he left the room, they all heard him repeat, "If only he had fallen into the North Sea. . . ."

The call to Heydrich in Prague went through immediately.

"It's not so bad, Martin," Heydrich said jovially from his luxurious headquarters in Castle Hradcany. "In fact, it's quite good here. Do you know that I don't have meetings—I grant audiences!"

"Hm. Perhaps you should start using the royal *we*."

"Oh, no, Martin, *we* would never do that!" Heydrich laughed. "What's happening in your neck of the woods? Any excitement lately?"

Bormann told him. Everything.

Heydrich howled with laughter. "Poor Hess," he said, calming down. "Well, he was due for a nice long rest. You know, Herr Reichsleiter, that makes you the undisputed number-two master of Germany."

"Yes," Bormann said pensively, "that is so, isn't it? Which makes Nibelung even more pressing, Reinhard. Is your man getting things moving in Paris?"

"He just got there, Martin. Give him time to get his feet wet, for God's sake!"

"Yes, you're right, I suppose. It's just that with Barbarossa only a few weeks away, we need to move quickly."

"I agree," Heydrich said with alacrity, "but aren't you counting the chickens a little too soon? Barbarossa has to have time to fail before we can move. Besides, how can you be so sure it *will* fail?''

"It will be a disaster, dear boy!" Bormann rang off.

The invasion of Russia—it can't but fail, Bormann thought to himself. *Delayed by precious weeks because of his tantrum against the Yugoslavs! He underestimates his enemy, as usual, and overestimates his genius*, he thought of his master. *And the summer will turn into fall, and then, winter! Fail? Oh, yes. Count on it. The military genius of the madman will be seen for what it is. Then Germany will be ready for another master.*

His hand still held the cradled telephone. He let go, noticing beads of sweat on the instrument. He rubbed his hands together, then tried to hold them steady in front of him. They trembled. He forced himself to relax, and the hands were steady again. Then in a violent spasm of excitement, his whole body shook. Little surges of nervous energy were making him lose control of his body in rousing paroxysms. He got up in a jerky motion and went to a filing cabinet and withdrew a bottle of cognac. He took a large gulp from the bottle, but still he shook. A second swallow made him tremble even more.

He leaned back in his chair and he remembered the only other time he had shaken like that—when as a youth he had lost his virginity. Through a crack in a barn door he had been watching a girl undress, and he tried to force his attentions on her. She had slapped him. As he had turned to leave, she felt sorry for him and invited him back, lying in the hay, pulling up her dress. As he stood over her, unbuckling his pants, holding his swollen penis, he knew that from then on he was going to do great and powerful things, and he began to tremble uncontrollably.

*   *   *

When the order to advance [on Russia] was given at three o'clock on the morning of June 22, [1941,] Hitler possessed the most formidable army the world had ever seen. . . . One hundred and forty-four German divisions . . . [and] more than 3000 tanks and nearly 2000 airplanes were ready to be thrown into battle. . . . In theory there was nothing to prevent Hitler's triumphant march through the rubble of Moscow before the end of the summer. (Robert Payne, The Life and Death of Adolf Hitler)

In November the cold winds came across the plains and the ice floes flowed down the Volga, while the German soldiers shivered in their . . . dugouts. Supplies broke down, there was never enough winter clothing. [The] Luftwaffe appeared to be grounded, and General Paulus was pleading for permission to abandon [Stalingrad]. [Hitler said,] "Stand firm!"

The Russian high command ordered the troops to resist to the last man. "Before you die, kill a German—with your teeth, if necessary." (Ibid.)

[Dannecker] visited Eichmann . . . and said that it would be necessary to propose to the French "something really positive, like the deportation of several thousand Jews." (Nora Levin, The Holocaust)

*   *   *

PARIS

WINTER 1941

Hans-Dieter von Bergdorf walked through the Tuileries gardens on his way to the Hotel Meurice. A yellow sun promised some warmth for the city, but he was in a sullen mood, a normal condition for him of late. He heard the chirping of a lonely sparrow in a barren tree and wondered what kind of foolish bird would stay in that dreary city when there were friends and warmth to the south. The contempt in which he held the simple bird characterized the depths of his spirit. And it was getting worse, this condition of his spirit, this restlessness and loneliness, even with Trudi at his side. The blueness gnawed at the pit of his stomach . . . all day . . . every day.

He attributed it to the job—what there was of it. At best, the job had him attending receptions of the highly ranked, a boring and fruitless activity; at worst, the job had him listening to the SD and Gestapo thugs at his headquarters, hearing the accomplishments of their flying squads rounding up foreign Jews for deportation to the east. Yes, he told himself, it was the job—the crushing, compressing boredom of the ugly job.

But deep inside he knew there was something else, something he forbade himself to think about—at least if he wanted to retain his spiritual integrity.

He had convinced himself that if he dreamed of her—and he did almost every night—he couldn't be held responsible for something his subconscious did. And he couldn't hold his soul accountable for wanting to be with her every second of his life, with every fiber of his being! he shouted to himself. Because he could not control his soul, his heart. She had been right, of course, when she told him that night—oh, so long ago!—that it could never be. And it was foolish even to consider the idea for one moment longer, the idea of holding her in his arms again, smelling her aroma, drinking her tears, tears of sorrow, tears of love! If only he could get back his command; if only he could be soldiering again, doing what he was trained to do. Oh, that swine, Heydrich! Then things would be right again in his soul, and his honor would not be compromised and he would be a good soldier again. Then, like all good soldiers when they are away from their wives, he could think of Trudi the way he used to, the way it was before. But now, Trudi was there and the aching was for someone else!

Bergdorf walked by the bare stumps of rose patches that, had they been in bloom, he wouldn't have noticed. He was thinking of Heydrich, and he was consumed with a loathing for him. He had sent several reports telling Heydrich that he hadn't been able to smell even a hint of a conspiracy against Hitler in the officer corps. If one were indeed brewing, surely he, Bergdorf, was the wrong man to find it. But Heydrich had told him to hold his ground, to continue his activities. In time, the rats would surface. He was trapped.

He sighed deeply, almost in anguish, as he reached the Rue de Rivoli and the Hotel Meurice, the headquarters of the German High Command in France. He knew there was only a small chance of finding von Trotha there on a Sunday, but he desperately needed to be with someone like von Trotha, whose scintillating and witty conversation might get him out of his mood.

As he crossed the lightly trafficked street, he saw something that did, in fact, alter that mood. At least, it drew his focus away from self-pity.

Two women were walking on the Rue de Rivoli toward the Meurice. Both women had yellow Stars of David on their coats. The women, he noticed in that brief moment, distinctly avoided the eyes of the two German sentries at the entrance. Then one of the women glanced up—only for an instant—at one of the two enormous swastika flags that emblazoned the building. She literally stole a glance, as if she were afraid of being caught looking. Then she looked down at her feet, and Bergdorf saw her look of resigned submission to the happenings of the times in her city, and her eyes betrayed the most anxious of her emotions—the uncertainty of her fate.

Bergdorf thought of his days as a student at the Sorbonne not too long ago. Had he been strolling down the Rue de Rivoli then and seen those same two women, they would have been just two more Parisians—one elegant, the other chic—on their way to some doing or another with complete freedom. Now, those two women were no longer free. Their existence was allowed—controlled—by the French police with the fragile cooperation of the German occupation authorities, while the Gestapo, like hungry wolves encircling the flock, waited.

He stopped momentarily at the hotel entrance and looked up at the huge banners of German might. Suddenly he saw grotesque meaning in the sizes of the two symbols that had been ironically juxtaposed a few seconds before: the massive swastika and the little Star of David. The large would swallow the small. It made morbid sense. The Jews did not have a chance.

He stepped up to a desk over which hung a large sign: DER MILI-TÄRBEFEHLSHABER IN FRANKREICH. An infantry captain, much older than Bergdorf, was the duty officer. Bergdorf pictured the older man's family back home: a plump, dutiful hausfrau and two teenage children—one, the boy, in the Hitler Jugend—and every night the family giving thanks to God that Papa was safe and sound in France and not on the Russian Front. Bergdorf asked for his friend, von Trotha.

"General von Trotha is not in," the captain said aloofly, not bothering even to look at Bergdorf, who was in civilian clothes. "But you may leave a message if you wish."

Bergdorf pulled out his calling card and dropped it on the desk. "You might tell him I came by. Nothing urgent."

The aging captain read the card and jumped to attention, almost knocking over his chair. "Pardon me, Herr General! I didn't know who you were. I—"

"As you were, Captain," Bergdorf said charitably, and wanted to add, *Don't worry, your safe job is secure.* "I'm not in uniform. Just relax. If General von Trotha should show up in the next hour or so, I'll be in the bar."

"*Jawohl,* Herr General! Again, please excuse me—"

Bergdorf waved off the apology and went to the bar, where he ordered a cognac from a passing waiter.

He sat down in a comfortable chair and looked out the window at the Rue de Rivoli. He could hear the growing sounds of the march music made by the German army band as it made its way down the Champs Élysées to the Place de la Concorde, a daily noontime ritual. That day they were capping off their triumphant parade with a ringing rendition of the Radetsky March.

He swallowed some of the cognac and lit a cigarette, exhaling the smoke in a long sigh. He tapped his fingers to the beat of the music, but his thoughts were with the two women who wore the yellow stars. His problems were inconsequential, even prosaic, compared to theirs. Or for that matter, to those of any other Jew in Europe, he thought.

It was inconceivable to him that his government would deprive a people of their freedom, of their rights, of their property simply because of their religion or ethnicity, and even deport those same people to God knew where—he had heard that the Jews were being sent to Madagascar—instead of treating them like other citizens of an occupied country. And German and Austrian Jews, Jews who had fought and shed their blood for the German and Austro-Hungarian empires just a few years before, were now being treated as aliens in their own lands and deported.

He was sure that the Germans were using the Jews as slave laborers, probably mistreating and underfeeding them. They were most likely victims of disease, he ventured. There was very little being reported by the Germans themselves as to the Jews' fate; there were only those horrible rumors. Dannecker told him of some himself: that the Jews were being eliminated (*exterminated* was the word) by the thousands by shooting and gassing.

That was what Dannecker had said, but Dannecker was a thug who enjoyed being a thug and was obviously a liar. Every war had its share of atrocity rumors on both sides. In some isolated instances they were true, but mostly they were exaggerated stories designed as propaganda to bolster the fighting spirit of the people. But for Dannecker to advance rumors to the effect that Germany, a civilized nation, was engaged in massive criminality as part of official policy was in and of itself a criminal act, Bergdorf had argued.

Dannecker had just smiled insolently and said in his most cynical manner, "Yes, a civilized nation owes it to itself to control its pests, to exterminate its vermin, which is exactly what we're doing!" Then he said something Bergdorf would never forget: he told him that in Himmler's SS bureaucratic, euphemistic jargon, they referred to the Jewish extermination program as the *Endlösung*—the Final Solution. At the SD and Gestapo, they were more imaginative, Dannecker crowed. They called it the Heydrich *Amt*. What did that mean, Bergdorf had wanted to know, the Heydrich office? *Amt* in this case, Dannecker explained, was an acronym of the names of the three leading death camps in Eastern Europe—Auschwitz, Majdanek, and Treblinka.

Bergdorf lifted the glass to his lips again and finished off the brandy. Dannecker's acronym story bothered him because Dannecker was an intellectual midget, certainly incapable of inventing something as potent as that kind of wordplay. Yet he was disturbed by the story; even though it was too impossible to believe.

He snuffed out his cigarette and got up to leave. Von Trotha was probably touring Paris with one of his two French mistresses. Or maybe both of them. Certainly he was not coming to the Meurice.

Bergdorf decided to walk across the street to the Jeu de Paume to see the Impressionists again, whom Trudi had shown little interest in. As he walked through the lobby of the hotel he noticed a rather unusual piano, a Pleyel. He stopped to examine it, intrigued.

The Pleyel was a long concert grand and judging by its elaborate design was probably from the middle of the nineteenth century. Bergdorf removed an oriental vase from the piano and placed it onto a nearby table, then opened the lid, revealing an idyllic scene of ancient Greece. He smiled at the kitsch of the work and pulled out the bench. He strummed a few chords in the bass; the tone was rich and flowing. He played the Schumann *Träumerei*. A few heads turned admiringly, appreciating the elegant, unobtrusive piece. He played for the better part of an hour, mostly for himself, as the music provided a sort of balm for his mood.

During an improvisation on a theme from one of Halévy's works, a voice behind him said in mildly accented German, "Most interesting! I've never heard it played like that before."

"Excuse me?" Bergdorf turned to the voice. It belonged to a man of medium stature, cheerfully stout and dressed in impeccable gray flannel. He wore a Homburg jauntily placed on a mane of white, and happy blue eyes smiled out of a face that could have been tanned in the south of France. A neatly trimmed silver moustache was anchored under a strong Gallic nose. He effused charm and joie de vivre.

"Ah, no," the man said, "it is I who should ask your pardon for interrupting. I was referring to the lovely music you were making, although I must confess I have never heard Halévy played quite like that."

Bergdorf at once felt the particular feeling, the unexplained reaction when two people meet and become aware of a mutual liking; the Spaniards called it *simpatía*. "Oh, yes, Halévy," Bergdorf said. "I was playing around with a theme from something of his; I can't think of the title now. I'm surprised you recognized it. It's rather obscure."

"You're right, most people wouldn't know it. That particular piece is from 'La Juive.' But before I impress you too much"—he leaned forward and smiled knowingly—"I should confess that Halévy was an ancestor of mine on my mother's side. A great-granduncle."

Bergdorf smiled and stood up, extending his hand. He spoke French to his new friend, a French by now polished and virtually without an accent. "I am honored, Monsieur—"

"Belfort. I am Guy de Belfort," the Frenchman said, taking Bergdorf's hand and removing his hat.

"And I am Bergdorf."

"Yes," said Guy de Belfort, "General Baron von Bergdorf, to be exact, senior SD officer in France, representing General Heydrich. Ah, your look of puzzlement causes me to explain to you that you and your exquisitely beautiful wife were pointed out to me by my friend General Blumentritt at the soirée of the Comtesse de Rémy-Villeneuve the other night."

Bergdorf smiled and nodded. "Of course, I remember now. You too were pointed out to me. I was told that you and I had a lot in common and that we should meet, but soon you were out of sight. And now here we are!"

"Fate, I daresay," Belfort said.

"Most likely," Bergdorf agreed, feeling better than he had for months. "But let's not stand here. Please join me in a drink."

They sat in the lounge and Bergdorf said, "Yes, Halévy. Beautiful music." Then as an afterthought and in the same tone, "He was a Jew, wasn't he? That makes you—"

"A Roman Catholic," Belfort finished the statement.

"I see," Bergdorf said, his chin cupped in his hand.

"We were always Catholic on my father's side. On the Halévy side they were Jews, but they soon converted. Even in those days it was the wise thing to do. No, I don't have to wear the yellow star. But if I were a Jew, I would wear it with pride."

There was a thoughtful pause. Then Bergdorf said, "I think I too would wear it with pride."

"Would you?"

"I'm not sure. I think I would. But then, it's easy to be brave when it doesn't count. I really don't know."

A waiter came by, and Bergdorf signaled him. He looked at Belfort for his pleasure. "A cognac, if you please. If it's still to be had, a Biscuit."

Bergdorf smiled. "At the Meurice? They'll have it, of course. I'm sure the German Army of Occupation has everything France can provide. It's called the spoils of war, is it not? Two Biscuits, please."

Belfort detected what he thought was a tinge of bitterness—or at least irony—in the remark, and he was about to respond in kind. He thought better of it. *Don't presume. Don't put him in the position where he'll have to defend what they're doing out of loyalty.* Belfort decided that there would be time later for "heart-to-heart" talks with his new German friend, as planned. For the moment, he wouldn't say anything that would force the German to backpedal his position.

"Yes, the spoils of war," Belfort said airily. "I recall, as a young lieutenant in the Great War, I accepted the surrender of a German company outside Strasbourg. Not only did I take the German commander's beautiful Solingen sword, but I ordered my sergeant to 'liberate' a case of a wonderful Neckar wine from them, which my men and I shared with the German commander and his adjutant. By the way, the sword still hangs proudly in my house, and I still have some of that wine—which I hope to share with you, my friend."

"I should like that very much," Bergdorf said.

Belfort proposed lunch at Maxim's, which was nearby on the Rue Royale. Bergdorf accepted with alacrity and newfound pleasure.

Like old friends, the two men—two men whose countries were at war, a fact temporarily forgotten by them—walked down the Rue Saint-Honoré. As they walked and talked of the arts and things meaningful to them both, the two gentlemen—two gentle men—were caught up in inglorious chance and circumstance and knew that a special bond had formed.

PARIS

SPRING 1942

"I just want to know one thing, Hans-Dieter," Trudi said suddenly, out of the silence, as if continuing a conversation. "Is it me? Is it that you're tired of me?"

"No, just tired," he answered softly without moving his head from the pillow.

Trudi continued to leaf noisily through a French fashion magazine, knees up under the blankets. "Tired of what? It can't be from making love, at least not to me. You haven't touched me in ages."

She was right. Since coming to Paris their lovemaking had dwindled to an occasional bout of corporal necessity, not a uniting of two people in love. In love? No, he realized, neither he nor Trudi had ever been in love with the other. They were married because, well, they made "the perfect couple"; it was a foregone conclusion. He sighed deeply at the thought.

"Is that your answer? A sigh?"

"It's the job, Trudi. I'm tired of it. Worse, I'm bored."

"You don't have to be bored, you know. You travel in high places, but you don't know how to take advantage of it. All those generals and high officials you rub elbows with—they could help you advance your career, you know. The right word in the right ear never hurts."

"I find it difficult to flirt with those high-placed gentlemen."
Then he added, to his immediate regret, "Unlike you, my dear."

"If I thought you were one bit jealous, Hans-Dieter, I would
defend myself by explaining that a little harmless flirting with the
right people can help your career in the SS. But then, I see that you
care very little about our future when you're seen all over Paris with
Guy de Belfort and his little gang of Jews."

"You don't know what you're talking about, Trudi. In the first
place, that is *my* business. In the second, they happen to be Frenchmen!" *The little fool,* he thought. *She knows nothing about this war,
nor does she want to know!*

"They may be French, but anyone can see they're Jews."

"If you're such an expert, perhaps you would do well in the
Reich Office for Racial Purity in Berlin. With your connections, I'm
sure you can get a job there."

"I'm glad it was you who brought up Berlin, Hans-Dieter," she
said, offended by his sarcasm. "I've not been happy for some time
now; I think you know why. You've changed, and I don't like what
I see—the indifference, the coolness. Yes, I will go to Berlin, as you
suggest, but with other goals in mind." She looked at him, waiting
for some comment on her announcement. "You have nothing to say
to that? Well, your silence is your permission."

"I won't stop you, Trudi. I wish you luck."

She arched one eyebrow. Her beautiful eyes were cold and
hard. "I see. Very well, I'll leave in the morning."

He turned to her and spoke gently, without rancor. "Yes, do
so, Trudi, for your own good." He stroked her arm in a last gesture
of affection. "And I hope someday you will understand the changes
in me and, above all, not hate me for them."

She looked at him. There was puzzlement, suspicion, and hurt
in her eyes. Wordlessly, she turned out the light.

PARIS

WINTER 1941–42

The Baron Guy de Belfort was dreaming that he was a lad on his father's estate in Alsace-Lorraine. He had removed his shoes and climbed the fruit tree, and the sun was warm, and the world was at peace. But for some reason he knew he should not eat the fruit. As he was about to find out the reason, the shrill sound of the telephone by his bed woke him. He said "Merde!" and turned on the lamp. The grandfather clock across the room said ten past two.

"Yes, yes, who is it?" he asked impatiently.

"Something has come up," said the voice of General Bergdorf. "I must see you first thing in the morning. Can you take breakfast with me at your usual place?"

"Yes, of course. Nine o'clock?"

"Make it eight." Bergdorf rang off.

At eight promptly, Belfort shook hands with Bergdorf and took a chair at a café on the Boulevard des Capucines.

"You look weary," Belfort said. "Is there something bad going on?"

"Yes, something bad. Here, I ordered rolls and coffee for you. Eat, then we'll walk and I'll tell you."

They ate quickly, silently, and apprehensively. Then they walked down the elegant boulevard, devoid of traffic except for a few bicycles.

"Last night I was called to Oberg's office," Bergdorf began. "You know who he is; the Higher SS and Police Leader for France, and Himmler's representative—therefore, my superior. Yesterday, as I'm sure you already know, there was an assassination attempt of a Luftwaffe officer on the Metro by some French youths, some of whom appeared to be Jewish, according to witnesses."

"Yes, I heard about it," Belfort said. "Damned foolish!"

"Yes, it was. Well, Oberg demanded of me what I was prepared to do about it. Before I could answer, he told me what must happen. First, he said, one hundred French hostages are to be shot immediately. Second—because it's believed that those responsible are, to use his words, Soviet-Judeo-Communist agents—the Jewish community is to be fined one billion francs forthwith. Third, he demands that one thousand French-Jewish professionals—doctors, lawyers, professors—be rounded up and deported to the east. This last assignment is mine; the other two he has already taken steps to handle. He finished up by informing me that all three phases of the reprisal have the blessings of Himmler *and* Hitler, which is his way of warning me that I had better do my job. Yes, Guy, something bad is happening."

Belfort's face was ashen. "Deportation means a one-way trip for them to places that we keep hearing about, like Auschwitz."

"Yes, I've heard of that place, too, but I think those are just rumors, Guy."

"Oh, please, Hans-Dieter!" Belfort said in exasperation. "You can't possibly believe that anymore! It's time you faced reality, the reality of what is happening to the Jews of Europe. They are being systematically exterminated!"

They walked in heavy silence for a few moments. Finally Bergdorf said, "Whether or not the rumors are true, we must assume that they are true and act accordingly. But what do I do? I'm but one man!"

"Yes, but you are in charge. That's a clear advantage. For what, I don't know yet. We must have time to think."

"Aside from my adjutant, Colonel Adler, I have no one," Bergdorf reminded him, "and on the other side, all those fellows at SD headquarters distrust me. They always have."

The Baron Guy de Belfort walked deep in thought, oblivious to Bergdorf's complaints. At last he spoke. "For months now, my contacts for Palestine and I have been trying to talk several of the so-called intellectuals—these professionals—into using our pipeline of escape out of Europe to safety so that they may later be part of a cadre, a nucleus, that will be needed to form the Free State of Israel. But these gentlemen would have no part of it; they think the Nazis are leaving them alone, honoring the Vichy government's request that they be left alone because they are first Frenchmen, then Jews. Now perhaps these babes in the woods will see the Nazis for what they really are.''

"What has all that got to do with the immediate problem, Guy? My orders are to round up one thousand Jews, for God's sake!''

"And you shall obey that order, my friend,'' Belfort said, now with purpose in his voice. "Just make sure that I get a copy of the list of deportees. In turn, I will give you names off that list, names of those whom we must get out of Europe, with your help.''

Bergdorf stopped in his tracks. "Would you mind telling me just how I am to do that?''

"We'll find a way, my dear General Bergdorf,'' Belfort said calmly. "You'll see, we'll find a way. I'll have the names for you six hours after you give me the list.''

"I wish I had your confidence, Guy. There's so little time—''

"Yes, I know. That's why we must hurry.'' Belfort grasped Bergdorf's hand. "I'll be in touch.'' He walked hurriedly across the broad street in the direction of the Place de l'Opéra.

Late the following afternoon, Bergdorf met with Belfort in a small apartment on the Rue de l'Arcade. With Belfort was a man introduced simply as DuBois. DuBois was an agent of Palestine Jewry and, more important, belonged to the Organisation Juive de Combat, one of several clandestine groups aiding French Jews with expertly forged papers—and funds.

"Here is the list,'' DuBois said to Bergdorf, handing him an official-looking document.

Bergdorf looked at the paper. It was from SS headquarters, Berlin. Or so it said. It was on the letterhead of the Wirtschaft und Verwaltungshauptamt of the SS Hauptamt. Bergdorf knew that was one of the many branches within the vast SS organization, the one that controlled and administered the concentration camps *and* the economic enterprises of the SS. The letter directed SS-Brigadeführer Bergdorf to place in *Schutzhaft*, or protective custody, the prisoners named on the list *zur besonderer Verwendung*, for special employment, in projects beneficial to the German Reich in France. It was signed Dr. Pohl, SS-Obergruppenführer, and stamped with the official seal of that office.

Bergdorf shook his head in silent admiration at the quality of the forgery and of the mind that had conceived the idea of making it appear to come from such a high and important office within the SS. No Gestapo agent would question the wisdom of using such valuable prisoners for "the benefit of the Reich." At least, not unless duty on the Eastern Front was more to his liking.

"Well, Hans-Dieter," Belfort said, "you asked me how one man can do it. What do you think?"

Bergdorf smiled. "I think that with this document, and my position . . . and with ice water in my veins, one man *can* do it!"

After the roundup the Jews were put in a holding camp at Drancy, just outside Paris, near the Le Bourget airfield. They and scores of foreign-born Jews would be processed before shipment to the camps of the "Heydrich *Amt*"—Auschwitz, Majdanek, and Treblinka—and other points east.

General Bergdorf, the author of the French list, came to the holding center accompanied by members of the French Security Police, a normal procedure. He showed the letter from Berlin to Dannecker, the SS man in charge, and began calling out names. Soon the rescued were back in Paris and were given papers and money, instructions, and the addresses of Frenchmen in Marseilles who would help them get to Spain for the duration of the war. And then to Israel.

AUSCHWITZ

SPRING 1942

IERF THCAM TIEBRA. Bergdorf tried to make sense of the strange words on the grillwork over the entrance, but the smell distracted him. His eyes scanned the cloudless blue skies of Silesia, and he thought for a few whimsical moments of turning around and going on a picnic. But he knew he mustn't, so instead he looked at the long and colorful flower beds on either side of the wide gravel path, a path similiar to one in any tranquil and perfectly kept German garden.

Höss was talking as the two walked leisurely down the garden path, talking about figures and statistics, but Bergdorf was only half listening. The smell was getting stronger, and he was close to identifying it when suddenly he stopped in his tracks and turned back toward the gate with the strange configuration of reverse letters. Of course, he said to himself, and he read backward: ARBEIT MACHT FREI. He was about to ask Höss whether work did indeed free those who passed through the gates when he remembered where he had smelled that peculiar odor before. It was when Trudi had dropped a knot of her thick hair into an ashtray where a cigarette had been burning. It was hair, burning hair.

Strange he hasn't mentioned the smell, Bergdorf thought. He hoped Höss would say something about it, something like, "We require all heads to be shaved, then we burn it in huge balls, and that is what you smell." But he knew Höss wouldn't say that. He also knew he shouldn't ask Höss about it, for it mightn't be in good form, but he asked anyway. "Tell me, Höss, the smell, is it what I think it is?"

Höss shrugged. "Yes, but one gets used to it after a while," he said with a touch of indifference. "I myself don't smell it anymore." He pointed beyond some rooftops to two giant smokestacks belching dark gray smoke, tongues of flame darting out of their mouths. "They're going all the time," he said. "With a population of one hundred forty thousand at any given time, we must keep them going day and night. But you get used to it."

Bergdorf wished he could place a handkerchief over his nose. Instead, he breathed in the smell, now getting stronger, very much like the smell of a pig being roasted over a spit on the Hungarian plains of his youth. Suddenly he felt like vomiting, and he prayed that he could hold it back. He would have to hold it back, although he didn't know why exactly. He made an empty comment on the flower beds.

Höss grinned broadly. "Ah, yes, the flowers. We'll have some beautiful roses this year. But you should see Frau Höss's garden in the family compound. She has the green thumb! Of course, we have an abundance of good, rich fertilizer here, which is needed because of the acidy soil."

Oh, please, dear Höss, don't tell me where you get your fertilizer, Bergdorf thought. He pointed to a railroad platform outside the main gate and asked Höss, "Is that the gate for arrivals?" Anything to change the subject from fertilizer.

"Yes. The trains bring them to that siding. In fact"—Höss consulted his watch—"a train is due within the hour. If you wish, you can see how our selection process works, how our medical director, Dr. Mengele and his staff, make the selections of those who are fit to work right there at the siding, saving a lot of time and costs." As an afterthought he added, "You know, we supply the various labor organizations with able-bodied men and women for the war effort. Todt, Thyssen, I. G. Farben—the lot. The Krupp concern will open a large facility here this fall, just outside the camp itself, and we will provide them with almost unlimited workers." He spoke with a certain pride. "Of course," he added confidentially, "because of the—the secret nature of our operations, we are not receiving the just recognition of our contribution."

"Of course," Bergdorf agreed. The smell was even stronger now—and sweeter. He gagged inwardly. Again he read the big block letters over the gate and wondered about those who were *not* selected for freedom through work, if indeed the words were sincere, which he doubted. Wondered? No, he knew. The smell told him.

"Höss, do you . . . do you have a little brandy? It's cold."

"Certainly, Herr Brigadeführer. In my office. I can also give you some hot tea with it. Come."

Bergdorf slouched in a chair in front of Höss's desk. He downed the brandy, its warmth making him feel somewhat better. The commandant poured tea for them both. Bergdorf put his feet up on the desk, trying to appear nonchalant.

"Yes," said Höss while he spooned a large amount of sugar into his tea, "with one hundred and forty thousand here on any given day, we are faced with continuing administrative problems, believe me."

"I don't doubt it. Tell me, Höss," Bergdorf said, pouring himself another brandy, "how many people do you kill in one day here?"

The suddenness of the question—its bluntness—unsettled the camp commandant, who was used to dealing in the euphemisms of the SS's extermination program—*Endlösung, Umsiedlung, Sonderbehandlung;* final solution, resettlement, special handling. Höss swallowed his tea. "I can't say with exactness how many we process in a twenty-four-hour period, Herr Brigadeführer, but I *can* tell you we are becoming more efficient every day. Look, let me show you something."

Höss put down his cup and led Bergdorf into a small storeroom with filing cabinets and a table. Several wooden boxes were piled up high on the table, one of them open and obviously empty. On the long side of the box was etched in brown letters the name of the manufacturing firm of its product: Deutsche Gesellschaft für Schädlingsbekämpfung—GmbH. The German Company for Pest Control, Ltd. On the short end of the box was the brand name: Zyklon-B.

Höss picked up the box and tapped it with his middle finger. "See this? This is what's increasing our production. With the little crystals that come in this, the time for processing has been cut nearly in half, as compared to other methods. And it is more humane, believe me."

Another odor invaded Bergdorf's nose—bitter almonds. "Humane?" he asked.

"Yes, humane. Even though we must be hard, we still have room for a little pity, you know."

"Yes, I see. Of course. Tell me, Höss, you mentioned 'other methods.' "

Höss rubbed his chin with large fingers, and a thoughtful look came to his eyes. "At first, the shootings," he said. "But that turned out to be expensive and inefficient. Of the large numbers scheduled for Special Handling, too few were done properly. We called it 'trench warfare' because large trenches were dug, and the people were lined up at the edge of it and shot, falling into the pit. Then the earth was bulldozed on top of them." His hands made a pushing motion. "You know, like a huge grave."

Bergdorf blinked several times. "I see," he said softly.

"The only trouble was," Höss continued, "many of them were still alive. I don't have to tell you what that did to the men involved in the operation—nightmares, drinking, requests for transfers to the Front, even. But I personally never used those methods."

"I can see why you didn't."

"Yes. Then Lange came up with the idea of using vans."

"Vans?"

"Exactly. They would load up vans with people, like cans of sardines. Then they ran a hose from the exhaust of the van to the compartment with the people and turned on the engines." He shook his head and began pacing the floor. "That too was inefficient—and cruel. They were supposed to die within fifteen minutes, but sometimes it took an hour. That was very bad, not to mention the effect it had on the men, the special Kommando doing this. They had to haul them out and bury them. Feces, urine, blood was all over them and inside the van. It was horrible, I tell you!"

Bergdorf's throat was locked in a spasm. In a way, he was glad he couldn't speak, for if he could, he would have said what he was thinking. But he was an SS-general and SS-generals did not cry and weep and tear out their hair in front of SS-captains.

Instead, he went on listening numbly, damning Heydrich to hell for ordering him to visit that place.

"Then Wirth came up with the idea of using fixed cubicles in which the exhaust gas was pumped," Höss continued, "and he raised the numbers in Belzec and Sobibor to six thousand a day."

Bergdorf still could not speak but his eyes showed shock and incredulity.

Höss smiled proudly. "Oh, we're well above that figure." He pointed to the box of Zyklon-B. "With this! Are you all right, sir? You look a little pale, if I may say so."

"I'm—I'm fine. It's the smell, probably. I congratulate you, Höss, on your efficiency." *I've got to get out of here,* he said to himself.

Höss grinned broadly at the compliment. "Thank you so much, Herr Brigadeführer. When we've worked out the various technical and logistic problems, the Reichsführer-SS will order at least three more camps built like this one. When he first summoned me and gave me this command, he told me that this would be but the first such operation in a major long-range program for even after we win the war. I like to think what I've done will justify his confidence in me."

"I'm sure it will." *God almighty, get me out of here!*

"We provide thousands of workers—men, women, and adult children—people who would otherwise die from starvation and sickness and disease."

Bergdorf didn't want to ask, but he had to. "What about the others, Höss, those not well enough to work?"

"*Na, ja!*" Höss sighed. "The majority are already half dead by the time they get here. But the transportation people are at fault there. So many Jews are already disease-ridden from the ghettoes that many die in transport." It was the first time he had used the word *Jew.* "I wrote a memorandum to Berlin pointing out the atrocious condition in which these people arrive. I even went so far as to complain directly to SS-Obersturmbannführer Eichmann himself, but he just shrugged it off as inconsequential. It's a terrible waste, you know."

"Yes, I can see that."

"If it's not imposing on you, Herr Brigadeführer, when you return to Berlin, a hint or two in the ear of Reichsführer Himmler would be helpful, and I would be grateful."

Bergdorf was astounded at the request from this rather gentle automaton whose chief concern in life was efficacy, even when the product was human life. He shook his head at the realization that the Hösses of the SS could reduce things to "output divided by input equals efficiency and a job well done" and incongruously ask a third party for help with his superiors. "I'll see what I can do." He sighed.

"Thank you, Herr Brigadeführer. You know, it's our job to process them, but how many more could still be employed in the war effort." Höss continued to sell his point to the young SS general sent by Berlin. "Do you know, sir, how much money goes into the SS treasury? Millions!"

"I'm sure." *Oh, God—please!*

"Krupp pays, Thyssen pays, all of them pay on the average of five marks per day per worker. Our selection criteria are very good; we gas only those who are better off dead anyway. We're not butchers, you know."

Bergdorf could only nod.

Höss, now agitated by his own words, walked up and down the little storeroom. "Go to Treblinka or Sobibor—you'll see, all they care about is killing. They're not concerned as we are with saving Jews for factory work. I don't think that was the intent of the program, just killing; and when we do it here, we're humane." He paused a few seconds. "Of course, because we are now the largest camp, our numbers are always greater, so that statistically, after the war is over, it may appear that we were bloodthirsty." He paused again. "Because of the numbers," he added softly.

"Because of the numbers," Bergdorf repeated dully.

"But we're not murderers. We don't take pleasure in putting people to death. That's why we use the Zyklon-B; it's fast and merciful. I think that if they knew it, they would go to the baths without so much as a whimper."

"Baths?" Bergdorf interrupted the monologue of sanguinary rationale. "What do you mean, baths?"

"Those coming off the transports who are not fit for work are processed at once. They are told that they will be bathed and deloused. They are taken to very large cubicles, rooms with many shower pipes, and the doors are locked. Then the Zyklon-B is introduced through the shower openings, and within minutes . . . they are no more. Fast and painless. Up to two thousand at a time."

Bergdorf choked back the vomit.

"You know, sir, I have nothing against Jews. In fact, I had many good Jewish friends before the war. I'm not a savage. To this day I've never beaten or mistreated a prisoner, and whenever I hear of one of my staff using excesses, I take firm and immediate action. That person usually ends up on the Eastern Front. We have definite policies laid out by the Reichsführer himself as to the treatment of prisoners. He makes it clear that extortion, sadism, cruelty, and otherwise un-German behavior will not be tolerated." A pause. "Neither will unauthorized killings be tolerated."

Unauthorized killings! Un-German behavior! Part of the Code of Ethics in the Brotherhood of Genocide? For the first time, Bergdorf felt pity for the kindly, otherwise prosaic taskmaster. He pitied that model of German obedience and compliance, that instrument of human annihilation who, with his wonderful insecticide, *humanely* exterminates "the pests." *The fly may be swatted to death, but don't pull off its wings or he agonizes for having violated the Code of Ethics.*

There was a long pause in which both men looked down at their hands folded in their laps. Bergdorf drank his third brandy, and as it seared his throat, he noticed he was actually getting *used* to the smell, the frightful odor of burning human bodies. He shuddered violently, hoping Höss would blame the brandy.

Then he asked, "Tell me, Höss. A while ago you mentioned that after the war you might be looked on as bloodthirsty. You don't really think that, do you? When we win the war, what will it matter? Or perhaps you're thinking that you would be judged a mass murderer if we lose the war."

Höss's eyebrows went up. "Lose the war? No, it's never occurred to me that we would lose. But now that you bring it up—hypothetically, of course—if I'm accused of such a thing, my response would be"—he pursed his lips as if opting between rice and potatoes with his meal—"that I was, after all, like a good soldier, only following orders. Yes, that would be my defense, I suppose."

Bergdorf looked at him in silence.

Höss pointed a finger at Bergdorf. "I see by the piping on your uniform, Herr Brigadeführer, that you are a Panzer officer, and by your Knight's Cross and Wound Badge that you were in combat. There must have been times when you, as a commander, ordered your men into the fight knowing that some would be killed. You were doing your duty as a soldier, following orders for your country. Well, it's no different for me here in the KaZet. I, too, am a soldier. My duties may be different, but I must obey the orders."

"Yes, yes, quite right, Höss. But let me ask you a question, if it's not too indelicate." Bergdorf leaned forward in his chair. He knew he shouldn't ask it of Höss or, for that matter, of any of the many Hösses wearing a uniform in the service of the Third Reich, the New Order. But still he asked. "Aren't there times when you ask yourself, 'Is this right? Is this moral?' when you've had all you can take of this, when the—"

Höss waved his hand in protest, interrupting the obvious and horrid question. "Please, sir! With all respect, I know what you're asking. I don't like to think of those things. With me, it can't be a question of morality or what is right or wrong when it comes to my duty to my country. I'm not political; I don't make my country's policies, nor do I question them. My God, what kind of order would we have if everyone questioned his superiors!" He lowered his voice to almost a whisper. "Besides, if not me, there are dozens, if not hundreds who would run this place."

Bergdorf rose to leave. Höss remained seated, staring at the floor morosely. "Good-bye, Höss. Your job is not an easy one."

"I do my duty," whispered the commandant of Auschwitz.

As Bergdorf left the camp, a train was unloading its cargo—Polish Jews, mostly, judging by the Polish and Yiddish he could hear coming from them. At the siding, a trio of striped-prison-garbed musicians were playing a lively Johann Strauss waltz, and the arrivals actually seemed happy to be there. A loudspeaker was telling them to line up so that they could be taken to the showers, after which they would all go to the mess halls for a good meal. But first, the camp doctors would select those strong enough for work units. *After the train journey, it must sound like paradise,* Bergdorf thought.

He looked at the prisoner-musicians again. He knew their smiles were out of sheer gratitude to be alive one more day in Auschwitz . . . one more week. Maybe more.

Auschwitz was in him, in his hair, in his pores. Every part of him had the soot and the ashes, and he scrubbed his chest and arms with as much soap and fury as he could get out of the hemp wash pad. He rinsed under the scalding water, and sniffed his arms and hands. He could still smell it, he could still smell and even taste the evidence of what was once human bodies. He scrubbed harder, in a panic, praying that the SS-corporal in the hotel in Kattowitz had bought enough wood for the boiler with the money he gave him. He needed the hot water to cleanse him, and the soap would— Suddenly he stopped scrubbing and stared hard at the white tile, the water running down his head and into his eyes. He stared through the steamy haze and asked himself aloud, "What will remove the soot *from my brain*?"

He pressed his fingers around his nostrils and blew hard into them, examining the mucus for bits of black. He did that several times until he saw tiny spots of blood from the force to his nasal capillaries. He washed his hair again, thinking, *It will pass, the nightmare will pass*. Then he leaned his head against the tiles in resignation, and he slowly slipped to the floor, his knees meeting his chest. He rested his forehead against his knees, moving his head from side to side in feeble impotence at the knowledge that his beloved SS—his country, for God's sake—was systematically, ruthlessly, unconscionably doing away with a whole people because those people were looked upon as a problem. And now the problem was being resolved. It was a solution, and the Hösses of the New Order were efficient. They all were efficient, Höss had told him, some more than the others.

Höss was right, he reasoned. If not him, there were others, perhaps some even more dedicated. The Hösses of Germany—of the world!—and their wonderful ability to obey. So easy. The men who can somehow put aside—at least for the duration—their sense of morality, their consciences, religious teachings, the lot, all for the greater benefit of the State, all for the—

Stop it! his brain screamed at him. He raised his sodden, aching head from his knees, staring once more at the nothingness of wet, white tile. *Stop it! You know about the Hösses. There is nothing you can do to stop them. The question is: What about you? What about the* Freiherren *and the* Grafen? *You, the so-called nobility, the "upper strata," the backbone of civility. You, the heirs of honorable blood! The masters of the castles! You, the overeducated, the philosophers! The intelligentsia! How dare you have asked poor Höss that question! You should be asking it of yourself. What are you going to do? Now that you know, now that there can be no more denial, no more convenient ignorance—what will you do?*

The clouds of steam had long dissipated, and the water had turned cool. He turned off the taps and sat shivering, but he did not know if it was from the cold or from his burning questions. He reached through the shower curtain and pulled in a towel, drying his face. Then he wrapped himself in the towel, hearing the drip-drip-drip of the lonely shower as he pondered those questions.

I'll tell him, he suddenly resolved. *That's what I'll do—I'll tell him what they're doing in his name. In his name, for God's sake! He will stop it. He must stop it! If only I can get to him, he will remember me. Those eyes, they looked into mine so deeply—he will not have forgotten me.*

But how can I get to him with that army of leeches around him? The leeches, yes, they know. They're the ones who dreamed up this abomination! Yes, and what about the giants of German industry that Höss mentioned—Krupp, Thyssen, Farben, Topf, and the others? My God, they too must know!

But . . . if they know . . . then he too must know! Oh, dear God, if he knows, then not just a handful of criminals are doomed— Germany is doomed! And Frederick the Great is doomed, and so is Barbarossa. Brahms, my beloved Brahms, and Beethoven—they are doomed, and even Bismarck is doomed! If he knows, then this obscenity is national policy. If it is, then we are all doomed, for who can forgive us?

Hans-Dieter, Freiherr von Bergdorf, major-general of the Waffen-SS, tank soldier, hero of the Yugoslavian campaign, rested his head on his knees and wept. His tears were of frustration and impotence, and of anger, disgust, and most of all shame. In his world of honor and civility, something new and alien and ugly was coming to pass, and the world was suddenly putrid. He felt alone, but now with his father dead, he had no one to counsel him, if only to remind him that he was a Bergdorf and therefore a man of honor.

One sob turned into a bitter, ironic laugh. He remembered a time at Oxford when he had been playing poker. He'd been dealt a hand that couldn't lose, and he didn't bet it. When asked why he had not bet everything he had on a sure thing, he had answered, "Ungentlemanly. It wouldn't have been sporting." Even in war there was room for idealism and civility. After the battle of the Tisza bridge, he remembered, the Yugoslavian commander had surrendered his troops to him by offering his pistol. He had saluted the Yugoslav and shook hands. Where had it all gone to, this chivalry, this decency, this sense of honor? Were they going to take it away from him? If the evil of Auschwitz was national policy, did they expect him to join it? The Reich, for good or for evil? Would his father expect him to do his duty for what had become the beast?

Yes, there was still something he could do, should do, one honorable thing in that world of dishonor.

He lifted his aching body out of the shower, dried off, and carefully buttoned his underpants. He carried his uniform belt to the bed and sat down. In slow, tired movements he unsnapped the black holster and removed the 9-millimeter Walther. He slid open the breech, admitting a round, and thumbed off the safety. The only indecision was whether the mouth or the temple. The mouth won.

He put the blue barrel beyond his teeth, his tongue tasting the acrid oil on the smooth steel. But the pistol was awkward in his contorted right hand. He shifted it to his left hand, right thumb on the trigger, remembering to point the barrel as high on the palate as possible so that with luck the bullet would destroy the midbrain first, then on its way out, most of the cerebellum. He shuddered at the thought of ending up a neurological invalid, unable even to end his life.

He squeezed his eyes shut, incongruously fearing the loudness of the explosion. But he knew he would hear nothing.

Then, in that almost-last instant of his life, he thought of Erika; and in logical sequence he thought of his wife. But Trudi didn't matter—only Erika mattered. Wait! He had to leave Erika a note. *My God!* he thought. *I almost left without saying—what?—saying something to her, my beloved Erika. I'll write her a letter. In fact, I'll write to them too, the men without honor, the criminals. I'll write them a letter. Otherwise, what good will my death be?*

Then, as he visualized the gendarmerie, or the military police, or whomever would be called, he knew that the letter would be turned over to that person's superior, then to the next, and so on down the line. And it would end up flushed down some toilet. And Erika? Would she get her letter? What if she didn't? What would she think of him? That he was a coward? *No, no. She's too fine and noble to think that.* And yet, the war may have changed her. If there were some other way of letting her know . . . *Wait. Maybe there is.*

Slowly an idea began to take form. He returned the mindless, irredeemable hammer back to its harmless position and tossed the gun casually onto the bed. Suicide, yes, but through more fruitful devices.

He jumped up with renewed vigor, the idea taking on a clearer and more definite form and intent. He dressed hurriedly, almost in a panic. He could still catch a military plane to Berlin, then on to Paris.

He knew it would cost him his life, but now, now he had things to do. From that moment on, he thought as he buttoned his uniform tunic, he would have things to do.

HRADCANY CASTLE, PRAGUE

SPRING 1942

Bergdorf studied the back of Reinhard Heydrich, the Protector of Bohemia and Moravia. The protector, in a perfect-fitting field-gray uniform, looked down from his private office window to the parade grounds of the great castle, seat of the Bohemian kings. He was now the reigning and supreme authority in Occupied Czechoslovakia.

Despite his hatred of him, Bergdorf was very much in awe of the blond Teutonic figure with the manxlike eyes and feline movements. He hadn't seen him since the previous year, but he was still the same imposing image of confidence and power. And yet he was different somehow. Before, he had represented a ruthless, arrogant, cynical man of great force, not just physical force but of great will crowned with self-assuredness. He had effused an almost perverse obstinance that would tolerate no challenge, brook no contradiction of his ideas or of his being. Now, as Bergdorf studied him, he acted like a benevolent dictator, a medieval lord concerned with his people, his serfs.

Heydrich came away from the window. "You know, Bergdorf, at first I wasn't thrilled about coming here, but now I see it was a blessing in disguise." He sat at his desk. "I've accomplished quite a bit in the short time I've been here. That fellow von Neurath, my predecessor, made a shambles of things, but now all is under control.

I've had to kick a few asses here and there, of course, and put some Czech agitators behind bars or in their graves, but all in all the people are responding well. They're working hard, but conditions are better for them overall, and their bellies are fuller. When bellies are fuller, there is less griping and rebellion. That's what counts, isn't it? Tell me, my dear Bergdorf.'' He smiled, leaning forward. ''How are things going in Paris?''

''You mean the salon-and-theater front? That's about it, I'm afraid. I've discovered no plots against the Reich, or for that matter the Führer, if that's what you mean. At least, all those I've come in contact with seem to be loyal. The army appears to be doing a good job running the show, and as far as my job is concerned, well, you know I'm only a figurehead.''

Heydrich made no comment. He just looked at him curiously. Then he smiled, nodding his head, waiting for more.

''But then,'' continued Bergdorf, ''maybe the consipirators don't trust me yet.'' He smiled nervously. A year ago he would have been pleading his case to return to active duty with his old unit, using the same arguments he had used with Heydrich at the Bristol Hotel— that he was a soldier, not a spy. But now things were different. He had to stay on.

Heydrich maintained his grin, enjoying Bergdorf's obvious discomfort. Finally, he picked up a letter opener and held it horizontally, gazing over it at Bergdorf. ''Tell me, Bergdorf, catch any Jews lately?''

Bergdorf had been prepared to discuss in general the activities of the SD in France as regards Jews. After all, it was now the SD's role to administer German racial policy, since the German ambassador to Vichy had given it up. And Bergdorf, at least in name, was the SD. But the sarcasm behind Heydrich's question upset him. ''No, not really. I leave that to Dannecker and his bunch. I must remind you of our meeting last year when you assured me that I wouldn't have to be involved in such activities.''

Heydrich recoiled in mock horror. ''My, aren't you the testy one! Why are you so defensive?''

''Respectfully, sir, I don't appreciate playing games in these rather distasteful matters.''

Heydrich studied him for a moment. ''Testy and sensitive, which is how I always remember you. And yet I see a contradiction in such a sensitive fellow who finds such matters *distasteful*, to use your word." He took out an official-looking paper from a folder. "This report indicates the opposite. It's an order, dated eleventh December, nineteen forty-one, in which SS-Obersturmführer Dannecker and his bunch are directed to round up one thousand French professionals—all members of the Hebrew persuasion—for deportation to points east as reprisal for an attack on a Luftwaffe officer." He leaned forward and whispered, "The order is signed by you, my dear Bergdorf."

"Yes, sir. It was my duty."

"Ah, yes, your duty." Heydrich grinned again. "Then your stock with Oberg and the others must have increased?"

The question was heavy with irony. "I really don't know; I didn't ask them."

Heydrich withdrew a sheaf of papers from the folder and began leafing through them. "Tell me, my friend, tell me about your fellow nobleman, the Baron Guy de Belfort."

Bergdorf was taken aback by the question but managed to hide it. "The Baron de Belfort? Yes, we became friends not long ago. He's very influential with the Vichy government, and he's helped me with a few problems." His pulse quickened as Heydrich pored over the many sheets.

"Hm. Could those problems be named? Let me see: Philippe, Paul; Varèse, Henri; Bressonière, Marc-Jean—shall I continue?" Heydrich smiled icily.

So, Bergdorf thought, *the moment has finally come*. He had thought of how and when it would come many times ever since his commitment to involve himself, actually to rebel and disobey orders, to betray his country and his oath. But he had done it in the name of an honor different from that of those who demanded loyalty and obedience. He had weighed it all, and he knew the risk. He had known it since that day in the hotel in Kattowitz after Auschwitz. And now he found that when the moment came, it wasn't so bad after all. He had opposed them, and he felt no guilt. Had he not opposed them, the guilt would have been lethal. He felt calm.

"Shall I continue?" Heydrich repeated, no longer smiling.

"No, there's no need. I know the names. They are French Jews whom I helped escape our policy of destroying them simply because they are Jews. I made it possible under my authority as your representative, knowing full well what I was doing and the consequences." He lit a cigarette. He noticed, as did Heydrich, the lack of tremor in his hand as he held the lighter to it. A look of serenity came over his face, a look not lost on Heydrich.

"You said you realized the consequences of your act."

"I did."

"And you still did it? Why, Bergdorf?"

"In view of the existence of places like Auschwitz and your Captain Höss and your Colonel Eichmann, I'm surprised you would ask me that question."

"But they're only Jews! Why have you given up your life for them?" Heydrich frowned his query.

"You're wrong, General. They're not *only* Jews—they're human beings, like me—like you—like the others."

"But you're a German!" Heydrich shouted indignantly.

"Precisely. It's because I'm a German. You may end up shooting me on the spot, General, but I will have died with the knowledge that what I did was honorable—as a German! In the face of the most dishonorable chapter of our history, I would be one German—and I'm sure there are others—who would rather die in honor than live in this disgrace!"

Heydrich applauded. "Bravo! How noble!"

Bergdorf stared defiantly at Heydrich, still panting in a combination of anger and fear. Heydrich's expression had changed to one of cold fury, his slit-eyes showing loathing and contempt. They glared at each other for a few moments, then Heydrich calmly pulled at the flap of his holster at his belt. He removed his Walther and pulled violently at the breech, snapping a round into the chamber, staring at Bergdorf all the while. He thumbed off the safety and pointed the gun at Bergdorf's chest. Bergdorf took a deep breath but remained stoically calm.

"I could kill you right now, Bergdorf, and the Führer would give me a medal for doing it. You have deliberately disobeyed his orders."

"I used to find it hard to believe that they were his orders," Bergdorf said impassively. "But at this point, nothing astounds me anymore. Not even your pistol. Go ahead, earn your medal."

Heydrich continued to stare. *What an idealistic fool,* he thought. *More so than I gave him credit for.* He pointed the pistol at the ceiling, pulling the safety lever and returning the hammer to its down position.

"Don't worry, Bergdorf, I'm not going to shoot you. Maybe you'd be more comfortable in Auschwitz. I hear that my friend Dr. Mengele likes musical accompaniments for his medical experiments. You're not a bad piano player, I hear. You could entertain the children of Israel with a few pieces by Mendelssohn."

"I would consider that an honor."

"Yes, I think you would. You have a sense for theatrics. Maudlin and melodramatic theater, you poor fool!"

Suddenly, Heydrich slapped his thigh as if inspired by a wondrous idea. "Better yet, I'm going to let you make a real hero of yourself. You're going back to Paris!"

"Is this another one of your sick jokes?" Bergdorf was beyond caution or civility.

"Even more cantankerous, eh? Well, I'll grant you that luxury for now if you'll grant me your attention. But first, let me ask you this: How much did you get from your Jewish friends for giving them their lives?"

"What?" Bergdorf was clearly outraged.

"Just as I thought—nothing. You know they would have paid with the gold in their teeth, don't you?"

"It was never on that basis!"

"No, of course it wasn't, my idealistic friend, but it will be in future. Remember when I told you that Nibelung and I have contingency plans? We're convinced more than ever that Hitler will be assassinated, or at best arrested. When that happens, we must be in a position to take over from him against the traitors. For that we need funds, lots of funds. And for that we need you selling French Jews their lives, for which they will be happy to pay."

"One moment, please," Bergdorf said. "You're asking me to assume my post again in order to extort money from these unfortunate people so that you and your—"

"Please, Bergdorf"—Heydrich grimaced—"spare me your naive, moralistic drivel. I'm giving you the chance to save some more of these unfortunates. In fact, as many as you want, provided, of course, they can pay. Remember this, and it may help you in the course of your 'extortion' activities: Those Jews are doomed; their assets will end up in the SS treasury anyway. It doesn't take a genius to see the alternative. Put it to them, your Hebrew friends. You'll see how quickly the line forms and the money comes out."

Bergdorf stared in disbelief. "You mean this, don't you? You really mean it!"

"Of course I mean it, you fool! What do I care if a few hundred, a few thousand Jews escape Eichmann and his boys?" He smiled. "Let's call it a tithe for our new church."

Bergdorf got up from his chair and walked around the room. This sudden inspiration of Heydrich's was what he had been looking for all along. As debased and dirty a plan as it was, it was a way. As for the money taken from the people, that could be replaced. Money can always be replaced—people cannot. Heydrich was right: the SS would end up with the money and their lives. *This is the way*, he thought. *But don't appear too anxious, make a small argument.* He stopped in midstride. "What about me? I'd be in direct disobedience of standing policy. Your spies would certainly report that, wouldn't they?"

"Don't concern yourself with my spies. There are only two people who know about your little display of conscience—Gutermann and Schroeder. They're both with the Waffen-SS in Russia with no hope of a transfer."

"You mean they're in Russia because they knew?"

"Of course not; how could they? I just now came up with the idea, which idea saved your life and that of your friends in the bargain."

"Yes, of course," Bergdorf said. Suddenly something in his head clicked, and things started to make sense. Within the space of a few minutes, he had been staring into the barrel of Heydrich's pistol, then had been threatened with Auschwitz. *Then in a flash, I'm let off the hook, my life, my future, my career, everything, spared. Then, the icing on the cake, I can go back to Paris and continue smuggling Jews out of Nazi Europe.* It made sense only if the whole thing were preordained, planned, plotted, *schemed* by that devil! He knew from the beginning how things would end up—a pistol pointed from across his desk . . . the brainless fish caught on the barb, then released, then snagged on another, smaller but more effective hook. *Fine*, thought Bergdorf, *I'll go along with his game, even with the first hook, the conspiracy-to-kill-the-Führer nonsense.*

Heydrich tossed a packet of Camels across the desk. He held a lighter up to Bergdorf. "Cheer up, man! You have a new lease on life—enjoy it!"

Bergdorf exhaled and smiled. "Yes, I'll enjoy it. You don't know how much I'll enjoy it, General."

Heydrich gave him a knowing look. "Good. Well, now that we understand each other, let's get cracking. I want you back in Paris immediately. You'll need help, obviously, which I shall give you. Two blockheads who won't question your orders, and this." He removed a document from the folder. It was the *Führerbefehl* that Bormann had obtained almost a year before.

Bergdorf read it and looked at Heydrich, puzzled.

"The date? Yes, I obtained it last year, just in case you ran into some problems in your assignment. But you never asked for help, so I withheld it. However now, with your new job, you probably will need it. It has magical powers, so use it judiciously."

Bergdorf folded it and put it into his tunic pocket. He had a feeling that he was in league with the devil, but at least now he could think along with him, if not ahead of him.

"Shall I continue looking for conspirators?" Bergdorf asked. If he were going to play along, he'd have to play it all the way, including asking stupid questions.

"Try to concentrate on your new assignment. Of course, if you should find that something is brewing, let me know."

"Of course." *You miserable lying swine!*

Heydrich held the incriminating sheaf of papers. "These are the only copies, Bergdorf. I think it would be prudent if we gave them a decent burial, don't you?" He struck his lighter, touching flame to the pages. He put the burning report in the fireplace, making sure all the fragments burned. He dusted his hands and smiled at Bergdorf. "It would have been a waste of talent to have shot you, don't you think? Besides, how could you have helped the children of Israel if you were smelling the violets from below?"

The next hour was spent discussing details of the plan: the minimum price; what securities and currencies would be acceptable; how to handle gold, precious gems, and so on. Heydrich made a point of tapping another source—the English Rothschilds and other British

Jews. American Jews could also funnel large amounts through England, he said. He had thought of everything.

The loot would be held in a *Bank privat* in Zürich, owned by a Nazi-sympathizing Swiss named Langfeldt. It was to be taken into Switzerland through a particular border crossing where the Swiss customs officials would look the other way. Bergdorf would be in control of the account.

"You would trust me with so much money?" Bergdorf asked.

"Let me put it to you this way," Heydrich said. "A, you won't steal from me, not as long as I'm alive. If I die, I couldn't care less, but Nibelung may have other thoughts in the matter. And B—more compelling—your honor is at stake. Not only your German honor, for which you were prepared to die, but your family honor. I ask you, Freiherr von Bergdorf, in the long and noble lineage of your family, would you be the first thief? No, of course you wouldn't. Does that answer the question?"

"It does."

Later, with Bergdorf gone, Heydrich picked up the phone and got through to Martin Bormann in Berlin.

"Hello, Reinhard. How did it go?"

"Even better than I expected."

"He'll stay in Paris?"

"Oh, yes. He'll do exactly as I say. The operation will begin immediately. Langfeldt will be alerted to expect the first deliveries within a fortnight."

"Well, Reinhard, I must say, you are a good judge of character! Did you have to use the Huntziger report?"

"No, I decided against it. There's no particular edge in letting him know that I know he's screwing around with his sister-in-law. We all do it—at least those of us with beautiful sisters-in-law. I didn't see the point."

"Yes. But on the other hand, I remember once, as a young boy, my grandfather caught me throwing away a piece of string, and he wisely pointed out that you never know when you might need even a piece of string. Think about it."

"Don't worry, I didn't throw it away. I just added it to the ball of string I already have."

"By now, Reini, it must be a big ball."

"It is, Martin."

"Yes. Well, pay my best respects to your lovely Lina."

Heydrich laughed. "I will, but you know, Martin, she hates your guts."

"My dear fellow, if I worried about all the people who hate my guts, I wouldn't be in my position today!"

* * *

[SS-Lieutenant Theodor] Dannecker pressed on with his plans as . . . deportation mania gripped the German police forces in Paris. Eichmann, on June 11, 1942, had called together his agents in France, Belgium and Holland to discuss deportation schedules for these countries, and a quota of 100,000 Jews was established for France for the next three months. On June 26, Dannecker drew up a set of rules for his territory. He fixed the age limits from sixteen to forty-five, and included French nationals as well as stateless Jews. Fifty thousand were to come from each zone; all were to be sent to Auschwitz. (Nora Levin, The Holocaust)

The Red armies had been crippled but not destroyed. Moscow had not been taken, nor Leningrad nor Stalingrad nor the oilfields of the Caucasus; and the lifelines to Britain and America . . . remained open. . . . The armies of Hitler were retreating before a superior force. That was not all. The failure was greater than that. [Chief of the German General Staff General Franz] Halder wrote [in his diary]: "The myth of the invincibility of the German Army was broken." (William L. Shirer, The Rise and Fall of the Third Reich)

* * *

PANESKÉ BREZANY

MAY 27, 1942

It was a sunny morning that Reinhard Heydrich chose to walk through the woods of aspen and birch of the Bohemian countryside. He breathed the pleasant aroma of moist earth drying in patches of sun, and he took in the other forest scents of the serene domain. The tranquillity was brought about by the least tranquil event of all—war.

But war was the farthest thing from his mind that glorious morning. He was thinking of fishing. He stopped at the bank of the stream that coursed its way through the vast estate, a stream abundant with trout, and skimmed a pebble into it. He promised himself that when he returned from Berlin he and the children would go fishing. Yes, when he got back from his meeting with the Führer. Oh, yes, and his meeting with Bergdorf. *Mustn't forget the meeting with Bergdorf*, he told himself. Nibelung was going full speed now, and he wanted an up-to-the-minute report. Certainly that swine Bormann would be pestering him for an update. He knew he couldn't leave Berlin without being subjected to Bormann's prying questions.

He checked his watch. There would be just enough time for a quick breakfast with his Lina and the children, some business in Prague, then the plane to Berlin.

Heydrich wiped coffee from his lips and bellowed for his personal bodygurard, giant SS-Sergeant Klein. He had dismissed his regular driver because Klein drove faster, and Heydrich was in a hurry that morning.

He strapped his Walther around his greatcoat, smiling at the assembled children. "Come, give Papa a big kiss. If you are good, Papa will bring you each a nice present from Adolf *Onkel*." The children and Lina lined up for their kiss.

"All set, Klein? Well, let's get a move on!"

Lina Heydrich watched from the steps of the mansion as her husband went off into surely more glory. It was such a beautiful day, and the birds were singing. She looked at him sitting proudly, regally, in the big Mercedes open touring car next to Sergeant Klein. He would be back to her soon, she was sure, with good news from the Führer. Yes, her husband had a way with the Führer. Their life was good, and it was only the beginning, she mused as the birds sang.

But she was wrong. For her and her husband, it was the beginning of the end.

"Faster, Klein, faster!" Heydrich, the protector, cried.

The powerful car tore down the country road, its heavy tires screaming against the asphalt and stone, leaving a violent storm of leaves and dust in its wake through the Bohemian forest. He enjoyed the speed of the car. It was in keeping with his personality—fast, furious, impatient, stormy, and violent. He showed the same aggressiveness in the politics of his position, and that combination of assertiveness and keen intellect made of him an effective protector. Not only had he subjugated the Czechs by ruthless means, he had succeeded in securing their cooperation toward the German war effort in their factories with what he called a policy of *Peitsche und Zucker*, "whip and sugar."

To the Czech government-in-exile in London and to the British, a man like Heydrich was as dangerous as ten Panzer divisions and therefore must be destroyed—at any cost.

The big 3.5-liter Mercedes engine growled like an irritable lion as Klein shifted into the lower gears, slowing it down. They were already on the winding cobblestones of the Rudé Armády, intersecting with Strelnicná, in Prague.

A *krummpp* from behind him made Heydrich's ears ring and his back hurt. A British grenade had been tossed into the open back seat of the Mercedes. The front seat absorbed most of the damage, but some horsehairs and other debris from the upholstery penetrated Heydrich's back. The wound in and of itself was not so bad. But the infection and the damage to his pancreas—which would result in an acute diabetic episode later—were.

Exactly one week later, Reinhard Tristan Eugen Heydrich, thirty-eight, died the way he had lived—by violence and pain.

* * *

[Soon after the attack on Heydrich, the following verbal orders were issued as part of the reprisals against the Czechs:] "Auf Befehl des Führers wird die Gemeinde Liditz von Frauen und Kindern evakuiert, die Männer von 16 Jahren auf der Stelle erschossen und die Gemeinde abgebrannt." *(By order of the Führer, the women and children of the village of Lidice will be evacuated, and men over sixteen will be shot on the spot, and the village subsequently burned down.) (John Bradley,* Lidice—Sacrificial Village*)*

"If an enemy bomber reaches the Ruhr, my name is not Hermann Göring: you can call me Meier!"

The bombing of Cologne starts just after midnight [May 30, 1942]. It is a terrifying experience for the city's inhabitants. . . . Raging fires devastate the city center and the whole of Cologne is enveloped in . . . dense, acrid smoke. Over 2000 tons of bombs have been dropped . . . 13,000 houses destroyed. . . . Hermann Göring wrote in his diary about the bombing of Cologne: "Of course, the effects of aerial warfare are terrible if one looks at individual cases. But we have to accept them." (A. Mondadori Editore, 2194 Days of War*)*

* * *

BERLIN

JUNE 9, 1942

The city was bathed in lazy sunshine that morning. Here and there crews of foreign workers carefully sorted usable bricks and timbers from bombed-out buildings. They would be used for repairs. The RAF nighttime raids were becoming a deadly but routine nuisance now. Berlin and other cities, especially the industrial and heavily populated ones, were starting to feel the brunt of the war more and more from the skies, as more and more British heavy bombers were penetrating the flak curtains, delivering their cargoes of death and destruction. In the rare moments of looking for mirth, Berliners more and more fell on the popular "Herr Meier" jokes.

The procession came down the broad avenues—the bomb damage had been hurriedly repaired—and on to the Kroll Opera House for the standing-room-only funeral ceremonies, attended by the entire German Reich leadership. Some genuinely and outwardly grieved Heydrich's death; most were genuinely and inwardly celebrating.

A contingent of military and political leaders slowly marched to the toll of funeral drums behind the swastika-draped coffin that was mounted atop a mechanized gun carrier surrounded by an honor guard of uniformed SD men. The coffin contained the once-handsome body of SS-Obergruppenführer Reinhard Heydrich, protector of Bohemia-Moravia.

An SS band played not the Funeral March from the Chopin sonata but excerpts from Wagner operas, while the crowds lining the route, disciplined and solemn, raised their arms in the old pagan German greeting, paying tribute to the fallen Siegfried on his way to Valhalla.

The coffin was set down amid thousands of flowers on the dais of honor inside the Kroll Opera. In the front row sat a solemn and angry Hitler; next to him was an equally solemn Göring, then the noncommittal Himmler. The two Heydrich boys, not understanding what was happening, sat next to their mother, Lina, who was pregnant yet stoic. In the next row, behind Hitler, sat his gray eminence, Martin Bormann. Then came Goebbels and other party leaders in their cloaks of sham sorrow.

Directly behind Bormann, in the third row, sat an SS-major-general in full parade dress: Bergdorf.

He had arrived the day after the wounding of Heydrich. Ignorant of the event, Bergdorf had gone directly to Heydrich's offices and found the place in chaos. He ran into Walter Schellenberg, head of SS Foreign Intelligence and one of Heydrich's confidants, who was preparing to go to Prague with Artur Nebe, chief of the Criminal Police, to investigate the bold crime. Schellenberg, in his usual wry manner, had filled Bergdorf in on the events, commenting that the British, with the help of some Czech resistance fighters, had introduced themselves "rather rudely to our dear Reini." Yes, he was alive, Schellenberg had said. "Oh, yes, Bergdorf, he gave me a message for you," Schellenberg had said airily. "He said you are to stand by in Berlin until further word from him. You are at liberty, but make sure the communications board at the Kurfürstenstrasse knows where you can be reached at all times."

"What's going to happen now?" Bergdorf had asked sincerely.

Schellenberg had laughed. "What a naive question! I don't know what will happen, my dear Bergdorf, but I do know that if Reini doesn't make it, the population of Czechoslovakia will be reduced rather significantly."

Bergdorf had waited idly, checking with the switchboard at RSHA headquarters so often that the operators got to recognize his voice before telling him there was no message. After a few days, it had seemed to him that Heydrich would survive. Then came the shocking message—from Reichsleiter Bormann, oddly enough—that

Heydrich had died of his wounds and to stand by for further instructions from him, Bormann.

The "further instructions" came by way of Bormann's written invitation to attend the funeral.

Bergdorf had sat on the edge of the bed in his hotel in an effort to regroup his thoughts, his plans. Because his relationship with Heydrich had run the gamut from friendly coercion to outright blackmail, Bergdorf had learned to be prepared for anything. But now he was gone. What would happen to Operation Nibelung? Was he free of it? No, there was Nibelung himself, the other partner. Was it Bormann? Probably. If so, what would he have to prepare for with the powerful Reichsleiter and Secretary to the Führer?

Now he sat behind Bormann, studying the back of his bull neck and his straight, coarse hair ending in bristles on his nape like a clothes brush. Yes, Bergdorf was convinced, Bormann was indeed Nibelung.

As Himmler droned on about his protégé, Bergdorf noticed that his hands were cold and sweaty. But when Hitler took the podium and as his impassioned speech shook the vast theater, Bergdorf's thoughts were elsewhere. Only when Hitler was finished with his moving and furious oratory did Bergdorf's thoughts come back to the Kroll Opera. He watched Hitler pat each of the Hedyrich boys on the cheek and grasp their mother's hand. He stared solemnly and wordlessly into her reddened, veiled eyes, in much the same manner that he had used during the presentation of the Knight's Cross that day so long ago in the Reich Chancellery. No words, just a baleful look. A look that was eloquent in its silence. Was it all an act, Bergdorf wondered, and had it been an act then?

As the Führer and his coterie filed out, Bormann stopped in front of Bergdorf. "Greetings, Herr von Bergdorf," he said casually. "Please wait at your hotel. I will call you within the hour."

Bergdorf looked at Bormann for a few moments. Bormann seemed to wait for an acknowledgment. "*Jawohl, Herr Reichsleiter,*" Bergdorf said.

Bormann looked at him, something close to a smile on his lips. Then he elbowed his way to Hitler at the front of the line that was going out into the fresh air of the summer day.

Forty minutes later the call from Bormann came. Bergdorf was to wait for a car to pick him up in front of the Adlon Hotel in thirty minutes. Precisely thirty minutes later, a large Daimler-Benz sedan came to a halt a few feet down from the main entrance to the hotel. The passenger door popped open, and Bergdorf stepped in. The driver was Bormann, in civilian clothes.

They drove in silence to the Tiergarten nearby and parked in a shady spot. Bormann turned, twisting his large bulk from behind the wheel. He offered his hand. "I'm glad to see you, Bergdorf, although not under these circumstances. But such are the fortunes of war, aren't they? I venture you know why we're meeting. The way you looked at me this morning, I would say that it would be redundant to introduce myself as other than Bormann."

"If you mean, Herr Reichsleiter, does the code name Nibelung mean anything to me, I would say yes."

"Of course. We're not schoolboys, are we, Bergdorf? Well, now, what did our friend leave us with as a result of his untimely departure? I imagine a discussion between us is in order, don't you think?"

"Quite in order, Herr Reichsleiter." *No expressions of regret at the death of a close associate*, thought Bergdorf, *not a kind word for a fallen soldier, no matter how insincere that word might be*. No. It was business as usual, cold and hard business.

"Very well," Bormann said. "First off, don't change your activities. Proceed as you have up to now, except speed things up if you can."

"I'll do my best." Bergdorf wondered just how much Bormann knew of those activities. Then he answered his own doubts: This man was even more astute than Heydrich, more practical and self-serving. No doubt he knew exactly what was going on with the Jews, and no doubt he could see the bottom lines of the ledgers, in which Jews were converted into pure profit without a single risk to himself. Still, Bergdorf thought of the nightmare Heydrich had put him through in Prague just a few weeks ago. He didn't want to go through that again, so he decided to lay everything out on the table with Bormann then and there. "I wonder, Herr Reichsleiter, if you know exactly what my activities are in France? I mean, what I do with Jews?"

"That you're shipping them out of Europe instead of to the camps? Of course, my dear fellow. I know it all, and in detail. Heydrich kept me informed, as well he should. You have my blessings; please continue your work with the Baron Guy de Belfort and his Palestinian friends. Except do it faster; use that document we gave you—use its power." There was a pause. Bormann came closer. "Look at it this way, Bergdorf: You're a moral man, doing what your conscience dictates. I, on the other hand, am an amoral man, doing what I see necessary for my survival. We both get what we want. What's a few hundred Jews from our seemingly endless bounty?"

BERLIN

SPRING 1944

Willi Bauer, of the Clean-up Brigade number 12 for Middle Berlin, walked precariously on the broken beams and slabs of plaster. He thought he spotted something in the rubble of what was once the third floor of the Adlon Hotel. He called out to his colleague, "Karl, come up here. I think I see something under this slab."

Karl Schmundt made his way up from the second floor. "Damn you, Willi, you want me to break my neck? What do you see that's so important?"

Willi pointed. "Look, Karl—a foot. See it? Sticking out from under that slab? It's a foot, I tell you!"

"You're right, Willi. Let's get a closer look."

The two men pushed and pulled at the debris until they uncovered a crumpled bed full of dust—with two bodies in it.

"Bloody hell," Karl said. "Look at that!"

"Yeah, but look at his face! It looks like he was in the act of creaming when he bought it."

"For God's sake, Willi, show some respect for the dead!"

"Unfortunately, I ran out of that ages ago," Willi said.

"Look at her face. She must've been a real looker."

"It's hard to look at faces when all I see are her legs wrapped around the poor fellow." Willi Bauer took a heel and tried to move it. It wouldn't budge; the legs were locked in rigor mortis around the dead man's waist.

"It's no use, Willi. Let them be, for God's sake!"

"Look," Willi Bauer said, "there's her purse. Let's have a look. Hm. 'Baroness Gertrudis von Bergdorf,' it says. Well, you have to give the nobility credit," Willi Bauer said, making his way down the debris-covered steps. "They know how to live and they know how to die."

"How's that?" Karl Schmundt asked.

"Fucking!" said Willi Bauer.

* * *

In the middle of March, 1944 . . . Eichmann was assembling at the Mauthausen camp in Austria the most devastating unit of Jewish killing specialists in the history of the Holocaust. . . . Wisliceny . . . Dannecker . . . Brunner . . . Krumey. . . . These men . . . came to Budapest . . . and formed the Sondereinsatzkommando Eichmann, the Eichmann Special Operations Unit. Their work elsewhere was finished; now all of their experience could be concentrated on Hungary. . . .

Eichmann himself, for the first time in his career, was to work in the open and become a public personality. The once-obscure and cautious deskman had now become a cynical, hard-drinking, luxury-loving Nazi satrap operating out of the Majestic Hotel, one of the best in Budapest. His ostentatious standard of living, however, had not changed his function. While hunting down the last Jewish prey left in Europe, he was, in his own words, a "bloodhound." (Nora Levin, The Holocaust)

* * *

TRANSYLVANIA

SPRING 1944

A blanket of hardened snow covered the rugged, wooded slopes and rooftops of Maroshéviz in the Carpathians, an area populated by Hungarian woodsmen and Romanian shepherds. A new storm was gently dropping fresh, small snowflakes. Here and there German soldiers in groups of two and three walked down the main street looking for warmth and schnapps in a saloon to help overcome the tedium of recovery from the wounds that had brought them there. Soon, however, those same soldiers would be sent back to the foxholes and the mud and the Russian shells—and death.

Erika Schuler sat in a small room of the German Military Hospital, a room that served as a lounge for the doctors when and if they could find a few moments to relax from the hours of treating the wounded. The room contained two cots and a table on which tea was brewed and a wardrobe stuffed with doctors' coats, some stiff with bloodstains. Erika sat on one of the chairs, her feet resting on a cot, sipping hot tea with rum. She had worked thirty hours straight and was now too tired to sleep. The workload was mounting every day: more and more wounded, more and more amputations, and fewer and fewer supplies. She looked out the frosted window and thought, *We're losing the war*.

Udo von Ost came in and poured himself a cup of tea. As he

opened the rum bottle, he said in a matter-of-fact tone, "We're losing the war, Erika." He pulled up the other chair and sat next to her, putting his boots up on the same cot.

"Those were the exact words I was just saying to myself," she said, still gazing out the window, "but we're wrong. We've already lost the war."

Udo von Ost, colonel in the Army Medical Corps and chief of the hospital, frowned. "Careful with that talk, Erika. You know what they do to defeatists." He took her hand and squeezed it with affection.

"Yes, I know," she said in a monotone, "but I'm beyond caring." She decided to change the subject. "What's the latest count?"

"Ninety-six, just this last trainload." He let go of her hand and lifted the teacup to his lips. He started to reach for the cup with his left arm and, realizing again that that arm was no longer there, cursed the arm, the arm that had been blown off his trunk some time ago. He cursed it silently, instinctively, as if it were the arm's fault that it no longer was attached to his shoulder to pick up teacups and hold surgical instruments and hug children. Now there was only an empty sleeve folded in half and pinned to his shoulder pad.

He still couldn't get used to the fact of not being able to command his left arm, the arm that had held and caressed his beautiful wife—now no longer living—had played with his beautiful children—now no longer playing. All of them were gone, along with his house, after an air raid. Afterward, when he again could think and act, that left arm had stayed in the fields of Kursk along with seventy thousand German bodies and God knows how many other pieces of bodies. His arm stayed at Kursk, but the rest of him journeyed to Maroshéviz, where he had found Erika Schuler.

"Ninety-six," he repeated. "For eighteen of them, the war is over. As for the rest, we'll see how many wrecks we can salvage for return to the Front, depending of course on how much baling wire we have left." His words were beyond the point of bitterness. It had been weeks since they had had a shipment of plasma and sulfa. Bandages were washed and reused; sheets were torn into strips for dressing wounds. Everything was in short supply—most of all, hope.

Von Ost put down his teacup. "By the way," he said casually, "there's a fellow downstairs from the Klausenburg Gestapo who wants to see you. Any idea what it's about?"

Erika looked at him vacantly at first; then a flicker of apprehension came into her eyes. "Didn't he say?"

"No, he didn't. He seemed to enjoy not telling me when I asked him. Rather crusty fellow. He did say the Budapest Gestapo people wanted to talk to you."

"Budapest!" She suspected now it was because of the Jews. Ilonka, Kálmán, Tibor, and the rest. Her assistants whom she kept on at the hospital as "essential personnel." She had been warned by the town officials.

"Yes, Budapest. He said they will fly you in from Maros Vásárhely and fly you back. This was in reply to my objections that you're badly needed here. It's about the Jews, Erika," he said very gently. "You can't continue to defy them; they must go."

She sighed deeply.

He opened the door and kissed her softly. "I love you, Erika. You know that, don't you?"

She touched his face, tracing the scars with her fingers down to his jaw. She nodded.

Despite the vast affection she had for him, she wasn't in love with Udo von Ost, and he knew it. He suspected that there was someone in her past who prevented her from loving him. He never asked, even when they were in each other's arms. He reckoned that eventually, should they survive the war, she would tell him. He didn't press it.

What was in evidence, however, was a certain emptiness in her, a hollowness of spirit, of emotion—of heart. He didn't have to delve into that at all because he too knew the feeling, he too shared that vacuum of emotion, that void made by an irreplaceable and irresoluble loss. Yet that same hollowness seemed to act as a bond between them because they saw it in each other's eyes. Then, slowly, the attitude toward life began to change in them both. The pervasive and continual atmosphere of death, which before had seemed to be a faceless but accepted part of their existence, now turned into a reality that they must face every day, and time and opportunity suddenly became precious. And he loved her, and she received him—his goodness, his loneliness, his needs. It was her salvation to give him all she had left.

Erika Schuler was cold and uncomfortable on that, her first airplane trip. The Junkers Ju-52, loaded with foodstuffs, lumbered slowly through the crisp night air, relatively safe in the darkness from Russian fighters. Various colored lights glowed eerily in the big plane's interior; the faint flush of SS-Lieutenant Brandt's cigarette brightened occasionally as he dragged on it. She had been unable to get anything out of the Gestapo officer other than to sense his peevishness for having been sent so far to fetch her—something a lower rank could've done, he said.

Erika thought of "her Jews," as everyone referred to them. Count Ormáncy, the burgomaster of Maroshéviz, had warned her about keeping them. She knew it would have been the better part of valor to go along with the German "request" regarding Jews and to have rescinded their "essential" status at the hospital. Instead, when the Hungarian prime minister, Miklós Kállay, defied Hitler and the SD regarding deportation of Jews, Erika had hired five more "essentials."

It wasn't long after that that Hitler summoned the Hungarian regent, Miklós Horthy, to Klessheim Castle near Salzburg. The German leader had pounded his fists at Horthy, demanding the immediate appointment of a prime minister who would be more sympathetic to the Reich's policies. Horthy, having stood up to Hitler for so long, was faced with an ultimatum: Give in, or Hungary would be invaded. Horthy broke down and named a virulent anti-Semite, General Sztojay, as premier, giving the SS a free hand in implementing the Final Solution in his country. The change also unleashed Ferenc Szálasi and his Hungarian Fascist "Arrow-Cross" Movement, who would, in the few months left of the war, go on a rampage of bloodletting on Jews and Gypsies that would make even the SS pale by comparison—and in disgust.

Count Ormáncy knew what was coming, and so he warned Erika. Now it was here, she thought to herself as the Ju-52 droned on to Budapest, where an unknown fate awaited her; those who sought vengeance were now in a position to wreak that vengeance.

She remembered the stories told her by a Waffen-SS officer who had been wounded in Russia, stories of the time he had been stationed in a place called Sobibor in which he had been part of the horror. He said it had been a choice of either dying of cirrhosis of the liver from his heavy drinking to alleviate his shame over his acts, or dying in honor at the front, as a soldier. Better the freezing cold and

Russian bullets, he said, than the nightmares of the gas chambers and the smell of roasting flesh.

The thought was so repellent to Erika that she forced herself to think of something else, anything else.

She remembered a visit to Budapest in her youth. She thought of the chestnut trees along the banks of the Danube where it flowed under the elegant Chain Bridge. The trees were displaying their Christmas candle-like blooms, very much like the chestnuts of Bistritz. It had been a long time since she had thought of her hometown and her family . . . and him. Her eyes moistened. She was wondering if she would ever see those chestnut trees again. Or her family. Or him. . . .

Her thoughts went back to Sobibor, and what she had heard of it and other places like it. She felt around in her coat pocket for the capsule, and as she caressed it with her gloved fingers she felt comforted. She marveled at the thought of the deadly power of the crystalline fluid contained in the little gelatinous tube: potassium cyanide, the dull, colorless, even prosaic fluid whose only purposes were aiding goldsmiths and taking lives. Quickly. Efficiently. And except for a few seconds of agony, virtually painlessly.

Erika Schuler looked out the window of the plane into the black, starry night. She hoped that wherever she was being taken she would be able to see once again the chestnut trees blooming on the banks of the Danube where it flowed under the Chain Bridge. Then she realized that they would not be in bloom, for it was too early in the spring, and she sighed.

It was almost dawn when Brandt and Erika arrived at SD headquarters. It was located at number 60 Andrássy-út, an elegant, treelined boulevard named for Count Andrássy, a nineteenth-century statesman said to have been the lover of Empress Elisabeth von Habsburg.

The place was teeming with activity even at that late hour. Cars and trucks came and went; SS men and Hungarian gendarmerie in groups outside the building and in the large courtyard talked in loud voices and drank coffee to ward off the cold of the dawn. Floodlights lit up the scene as large buses unloaded groups of people who were then herded into the building by barking SS troopers. Erika stole a glance and thought, *Jews*.

Brandt took Erika into a large room and told her to find a seat and wait until called. There were about sixty people in the room. Aside from a small group of Gypsies, they were all Orthodox Jews, Erika noted, wearing the long caftans and beards and *payesses* and the characteristic black hats. Erika studied the family groups. Aside from the children, who were playing or asleep, they all seemed to have looks of resignation on their faces. She thought it strange that no one looked scared or apprehensive. They just talked in low murmurs, creating a din in the cavernous hall. One of the SS suddenly shouted to them in German to be quiet. Then a man stood up, as if propelled by the officer's shout, and began what appeared to be a prayer in Hebrew. He was almost wailing as he rocked back and forth, back and forth, holding a small, dog-eared book. *"Sh'ma Yisroel, Adonai elohaynum, Adonai echod. . . ."* There occurred a deathly silence in the room as everyone's attention was riveted on this bearded man in a black hat. They knew the prayer he was reciting. Pious men said every morning and evening—and when facing death. The man continued his mournful chant, rocking from the waist so violently that his hat flew off his head. *"Adonai elohaynum. . . ,"* he wailed in his Chassidic intonations of the Hebrew. Erika concluded that when the SS man had shouted, the bearded man finally lost the stoicism that had sustained him up to then, even though he knew that his destruction was only a short time away. Now he called upon his God to sustain him—not in this life, but in the next.

Then, as if on cue, the rest of the group began murmuring the same prayer, the *Sh'ma.* This only served to irritate the nervous SS man. He walked over to the instigator, the bearded man, and with the butt of his Schmeisser struck him a savage blow to the back of the head. He fell on his knees, then the rest of him went forward, hitting his forehead on a bench. He twitched for a few seconds and finally lay still, the life gone from his lips.

"Goddamned Israelite bastard!" the SS man yelled at the fallen figure. "See what you did? Didn't I tell you to shut your trap?"

A few women tried to stifle their sobs for the dead man and for themselves, but the wailing took on a high pitch. The German raised the Schmeisser above his shoulders and yanked at the bolt; the sound of metal against metal created a terrible, ominous noise in the high-ceilinged room. *"Shut up, I said!"*

Suddenly there was quiet.

Erika, wide-eyed and scared and sick to her stomach, felt in her pocket for the capsule and held it firmly.

A few minutes later, while the body of the Jew was being dragged away, Brandt returned and motioned for Erika to follow him up a flight of stairs to a large office. The room contained three wooden desks and a long, wooden bench, along with some metal filing cabinets. Boxes of papers and other materials were stacked in a corner. A picture of Hitler and another of Himmler were hanging on the wall. The place smelled of bureaucratic efficiency.

Brandt directed Erika to sit at one of the desks and said Colonel something-or-other would be with her in a minute.

A few minutes later, two SS officers came into the room talking animatedly. One, a captain, was short and dark with a thin moustache. The other, with the four pips of a lieutenant-colonel on his collar patch, was tall and blond. Pale blue eyes and straight white teeth made him rather handsome in Erika's view. He looked at her and smiled, creating dimples in his somewhat craggy face.

He came over to her and in an Austrian accent said, "Ah, Frau Doktor Schuler! I hope you're not being inconvenienced too much." He took her hand and brushed his lips on it. She almost pulled back her hand in displeasure at his oily charm.

"It's just that we're so short handed at the hospital," she said softly.

"Ah, yes, the hospital. You're a long way from home, my dear lady. Well, we won't keep you too long. Actually, you are our first, shall we say, customer." He laughed at his joke. "Yes, we just got here yesterday. You see," he said, waving his arm in an arc, "we're still moving in."

"Yes, I see," Erika said, thinking maybe things were not so bad after all. He seemed decent, even nice.

"Before we get to the business at hand, Frau Doktor, let me introduce my colleague, SS-Hauptsturmführer Dieter Wisliceny. And I am SS-Obersturmbannführer Karl-Adolf Eichmann, at your service."

He sat on the corner of the desk and offered a cigarette to Erika, which she declined. He lit one, blowing smoke upward to the ceiling while he examined Erika. Despite her haggard appearance from the long trip and lack of sleep, he found her serenely beautiful. A physician, he thought as he studied her, an educated woman, obviously as cultured and well-bred as he considered himself. He allowed his mind a flash of fantasy with the lovely woman, all the while trying not to think of his bourgeois wife back home in the Schöneberg District of Berlin parroting platitudes. Yes, he could imagine very nice things with this one. Maybe a post here in Budapest, in a German hospital. He pocketed the matches and tapped ashes into a tray.

"The Führer and Chancellor of the German Reich," he began stiffly, "has met in the past twenty-four hours with Admiral Horthy in Salzburg, during which meeting was discussed the need of Hungary to have the full support of the Reich in her struggle with Bolshevism. Consequently, it has been decided that, as an ally of Germany, and in order to deal with our mutual enemies during these times of crisis, Hungary shall be occupied by German forces immediately. Of course, German policies and laws will now play a greater part in the struggle for victory. One such law concerns Jews, since they are considered enemies of the state." Eichmann dragged on his Player and removed a bit of tobacco from his lower lip. "Do you understand what I say to you, Frau Doktor?"

"Yes, I think so."

"Good! Then I think you will recognize that you have been violating the law. You have been harboring Jews in your hospital despite numerous admonitions from the authorities." He fixed her with an icy stare, although more for effect in front of Wisliceny. Under the stare, he was still admiring her.

He paused for a few moments. Erika became more uncomfortable. This was going to be more than just a lecture. *Why would they go to all this trouble?* she wondered.

"I don't know what to say. I wasn't deliberately violating the law. I didn't know it existed."

"Oh, it exists all right. It was just not being enforced by your Hungarian compatriots. That's the reason we are here, to see that it is enforced." Eichmann was lying. No such law existed in Hungary in regard to Jews—only sets of guidelines that prompted stricter, but not severe, treatment, which included conscription into labor units, consfiscation of property, employment restrictions, and the like.

"I'm sorry," Erika said. "I'll do better in the future."

Eichmann was disconcerted by Erika. Interrogating an individual—especially a harmless one—was not in keeping with his vast authority. He was Eichmann, head of Section IV B 4, the Office of Jewish Affairs of the RSHA, a man who dealt with ministers and generals and chiefs of police. He sat with heads of other SS departments and, despite his lowly rank of lieutenant-colonel, gave orders to Kreisleiters and Gauleiters. So powerful had IV B 4 become that he rammed SS policy down the throats of field generals. In a few short years he had risen from a clerk corporal to become Himmler's "Jewish expert." He spoke Yiddish and his Hebrew was passable, learned, ironically, from a man he greatly admired, Rabbi Leo Baeck.

The clever Eichmann had turned his questionable relationship with the Jews of Vienna into tremendous power. His mind, like that of his late chief, Heydrich, was continually clicking off his advantages in his quest for power. But he did it in a smaller scale than Heydrich, less boldly, but with the tenacity of a bureaucrat, effectively employing the little authority he was granted, and obsequiously accepting promotions for jobs well done. This perfect Nazi functionary had purposely held back applying for higher rank, he had told his subordinates the night before at a party in a quaint cellar café.

Over bowls of *gulyás*, stuffed cabbage, and gallons of red wine from Eger, he had entertained his six Horsemen of the Apocalypse for the Final Soution—Krumey, Nowak, Abromeit, Hunsche, Wisliceny, and Dannecker. He told them in the spirit of confidential camaraderie that tends to flow from wine bottles that he could very easily wear the oak leaves of a general but for practical purposes had avoided promotions. "They'll go after the generals when this is over, not us small fry," he said to them.

Hunsche, using the familiar *du*, protested, "But, Adolf, you talk as though we've lost the war—"

"We have, you drunken fool!"

"Well, goddamn it, why are we here to kill Jews?"

"Very simple," Eichmann had said between sips of Bikavér. "Because they're here."

Eichmann lit another Player and stared at Erika. She was becoming more and more desirable to him. Her soft, unmodulated voice lingered in his ear like a delicate kiss. He had visions of parting her thin, shapely legs with his knees. And it wasn't only that she was so lovely; no, that was just the icing on the cake. It was Huntziger's report that fascinated Eichmann. The report that said that Erika Schuler was the sister-in-law of that swine Bergdorf! Bergdorf, the aristocratic snob who had dared to order him, Eichmann, out of his office in Paris! That hypocrite who, according to the *V-Mann's* report, had tried to fuck his wife's sister under her own roof in his medieval *Schloss*! Oh, it was wonderful to have found that report! How he'd love to see Bergdorf's face now! He felt a swelling in his crotch and didn't know if it was from hate or desire.

"Yes, dear lady, I'm sure you'll do better in future." He got up and walked to a window, opening the draperies. The gray light of dawn came in. He turned to Wisliceny. "Leave us for a few minutes, will you?"

Eichmann came around the desk to Erika, putting his hand on the back of her chair. "You have been a bad girl, Erika. May I call you that? Thank you. Yes, a bad girl. I could very easily send you away, you know." He was almost whispering, his face close to hers. She smelled the acrid tobacco on his breath. She hadn't eaten except for some dry cheese sandwiches on the plane, and her empty stomach, already weakened from the sight of the blood of the Chassid's battered head, was rapidly giving in to nausea. She leaned away from Eichmann, waiting for his next words.

"I'm sorry if I offend you. At this time of night, after working all day, I'm sure none of us smells too good!" He laughed at his own humor. "As I was saying, Erika, your position is rather precarious, wouldn't you say? But to show you that I'm not an unreasonable man, I would like to make you an offer."

She looked at him with open suspicion. "Offer?"

He walked a few feet away, hands behind his back. "How would you like to be the official SS doctor, with your own apartment, your own personal staff, here in Budapest? I'll bet it's been some time since you attended a concert or the opera, which by the way are quite good here. Or had your laundry done by someone other than yourself, or had breakfast served in your own soft, warm bed. Your hours? Well, shall we say: as needed. I'll see to it that you aren't worked too hard. You'll have all the real coffee you want; butter, eggs, cigarettes, Scotch whiskey, if you like. In short, you'll need nothing. Well, what do you say?"

"Why? Why do you offer me such a life, Herr Eichmann?"

"Why not? We need a physician here, someone who can speak German."

"I know of no Hungarian doctor who doesn't speak German."

"But they're Hungarians, aren't they? You're German."

Erika had no retort. She looked at him with suspicion.

"Besides, I like you, Erika. Yes, damn it, I like you as a person! There"—he slapped his hands together—"I've said it!" He smiled. "I really do like you," he said softly, "everything about you . . . as a woman."

"You want a mistress then, is that it?" She was furious now that it was out. For this they had brought her here? "You don't want a doctor, you want a mistress!"

"Please don't be vulgar," he frowned. "I'm offering you a choice position. Anyone would lick her fingers—and kiss my boots—to have it, you know. The Russians are not too far from Eastern Transylvania. We won't fight them there; they can have it. You'll be overrun in a month, and you'll be raped, Erika, raped over and over again. On the other hand, we will push them back at Debrecen and Arad. You'll be safe here in Budapest. In any case, I'd see to it that you were taken west if it got too hot here." He softened his voice. "Don't be a little fool; I'm not so bad. Just give me a chance." He took her by the shoulders and tried to kiss her.

She pushed him away. "You disgust me!" she said. "You smell of death!" She slapped him hard on the face.

His hand went to his cheek. "You little bitch!" he hissed. "I've offered you not only a life of ease, but life itself! But I see I'm not good enough for your kind, Frau *Doktor!* Your kind will spread their legs only for the aristocracy, won't they! Tell me, my dear lady, is your aristocratic brother-in-law, Freiherr von Bergdorf, such a good lay?"

Erika leaped from her chair and threw herself at him, scratching at his face. "You bastard!"

Eichmann grabbed her arms and roughly pushed her down, slapping her with the back of his hand. "Your own sister's husband!" He took her hair, pulling her head back viciously, and slapped her across the mouth with his knuckles. *"Swine! Both of you!"* He knocked her down, and she crumpled into a heap, crying in anger. "Look at her, the high-born whore! Get up!"

Brandt and Wisliceny came in. "What's going on?" Brandt said. "We heard a commotion."

"Never mind," Eichman said, looking at Erika, "I've handled it myself. Get this baggage out of my sight."

"Where to?" Wisliceny said.

Eichmann straightened his slightly mussed uniform jacket and lit a cigarette. He looked pathetically, disgustedly at Erika, now sitting in a chair, blotting her bleeding lip with the back of her hand. "Send her with my compliments to our friend Mengele. If she's lucky, he'll send her to the showers for 'delousing.' But who knows, he may take a fancy to her and make her an assistant." They laughed.

"Right," Wisliceny said, lifting Erika by the arm. "Will it be Auschwitz or Birkenau?" Birkenau was the women's camp in the Auschwitz complex and was not an immediate killing camp.

"All Jews from Hungary—and Jew-lovers like this one—go through Auschwitz. You should know that, Dieter. I'm surprised you ask."

"Of course I know that," Wisliceny said, offended. "I only thought, considering that Dr. Schuler is a German—"

"I said Auschwitz!" Eichmann shouted. "She made her choice, damn it!"

Erika's senses returned. Auschwitz. *No*, she thought calmly, *never*. She had her hand in her coat pocket and casually pulled out the capsule. *Now*! Her hand went to her mouth. Brandt saw what she was doing, and like a cat he leaped at her and grabbed the back of her hair, but the capsule found its way in. She tried to place it between her molars so that she could bite down on it, but Brandt was too fast. He pulled at her hair, causing her mouth to open slightly, preventing her teeth from crushing the capsule. In the same motion he rammed his balled-up fist into her solar plexus, forcing the wind out of her, together with the capsule and the contents of her stomach.

As she vomited bile, she crumpled to the floor. Brandt picked up the capsule and examined it. "Cyanide," he said.

Eichmann raised his eyebrows. "Cyanide? Well, well! Her Highness came well prepared. That shows her guilt straight off, doesn't it, gentlemen?"

He bent over Erika's passive form. In her ear he whispered, "This is your last chance, Erika. The offer is still good."

She put her arms around her aching stomach and her reddened eyes looked over her shoulder at him. Her look of repugnance and revulsion was her answer.

Eichmann stood upright. "Right. Get her out of my sight! Brandt, get someone up here to clean up this muck on the floor."

PARIS

EARLY SPRING 1944

The telephone by the bed rang urgently several times before Bergdorf awakened. It was 6 A.M. in Paris, at his home in the fashionable Rue des Capucines.

"Yes?" he said dully. "Bergdorf here." He could hear the crackling of the long-distance wire. Berlin, no doubt.

"Heil Hitler, Bergdorf. Nibelung here."

It was out of character for Bormann to call, especially at that hour. "Yes, is there something wrong?"

"I'm afraid so. It seems an overeager SD chap from Berlin RSHA has arrested your sister-in-law, Dr. Schuler."

"What! Where? Where is she?"

"Locked up by the SD in Budapest. She was denounced to the Gestapo for political crimes against the Reich."

"Political crimes! That's ridiculous. She's a doctor; she doesn't even know the meaning of those words! Are you sure, Nibelung?"

Bormann sighed loudly. "Yes, Bergdorf, I'm sure. Something about using Jews in her hospital to keep them home. Quite against policy, you know."

"Oh, for Chrissake! Everyone uses Jews for his own purposes. Himmler employs hundreds of thousands in the Ruhr. And what about Krupp and Siemens?" he demanded.

"My dear fellow, you're yelling at the wrong man. It's Eichmann who has her, not me." Bormann chuckled as he spoke. "Don't forget, you chaps in the SS make policy for Jews, not we in the party."

It was Bergdorf's turn to sigh. "Yes, you're right. Eichmann, you said? I remember him now. He's a miserable prick, that one. He came to Paris last year with some of his people. Gave us a rather hard time of it. He came to assist us, as he put it, in the rounding up of Jews. He seemed obsessed with the Jewish thing. I sent him packing, him and his thugs. Do you think that has something to do with Erika's arrest?"

"Of course, Bergdorf, that's it! I should've figured it out myself."

"What?"

"I recall Kaltenbrunner's report to Heini about you throwing this Eichmann fellow out of your office. I get copies of those reports, in case you didn't know. Heini himself sees to it for favors he owes me. Anyway, this fellow Eichmann probably holds a grudge against you for that, don't you think? He must've found out that Dr. Schuler is related to you by marriage and decided to take it out on her, don't you see?"

"Look, Nibelung, at this point I don't give a damn about the workings of Herr Eichmann's mind. All I care about is getting Erika out of this mess. By the way, how did you learn of it?"

"Winkelmann, the SS and Police Führer for Hungary, called me a few minutes ago. He saw Dr. Schuler's name on the daily arrest report. It seems he knows you and—"

Bergdorf interrupted, "Yes, we're friends."

"—under the circumstances called me direct."

"Why didn't he release her, for God's sake?"

"He said that he normally doesn't interfere with Gestapo business; it would be exceeding his authority. He's also a little afraid of Eichmann, I think. From what I hear, Eichmann can be quite ugly. In any case, she's scheduled for the next transport to Auschwitz."

Bergdorf jumped to his feet, almost dropping the phone. "Auschwitz! That's impossible! You've got to do something, Nibelung. You've got to stop this madness!"

Bormann purred. "Does it mean that much to you?"

"Yes," he said softly. *He may as well know it all, if he doesn't already know it.* "It means everything to me."

"All right, I'll call Winkelmann. What should he do with her?"

"I . . . I want her here. In Paris. With me. Can you arrange that, Nibelung?"

"But what about your wife, Bergdorf? Certainly she'll know, as I do, that it's more than just familial anxiety that concerns you."

Bergdorf gritted his teeth in anger. "Trudi died last month. Can you arrange it?" he said evenly, convinced that Bormann knew, as he knew all things large and small.

"Yes, I can arrange it. My condolences, dear boy. How and when did it happen?" Of course he knew. Himmler had told him even before Bergdorf was notified.

"In Berlin during an air raid." He wondered if Bormann knew the circumstances of Trudi's death at the Adlon Hotel.

Bormann was about to say, *How convenient for you,* but even he knew limits of decency. Instead he said, "I'm sorry, Bergdorf. Don't worry about Dr. Schuler; she'll be on her way to Paris at once. I'll notify you with the details."

"Thank you."

"Bergdorf, you'll owe me on this one, you know."

"I know."

"Fine. Now, do you have a report for me? How many units do we have now?" Translation: How many Swiss francs on deposit in Zürich?

"Over two hundred." Translation: Over 200 million.

"What color?" Translation: Paper, gold, or other.

"One hundred yellow, over one hundred white." Translation: 100 million in gold, over 100 million in diamonds.

"What was our cost, Bergdorf?" Translation: How many Jews bought their way out of Europe?

"One thousand or so."

"One thousand it cost?" Bormann sounded bored.

"Yes, more or less."

"Cheap, eh, Bergdorf?"

"Yes, Nibelung, cheap."

"Thank you," Bormann said in sing-song and rang off.

Bergdorf poured a large whiskey and downed it. Then he sat down and put his face in his hands and wept with relief.

PARIS

SPRING 1944

The Gare du Nord reverberated with announcements, both in French and in German, of arriving and departing trains. Like industrious ants, people scurried, bumped, then scurried again in opposite directions. German soldiers on leave from the provinces of the English Channel, excitement and anticipation in their eyes as they visited the City of Light for the first—and for many the last—time. Civilians fortunate enough to have scrounged a *Reisegenehmigung* from the authorities, the precious travel permit, judiciously side-stepping their entrenched guests.

Bergdorf walked up the busy aisle with his aide, Lieutenant-Colonel Adler. They wore the field gray of the Waffen-SS, and as if with the aid of an invisible but powerful bulldozer, a path opened for them as they walked, searching the faces for a solitary woman.

Then he spotted her.

Her hat half hid her thin face, but he recognized her walk. She was carrying a small suitcase, and her shoulders drooped with fatigue. He stopped five or six paces from her; she stopped when she saw the military boots. She looked up from beneath the wing of the floppy hat and her eyes grew large, a thin, uncertain smile on her lips.

He smiled at her. "Welcome to Paris, Erika." He reached for her with open arms; she offered her hand. He hesitated, then took the hand, a quizzical smile fading on his face.

She nodded formally. "Hans-Dieter," she said, blinking rapidly, holding back tears, tears that had flowed freely on the long journey to Paris—for everything and anything, so injured and sensitive was her psyche.

Bergdorf saw the reddening of her eyes, and despite her cool formality, he understood. A lump formed in his throat for a few moments. He coughed and nodded to Adler. "May I present my adjutant and friend, Colonel Franz Adler."

She offered her hand and nodded formally again. Adler clicked his heels and saluted in the military manner.

"Now, Erika, come," Bergdorf said, "let's go home." To Adler, who had picked up Erika's bag, he said, "Franz, please be good enough to drive us."

The lights of Paris were taking effect as they made their way down the Rue de La Fayette. Bergdorf began to comment on the beauty of the city—just to say something, so oppressive was the silence in the car—but he decided against it in view of her coolness. No doubt she had gone through a great deal with that dog Eichmann.

Adler slid the Mercedes onto the Boulevard des Italiens. "Look, Erika, the Opéra! Isn't it beautiful?" Bergdorf said with enthusiasm.

"How fortunate you are to walk in a city in Europe where the buildings are still standing," she said dryly.

The Rue des Italiens became the Boulevard des Capucines, and around the corner was the tiny Rue des Capucines, where he lived. Home was the townhouse of the Baron Guy de Belfort, who had left the place to Bergdorf when the baron felt Paris become too warm even for Catholics who had only a one-eighth Jewish ancestry.

Belfort was in Geneva waiting for Germany to lose the war. At first, Bergdorf had resisted the offer. It was only when the baron had pointed out that if not he, some other German—one not so considerate—would take it over. Then what would happen, he had asked, to his priceless collection of oriental carpets, tapestries, and paintings? Besides, André, the longtime Belfort retainer, needed looking after.

André greeted them at the door. *"Bonsoir, André,"* Bergdorf said, stepping into the foyer. *"Je te présente Madame le docteur Schuler."*

"Bievenue à Paris, Madame," the butler said, bowing. *"Je suis à votre service."*

Erika smiled warmly and said in her school French, *"Merci beaucoup, André."*

The warmth of Erika's greeting to André encouraged Bergdorf. He sensed a thaw in her. "Come, let me show you around, if you're not too tired." He took her arm, but he felt a slight stiffening and immediately let it go.

She looked over the impressive salon, the marble floors graced by silk Tabrizes and Isfahan runners, old Gobelins on the wall, with oils by Hals and etchings by Dürer.

As soon as Adler and André left them, she said, "So this is where you live?"

The way in which she posed the question made him feel uncomfortable, even guilty. "Yes," he said, "this is the house of a friend. I'm looking after it while he's away."

"A Frenchman, I presume," she said, examining, touching, admiring. "If so, why do you apologize? After all, you came here as a conqueror, and to the victor go the spoils."

Her sarcasm was like a slap. He knew the war had changed many things, and he wondered if he was seeing the most disturbing change of all. "You're wrong on both counts, Erika," he said softly. "I neither apologize nor came here as a conqueror. Germany's armies did that before I came. I'm here because of orders."

"And I too am here because of orders. Your orders?"

Bergdorf finally lost his patience. "You're here because you were damned lucky! Lucky that I have friends in the right places, or you would be in Auschwitz at this moment! Did you think you could get away with defying them? Did you think you were rescuing those Jews? You were only postponing the inevitable and putting your own life in danger."

"My life? What's one life compared to the thousands you people are taking?" She spat the words. "Defenseless women and children who—"

He whirled on her. "What do you mean, *you people?*"

"Trudi wrote me. She told me of your life here, the theater, the soirées, and of your position as head of the SD in France. The SD, Hans-Dieter, the same organization that your man Eichmann belongs to, the same people who are killing the Jews of Transylvania and, I'm sure, of all of Europe!''

Bergdorf took a deep breath. He wanted to take her in his arms and kiss her and tell her that they were on the same side, that he was proud of her foolish acts, that he was doing something about it, too. But he couldn't. Not then. Not yet.

Instead, he exhaled in frustration. "Erika," he began quietly, choosing his words, "what Trudi wrote you is, well, it's only part of the truth. It's the truth seen through her rather peculiar eyes. She saw only the glamour of my position, but there is actually very little glamour. Appearances—many times they are misleading, deceiving. It has not been what you think, what you imply, what you accuse. I ask you to trust me, to believe in me." He looked at her eyes, her large, inquiring, demanding eyes that waited for the answer he was not ready to give her. He saw her eyes ask, *Who is this man living in a mansion in Paris? What has he done with the man I love?* Now as he looked at her, *his* eyes became hard. "Well then, you'll simply have to take me at face value."

He reached for his coat and hat. "I think you'd benefit from some rest. When you're ready, André will show you to your rooms. I have some business to attend to; we'll talk some other time, when you're rested."

He started to leave, then turned to her. "For what it's worth, Erika," he said, eyes softening again, "welcome."

Despite the fatigue and the hot bath and sleeping powders, Erika could not sleep. Instead, she agonized.

Everything had happened too fast, and what had happened was too horrible. Winkelmann telling her of Trudi's death and the ambivalence that created in her. The sudden and confusing fact of being snatched from the horror of the cell in Budapest and being put aboard a train that would take her to Paris—and to him. To the safety of him, of his arms, the answer to her dream. But now this was no dream anymore, this was real! He was real, the death of Trudi was real! *Oh God! I never wished her death! You know that!*

But if I'm not to feel the guilt, she thought, staring into the black of her closed eyes, *the guilt of taking what he has to offer me now free of sin, do I take it from this man? This man whom I may not know? This man who is one of them? I'm so confused—so guilty—so dishonest to myself!*

The next morning a note was on Erika's breakfast plate.

> My dear Erika,
>   I hope you slept well and that you feel better this morning. I had to leave early. Adler will show you around. See you tonight.
>   Yours,
>   Hans-Dieter

Franz-Christian Adler rang the bell at the Rue des Capucines. André admitted him, and a few minutes later Erika came down the stairs in a skirt and sweater. She was cordial and correct, and he saluted her.

They went to the Louvre to view what Marshal Göring had left of France's art patrimony. After viewing some of the smaller works, they sat on a bench in front of the massive painting by Jean-Louis David, "The Self-Coronation of Napoleon at Nôtre-Dame."

Adler noticed the unhappy look on Erika's face. "Frau Doktor," he said, "it is your right to tell me to mind my own business, of course. But I must say that you appear to be most miserable since I first saw you at the Gare du Nord. And further, my chief, quite unlike himself, appears to share your misery. I saw him this morning, and instead of beaming happiness, which is what I expected with your arrival, he seemed downright depressed. I take the liberty and breach of my position only because I see that there is something obviously wrong, and perhaps I can be of some help."

Erika turned away from him without comment.

After a long and discomforting pause, Adler cleared his throat. "I see," he said. "Excuse my intrusion."

She looked at him. "I'm sorry, Colonel. It's just that I can't get used to the idea of touring Paris with a member of the security service, the same security service of which my brother-in-law is chief, and the same security service that is deporting Jews from my homeland and other places—and killing them." She had spoken evenly, without emotion.

Adler stood up, visibly shaken. He took a deep breath and compressed his lips. "So," he said, fixing her with a pointed look. "Did you voice these same misgivings to General von Bergdorf?"

"I made my feelings known, yes."

"I assume, Frau Doktor, that he did not see fit to offer you any explanation of his activities here?"

"You said it well, Colonel Adler. He did not see fit to explain anything to me. He simply said I would have to accept him at face value."

"I see," Adler said. After a few moments, he turned to her. "Would you mind taking a walk with me? There are some things you and I should discuss regarding your brother-in-law's activities."

As they walked through the gardens of the Louvre, Adler began. "I have served with General von Bergdorf since nineteen forty in Belgium, and we were in the fight together in Yugoslavia. I know what kind of man he is—there is none better, believe me. He resisted coming here; he wanted his old Panzer command again, but that couldn't be. Since he's been in Paris, however, he's been involved in . . . in something far more dangerous than the field of battle." He looked around. "I know I shouldn't be telling you this, he will tell you himself someday, but I can't allow you to draw such conclusions about him any longer." Adler took a deep breath. "He is here because he sees his duty, not to the Fatherland, whose policies are shameful, but to humanity."

She looked at Adler wide-eyed. "What do you mean?"

He looked around again. "Since nineteen forty-one he has been risking his life by disobeying standing orders regarding Jews. In other words, he has been rescuing Jews, Frau Doktor. We have lost count now how many, but there isn't a day that goes by that his life is not in danger. That's why he chooses to stay here, using his position, his rank, his brains, and above all, his courage."

Erika put her fist up to her mouth. Her eyes grew even wider. "Oh, my God, I didn't know! Why didn't he tell me?"

"He couldn't, don't you see? Even if he wanted to, he couldn't. If you knew, you would be implicated, and he had to protect you. That's why he told you to accept him at face value"—Adler smiled—"that is, if you loved him as he thought you did."

"Oh Franz, I do! I always have! I just didn't know how to accept this new and wonderful turn of—oh, I don't even know what

I'm saying—my sister is dead, and that is a tragedy, I know. But I didn't wish it, Franz, I—'' She looked at him, eyes pleading understanding.

"Erika," he said warmly, "you must take what is given you. Take it freely and without guilt. Yes, your sister died, but neither you nor your brother-in-law had anything to do with that. There is nothing you can do to change it. If you allow any guilt to come between you and your happiness with him, you will be doing a terrible disservice to you both. Especially now that his life has some meaning for him. Don't disappoint him, Erika. He loves you so much.''

Her eyes filled with tears. She kissed Franz Adler on the cheek. "Franz, thank you for telling me, for talking to me like that. I hope he forgives me. Please take me home. I want to be there for him!''

That night Erika's head rested on her lover's chest. He stroked her hair, not thinking, either of them, allowing the feeling of sheer, undiluted, uncomplicated joy to course through their beings. The long-sought-after dream was a reality.

She stirred under the sheet, her fingers moving across his shoulder. "I've never known such happiness," she whispered. "If I should die tomorrow, I will have died a happy woman, my darling, my darling, my darling!''

He drank in her words silently, savoring them. Finally he spoke. "Things are different now, Erika, and for the first time I'm afraid of dying. I want you to listen carefully. We must make plans to safeguard our future.'' She raised herself and looked at him in the soft light. "I love you, and I want to marry you.'' She moaned and kissed him, and he breathed the perfume of her lips and mouth. "Please listen. I've got to get you out of Occupied Europe, to Switzerland, to my friend, the owner of this house. He will see to you.''

"Why can't you come, too?'' she said anxiously.

"For several reasons. First, it would be desertion. I can't do that. Second, I have to return to Germany. The Allies will be on the continent soon, within weeks, if our intelligence is correct. German soldiers will be taken as prisoners of war, but those of us in the SD and Gestapo will be arrested as war criminals. I can't carry out my plans for after the war if I'm hanged or imprisoned for years. Someday I'll tell you of those plans, but for now it is imperative that when this is all over I escape. Then I'll join you.''

"But if you go back to Germany, you'll be in danger, too. If Hitler fights to the end, you may be killed!"

"No, no, I won't be. I'll find a way, I promise."

She looked at him in panic. "You can't guarantee that, Hans-Dieter!" she said. "Please, let's go to Switzerland while we can! Oh, please say yes!"

"I can't, Erika. It is one thing to violate my oath; it is another to desert. Besides, I still have things to do. Otherwise, it will have been almost meaningless. You must trust me in that. You must do as I say!" He leaned on his elbow and looked at her lovely, worried face. He smiled and said, "Besides, now I have everything to live for."

OBERSALZBERG

SUMMER 1944

The terrace that Bergdorf stood on overlooked the valley and the mountains to the northeast. Shafts of afternoon sunlight cut through the evergreens, gentle breezes stirring their branches. *What incomparable beauty of land*, thought Bergdorf, *and look what this man is doing to it*. When is enough enough? How can the power of the will—the will of one man, one nihilist—be so great as to destroy a whole continent? One man against the world, and he was succeeding. Not winning, but succeeding in dragging everyone else with him down into the pits of hell!

A voice behind him startled Bergdorf out of his thoughts. It was Bormann. "There you are, Bergdorf. I was looking for you." The rays of sun warming the green valley below and playing off the snow on the mountaintops caught Bormann's eye. "Hm. This is the kind of sight the postcard publishers dream of. I wonder if there's time to get my Leica. Oh well, never mind," Bormann said blithely, "there's a better show inside. Come on, we're going to the movies!"

As they walked through the vast living room of Hitler's house, Bergdorf knew by Bormann's enthusiasm that it would not be another Shirley Temple film. He wondered what was so special about this one.

The lights in the projection room were still on. Several political leaders and high-ranking military officers had taken their seats. They were talking animatedly, smiling in seeming anticipation. Bergdorf noticed, however, that the Führer's two secretaries, Frau Traudl and Frau Dara, and of course Fräulein Braun, who always attended the movies, were absent. *I see*, thought Bergdorf, *we're going to have a stag film. Curious, I never knew Hitler to go for that sort of thing.*

A minute later the Führer came in. Everybody rose; he motioned impatiently for them to sit. *Let's sit back and enjoy the show!* he seemed to be saying. He sat next to Bormann; Bergdorf sat one row behind. The theater darkened, and the projector whirred into life.

The color film—the first Bergdorf had seen—flickered with several numbers for a few dozen frames. Then, with no sound other than its own, the film steadied and showed a scene in what appeared to be a butcher shop because of a close-up of large meat-hooks coming out of the ceiling. Then three men came in. Two were in shirt-sleeve SS uniforms; the other was a convict of some sort, judging by his broad striped pants. He was stripped to the waist and had a look of resignation in his eyes. (At that point, Hitler mentioned a name Bergdorf didn't catch.) The convict's hands were tied behind him. Then, a close-up of other hands holding what looked like wire with a loop on the end of it. Then—*oh my God!*—the wire was put around the man's neck. The man's eyes grew large; then he shut them tight as two men pulled on the end of the wire, hoisting the man up in the air. *These are real films. Holy Mother of God, these are actual films!* The man's eyes were bulging now, his tongue shot out of his mouth, and even though it wasn't sound film, Bergdorf could hear the gurgling as the veins in the man's head and neck were close to bursting like a toy balloon. Bergdorf's eyes were frozen on the film, on the evil of it. He could hear sounds from the audience, boisterous sounds—nervous laughter, throats being cleared. He tried to force his eyes shut, but he could not, and he watched the man's body twitch in terminal agony. Finally, after an eternity, clement death. Merciful death.

Bergdorf asked himself the obvious question: *Who was this man? Why are we viewing this?* Of course! The name he hadn't understood—Stuelpnagel! General Karl-Heinrich Stuelpnagel, military governor of France, one of the conspirators of the July 20 plot to kill Hitler. This, then, was a film made in Plötensee prison, where he and the others had been hanged for their part in the aborted coup. No wonder he didn't recognize the old general—beaten, tortured, broken. How many times had Bergdorf lunched with this fine man in Paris? He looked at the screen again to confirm his fears. Yes, the grotesquery that was hanging was indeed Stuelpnagel. Bergdorf looked askance at Hitler. He could not see his eyes from that angle, but he didn't have to see them to feel the enormous capacity to hate.

"I was standing by the table," Hitler was saying to those who would listen, "when the bomb went off near my feet. Just opposite me an officer was literally blown out a window. My clothes were in tatters and I was burned, but still I was alive! What this incident points out clearly is that nothing will ever happen to me, gentlemen. Providence has seen to it that it is my fate to bring my task to its completion."

Another prisoner was brought into the Chamber of the Hooks. "Witzleben," Hitler informed his guests. Field Marshal von Witzleben, unshaven, his false teeth taken away, looked happy to die at last. Generals Hoepner, von Hase, and Stieff were next. Peter, Count von Wartenburg, was the last. At the end the cameraman, in an attempt at artistic cinematography, shot a wide angle, encompassing the whole cast as they twisted slowly, like abused marionettes.

The lights went on. Several viewers had sneaked out, but the Führer didn't seem to notice. "You see, Bormann," he said, rising, "shooting them, as Jodl suggested in view of their military station, would not have been appropriate."

"They didn't behave according to their military station, my Führer," Bormann said. "They behaved like traitors, and they died like traitors."

"Exactly," Hitler said. "You see my point, then."

"You made it quite clear, my Führer." Bormann looked over his shoulder at Bergdorf and motioned with his head to wait for him.

Bergdorf waited, wandering around Hitler's oversize living room, brooding over the film he wished he hadn't seen. He knew the images would haunt him for the rest of his life. Images of once-proud men reduced to common criminals, their honor stripped away by a dishonorable man.

Yes, they were guilty of treason. They gambled and they lost, and for that they had to pay. But in that manner?

He shuddered at the thought of how close he himself had come to joining Operation Valkyrie, the code name for the attempt to kill Hitler. He had learned through his connections in the Jewish underground that most of the military leadership in France was involved in the conspiracy. He had been approached by a fellow noble, Count von Moltke, a senior officer on Field Marshal von Witzleben's staff. Von Moltke wanted to know if Bergdorf sympathized with the plan, and if he did, would he join it. Bergdorf had been tempted and had asked for a day to respond; then he decided against it for several reasons: One, he thought it wrong for the generals who had followed Hitler in his triumphs to kill him or depose him now when things were going badly; two, even if he wanted to join, his contribution would be minimal, considering that the SD forces in France could not be ordered by him to join the conspiracy, or at best to stand by idly; and three, his activities with the Underground would be sidetracked from the main goal—rescuing Jews. The first two reasons were conveyed to von Moltke, who understood and respected the reasons. Bergdorf told von Moltke that he would not join the plot but would not turn in the plotters. In fact, he wished them luck. The monster that was destroying Europe needed to be destroyed himself.

How shrewd and cunning Heydrich had been, Bergdorf thought. When he had sent Bergdorf to Paris on the "conspiracy" mission, he most likely had had no knowledge of any conspiracy at that time; it had only been a pretense for the ambitious Nibelung operation. Yet he had been right after all. He had seen the writing on the wall and predicted the treason. Had he lived, he would've killed two birds with a single stone: defeated his enemies and seen Nibelung a success. Or even seen the death of Hitler and himself taking over the reins!

"All right, Bergdorf," the voice of Bormann said, shaking him out of his musings, "let's go to my office. I want to talk to you."

They went into Bormann's small suite. "Well, what did you think of our premiere?" He smiled.

"Graphic, to say the least," Bergdorf said dryly.

"The Führer wants it shown in every officers' barracks at home and at the Front as a lesson in loyalty. I'm sure he will want to view it again when he's bored!" He laughed.

Bergdorf remained silent. "Anyway," Bormann went on, "the purpose of this chat is not the film, Bergdorf, but to give you some good news, an item hard to come by these days. You will live to see the end of the war, unless you get run over by a trolley or some such stupid thing. You are going abroad."

"Abroad? Where and why, Reichsleiter?"

"Switzerland. Zürich, to be precise. You may even have your

lovely sister-in-law join you''—Bormann leered—''unless, of course, she's there already. What have you done with her, you scoundrel? I know you got her out of France. Oh well, no matter. Just so you get yourself to Zürich. Why, you ask? It doesn't look right—you, a combat officer, hanging around here. The Führer may order you to the Front. He intends to fight to the bitter end, you know, which means that we will all be done for unless we are clever, something of which I have been accused. Anyway, I want you safe. You might say I'm protecting my investments.''

"Meaning the money," Bergdorf said. He had promised Erika he would see her again. He didn't know how, and short of deserting, he hadn't found a way. Now it was being handed to him, and suddenly there was a swarm of butterflies in his stomach.

"Yes, the money," Bormann repeated. "The way Heydrich set up the operation, you have the only key, shall we say, to that account. I'm counting on you to remember to whom that money belongs. Meaning I have complete faith in you."

Bormann paused for a reaction. Bergdorf maintained his silence, but his eyes asked the question. "You are thinking, my dear Bergdorf, how can I trust you with so much money. Well I've been observing you since I sent for you to join me here. I must admit that our late friend Reini was right about you. You're a starry-eyed idealist and too much of a gentleman to steal from me, and that's what it would be—stealing. As Heydrich pointed out to you, your honor is too much a part of your heritage. If it were not, you too would be hanging from one of those meat-hooks we saw in the film. You look shocked. I know how tempted you must have been to join the conspiracy of July twentieth. You could have, but you didn't, and that says it all. No, I don't worry about you, Freiherr von Bergdorf."

The next day Bergdorf crossed the border into Switzerland. He was in civilian clothes, with a Swiss passport. He met with Dr. Heinz Langfeldt, the banker. The vast amount of money in the numbered account was protected and would remain in Bergdorf's exclusive control.

He found Erika.

Soon after, with the help of Guy de Belfort, Bergdorf and Erika fled to the safety of Spain. They settled in a small fishing village on the Costa Brava, San Feliú de Guixols, and waited out the end of the war—only the two of them, for whom a new life was just beginning.

INTERLUDE

1945–THE PRESENT

The greatest war known to man in terms of total destruction and loss of life ended a few days after the suicide of the single person who willed and began it—Adolf Hitler.

There were survivors. But few of them returned to the lives they once led. For most of them, their lives were changed forever.

Two of these survivors were Erika Schuler and and Hans-Dieter von Bergdorf.

They spent the last few months of the war and the first year after in the quiet Spanish fishing village, where no one took notice of them or asked them questions. Not their neighbors, not the local police, not even the Guardia Civíl. In those days, there were many new residents in Spain who spoke nothing but German, but no one disturbed their peace. The cause for that was most probably that Generalísimo Franco, although never an ally of Hitler, was still a Fascist chief of state and not totally unsympathetic to the vanquished Nazi regime and its survivors. Los Falangistas Españoles, although not extending an open invitation to escaped Nazis, did provide a temporary look-the-other-way haven for them during the postwar storm.

Then came the Nuremberg trials of the major war criminals and the testimony and evidence of barbarity that was too horrible for the world to believe, let alone understand.

So like a swarm of cockroaches startled by sudden light—in this case, the light of truth—the Nazis scattered, looking for new cracks to hide in. Many found those cracks in Paraguay, Chile, and Perón's Argentina, the very bold ones even found their sanctuaries in the United States under the aegis of elected officials who considered the Nazis anti-Communists and therefore acceptable.

By that time Bergdorf had established a firm and warm relationship with Swiss banker Gerd Langfeldt, in whose vaults the Bormann treasure was lounging in accounts controlled by Bergdorf. Later, Bergdorf learned that the French National Military Tribunal, whose duty it was to prosecute war criminals, had an order out for his arrest by virtue of his position as Heydrich's deputy and chief of SD forces in France. Even more damaging were documents discovered ordering the deportation of French Jews over his signature. If found, he would have immediately been returned to France to stand trial as a war criminal. Passions were too great, blood too hot, and vengeance too swift to have risked a trial. Something imaginative had to be done.

From that insecure footing and with the urging of Langfeldt and the consent of Erika, Bergdorf decided to bury Hans-Dieter, Freiherr von Bergdorf. From that decision, and with Langfeldt's expert help, a new identity was born—Peter Kramer.

Langfeldt's trusted operatives, long experienced in banking secrets and related privacies, provided Kramer with a scrutiny-proof background. Swiss birth and academic records were produced and placed. A set of parents, deceased, were provided, a record of a student loan from a finance company whose files were subject to public examination was suddenly in place. A court-docket entry in the canton of Zug showed a fine of fifty Swiss francs levied against a young Peter Kramer for speeding in 1938. A set of fingerprints was on file. An authentic Swiss passport was issued for Peter Kramer and one for Erika Schuler.

During the last few months of their residence in Spain, Erika and Peter were married.

For the next few years Switzerland was home for the Kramers. It was from there that Kramer made contact with his former adjutant and friend, the trusted Franz Adler. He needed Adler to implement his plan for *Wiedergutmachung*, as he called it—atonement.

Neither man had any idea whether Martin Bormann was alive or dead. It didn't matter: Kramer had never followed Bormann's instructions to place a monthly advertisement in the classified section of the *Frankfurter Allgemeine Zeitung* with a code to indicate Bergdorf's location. No, it didn't matter. The treasure would go to the survivors of those whose ashes still mingled in the soil and rivers of Europe, those who didn't make it, those whose sheer numbers made it possible for others to have made it.

Soon an organization was put together by Kramer and Adler, one made up of trusted, loyal Germans, former combat soldiers whose consciences were clear but who shared the collective guilt of their Fatherland and who needed to make amends. They formed a working group, each with specific responsibilities, primarily to launder large sums for placement with Israeli intelligence units to help finance the search for the killers of their people. It was necessary to operate in that way in order to protect both the fund and Kramer's identity.

It was then that the Q-B group was born. Q-B, pronounced *kuhbeh* in German, was named in memory of Wilhelm Kube, the Nazi Gauleiter of East Ruthenia who had defied the SS leadership by protecting Jews and openly voicing his opposition to the Final Solution. At first, Kube had been an ardent Nazi; then his decency came through. Ironically, he had been killed in his bed by a Russian partisan's bomb.

As time passed, however, many of the old Nazis came out in the open. Most had received what amounted to a slap on the wrist by way of a prison sentence and were now free to come and go as they pleased. Many received financial help from two organizations made up of former SS men—some of them still unrepentant Nazis—ODESSA and *Die Spinne*, "The Spider." Suddenly, Switzerland was no longer safe for Kramer. He and Erika decided to leave for the United States, where they could lose themselves in the huge melting pot, where the people, with their natural and forthright disposition, would be less inquisitive, less suspicious of foreigners, than Europeans.

A suburb of Boston became their new home. Other than having a few yearly meetings with Langfeldt and the Q-B group, their life was routine, normal, and well in hand. The fund, despite large amounts funneled to the Israelis, continued to grow under Langfeldt's keen, expert management. With little else to do, Peter enrolled at Harvard University, earning a Ph.D. in Middle Eastern history—a decision of consequence, as it turned out—and Erika earned her U.S. medical boards after presenting the appropriate "diplomas" supplied by Langfeldt and taking the required examinations for foreign medical graduates.

The years in Cambridge were happy years for them. Peter began teaching at Harvard, and Erika, after a residency at Massachusetts General, stayed on in a fellowship in laboratory pathology for cancer research. They were both so heavily involved in their careers that they had little time for each other. But when they were together, they shared the most satisfying and tender relationship either had ever known.

And they had taken steps to insure that the past was just that—the past. Especially Erika. There were no reminders of it, of Europe; not even a decorative pillow or a piece of porcelain. They lived not as transplanted Europeans but as Americans. They spoke English, although during some intimate moments, when their guards were down, they lapsed into German. Despite the stress these "rules" caused them, those years were their happiest.

There were times when Peter had his own private strife, however. On certain nights—or days, it didn't matter; it was all a question of when the feeling hit him—he felt a dull ache in his gut, in his heart really. It came whenever he realized that with the "death" of Hans-Dieter von Bergdorf, he had also allowed his family name to die, his history—their history!—his great ancestors and their names. The title Freiherr had been bestowed upon some ancestor of his by his prince for deeds noble and gallant, honorable and perhaps even heroic. Now, in a decision that had taken only seconds, a decision reached by fear or at least for preservation of body—not of soul and honor—that title and its history were gone forever. Gone, thanks to him.

But after these agonizing self-indictments he would always come back to the reality of things. The reality was that he hadn't been afraid for his life. He had proven that time and time again in Paris, then in the confrontation with Heydrich. No, his fears were of somehow being thwarted in carrying out his plans, the plans born of the vow he made to himself that horrible day in the hotel near Auschwitz, in that shower, as he washed the human soot from his body but not from his mind or his soul. That was why he ran.

If he was living a lie, at least it was a noble lie.

And to him, it was the unresolvable contradiction—the great paradox.

Then came a job offer for Peter from George Washington University. And a paper he wrote on the Middle East crisis.

Then came a call to duty from the charismatic and enigmatic President of the United States, Simon Bolivar Jensen.

THE WHITE HOUSE

THE PRESENT

He surveys his surroundings, the trappings of power. The bank of telephone lines on his desk and the awesome black one in a drawer. The pens with which he signs bills into the law of the land. The communication system with which he summons efficient aides to his calling; even generals and admirals who now address him as "sir" because he is their commander in chief. The sophisticated computer by which he has instant intelligence of the location and deployment of his nuclear arsenal and, he hopes, that of his enemy. He surveys these surroundings and acknowledges once again, as he has countless times before, that he is the most powerful man in the most powerful nation on earth. But after drawing that portentous conclusion, he draws yet another: he believes himself to be the loneliest man on earth.

He has lost his friends, even those whom he once considered intimate. Since his inauguration they call him Mr. President. And yet he knows that that is correct, since they must respect the office and with it the man in the office. Since assuming the presidency only his wife calls him by his first name, but she doesn't call him Si as she once used to. Now she calls him Simon. He misses that awful little bedroom joke: "Oh, Si, you make me sigh!" Now she doesn't sigh with him any longer since she sleeps in another room because, she said, "of all those phone calls in the middle of the night."

She calls him Simon and sleeps in another room. He knows why. He knows it's because of the screams. His screams that always end the dream. And since the very first night after the inauguration—three years now, for Chrissake—the dream has been more and more insistent, more and more upon him like a perverse haunting. Yes, it's the dream and the screams and the soaking bedclothes and the changing of pajamas—more than that, his refusal to talk about it—that make her sleep elsewhere.

He doesn't blame her. She can run from it; he cannot. If he could hide from it . . . but he cannot.

And yet . . . and yet, the dream, horrible as it is, unwelcome as it is, the only thing in life that dares not respect his presidency, seems to be telling him something. There is a message there in the dream, a vague and murky communication that hints—no, promises—to reveal itself. The details are unknown to him still, but he knows that the dream is trying to tell him who his enemies are. Yes, that's it. The dream and its obscure characters and dark proceedings are trying to tell him that.

All presidents have enemies, he knows; it's only natural. Sometimes even old friends turn on you. He adds a line to Truman's famous THE BUCK STOPS HERE desk plaque: SO DO THE FRIENDSHIPS. He is reminded of a popular baseball player who, in the twilight of his playing days, was appointed coach on the same club. He sent a letter to his player-friends that started, "Dear ex-friend . . ." That's understandable; you have to draw the line; you have to put up a wall if you want to govern properly.

But you must be prepared to pay the price.

The price is high, for now he has more than just political enemies. Now he has enemies from within. And some may be trying to destroy his accomplishments—and him.

His accomplishments are great ones—of that he is convinced. And with a second term looming so close, when the truly great achievements will come, it is important—vital, goddamn it!—that he know who his enemies are.

The dream, the terrible dream, is somehow going to tell him who those enemies are.

Simon Bolivar Jensen, in shirt sleeves, leaned back in his big chair, putting his feet up on the table that was his working desk. The other desk, the elaborate one that faced the entrance to the Oval Office, had been given to President Hayes by Queen Victoria and was used mostly for ceremony.

Jensen cradled the phone. "That's fine, Pete," he said to Peter Kramer, who was calling him from the American Embassy in Paris with a preliminary briefing of the situation in Cairo. "But we've still got to get the damned show on the road before November. What are the chances of that?" Jensen listened. "Okay. You can give me the details when I see you. We're going down to the ranch tomorrow. Come on down and bring Erika with you. Oh, you think not? She can tell those people at Bethesda that the President wishes it. I see. Well, if she can find a way, I think she'll enjoy it. See you here." Jensen rang off.

He looked out the window at the Washington Monument, but he didn't see it. He was too deep in thought. His usually cheerful tone had been restrained with Kramer. Despite the news of progress with the treaty time frame, he failed to get excited about it as he normally would, and he wasn't sure if it was because of his periodic suspicions about Kramer or simply because of the hangover from the dream. He sighed, thinking of his old antagonist, the dream. He was used to it by now, and he had grown to tolerate it. Like a visit from relatives—unwelcome but tolerated until they left, yet knowing they would return next year, and the next.

The dark cellar was long and dank, and it had vaulted ceilings. On either side of its high, indistinct walls were rows of tables with human forms lying on them. Dead or asleep, he couldn't tell, because they were wrapped in white sheeting, something like mummies but not quite. His job—obligation, really, because he didn't seem to have a choice—was to take four of them to a car-truck-bus outside. Which four he never knew until he was told by the pointing finger of the keeper of the place, a tall, gaunt man in a gleaming white uniform. He always carried each sleeping or dead figure in his arms, not over his shoulder, but delicately, tenderly in his arms. He made the trip down the damp staircase, slipping from time to time in some sort of cleated shoes—golf shoes, probably—until he had brought the last one and placed him-her-it next to the others in the vehicle, which looked like a school bus. He started the engine. Going where? He never knew—he never got there; he gained speed down the street, and it was suddenly daylight. Then the puppies came. Sweet, playful little puppies wagging their tails, tongues hanging out, almost smiling, romping across the street in front of his car.

Suddenly he was on his back, looking up at the blue, blue sky, a bird flying over, the only sound a roar. He looked in the direction of the roar and saw fire in the lake-river-ocean, whatever body of water it was. The forms in the wraps were standing there, but now with faces—the faces of his four offensive linemen at USC when he quarterbacked the team to a one-point win in the Rose Bowl.

He tried running toward them to rescue them from the flames, but his legs responded in slow motion and with impotence, barely closing in on them. Then one came out of the flames, holding a football—and he and the others started to disintegrate in flames.

The muffled *aaaahh!* used to bring Secret Service men running into his bedroom, but now they were used to it since it happened two or three times a week. Now they simply listened to the sounds of the President stumbling to the bathroom to splash cold water onto his face and change his soaked pajama top. Then sleep. Until the next time.

The President gazed out his window at the pompom dahlias that the White House gardener was so proud of, but he didn't see them, either. There were several documents and memoranda on his desk for his signature, but he seemed paralyzed, unable to get to the business of government. He was brooding over the dream. Not because of its terror—no, he was inured to that—but because he was suddenly starting to analyze the dream, to dissect it, looking for a meaning, a sign. What, he didn't know . . . yet.

He buzzed his appointments secretary, canceling lunch with the Senate majority leader, pleading pressing business.

He closed his eyes and did something he had always resisted: He allowed himself to drift back in time to 1945 . . . and to remember.

Second Lieutenant Simon B. Jensen arrived in Deggendorf, Germany, during the last month of the war. He had come as a green replacement but was quickly assigned a platoon of Sherman tanks. His greatest worry was not that he would catch the last bullet of the war but that the war would end before he got his chance at combat. It was with that élan that he volunteered for the one unit that could guarantee him his wish: Patton's Third Army.

Patton's juggernaut had ripped through Germany at lightning speed and was already at the Danube, hammering the last nails of defeat into the Nazis' coffin. It was only a matter of time now, he remembered being told, but there was still plenty of action ahead, which was what the young tank soldier was looking for.

He had been getting ready to join XII Corps when his regimental commander called him in.

"Who wants to see me?" Jensen had asked, amazed.

"The Old Man, you idiot. The commanding general, Third Army—George S. Patton, Jr." The colonel apparently had little patience with the "ninety-day wonder" who for some unexplainable reason had been asked for by the army's Almighty.

Jensen remembered the meeting with Patton. He looked taller than tall in his jodhpurs and high boots, with rows of stars on his cap, on his collars, on his fur-lined jacket draped over a chair back, on his enameled helmet liner posed on a map table, and on his pistol-grips—not the famous ivory-handled pistols but a lone .45 automatic.

There were other stars in Patton's headquarters, but they were the lesser stars of his division and corps commanders. The room was the Milky Way of the U.S. Army, and Patton was a comet, preparing his final trajectory into Austria—and the end.

Patton greeted him warmly, like an old friend. As a little boy, Jensen and his father had visited the Patton ranch near Pasadena, where the Jensen ranch abutted. There, Georgie Patton and Si Jensen, Sr., used to play Civil War games, with Georgie playing the part of his idol, Confederate General Stonewall Jackson.

Now, with his own reputation overshadowing that of his hero, George Patton stood ten feet tall in a captured city hall in Deggendorf in 1945, holding sway the captive audience, an audience of a curious mix of love and hate, of admiration and criticism. Hands on hips, he stood in the middle of the large hall, captivating and infuriating, invincible and, by his own admission, vulnerable. To Jensen, he had the look, the swagger of one who had just won the last pot of the night at poker and could hardly wait to play again.

"Gentlemen," Patton announced, "allow me to introduce Second Lieutenant Simon Bolivar Jensen, the hero of the Rose Bowl. He descends from the illustrious *hidalgos* of Spain, sent by their king to unheathenize the heathens and from those intrepid warriors of the seas, the great Vikings. And now, generations later, gentlemen, the scion of those noble ancestors comes to us a pure American, sent by his country to kill Germans!"

President Jensen felt a shudder course through his body at the memory of Patton's words. He opened his eyes and looked at the dahlias in the garden. His eyes closed slowly again.

"Son," Patton had said softly to him, taking him by the arm to an anteroom, "your father and I are old friends, and he knows there is little I wouldn't do for him. He wrote me a letter in which he asked that I look out for you. Mind you, he didn't ask for special favors of me—that wouldn't be like him—but I see nothing dishonorable in your serving your country attached to my headquarters. You are the last of that great family, Lieutenant Jensen, and if something—"

"Respectfully, General," Jensen interrupted, "I volunteered for service in the Third Army because I knew that if any outfit was going to see action, it would be this one. Unlike my father, *my* biggest worry is that the war will be over before I can get my licks in. As you said, sir, I came to Germany to kill Germans."

Patton's eyes became slits and his mouth held a tight grin. "Goddamn it, I knew you would say that! Yessir, I just *knew* you would say that! Listen, son, I saw you beat the pants off the Buckeyes that day. Now, that's what I want you to do to those German bastards—beat the pants off them!" Then Patton lowered his voice to a hoarse whisper: "And if you should die out there, son, you will have died a hero, and there is no sweeter thing that God can give you."

The Sixth Armored Division finished its refitting and was once again part of XII Corps, now on a steady drive southeast along the Danube. Little towns and big towns along the way, as if by mass prearrangement, flew white flags of surrender in the windows of their Hansel and Gretel houses, and townspeople quietly cheered the American conquerors, thanking God and General Patton for having gotten to them before the Russians.

Lieutenant S. B. Jensen sat high in the turret of his Sherman and observed the easy conquests, feeling frustrated. He saw hordes of captured German soldiers, some glum in defeat but most with looks of resignation and relief after so many years of armed struggle—and he felt more frustration.

Then as if in answer to a prayer, his earphones crackled with sound: "Okay, Jensen, you're gonna get your chance." It was the voice of his company commander. "G-two says there's a bunch of SS guys holed up in a brewery—maybe thirty, forty 'em—in a little berg called Ruhmannsfelden, just off the main highway, coordinates forty-nine degrees north, thirteen degrees east. Go get 'em, cowboy!"

Jensen felt elation he hadn't known since his sophomore year at USC, when the coach had told him he would start the second half of a game as quarterback. The game was virtually won by the time they gave him the ball, but it didn't matter; he still put three touchdowns on the scoreboard. He had acquitted himself with poise and leadership and a certain flair that was to be his trademark in coming seasons. Now, once again he was being handed the ball when the game was almost over, but he knew he could score just one more touchdown. He had to. Patton expected it of him, and he demanded it of himself.

In less than an hour, Ruhmannsfelden was secure. The SS men, remnants of the Seventeenth SS-Panzer Grenadier Division Götz von Berlichingen, had fought bravely to their deaths. Jensen had given them a chance to surrender, but SS troopers seldom did—so they died.

Jensen went into the brewery. And then he came out.

He sent medics into what was left of it, and the medics came out saying that they weren't needed in there; a burial detail would do. He gave orders to round up some of the townspeople and a tractor to quickly dig a mass grave.

He announced that he would take his tank to a nearby hilltop to reconnoiter the area. Up to then, the SS men had been a faceless, dangerous enemy; now they were dead, and he didn't want to see them again as they lay destroyed, fanatical but valiant young warriors for whom all wars were over.

At the top of the hill in that peaceful land, with the echoes of the battle still in his ears, Jensen looked around. He thought of telling his driver to turn off the idling engine, just so he could hear the quiet he had caused. But he saw movement in a clump of trees nearby.

He swung his big Browning .50-caliber machine gun around to the movement that was parallel to the tank. Over his machine-gun sights, he saw two figures in steel helmets. One was carrying a *Panzerfaust* already loaded with the bulbous antitank shell in its muzzle. But the figures weren't men, they were boys, not more than twelve or thirteen, with red cheeks and beardless faces lost in the large helmets. They were trying to position themselves to fire, but they kept tripping on their oversize greatcoats. Jensen wanted to laugh, to shout at them, "Come on, boys, that thing's loaded—you're gonna hurt yourselves!" Suddenly he realized that they were serious in their game, that they were trying to hurt him and his tank.

He shouted to them in the only German he knew: "*Halt!* Stop! Give up! You're too young to die like this! The war's over, for Chrissake!"

He fired a burst over their heads, hoping they'd drop the damned thing and scatter and go home where they belonged, but they didn't. They were lads of the Volksturm, the hastily organized home army made up of old men and young boys, and they were told that the nation—the Führer!—depended on them, and that they were to be brave like their fathers and sons who died at Stalingrad. He could see the scared eyes under the comical helmets. General Patton had said, "Kill the sons of German bitches!" But these weren't sons of German bitches—they were little boys, the future of a defeated nation. *Please, don't make me kill them!*

Then he was looking up into the cloudless skies of Lower Bavaria. He realized he was on his back on the soft turf. A voice kept repeating through the loud ringing in his ears, "Lieutenant, are you okay? Don't move. Are you okay?"

He giggled and asked the voice, "What happened?" He felt incongruously embarrassed, as if he had run into a lamppost or some other slapstick thing.

The voice was that of an infantry sergeant, and the tone was far from jovial. "Don't move, sir," he said. "A medic's on the way. You're bleeding from a head wound, and your arm's limp. It looks broken."

"What about my crew, Sergeant? They okay?"

The sergeant ignored the question. Instead, he yelled, "Hey! Where the hell's that medic, goddamn it!"

Jensen grabbed his sleeve. "I asked you about my crew!"

"Uh, you were hit by a rocket, sir. Gas tank exploded knocking you outta the tank." He looked over at the burning hulk.

"Look, you son of a bitch, what about my crew? Are they okay?" Jensen screamed.

"No, sir," the sergeant said softly. "They didn't get out in time."

The roar of the Rose Bowl throng was still echoing in his ears as he and the other ten huddled. The smell of sweat and leather and that special scent of wondrous excitement were in his nostrils. They were giddy in their elation at having come within one point of tying the game with Si Jensen's long pass to his receiver, and now all they had to do was to kick the point-after to tie and remain undefeated for the year. With Si Jensen holding and the best kicker in the conference booting, they couldn't miss.

But it would be a tie, not a win.

"Give me the ball, Si," the fullback panted. "I can get it over. Let's win this sonuvabitch!"

"Yeah," chimed in the center, "a tie is like kissin' your sister. Let's go for the win!"

Si Jensen took his last allotted time out. He was going to try to talk the head coach into going for the two-point conversion by running the ball in. The coach saw him and motioned him back to the huddle. He was on his own.

"Okay, you guys, do we go for broke?" he asked the others.

"Hell, yes!" they chorused.

Si Jensen, quarterback, called the play.

USC came out of the huddle and lined up to kick the extra point. The crowd groaned and booed. Si Jensen, as usual, was the holder; Harry "the Boot" Goldfinger was the kicker.

Jensen received the snap from center, and Harry kicked at empty space. Jensen swung left to pass to the tall tight end. The fake was on.

The tight end was double-covered, as were the other receivers. The Buckeyes smelled the fake kick.

In the second or two he had to decide, Jensen did the only thing left to do: he ran. He ran to the goal line—it was only five yards away but looked like five miles. He was met by a ton of Ohio beef in the persons of two linebackers and a safety. His legs churned into the Pasadena turf, and all he could see was the hungry look of the ten guys who had said "No tie!" His legs dug and his body twisted in one last effort before going down. In a panic he thought that this was now a loss, not even a tie, let alone a win.

He couldn't see the referee's signal, but the explosion of sound from the stands told him that the zebra-striped arms were pointing toward heaven. He was over! He had scored the two points for the win. No tie, goddamn it!

He looked at the burning tank. The reality of what had happened—what he had allowed to happen—hit him squarely. He knew that his men were dead, but he couldn't bring himself to ask the question, as if . . . if he didn't hear the words, it wouldn't be so. But his eyes asked it, and the sergeant gravely nodded the terrible answer.

The Germans—the little boys—the kids! He remembered their eyes—frightened but determined; the fright had been fear of failing, not of dying, he thought. That's why he had spared them. He spared them when he could have killed them. He hadn't wanted to live through what he had done in the brewery—not again, not with little boys, dear God! But he had made the wrong decision—he had fumbled the ball in going for the win. They had counted on him, and now they were dead.

Second Lieutenant Simon Bolivar Jensen, already a leader of men in his young life, knelt on a soft, grassy mound of Lower Bavaria and looked up to the sky. From his parched throat came an agonizing cry.

"At ease!" The voice in the large hospital ward in Nuremberg wakened Jensen. "As you were!" echoed the same voice.

Jensen closed his eyes. Whoever it was would have to wake him.

"These are a bunch of brave boys, General," said the same voice.

"Goddamn it, Colonel, these are not boys; they are brave *men!*" It was the unmistakable high-pitched thunder of George S. Patton, Jr. "These are wounded soldiers, Colonel Harris. Next to the dead, there is no higher standard by which to confer upon them the title, brave men!"

Jensen gritted his teeth and squeezed his eyes shut. He felt sudden wetness on his cheeks, running into his ears.

The voice of Patton almost whispered, "Here's one who is an especially brave man: Lieutenant Simon Bolivar Jensen." He sat on Jensen's bed. "Please leave us, Colonel. I wish to be alone with this soldier."

The general removed his gleaming helmet liner, emblazoned with the four stars and the Third Army emblem. Jensen opened his bloodshot eyes and looked up at the ceiling.

"Nice to see you again, General."

Patton spoke softly. "Listen to me, soldier. You have done a brave thing. You led your men into battle, and you killed the enemy. I have written a letter to your father, and he will be proud of you, as I am proud of you. God chose to spare your life as He has chosen to spare mine. I firmly believe this because there is a reason for it from up there," he said, pointing above. "You have lost four brave men, and now you weep for them. I have lost thousands of brave men, and I weep for them every night when I'm alone. But every night I remember that they now lie in the field of honor, their sacred duty served, where none but the brave are entitled to that hallowed ground! Do you hear me, Lieutenant Jensen?"

"Yes, sir." *Is this how God works?* Tears streamed silently down his face.

"For some reason God has decreed that I not share this glory with those men," Patton said, looking away in troubled thought. "I can only pray that He spare me meeting my end slipping in a bathtub or some other ignoble and despicable thing." He looked back at Jensen. "You, on the other hand, will do great things. I know. You are a leader of men, Lieutenant Jensen. Now that this great war is over, you will wait for other great struggles, and you will take your armies and fight those battles for your country. And maybe one day you too will lie in the field of honor alongside your fallen comrades."

The mounds of bodies were gone by then, but the stench remained. So were the barracks still there, and the rotting smell of lice-infested straw, and the odor of tuberculosis that stank of mouse urine. And the fetor of typhus, dysentery, and starvation—those were still there, too. The interrogation block, the rubber truncheons, and the whips and the shouts and the threats; sadistic laughter lingering, mixing with the screams of pain and the moans of hopelessness—those remained. Oh, yes, and the ovens of charred brick, blackened with human soot, pregnant with the ashes and bits of bone, those too were there. And one might even hear the sounds, the echoes of merciful death.

The former masters were still there, but now as prisoners in their own house. Once-natty uniforms now looked like slept-in beds, trousers were baggy, and field caps were floppy behind the barbed wire they themselves installed for "protective custody"; SS runes were still on their collars, smirks were still on their faces—whistling in the dark of coming vengeance.

Simon Jensen walked away from the camp at Dachau with hate forever implanted in his bosom.

RANCHO SAN BUENAVENTURA, CALIFORNIA

THE PRESENT

Peter Kramer stood on the veranda admiring the President's ranch. It was a warm September afternoon, and Kramer sipped the icy dark Mexican beer brought to him by an attendant. He looked at the husky live oaks that interrupted the otherwise smooth flow of neatly trimmed grass that undulated down to a sunbathed lea; it reminded him of the Transylvanian meadowlands of his childhood. Here, he reflected, he could be completely happy in secluded retirement. Here he could write. Fiction perhaps, smiling at the chimerical idea. Memoirs? *No*, he admonished himself, *who would believe them?*

There was a quick knock on the door, and Simon Jensen entered. He wore a loose-fitting sweater and slacks. A drink was in his hand. He looked and moved in a relaxed, airy manner, but Kramer noticed lines of tension in his face, especially around his eyes and mouth.

"Hi there, Pete," the President said, flopping into a chair. He put his feet up on Kramer's bed, gesturing toward the view from the veranda. "This is the land I was reared in," he said. "If the world were as peaceful as this place, you'd be out of a job."

"A job I would gladly give up, Mr. President."

"Yeah. Well, if there's one thing I would want Si Jensen to be remembered for, it's that he was a peacemaker. And I think I can do it. Yessir, I think I can do it."

"All the indications are that you can, Mr. President."

"That's right." He paused for a few moments, a faraway look in his eyes. "You know, Pete, the guy said, 'War is hell'—three little words, but they go deep for those of us who know it. I know it because I was there, I went through it. It *is* hell." He turned to Kramer. "You Swiss were really smart, staying out of it."

There was a hint of provocation in the words and in the manner in which he spoke. Kramer said, "Only a madman wants war, Mr. President."

"Yeah. Well, let's get to your report."

The next hour was spent discussing Kramer's mission to Cairo and its ramifications. Jensen was pleased.

"Well," Jensen said, getting to his feet, "we're on the goal line, and short of a fumble, we will score. We've got them by the short hairs, Pete."

"By 'them' you mean—"

"The Russkies, damn it! This perpetual shooting match in the Near East, this pressure cooker threatening to blow its lid, that's what the Russians want. They want to come in the back door in Iran, but I won't let them—that I can promise you. They're looking for eventual control of the Persian Gulf, and political stability in the Middle East will be an obstacle for them. Well, that's just what they will get, because they're going to be playing *my* game by *my* rules! You know what I mean? No, I see that you don't." He smiled at Kramer as he paced. Suddenly he pointed a finger at him. "You people, the Europeans, you've given football a bum rap. You consider it a game of brawn and violence. That's because you don't understand it. Well, it's far from that."

Kramer reeled in confusion. In one breath, American foreign policy was discussed by the nation's chief executive; then, in the next, a spirited defense of a *game!*

"Football has as much an intellectual aspect to its strategy as does chess, the Russians' game," Jensen said with enthusiasm. "To take it even further, as does high-powered diplomacy. But the object is to have a blend of the intellect and the supreme physical conditioning necessary for the ultimate use of force, because unlike chess, where the loser graciously accepts defeat, in football your body fights with its last drop of sweat and blood!" The faraway look came back for a moment; then, smiling again, he said, "Ours is to win, Pete, to win!"

Then as if struck by a brilliant idea, the President put his finger to his temple. He went to the telephone by the bed and dialed a number. "This is the President," he said, grinning at Kramer. "Tell the fellows—all of them—to suit up for a game. We'll meet at the meadow in fifteen minutes. Yes, him, too."

Jensen went to a dresser and pulled out a sweatsuit and tossed it to Kramer. "Here, put this on. You'll find some jogging shoes in the closet that should fit you. You're going to play your first game of football."

"But Mr. President, I—"

"Don't worry, nobody'll get hurt; we're all a bunch of old fogies. I won't take no for an answer. C'mon, hurry up," he said, smiling. "I'll see you in the meadow."

Fifteen minutes later two teams were fielded for touch football. They were made up of the Secret Service contingent and some of the most important and influential men in the country, including the White House chief of staff, the presidential press secretary, and Senate Majority Leader Alan Heller of California.

After the first two plays, with Kramer blocking, Jensen said in the huddle, "Okay, Pete, I'm gonna hand off to you. All you have to do is make two yards. Just follow our block."

The ball was snapped to Jensen, the quarterback. He slapped it against Kramer's heaving chest. Kramer had run a yard when a Secret Service agent broke the block and crashed into him harder than the rules called for. The ball squirted out of Kramer's arm. With a shout of glee, the agent recovered the fumble.

Jensen knelt by the fallen, laughing Kramer. His face was distorted by anger. "You fumbled the ball, Kramer."

Still laughing, Kramer looked up and said, "That fellow plays rough, but I'll be ready for him next time. Just give me the ball again."

Jensen stood up straight. His body was rigid. "There won't be a next time. *You fumbled the ball!* No one on my team fumbles the ball, Kramer, because if he does, the other side kills you. Or didn't you know that?'' His words were angry, his tone serious.

Kramer got to his feet. The others stood around looking at one another, mouths open. ''Mr. President,'' Kramer said, brushing himself, ''if this is some joke . . .''

Jensen stared at Kramer, then at the others. He looked confused, uncertain.

''What?'' Jensen asked softly, eyes dull and flat. ''A joke? Yes, it was only a joke. C'mon,'' he said, picking up the football, ''let's play some more.'' But he walked to the house instead. The others watched the drama, eyes blinking in confusion and bewilderment.

The press secretary, Justin Powell, an intimate of Jensen's from his days in the Senate, turned to the others. ''Look, fellas, take it easy; he's overworked. Don't go off half-cocked.''

''Maybe he needs a real vacation, Justin,'' Alan Heller said. ''He's carrying too much on his shoulders, don't you think?'' But a look of deep concern was in Heller's eyes as he peered uncomfortably at Kramer. ''He's got an awful lot on his mind, Peter. You mustn't take it personally.''

Kramer grinned broadly. ''Of course not, Senator. The President takes football seriously. Just before our game he lectured me on it as it equates to foreign policy and diplomacy. I found his discourse fascinating.''

Alan Heller put his arm around Kramer's shoulder as they made their way back to the ranch house, the tension suddenly lifted by Kramer's blithe remark. ''Peter,'' he smiled, ''no one has to teach you anything about diplomacy.''

Later, Peter Kramer tossed and turned in an effort to nap after a shower. He couldn't get the bizarre incident with Jensen out of his mind. What had it meant? Would that have happened with someone else? Or had the President singled him out? It was a childish outburst, no matter how it was mitigated by him and the others. Was it overwork? Everyone, world leaders included, was overworked. But did they react in that way? Was this the man with the finger on the button?

He had noticed a certain coolness in the President lately whenever they spoke. Well, perhaps *coolness* was too strong a word, he judged. Distant, withdrawn, not quite as amiable. Was the change due to his burdens, or was there a change in their relationship? If only Erika had come with him. Her keen perceptions of these things were always uncannily correct. Yes, Erika would know. Strange, he thought, thinking of Erika, she didn't seem to like Jensen. She never said it, but he knew. Maybe it wasn't dislike, perhaps it was distrust. At first Peter thought it was because Jensen was demanding so much of his time, taking him away from her. But so was Hetherington, and she liked Hetherington and was warm and cordial to him, in contrast to her aloofness with the President. Why was that? He would have to ask her someday. It was delicate, however. He didn't want to open a Pandora's box by broaching the subject with her. She was upset enough as it was without adding more reasons.

A soft knock on the door brought him out of his worried thoughts. It was an aide to Jensen asking him to come down to the President's study.

Kramer dressed quickly and went downstairs. He knocked and entered.

"Come in, Pete. Sit down," Jensen said amicably. He called him Pete, a sign of friendship. "The press is badgering me for an off-the-cuff statement about your trip to Cairo. I'd like you to participate in a news conference. Okay?" Jensen smiled his usual warm, charismatic smile.

Kramer smiled, too, the football game suddenly ages away, a thing of the past, forgotten. All at once the darkness of his relations with Simon B. Jensen had been lifted. "Of course, Mr. President," Kramer said. "I'd be happy to."

The news conference was held on the patio of the Western White House, in the shade of a huge live oak. Jensen and Kramer sat at a redwood picnic table and the half-dozen journalists who covered the presidency were given a bench to share. Jensen ordered it placed in the hot afternoon sun, a tactic to make the journalists uncomfortable, thereby keeping the session short.

The President opened with a statement about the impending railroad strike that was threatening to cripple the country. "Secretary of Labor Strauss has just called me with the good news that both sides have agreed to binding arbitration, thereby postponing the strike for one week," Jensen said, starting on a high note.

Joe Crutcher of *The Los Angeles Times* raised his hand. "Mr. President, you once said that the railroads would continue running despite a strike even if you yourself had to drive the first train out of the Washington roundhouse. Is that still operative?" Everyone chuckled.

Jensen grinned his broadest. "Joe, you know I never break a promise. Trouble is, I'd have to find some fellow to teach me how to drive a train, and he'd probably be on strike." A roar of laughter.

Kramer was looking at the Jensen he knew before—witty, confident, comfortable in the face of any adversity, gifted with that quality few men have. He was proud to serve him.

Someone asked about the Arab-Israeli peace treaty. "At this point," Jensen replied, "I'll let Ambassador Kramer field your questions. As you know, he just returned from Cairo for a meeting with the Israelis and our Arab friends. Although he has briefed me on some of the highlights, I haven't had a chance to read his detailed report."

William Carver of UPI looked at Kramer. "Mr. Ambassador, do you have a treaty?" he asked.

"Not yet, Mr. Carver, but we have the foundations for one. The five major points have been agreed on in principle, and other than bringing them down to specifics, which are to some extent negotiable, all parties seem harmonious."

"With respect, sir," Carver said, "that sounds a little equivocal. On a scale of one to ten, ten being a certainty, where would you rate the chances for a treaty by the first Tuesday in November?"

Kramer looked at Jensen. They smiled knowingly at the political tenor of the question. "I would rate it a nine, Mr. Carver," Kramer said, enjoying a press conference for the first time since his arrival to prominence.

Sylvia Weisskopf of *The Washington Post* raised her hand. "Uh, could you be a bit more specific as to those five major points, sir?"

Kramer nodded with amiable tolerance. This was a subject that had been discussed at length at previous news conferences. "Certainly, Ms. Weisskopf," he said. "As you may remember, these points stem from the basis of the accord, the foundation of which I addressed before, which is, of course, that the Israelis recognize the Palestinians, and that the Arab participants in turn recognize Israel's right to exist. This is now a reality.

"Now, to the points," Kramer continued. "The first three deal with the geographical structure of the Palestinian homeland—that is, the territorial cessions by Israel, Syria, and Lebanon.'' Kramer turned to an aide. ''It might help if we had the map.'' An easel was put up to hold a large map of the Middle East. Kramer picked up a pointer.

''Israel cedes its territory from here, at Nahariya at the thirty-third parallel,'' he said, pointing to the map, ''to here, the border of Lebanon at Mishmar HaShofet. Then, south along the Syrian border to here, at En Gev, on the northeastern shore of the Galilee.

''Point Two: Lebanon cedes the land from its border with Israel here, north to the Litani River, including the port city of Tyre, then east to the Syrian border at Metulla.

''Point Three: Syria cedes the territory of AlQunaytirah, here''—he circled with his pointer on the map—''south to the northeast shore of the Galilee.''

Bill Merrill of the Associated Press stood up. ''But that includes the Golan Heights, Mr. Ambassador. I thought the Syrians were inflexible on the Heights.''

''Inflexibility, Mr. Merrill, is not a condition that furthers diplomacy or the cause of peace,'' Kramer said. ''One may as well not come to the table. The Syrians are practical enough to recognize that, short of war with Israel, the Golan Heights are Syrian no longer. Besides, what better gesture can be made by the Syrians than to graciously cede that land to their Palestinian brothers?''

There was nodding of assent among the journalists and a general feeling of admiration for the special envoy.

''Now, to Point Four,'' Kramer said. ''The governments of Saudi Arabia, Qatar, Bahrain, Kuwait, and the Arab Emirates—nations that form the United Arab Alliance—will commit their economic support for the formation, development, and maintenance of a Palestinian homeland.''

''Under what conditions, Mr. Ambassador?'' asked Crutcher.

Kramer sat down. ''Under the framework of the Pan-Arab Monetary Fund, as outlined in Article Four. With one condition: that the Palestinians agree not to explore or drill for oil during the life of the treaty, which is to be fifty years.

''And finally, Point Five: The State of Israel commits technological assistance in the development of the Palestinian homeland. Technology dealing with agronomy and agriculture, water resources development and explorations, irrigation and fertilization techniques, and other areas of necessities such as highways, communications, medical and health delivery systems, and so on, together with the establishment of trade and commerce between the two nations."

"Ambassador Kramer, I take it that the West Bank of the Jordan is definitely out as far as the Israelis are concerned," offered Kenneth Ladd of *The Christian Science Monitor*.

"That is correct, Mr. Ladd. The Israelis won't budge on that. They want it as a 'buffer zone' against their new allies, the Jordanians." Everyone laughed. "It makes sense geographically, I think," Kramer added.

Sylvia Weisskopf raised her hand again. "Mr. Kramer, you didn't mention a Palestinian army. Is there to be no Palestinian army for national defense? I mean, how will they defend themselves if attacked?"

The other reporters looked at one another. It was a negative question, one better saved for the editorial pages of her newspaper, one of the few that were anti-Jensen.

"The new name of the Palestinian homeland should give you that answer, Ms. Weisskopf. It will be the United Nations Protectorate of Palestine."

Alden Wadleigh of Reuters was recognized. "Shaffir Mahamet of the PLO has vowed that, unless the West Bank is a viable point of negotiation, he will not agree to a treaty. What is his position at this time, Mr. Ambassador?"

"As you know, Alden, I met with Chairman Mahamet in Cairo a few days ago. He sees the obvious goodwill on the part of the Israelis, particularly that of Prime Minister Ben-David. Since the prime minister has assured King Hussein that Israel will not settle the West Bank, and since the Jordanians are not thrilled with the idea of the Palestinians moving in, Chairman Mahamet assured me that he can live with the terms of the treaty."

Sylvia Weisskopf raised her hand yet again. "Washington is rife with rumors in regard to the Arab-Israeli peace treaty, one of which is that you will be nominated for the Nobel Peace Prize if it goes through. Another is that you will replace Secretary of State Hetherington. Uh, do you have any comments?"

Kramer turned beet red. He took a deep breath and in a low voice, almost shaking in anger, said, "Ms. Weisskopf, I fail to see, even in the most remote way, the relevance of such questions in this news briefing. First of all, such rumors, if they exist at all, are unfounded, rash, careless, and injudicious. Second, I suggest you remember—all of you—that I am simply an agent of the President of the United States, and that it is his judgment and his wisdom and his foresight that have stimulated the parties to this accord into a peaceful settlement, something that was once considered an impossibility.'' His jaws were dancing in fury. ''As to my ambitions, Ms. Weisskopf, as long as you brought up the subject, I can only tell you that my goal is to do the best possible job for the President in my capacity as his agent and then to return to my former life as a teacher. I hope that answers your . . . question.''

Simon Jensen stood up. He had a frozen smile on his lips, but his eyes were hooded in a cloak of anger. ''Well, I guess that's all for now. As soon as we have further developments we'll let you know.'' He left the patio, Kramer behind him.

Dinner at the Western White House was held on the patio. The weather was balmy; fragrances of blooming flowers mixed with the aroma of broiling steak. The President of the United States made the salad; the conversation was light and humorous. The majority leader told some of his best jokes, and cold beer from a keg made them even funnier to the relaxed group. The press corps had been invited to the barbecue but had elected instead to have their dinner at the nearby Ojai Inn, where libations could flow more freely than at the President's table, as could the gossip and speculations.

Over dessert, Jensen asked the question. Nothing in particular that anyone could think of later brought the question about; Jensen's mood was jovial, if anything. It was out of the blue, as Alan Heller would say later.

''Tell me, Pete,'' Jensen asked between spoonfuls of pineapple sherbet, ''what did you do during the war?''

The question came like a slap. There was no doubt—and the sudden silence at the table confirmed it—that the question was insolent and was meant to humiliate Kramer, and President or not, Kramer could not allow it. He was about to answer that the President well knew that he had spent the war in Switzerland, and further, that the query was beyond his understanding.

But before he could reply, Jensen answered his own question. ''Oh, yeah, you guys were neutral, weren't you? Well, I wasn't so lucky. I fought the Krauts with General George S. Patton. I did luck out in one respect, though. I was wounded a couple of times, not bad enough to cripple me but enough to get me a couple of medals, which got me elected to the Senate. Of course, my father lucked out, too, by me not dying for my country"—his voice dropped low—"like my tank crew." His voice turned sullen. "Old Dad got a live hero, didn't he?"

The atmosphere at the table turned thick and cold. Lorelei Jensen, the President's beautiful and cultured wife, cleared her throat as a prelude to breaking the oppressive silence. "Tell me, Senator Heller, did you ever control that citrus fungus on your orange trees?"

"No," Heller said, "as a matter of fact, I didn't, Mrs. Jensen. We finally had to clear away the orchard, which in these days was a luxury we couldn't afford anyway. We ended up selling the land to some developers." Everyone seemed grateful for the talk about citrus fungus.

"Must've been nice"—the President smiled, ignoring the new topic—"spending the war skiing and mountain climbing, hey, Pete?"

Justin Powell broke in in an attempt to rescue Kramer from the mysterious presidential attack. "I don't know, Mr. President, if I would have traded places with Peter, since I spent the war behind a desk in Honolulu attached to Headquarters, Pacific Fleet. After a bad case of sunburn, I put in for a Purple Heart, but they turned me down!" Everyone laughed except Simon Jensen.

"Tell me, Pete," Jensen pressed on, "what with Switzerland being made up of Italians, Frenchmen, and Krauts, what do you consider yourself—Kraut?"

Peter Kramer took a last sip of coffee and wiped his lips. "Swiss, Mr. President, just Swiss. Now, if you will excuse me," he said, rising, "the jet lag seems to have caught up with me, and I must bid you good night, sir. Mrs. Jensen, gentlemen."

As he left the patio Kramer heard the voice of the President. "Andrew," he said to an attendant, "bring us some brandy. I want to toast the next Nobel Peace laureate, Peter Kramer!"

THE DEAD SEA

THE PRESENT

The helicopter with the blue and white Star of David on its sides settled down in a cloud of desert dust. The whine of its turbines diminished into a groan, then stopped altogether, creating an uncertain silence. The two men stepped down the ladder into the oven that was the western shore of the Dead Sea near 'En Gedi, a place forsaken by God but not by Jews. The prime minister of Israel sat on the bottom rung of the helicopter ladder and removed his shoes and socks. Then he slipped on rubber Japanese sandals. Blithely he watched his lanky guest stare in awe at the vast nothingness, his hands in his hip pockets, his shirt already wet with perspiration.

Baruch Ben-David handed Peter Kramer a pair of sandals. "Here. Put these on. We can walk to the water without burning our feet." He studied his friend's face. "You look as if you're in pain," he said, smiling. "I chose this place because it offers some privacy."

"And I take it hell was too crowded," Kramer said.

They both laughed. "No, it's not Palm Springs," Ben-David said, "but it's home. Give us a few more years, and you'll see what we do with it." They donned floppy sun hats and walked toward the shore of the mineral-pregnant lake.

Ben-David still had not indicated his reason for wanting to talk to Kramer, not even on the helicopter trip from Jerusalem. In his phone call he had stressed urgency, and Kramer had known better than to press him. Ben-David's way was reserved; he was not given to rashness. His deliberate ways often angered both his colleagues in the Knesset and his political opponents, most of whom were Ashkenazi firebrands who were short on patience when it came to Israel's future. They were all quick to point to his Sephardic ancestry, claiming that Sephardic Jews, especially those from France or Italy, lacked the fervor and patriotism of the Eastern Ashkenazim who had endured the pogroms and the ghettoes.

Perhaps it *was* his Gallic upbringing that made him more diplomatic than his predecessors. Before the war, he had been more a Frenchman than a Jew.

Baruch Ben-David had been a young lawyer in Paris in 1941, part of the legal team that defended another French Jew, Léon Blum, before the Vichy courts that were accusing Blum of something close to treason. Also during that epoch, Ben-David had been an associate of yet another notable French Jew, Pierre Mendès-France. Blum, who had already been a French premier, died a Frenchman; Mendès-France, who was later to become a French premier, also died a Frenchman in the country of his birth. It was the third member of the trio, the young Henri Varèse, who would end up as the Israeli statesman named Baruch Ben-David. The Nazis made him a Zionist; the British, in their opposition to a free state of Israel, made him a Jewish patriot.

They waded in the ankle-deep hot waters, and a slight breeze tried to cool down the desert. They spoke French, their usual language when they were alone.

They talked about the time in Paris when Ben-David had been a law student and Kramer was at the Sorbonne. They reminisced, each man with his own memories of those seemingly carefree days before the war.

They went on like that for the better part of an hour, taking a brief detour from their ponderous business, pausing now and then to drink chilled Haifa orange juice from insulated canteens.

Then as the red orb that was the Middle Eastern sun was beginning to set, Baruch Ben-David sighed and said, "Then came the war."

Peter Kramer nodded. "Yes, the war."

Ben-David asked casually, "Where did you say you spent the war, Peter?"

"In Zürich," was the equally casual answer.

Ben-David stopped walking and placed an affectionate hand on Kramer's shoulder. He looked at Kramer through troubled eyes. "My dear friend, in spite of our friendship, our closeness, is that your answer to me?"

Despite the blazing heat, Kramer suddenly felt cold. Decades of fear, of living a lie, were going to end then and there. "What an odd thing to say, Baruch."

They resumed their walk in the hot surf. Then Ben-David said, "Peter, I'm going to suggest something to you. You can admit it as true, in which case we'll work something out, I promise. If, on the other hand, you deny it, I will accept your denial without question. I shall never mention it, and I will ask you to forget that I ever asked it in the first place. Do you agree, my friend?"

"Of course," Kramer said with alacrity. A heaviness had crept into his chest. He knew what was coming. He had dreamed of it countless times—the confrontation, the finger pointing, accusing.

Baruch Ben-David took a deep breath. "Very well. I suggest that you did not spend the war in Zürich. You spent it—or at least part of it—in Paris, as SS-Major-General von Bergdorf, Chief of the SD-France and representative of SS General Heydrich."

He looked at Kramer for a reaction, but Kramer's face was impassive.

"I further suggest," Ben-David continued, "that I met you one unforgettable night in the transit camp at Drancy where I and others were being processed for Auschwitz. The date was June seventh, nineteen forty-two. You had a fellow working for you—Denker, or Drenken, something like that—an ugly SS thug who hardly spoke French. You ordered him to remove certain ones of us from the transit manifest on the pretext that we were professionals—doctors, lawyers, et cetera—and that the SS leadership in Berlin had other plans for us. Do you remember? Shortly after, we were on our way to Marseilles and freedom—and life!"

He searched Kramer's stony face for some sign. "Surely you remember that night, Peter! It was cold and rainy, and you stood in front of me in your uniform, with beads of raindrops on your cap visor and on your boots. You even asked me in perfect French if I was the Henri Varèse who had defended Léon Blum. Damn it, you *must* remember that night!" he roared in frustration.

Kramer removed the sun hat. He stopped and scooped a palmful of water and splashed his neck.

"Then I was wrong. It wasn't you. Or . . . you deny it." Ben-David spoke softly now, resigned to his disappointment.

Kramer sighed. In the dream, the finger was always attached to a faceless form; now the form had a face. Now the moment he had dreaded for so many years had come, but he discovered that it wasn't as bad as he had imagined, and he almost felt relieved. Yet the years of silent denial still dictated to his instinct of self-preservation, and he said only, "What an extraordinary story, Baruch!"

"Well then, I was wrong," Ben-David repeated heavily. "Forgive me for having put you through that. It was stupid of me, since if you really were von Bergdorf, you would deny it anyway because of the implications it would have for the peace treaty. Very well, you deny it, and I accept it as I said I would, with no reservations." Ben-David smiled wistfully. "And yet it would have been . . ." The words trailed off.

Kramer well understood the half-spoken phrase, the trailed-off words. The thin thread of deceit snapped under the weight of affection. "Dannecker," Kramer said as they walked. "That was his name. Dannecker."

"What?"

"And you were very thin then, and with more hair. You wore a moustache, didn't you?"

The prime minister of Israel tried to smile, biting his lip as tears welled up in his eyes.

He munched on a piece of crusty bread with some cheese on it, and because he was hungry, it went down well. He sipped the hot sweet tea, and that went down better because he was trying to warm his insides, which were shaking with what he thought was cold. But his brow had beads of sweat and his underarms were damp. He looked out the window of the large building in the direction of Le Bourget airfield and wondered how the place looked when Lindbergh touched down in 1927 amid the lights and the cheering crowd. He turned to look at the other crowd now, the one occupying the building, but it wasn't cheers he heard, it was more a low, thundering din of voices, anxious voices in a babble of foreign tongues—Polish, Slovakian, German, and Yiddish—none of which he understood.

He held the hot cup in his numb hands and watched more with curiosity than with interest the long lines forming across the room, lines made up of men with beards, young boys with long curls adorn-

159

ing their cheeks, and women in heavy, serviceable fur coats holding playful children by the hand. Ashkenazim, he said to himself with a trace of distaste. They all wore a six-pointed yellow star on their breasts—much like his own, he realized with uneasiness.

A man from his group who was French but who also wore the star spoke reassuringly. He said that the people in line were exchanging their francs for Polish zlotys since they were being sent east to help Germany in the war effort—or so they were told by their hosts, the men in the gray uniforms with the diamond patch on their sleeves with the letters SD. He remembered that that stood for Sicherheitsdienst, the security service of the SS—the Gestapo.

Another man spoke, but in hissed whispers. There are camps, he said, in which Jews are being killed—exterminated, he said, using a term he had heard applied only to pests before. The boches were going to kill them all, the man said, his voice shaking in fear and anger, and the French were allowing it! They were not taking them to work, he maintained, they were taking them to die. The man had answered the unasked questions: What were they doing there? Where were they going?

He walked away from the man in disgust. What ugly rumors! He bit into the bread, but his mouth had become dry. He took some more tea, swallowing it with difficulty. What ugly rumors! he reiterated. He was a lawyer. He knew that there were laws protecting French Jews from deportation, and even the Germans had respect for the law. He and the other Frenchmen would soon be released—and with apologies! He wiped his cold, clammy hands on his coat front, and he felt the cloth star. He recalled that the Germans had agreed that French Jews would not have to wear it. And yet they were wearing it now. The edict had been issued only a few weeks earlier, and it had seemed proper to comply. After all, the Germans had behaved rather decently, hadn't they? They were brutally stern with saboteurs and members of the Resistance, he knew, but he and the others were not saboteurs. And yet, they had to wear the star. . . . Why did they have to wear the star? he wondered. He looked around for the man who talked about the camps; maybe he knew something else. He couldn't find him now. His mouth became dryer.

Two SS officers and a captain of the French gendarmerie came up to his group. The taller one said he was SS-Obersturmführer Dannecker and that the French Jews were being drafted by the German

Reich in its fight against Bolshevism. They were not to worry, he said, they would be well treated if they cooperated. They were to line up for an exchange of currency and then board the transports.

A wail of protest went up from the Frenchmen. Dannecker shouted to them in German. He couldn't understand the words, but the manner was threatening. Then two other SS men appeared. They were dressed in the field gray of the Waffen-SS, and their sleeves had regimental armbands indicating that they were combat soldiers. One had the stripes of a general on his trouser legs and wore a large Iron Cross around his neck. The general spoke calmly to Dannecker, who argued angrily. The general then spoke harshly to Dannecker and took a list from his pocket. The general began calling out names. Finally he heard his own name called. The general said something to him about the defense of Léon Blum. Unlike Dannecker, the general spoke perfect Parisian French.

They were marched to a bus, still in a state of fearful uncertainty despite the reassuring words of the French policeman who accompanied them. The bus took them back to Paris, to 36 Rue Aimellot—he would never forget the address—and they were given false identity papers, ration cards, and travel passes signed by the German authorities. They were told to go to a Capuchin monastery at 51 Rue Croix de Regnier in Marseilles—he would never forget that address, either—where the father superior would provide them with new papers and money and arrange for their smuggle into Spain, then to Palestine!

They had time, they were told, only to go to their homes and pack what they barely needed, to say a quick farewell to their loved ones, and to take the train, posing as workers for French industry in Marseilles.

He asked what would happen to his family. Whatever could be done would be done, he was told, but not to count on much. He asked where they would have been taken from Drancy. A place called Auschwitz, he was told, where the SS had built gas chambers and ovens, and from the ashes of Jews they made fertilizer. Why had he been rescued? he asked. Because he, and others like him—as many as could be gotten out through the Jewish underground—were the future of Medinat Yisra'el, the state of Israel, and that from the ashes of Auschwitz, it would rise.

Who was the SS general who had rescued them? he asked.

The reply: A friend.

Baruch Ben-David clasped his hands in front of his chest. He looked up to the cloudless sky as if offering a prayer of thanks. "I knew it!"

Ben-David grabbed Kramer in a bear hug. He gave way to his emotions and wept. Kramer returned the embrace, weeping too on his friend's shoulder.

And far off on a hilltop was the only witness to the scene of such importance to those men of such importance—a lizard of the Dead Sea.

Baruch Ben-David disengaged himself from Kramer, pulling out a handkerchief. "I knew—I felt in my guts that it was you, Peter." He blew into the handkerchief. "And now I can at last thank you for what you did. You know, over the years I tracked down the resting places of some of those people who helped us—gentiles mainly, like the good Father Marie-Benoit of Marseilles. I put flowers on their graves as thanks for their unselfish acts that cost some of them their lives. But I could never find your grave, Peter. It was as if you had disappeared off the face of the earth."

Kramer dabbed at his eyes with his shirt sleeves. "Come on, old friend," he said, taking Ben-David by the arm, "let's go."

They resumed their walk in the gentle surf, pant legs rolled up to the knees, floppy hats adding a touch of the comical to the weighty subject.

"I imagined that you were dead," Ben-David continued, "buried by the Gestapo in some unmarked grave. I imagined all sorts of things. I became even despondent over not finding you, over not being able to thank you. And now . . . and now I can thank God that I didn't find your grave!"

"But how in the world did you make me, Baruch? After all these years, how did you make me?"

"Ah"—Ben-David smiled—"it's this damned ear of mine. I have to go back to that night at Drancy." The smile left. "You know the night. This SS-general who spoke such perfect French—I wasn't paying attention to what was said because I was too scared, too worried—but he spoke a particular phrase that has stayed with me all these years. Whenever I tried to remember that night, it was that phrase—'il ne croit plus à rien'—that stuck with me. Not the meaning of the words, but the pronunciation; the *cr* of *croit*. It had just a touch of an accent; the *r* was almost rolled. Later, every time I relived that night, I remembered that slight imperfection of his French, while repeating over and over again that phrase."

Kramer said, "I'm afraid I don't understand—"

"Wait, I'm not finished. This mental exercise, as with all things connected with the memory, was finally forgotten. Or rather filed away in the 'inactive drawer' up here." Baruch Ben-David pointed to his large head. "Then, two weeks ago, when I agreed at your urging that you and I meet with Shaffir Mahamet and the other PLO fellows, there was a point in the rather emotional discussions in which Mahamet doubted our sincerity. You turned to me and whispered in French, 'He no longer believes in anything'—the exact words I heard that night in Drancy, and with exactly the same trace of an accent in the *cr* of *croit*. It took a few days to unlock the memory storage drawer in my brain, but when I did . . . well, you know the rest. Of course, I still had to ask you."

"And so you did." Kramer shook his head. "Incredible! To think a tiny sound—"

"I told you, it's my ear. It's like a curse," Ben-David said, smiling, pleased with himself.

They turned in unison and began walking through the wilderness back to the helicopter. The Middle Eastern sun had disappeared behind the craggy hills of Judea, creating a pale blue sky with splashes of magenta and orange. A doggish wind suddenly snapped at their hat brims.

"Tell me, Baruch," Kramer finally said, "now that you have this knowledge, what will you do with it?"

"Nothing. Other than Simon Jensen, who needs to know? Your secret is safe with me, if that's what you mean."

"I know it is, Baruch. It's just that . . ." Kramer bit his lip in thought. He wished he could convey his feelings about Jensen the man, as opposed to Jensen the President of the United States; the latter, however, was the way Ben-David was considering him.

But how could he say that there was something abnormal about Jensen, that he seemed to harbor a hatred toward Germans because of something that had happened to him during the war and that was now affecting his judgment as President, as a leader in the peace process? That judgment affected the most far-reaching decisions for his country and for the world. How could he relate his apprehensions, his uneasiness, about the President, when they stemmed only from vague and undefinable events and moods and words, events that of themselves were no cause for concern but taken as a whole could spell doom for the peace treaty?

He had thought long and hard about the strange occurrences that evening at Jensen's ranch: the football game, the press conference, the dinner. His initial feelings—lacking any evidence of other, more sinister motives—were that Jensen resented the amount of publicity and credit that Kramer was getting for the peace treaty. Now he felt that that was too simple—there was something else, something to do with his Germanic background, something obscure that veiled the future of the treaty in a shroud of danger. But there was no way he could share those misgivings with his friend. How could he tell the Prime Minister of Israel what he was really thinking? How could he dare think, let alone say to another world leader, "I think the President of the United States is mad"?

"Look, Peter, I can understand your hesitation about telling Jensen; it's a secret you've lived with for so long. But he must be told, don't you agree?"

"Must he? He's not overly fond of Germans," Kramer said softly. "I can't predict how he'll react to the news that I'm not the Swiss historian I pretend to be but one of those Germans he fought in the war. And a wanted former SD man, on top of it."

"Yes, he's a little impetuous, and he'll probably sack you," Ben-David said without emotion. "But not until after the treaty business is concluded," he added quickly. "He won't jeopardize the treaty, I assure you."

After a pause, Ben-David turned to Kramer. "Good Lord, Peter. How can we *not* tell him, now that I know? What if he were to find out through other sources and learn that I knew? Our relationship—his and mine, our nations'—is based on trust and openness. It would most severely strain this relationship if he should learn about it from anyone other than you or me."

Kramer sighed. "Of course you're right. I'll tell him as soon as I return to Washington. No matter what his reaction, he won't jeopardize the treaty."

They walked in silence; the desert wind still blew in small erratic gusts, and the heat was quickly dissipating into the long and weird shadows of the hills. Peter Kramer looked at the soil upon which they walked, and he wondered about other feet, sandaled feet, that had trodden it, feet belonging to other troubled men: one of them who led his flock to the Land of Canaan thirty-five hundred years before, and another, a carpenter, who led his smaller flock into a future in which what others did in his name he could not sanction.

The sound of Ben-David's voice brought Kramer back to the present. "Tell me, Peter, why didn't you deny it? You could have played dumb, and I would have understood. For my part, I had to ask, but you didn't have to admit it. Why?" His voice was soft, undemanding.

"My first instinct—an instinct I've developed over so many years—was to pretend I didn't know what you were talking about. My attitude in any confrontation has always been categorically to deny all that wasn't consistent with the persona of Peter Kramer, Swiss-born college professor and part-time diplomatic negotiator. No one has ever been able to prove any different, so air-tight was my new identity.

"But that doesn't answer your question. I don't know why, Baruch. Perhaps it was being here in this place, with its momentous history that has a way of humbling one, making one vulnerable to the truth, especially when asked about it by someone I esteem. Those reasons alone are good ones, I think, and I hope Erika will understand them when she finds out.

"But there is still another, which goes more to the core: I felt an elation, a joyous relief in telling you. I suppose it's that old cliché—confession is good for the soul. It certainly was good for mine. You know, Erika and I have lived a lie for a long time. It gave us the security we needed. But the lie has become a private hell. I think I've secretly wished sometimes that I *would* be discovered. Well, thanks to that ear of yours"—he smiled—"I finally was. And I feel ten pounds lighter!"

Ben-David nodded in understanding as they approached the helicopter, still off in the distance. "One more thing, Peter. Why did you run? You weren't a war criminal; you had nothing to hide."

"It's a long story, Baruch. I'll tell it to you someday. But you're wrong about one thing—I was a war criminal. The orders for the deportation of the Jews came from my office on Avenue Foch, over my signature. That bit of doing constitutes a crime against humanity. I would have been arrested and bound over for trial and perhaps even convicted, the passions of the time being what they were. I couldn't face a trial. And there were other reasons, and I had things to do, so I ran," Kramer said, immediately regretting his candor.

"What other reasons?" Ben-David pressed. "What things did you have to do?"

"I told you it was a long story, and someday I'll tell it to you. In the meantime, please don't press me."

"Very well. But as far as you being tried, you must know that we—those of us you saved—would have testified in your behalf. Guy de Belfort was still alive and would have come forward. He was a cabinet minister under de Gaulle, and his testimony alone would have carried a lot of weight."

"It wasn't that simple, my friend," Kramer said. "You're forgetting that I was a German officer. Despite the crimes in which my government was involved, I was disloyal. I had taken an oath, and I violated that oath."

"Excuse me, but I fail to see how that would've prejudiced your case with the judges."

"I'm speaking of my German judges, Baruch, those who sit in the security of their pensions, writing their memoirs. They sit in judgment as they drink beer with their former comrades and assert that they had to perform unpleasant tasks during the war, but they didn't violate their oath, their honor. No, I just couldn't face that."

"But what about Stauffenberg and the others?" Ben-David said, pushing his point. "They certainly weren't condemned for opposing Hitler, and they were Germans."

"If you think they were judged kindly by their countrymen, then you've been influenced by romanticized but inaccurate history. There are few monuments to Count Stauffenberg in Germany. The yardstick by which Germans measure honor and loyalty is unlike any I know. In their view, the view of the officers who didn't join the conspiracy, Count Stauffenberg and his followers were traitors. And they don't give medals to traitors. It all goes back to the Teutonic principles of duty to the Fatherland, respect for authority, and obedience to leadership. This national character of the Germans is well known, Baruch, and I'm sure I don't have to detail it more."

"Well, they still have no right to judge a man of conscience and decency like you! No matter what the traditions!"

"Perhaps," Kramer said, "but they are traditions, nevertheless.

The same ones I was raised with, and they make me guilty in their eyes."

"I don't understand, Peter. You accept this guilt, then?"

"In my own case, whether I bear guilt is too subjective an issue for me to judge. If I had to do things all over again, there is no question that I would act in the same way, because my conscience would so dictate, as would my intellect. That is, from a moral position I bear no guilt. But as a soldier sworn to a blood oath, I am guilty of violating that oath. In any case, I will leave it to others to hand down a verdict. After all, I handed down my verdict on others long ago."

"You mystify me, Peter. All I can say is, thank God I'm a Jew. Our guilt we can live with!"

The helicopter deposited the two men at the military airfield just outside Tel-Aviv. They boarded Ben-David's Mercedes; two other Mercedeses with security agents followed them to the Dan Hotel, where Kramer was staying. As Kramer opened the car door, they shook hands warmly and looked at each other in newfound understanding and sympathy.

Ben-David said, "You'll talk to the President?"

"Yes. Tomorrow, if I can get him alone. I'll call you."

"Yes, call me immediately. Are you sure you can't come with me to supper? Rivkah will be terribly disappointed, you know."

"Not more than I," Kramer said. "I have just time enough to shower the Dead Sea off me and to catch the El Al flight to New York. I want to get back without having to offer awkward explanations about my trip here. Please kiss Rivkah for me and extend my apologies."

The three-car convoy drove up ha Yarkon to Ben-David's modest apartment on Keren Kayemet. He and Rivkah had lived there for a number of years, and despite his high position, they found no reason to change their comfortable lodgings to a strange place. It was only a forty-minute-or-so drive to Jerusalem anyway.

He found his wife in the kitchen, putting the finishing touches on the evening's dinner. She wore a starched white apron and, underneath, an evening dress for the occasion.

Ben-David sniffed the air. "Mm, what smells so good? You or the food?" He kissed her on the neck.

"That's the perfume Peter gave me," she said, wiping her

hands on the apron and looking around the apartment. "So? Where is Mr. Ambassador Kramer? In the living room?"

"Here, my Rivi," he said, kissing her on both cheeks, "that's from Peter. He's not coming. He had to get back to Washington tonight, and he sends his regrets."

She pushed her husband back. "Not coming? *Jaj, borzasztó!*" she wailed in Hungarian. "That's terrible! Look at all this—the chicken *paprikás*, and the *krumpli* . . . and my *mákos beigli*—what am I going to do with all this?" she asked in Hebrew, which was their common language; she spoke no French, and he no Hungarian.

He looked at the spicy chicken and potatoes and her poppy-seed roll. He smiled sadly. He knew that much of her disappointment lay in not being able to do what she enjoyed most, which was visiting with Peter Kramer and speaking German, the cultured German of Thomas Mann and Kant and Schopenhauer, the German she had learned in the private schools of Budapest that her father had sent her to because, irony of ironies, he was a Germanophile.

He held Rivkah's hands and kissed them tenderly, the lovely hands that were still calloused from a thousand hoe handles on the many *kibbutzim* and from the thousand rifles she had carried during her days in the fledgling Israeli army. And she had other scars, because she too was a survivor, one who had come out alive from Auschwitz-Birkenau. Alive, but with scars on her body.

She had been very young and beautiful when Dr. Mengele had taken a special interest in her, and it was he who had operated on her. The physical scars were still there, but she was used to them; what she wasn't yet used to was the scarring of her psyche, from which the haunting dreams still came, dreams that made her scream in the night, dreams shared only with her husband as he cradled her in his arms and wept with impotent fury at the thought that Josef Mengele, Doctor of Evil, might somehow know that Rozsa Kuhn, late of Budapest, whom he had touched in scientific debauchery, whom he had soiled with his scalpel and . . . other instruments . . . was the wife of the prime minister of the State of Israel—and that he might sit in his jungle compound and laugh!

Rivkah shook her head. "*Jaj, nekem!* Oh dear, look at all this food. What will I do with it?"

"I'll tell you what you'll do with it, my Rivi," her husband said, putting his arm around her. "You'll fix me a little plate and bring it into my study. Then have the boys downstairs come up and sit at our table. By the time you blink, it'll all be gone. What do you say?"

She smiled. The boys from the security detachment—they would be hungry. They always were.

Baruch Ben-David pushed away the plate of chicken. He drank some wine and looked at the picture of Peter Kramer on his cluttered wall. He was replaying something Peter had said as they walked back to the helicopter at 'En Gedi earlier that day. He had asked Peter why he had fled, and Peter had given his reasons. Then he had vaguely added, "There were other reasons, and I had things to do." What had he meant by that? Then he had made a cryptic remark about the guilt of others. What others? What guilt?

A connection started to click in Ben-David's mind, a blurry image of a report he once read years ago when he was deputy defense minister. Prime Minister Ben-Gurion had called him in to ask his opinion about a report brought to his attention by Isser Harel, the then-chief of Mossad, in which a German-speaking Mossad agent had made contact with an ex-SS man in Barcelona. Ben-David now remembered that the agent had befriended the German over drinks and that the German became talkative, which had been the agent's objective.

Sometime during the evening, the agent had spoken of belonging to a group of ex-Nazis whose purpose was, according to the drunken German, to make amends for Germany's crimes against the Jews. How they were doing it, the German had said, was nobody's business. But there was money—lots of money, he had said in alcohol-induced candor. Once, during the binge, according to the report, the letters *QB* were alluded to.

Isser Harel had offered Ben-Gurion his opinion regarding the matter, which was that he gave little credence to the German's story inasmuch as he could not believe that former Nazis would want to help those they had so recently sworn to exterminate. Still, Isser the Little had instructed his agents to check out this man. Who knew? Perhaps he and his friends might be of interest to Mossad for other reasons. And the matter had ended there, years earlier.

Baruch Ben-David dialed a number with one hand and held a drumstick with the other. He chewed as the number rang at Mossad headquarters, Israel's main intelligence agency. The deputy chief, Eliahu Allon, answered the phone. "Who calls me at this hour?" he said.

"Good evening, Eli," Ben-David said, "it's me."

"As if I didn't know," Allon said. "Who else would have the cheek to call at this hour, chewing in my ear? What are you eating? It sounds good."

It was a typical conversation between the two old fighters, close friends since the days of the Haganah battles with the British. Ben-David had made Allon deputy chief of Intelligence, not out of the strong friendship but because of Allon's great skill and unique instincts when it came to Israel's security.

After the Yom Kippur War Mossad had become too "political" for Ben-David's taste, eventually becoming controlled by Sharon's people in the Ministry of Defense, bypassing the prime minister. After the godawful *michdal* in Beirut, there was a major shake-up in Defense, and along with it in Mossad. That was when Ben-David installed his confidant, Allon, with whom he could work better, more closely, and with more freedom.

"It's a piece of Rivi's chicken," Ben-David said into the phone. "Listen, Eli, from over there in your shop, do the German letters *QB* mean anything to you?"

"No. Should they?"

"If you were the real *memuneh* that you think you are, they would, but they don't, and that's why you're only deputy. Now, go over and bring me the file—whatever else is there, too—on Q-B. I want to take a look at it."

"Tonight you want it?"

"No, *chamor*, next year! Of course tonight. Now! And Eli," Ben-David said in more intimate tones, "this is only for our knowledge, yours and mine."

"Understood, Baruch. I'll bring it over myself. If it is there, of course."

Good old Eli, Ben-David thought, *I can always count on him through all his insolence*. "Of course it's there," he said with mock irritation. "Isser put it there himself."

"Understood, Baruch. Shall I read it?"

"Now that you mention it, Eli, I would prefer that you didn't," Ben-David said, knowing that a lesser man would take offense at such a request. "It may concern a good friend of mine. I hope you understand, old pal."

"No problem," Eli Allon said offhandedly.

Eliahu Allon delivered the package to Ben-David. They ate poppy-seed rolls and exchanged good-natured insults. Then, sensing the urgency of the file, Allon left.

Ben-David perused the first two pages; they were substantially what he remembered, except the names, which he had forgotten. The Mossad agent was called Manuel, and the German's name was Odilio Kellermann.

The next entry was a memo to the file from Manuel's section chief noting that nothing had turned up on Kellermann, if that was his real name. His photograph also produced a blank, which, if anything, proved that he was too small a fish for Mossad to be further interested.

That was followed by a memorandum to Isser Harel from his expert on Nazi assets still unaccounted for. By their very nature these assets were of great interest to Mossad, since Mossad wanted to stay on top of any possible "Fourth Reich" movements that could spring up in different parts of the world. The memo listed the names and titles of various Germans, most of them unknown to Ben-David. Next to their names were estimated amounts of assets, all in U.S. dollars; adjacent to the names were the sources—Poland, France, Hungary—places where there had been mass deportations of Jews.

Circled in blue pencil was France. Isser Harel liked to use a blue pencil.

The next entry—all were in chronological order—was the original of a report from two Mossad agents about Kellermann. It told where he lived, that he was married to a Spaniard, the number of children, and that he worked as a construction estimator for a firm by the name of Constructora El Águila, Sociedad Anónima, with a Barcelona address. Again there was the blue pencil of Isser the Little, this time circling El Águila, and a notation: "*Águila* = Adler—not very clever!"

Ben-David could hear Harel's sneers as he deciphered the coded name of the firm, if indeed it was meant to be a code. *Águila*. In

French, *aigle,* or eagle. In German, Adler, of course. All very interesting, in the world of intelligence, of spy and counterspy. But it got him no closer to what he was looking for. He wondered if his instincts had been wrong, if they were muddied by his affection for Kramer. Was he trying to find meanings in his words, noble meanings that were not there? The Q-B file was drawing a blank as far as Kramer's connection with it was concerned. He was tempted to skip the few remaining pages and read the back of the file, but he resisted. The next entry was a photocopy of a memo to "B.-G." from Harel.

The memo alluded to follow-up conversation between Harel and Ben-Gurion regarding large sums that Mossad had been receiving from anonymous sources. The anonymous grant had a condition: that the funds be used to bring to justice those "war criminals of the Holocaust." Harel pointed out that his office had tried to trace the source of the funds, but they had been laundered down the line, ending up in several Swiss banks, which, at that point, made it impossible to go farther, considering Swiss banking security.

The next two pages contained what Baruch Ben-David was looking for. It was an intelligence report on one Francisco Adler, managing director of Constructora El Águila, S.A., of number 36 Calle Joan Güell, Barcelona, Spain. Born Franz-Christian Adler in Bayreuth, Bavaria, he had enlisted in the Waffen-SS, rising to officer's grade. He was in combat in Belgium and Yugoslavia, then was assigned in 1941 to the *Sicherheitsdienst Kommandantur* in Paris; he was promoted to SS-Obersturmbannführer as adjutant to SD-commander Bergdorf.

"There it is, the connection!" Ben-David said aloud. "My instincts were right!" He read on, excited now.

Franz Adler, the report went on to say, was arrested soon after the war and tried for membership in the SD, an illegal organization. He received a six-month sentence in Dachau, as prescribed by the denazification processes. No war crimes were attributed to him. He left Germany in 1947 and was reported in Switzerland for the next four years, until he moved permanently to Spain. There he established a construction business in 1951 in Barcelona. Today, the report said, his firm is successful and well known, with an AAA credit rating. Adler lives well but not lavishly in an apartment on the Plaça de Catalunya and has a weekend villa in San Feliú de Guixols on the Costa Brava, where he has berthed a sailing ketch, the intelligence summary went on to say. He makes frequent trips to Switzerland and the

USA, ostensibly for business. He is married to the former Ursula Hahn, a Spanish citizen of German birth; they have two married children. Final note: Of the many organizations and clubs of Germans living in Spain, Adler belongs to none.

Ben-David put a paperweight on the page. He knew he was right, but he didn't want to prove it too fast; he wanted to savor a bit longer. He went to the small kitchen and put a kettle on. Kellermann to Adler to Bergdorf, he reasoned as the water began to boil—those were the links to Q-B. Adler, a serious businessman, clearly avoiding the other Germans, the *Alte Kamaraden*. He knew he was right!

He put instant coffee into a cup, then peeked into the living room and saw Rivkah asleep with a copy of her favorite poetry by the Hungarian Sándor Petöfi in her lap. Next to her was *The Sorrows of Young Werther* by Goethe, in German. He shook his head sadly and smiled knowingly. Despite what they did to her, she was willing somehow to forgive. He flirted with the idea of telling her about Peter. Oh, how she would react, knowing that the by-now legendary Bergdorf of their private conversations, of their deepest gratitude, was none other than Peter Kramer, whom she loved so much anyway!

The whistling of the kettle put an end to the notion, at least for the time being. Peter had not given him permission to tell even Rivi. He fixed the coffee and went back to the file.

Another photocopy marked "Q-B File" from Harel to Ben-Gurion was next. In it Harel noted in his own handwriting, "Regarding Martin Bormann, hard evidence is that he authored Aktion Feuerland, an operation designed to remove great parts of the hoarded SS loot from the Reich Bank to his future haven in Argentina. This began in 1943 from assets of European Jews. Soft evidence is that several U-boat shipments were landed at a port in Patagonia, southern Argentina."

Feuerland, thought Ben-David. German for Fire Land, and in Spanish, Tierra del Fuego. He imagined German U-boats steaming under the ice of Cape Horn, loaded with gold bars—gold taken from the teeth of gassed Jews. He shook his head in a quick, violent motion. Grimly, he sipped his coffee and continued to read.

"Soft evidence," the memo went on, "from a statement given by Albert Thoms, former clerk in the Reich Bank, indicates that a considerable amount in gold coin and diamonds was cached in banks in Switzerland just before the end of the war, and that Bormann's trustee disappeared, presumably captured by the Russians or killed in the Battle of Berlin. There is no evidence that this part of Bormann's treasure arrived in Argentina. Therefore, it must be assumed that the trustee disappeared with the loot. If so, the few facts we have point to Franz Adler or his wartime boss, Bergdorf, as the trustee of the Swiss account. If we are to believe any part of the story that Odilio Kellermann told agent Manuel, it may solve the riddle of Mossad's anonymous benefactor. My view at this time—that is, until something more concrete turns up, if it ever does," Harel wrote, infuriating Ben-David with the supercautiousness of his words, "is to believe the Kellermann story, for what it's worth."

" 'For what it's worth'!" Ben-David repeated, exasperated with the former spy-chief's guarded manner.

There was a final paragraph: "Conclusions: a) Martin Bormann landed in Argentina, preceded and followed by submarine shipments of vast sums; b) an undisclosed sum destined for Bormann ended up in Switzerland under the control of Bormann's trustee, used ultimately for purposes other than Bormann's; c) Kellermann's story of the Q-B group is probably authentic; and d) either Adler or Bergdorf is the trustee. (My view is that Adler, due to his high visibility and traceable background, is unlikely, thus leaving Bergdorf, about whom we know very little and who has 'vanished' from the scene, as the probable trustee and anonymous benefactor of Mossad."

"Isser the Little," Ben-David said aloud, "I couldn't agree with you more!" He turned to the next page.

A handwritten note from David Ben-Gurion to Isser Harel said, "My dear Isser, I thank you for the hard work you put into this inquiry. As usual, your dedication and tenacity serve our nation and our people well.

"After having studied this case, I am now satisfied that we should cease further inquiry into this unique matter." It was signed, "David."

Baruch Ben-David emitted a long sigh and closed the file. The clock on his desk said it was after 2 A.M. He spun the Rolodex in front of him and found a number. He hesitated a few seconds, shrugged, and dialed.

"Harel here." The voice was alert despite the hour.

"Isser, this is Baruch. Did I wake you?"

"No, I have trouble sleeping of late. How can I help you, Baruch?" Straight to business, as usual. No greetings, no niceties, no formalities. He hadn't changed, observed Ben-David.

"Have you tried a warm bath? It works for me."

"I wasn't complaining, Baruch. It gives me the opportunity to review my life and my service to Israel."

"Perhaps you should write your biography, Isser. I'm sure it would make exciting reading," Ben-David said.

"Yes, I suppose now I have the time. But"—he laughed with a touch of irony—"everything interesting I could say in a book I myself classified as secret. That leaves only the dullness of the job. However, you didn't call to discuss my boredom, Baruch. What can I do for you?"

"Yes, well. I just finished reading a Mossad file—for reasons that are my own—on a group called Q-B. Do you remember that file, Isser?"

"Of course," Isser the Little said curtly. "What about it?"

"One of the—ah—principals was a man named Bergdorf."

"What about him?"

"That's what I was going to ask you. What do you remember? What do you know about him? I know it's old stuff, but—"

Harel interrupted. "Bergdorf, Hans-Dieter, Freiherr von Bergdorf, SS-Brigadeführer and Generalmajor der Waffen-SS, posted in Paris, nineteen forty-one to forty-four, Chief of SD, representative of Heydrich; reassigned to Reich Chancellery as SS liaison to Reichsleiter Bormann. Fled Berlin with Bormann during the Russian attack, believed killed or captured by Russians. Yes, it is old stuff, as you put it, but my memory still functions despite my retirement."

Ben-David laughed nervously. "Isser, you're remarkable!"

Harel's voice softened a bit. "I wouldn't go that far."

"I noticed that Ben-Gurion asked you to stop further inquiry into the matter, Isser. Did you ask him why?"

"No. He was the prime minister; he didn't need a reason. He just said, as you did, 'for reasons that are my own.' "

"And so you ceased all activities on Q-B?"

"Yes. Of course, I updated the file before putting it to bed. I don't like leaving things hanging."

"Then, you did follow up some more . . . just to close the file."

"Yes, but I didn't have to go beyond our own walls, Baruch. I just looked in our files under high-ranking SS whose status were still undetermined. His service record is still there."

"Ah, of course!" Ben-David said, silently kicking himself. It had never occurred to him. "Tell me, Isser, did you ever wonder? Did you ever ask yourself . . ." The question died on his lips.

Harel finished it. "Who he was? Prime Minister, I'm a man of action and of facts on which to act. I'm not a philosopher, I don't— I didn't have time to wonder about things. As long as the security of Israel wasn't threatened, I was satisfied, and we went on to other more important and current things."

There was a pause. Ben-David was thinking, assessing this cold, impersonal man who did not sleep nights and whom it was all right to press back into service, if only for a few minutes on the phone—this diminutive but giant watchdog of his nation's security, this pursuer and apprehender of Karl-Adolf Eichmann, this single-minded, dedicated servant of Israel, now retired because of a falling out with David Ben-Gurion . . .

"Isser, I'd like you to know, just in a few words, who this man was."

"If you wish."

"Freiherr von Bergdorf was the man who saved me from the gas chamber, me and many others. I tell you this, well, because"— he paused—"I really don't know why I want to tell you, Isser. I just want you to know who it was that your file and your investigation so long ago were about. Not just a name on a report, but a person, a real person. Just that, Isser."

There was a long silence. Then Harel spoke. "If it means any-thing to you, Baruch, I think Bergdorf was our anonymous benefac-tor. I'm happy to hear what you tell me; I'm not the cold man I repre-sent. One more thing: When I asked David Ben-Gurion who this man was, he simply said, 'He's a friend of the Jews.' "

THE WHITE HOUSE

THE PRESENT

"Come in, Pete," Simon Jensen said, pointing to a chair. "I understand you asked for no more than thirty minutes. I hope we can wrap it up sooner; I'm running behind today. Now, what's on your mind?"

Kramer knew by the President's tone and his quick, unrelaxed way that he had picked a bad time for what he had to say. No softening preamble to his confession was going to be possible; yet he just couldn't blurt out the potentially damning words.

"Sir," Kramer began, "I've just been with Prime Minister Ben-David. I was with him in Israel yesterday, and we had a long talk, the subject of which you should know."

Jensen was surprised. "Oh? You were with Ben-David?" he asked, slightly chagrined. "I didn't know you had gone."

"I know I should have cleared it with you first, Mr. President, but the situation called for an immediate meeting with him, and it was simply not possible to inform you. You will understand when I tell you."

Jensen leaned forward in his chair. "What's going on, Peter? Is there a problem with the treaty?"

"No, sir. It has nothing to do with the treaty—at least, it shouldn't. A situation has come up rather—"

"What the hell's happening?" Jensen said, eyes narrowing. "What do you mean, 'at least, it shouldn't'?"

"I'll get to that in a moment, Mr. President. But first, let me tell you the—let me inform you of this rather sticky but not insurmountable situation that has arisen." Kramer paused, searching desperately for the right words, intimidated by Jensen's impatient and irascible manner. "Sir, for reasons I'll explain in a moment, I've gotten myself—and perhaps you—into an awkward position. All of us make at one time or another decisions that later prove to have been mistakes, errors in judgment. I made such a decision in miscalculating the length of time and the extent of my service to you, Mr. President, in the effort toward a peace treaty, and now—"

Jensen interrupted again. "For God's sake, man, get to the point! What do you mean you've gotten me into an 'awkward position'? Skip the commercial and get to the point!"

Nervously, Kramer lit a cigarette. "Yes, sir, I'll get to the point. I hope you realize you're not allowing me to properly prepare you for this, but I'll get to the point." He sighed deeply. "You see, Mr. President, I'm not who you think I am. That is, my name is not Peter Kramer. That is an assumed name and part—"

"What the fuck are you talking about?"

"—and part of my assumed identity which I've maintained for many years. My real name is Bergdorf."

Jensen stared. "Go on," he said darkly.

"I am Hans-Dieter von Bergdorf, a former officer of the German armed forces," Kramer said, knowing he had gone beyond the point of turning back, knowing the die was cast. "A former SS officer, in fact."

Jensen's mouth opened in amazement. *"What?"*

"I am wanted by the French and West German governments on charges of . . . war crimes, crimes that—"

"What?" Jensen repeated. "Is this a dream?" he said.

"—I didn't commit."

"Wait! Wait! Wait just a damned minute," the President said, his face red with anger. "Am I hearing you right? Are you telling me that you're a Kraut? A goddamned Nazi? On my staff? Doing business for *me?* I don't believe it! *I don't fucking believe it!*" He got up from behind the Hayes desk and began pacing like an indignant panther behind bars. He looked several times toward the door of the office as if he needed witnesses to what he was hearing.

"Mr. President, if you will allow me to explain—"

"A Nazi! Hang me by the balls, I got a fucking Nazi on my team!" the President of the United States shouted. He shot a look at Kramer, who was sitting with legs crossed and holding a burning cigarette, looking penitent. "I knew there was something about you, mister; I just couldn't put my finger on it. Jesus Christ!" he said, running his fingers through his hair, "do you know what the opposition will do to me with this? They'll pluck me like a dead chicken! Jesus fucking Christ!"

"If you would just let me finish—"

"Finish? Oh yes, you're finished," Jensen said. "You can be sure of that, Herr—"

"Bergdorf, Mr. President," Kramer completed the sentence for him, with the knowledge that he was not dealing with a reasonable man.

"Bergdorf," Jensen repeated. "A good Nazi name!"

"Sir, I was never a Nazi or a war criminal; but it seems you have no interest in hearing that."

"No, you were all just a band of Boy Scouts, weren't you? But you forget, I was there! I saw what you SS killers did! I went to Dachau, you bastard! And you killed my crew—" Jensen's expression suddenly changed. "You burned my boys—you turned them into torches," he said softly, "and because your life was spared . . . they died . . . and I didn't . . . and you should've died . . . and . . . I—I—" He turned and looked out the window at the dahlias.

Kramer looked at the back of the President's head in the awful silence that followed. He saw the head of a young man in olive drab, trousers stuffed into combat boots caked with dried mud and blood. Suddenly he knew the reason for his now-obvious hatred—his impassioned hatred—of the Germans. A wartime experience—one experience among the thousands that occurred on both sides, cruel and painful experiences—still burned inside him. But unlike most of the others, the President had been unable to dissolve it with the passing of time or to extricate himself from its horrors, even decades later. It was understandable, even sympathetic, in others, yes. But he was the President of the United States now, with his finger—every day, every minute—on the button of life or death.

"Mr. President, I'm so sorry—"

Simon Jensen turned. His eyes were full of hate and determination.

"Look, mister," he said, "you lied to me. Nobody lies to me—nobody!" He was back to his old self now. "I don't give a damn what your story is, you lied to me. You could have told me up front when I hired you for this job. You knew you had to be clean; that's what the security check is all about. Well, heads are going to roll, including yours, make no mistake!"

Kramer jumped up. "Mr. President! No heads, other than mine, should roll. My dossier as Peter Kramer is air-tight! I was going to tell you that I would tender my resignation—without compromising you in the least—as soon as the treaty is signed. However, you didn't give me a chance."

"Oh, really? Don't delude yourself with your importance. As of this moment, my friend, you are fired."

"I cannot believe you would endanger the treaty!" Kramer said with passion. "Think what you are doing, sir."

"The American people are not going to be taken in by your—your duplicity any longer, Bergdorf. It's my duty as President and architect of the peace accord to expose you. Yes, I said 'architect of the peace accord,' or did you forget that it was I who put it together, who engineered it from the beginning? Don't worry, I'll find a way to put the pieces together and bring it to a successful end. In the meantime, I will inform the West German government and the French authorities of your existence. Our own immigration office will deport you, no doubt, for having lied under oath about your past."

Kramer saw clearly for the first time the flaws in Jensen's psyche. It was not only the old war wound that was tearing at him; even in his normal state of mind he was being overcome by resentment—and jealousy. The President saw him as a rival.

"No one doubts that the treaty is due to your efforts and statesmanship, Mr. President," Kramer said, now calm. "But what useful purpose would it be if you exposed me at this time? Surely the Soviets would—"

"What makes you such an expert?" Jensen's eyes became slits. "But then, I see where you're coming from; I've seen it all along. You see the Nobel Peace Prize slipping away from you. You see your career as the world's savior coming to a grinding halt, don't you?"

"I never entertained for one minute—"

"I've had my eye on you, Kramer—or Bergdorf, or whatever your name is—I saw how you took over, shoving Hetherington aside in the process. And me too, whenever you could. I knew there was something odd about you. Oh, not at the beginning—you were too clever—but later on I saw your true spots come out. The way you handled that reporter at the ranch when she asked you about the peace prize and Hetherington's job at State. I saw the look on your face; it was there for only a flash, but I saw it, Bergdorf. You were creaming in your jeans!''

Kramer picked up his briefcase. ''I see no use in continuing this discussion, Mr. President. You've made up your mind in this matter. You will have my resignation on your desk before the end of the day. I can only hope that you will find the wisdom to remove the webs of hate from your eyes and with a clear vision turn once again to your goal of world peace.'' Kramer thought for a moment. ''Good-bye, sir. To use your metaphor, the ball is in your hands—don't fumble it.''

THE WHITE HOUSE

5:20 A.M.

He walked down the steps, and the metal-fitted shoes echoed in the huge hall-church-vault-dungeon-catacomb, whatever the place was. The stone steps were worn with age, and he kept slipping on the sooty fluid that coated them. Then, out of nowhere—but somehow logically—hands came up to help him, hands holding him in a tight grip, hands attached to bodies in football helmets. But they weren't football helmets after all: they were tankers' helmets made of heavy leather with ear flaps. He looked at each body's face then, and as he recognized the faces, he sobbed. They were Rizzo, Fernandez, Jonesy, Sulley. Then he knew why he couldn't make it down the staircase alone—he was thirsty, oh so thirsty! Sulley knew that and pulled his canteen off his webbed belt and handed it to him. He drank. "Aagh! It's gasoline!" he said, spitting it out. "Yeah," said Rizzo, "we were drinking a toast to you, Lieutenant." They all laughed, and he laughed, too, and then Jonesy handed him the canteen for a drink, but he said no, he had to take care of them, and they all laughed. And then, as was right, they huddled, their arms around one anothers' shoulders. He knew they were dead, but they had come back to him and he loved them and he started to weep again in happiness or in sorrow—it was hard to tell which. "Don't do that, Lieutenant," Fernandez said. "Just call the signals. They're waiting for us over there, those guys behind the wire." He looked behind the barbed wire, but he could see only one of them, the one with the cigarette hanging from his lips, the guy in the black uniform with the silver flashes on his lapels, the guy who was smiling at him. He tried to make out his face, but the light from the lightning flashes on his lapels was blinding him, and all he could see was the guy holding a match, ready to strike it into flame. He again huddled with his team and called the signals: "Our Father, who art in heaven, hallowed be Thy name. . . . Where's the ball?" he asked Sulley. "It's in the tank turret, Si, where it always is," Sulley said. They broke the huddle and started for the tank. A tall, gaunt figure in a gleaming white uniform stood by the four slabs under the vaulted ceiling, hands on hips, feet apart. He wore a shiny silver helmet that hooded his brilliant eyes. He asked the figure, "Who is the guy with the lightning on his collar?" The figure said, "You know who he is." "But my crew is drunk with gasoline, and he's got the match! What shall I do?" he asked. "You must not ask me, Lieutenant. You are the quarterback; it must be your decision," said the tall, gaunt man in the gleaming white uniform.

Simon Bolivar Jensen opened his eyes to the semidarkness of his bedroom. He hadn't screamed or even moaned. Lying in his sweat, he reviewed the dream, especially the conversation with the tall, gaunt man. He made a judgment.

He went to the bathroom and splashed cold water onto his face and chest. As he dried off, he looked at his image. Then, for the first time after the terrible dream—a dream that always brought about fear and anguish—he saw the eyes of resolve and tenacity. Now he actually looked forward to the next dream, when he would at last know his enemy, and knowing that enemy, he would destroy him. And Rizzo and Sulley and Fernandez and Jonesy would be avenged.

ARLINGTON, VIRGINIA

5:23 A.M.

Peter Kramer sipped coffee and lit a cigarette. He dialed the long area code for Israel and Ben-David's private number in his office in Tel Aviv. He listened to the melodious ticking that made the connection and looked around his small study. He wondered if Erika would stay on in Washington if he had to go back to Germany. She would want to go with him, he was sure, but he would advise her against it. The awful chore of packing made him shudder. That was his only worry at that moment; he couldn't think beyond that just then.

The voice of Baruch Ben-David came on the line. "Yes, who is it?"

"Baruch, it's Peter."

"Peter! How are you? Did you talk with him?"

"Yes, I did."

"Peter, you sound depressed. What's wrong?"

"It was a disaster, Baruch. Much worse than I imagined. To begin with, he fired me, but—"

"What! He fired you?" Ben-David shouted into the phone.

"Yes, but that doesn't concern me. What concerns me is the timing. I couldn't convince him; he wouldn't listen to anything I had to say. He accused me of campaigning for the Nobel Peace Prize," Kramer said, almost in shame.

"But that's incredible, Peter!"

"That is endurable. But he says he wants to expose me to the French and West German authorities—now! Not after the signing, if there is to be one."

"But that's impossible! Mahamet would jump on this. The thing is far too fragile. The Soviets would have a field day! I can't allow that. Who does he think he is, damn it all?"

"That is the question, Baruch: Who is he? I think we're dealing with a man who is . . . not normal. If you could have seen the rage, the hate. I tried to reason with him, pointing out the importance of him not doing anything until after the signing, at which point I would immediately resign and he could do what he might. But he wouldn't listen. Baruch, he must know that the treaty will be in danger, that it could collapse, but his hatred is far too great for that to matter."

"I cannot accept this," Ben-David said. "I too have a responsibility to my country. I'll call him. What time is it over there?"

"It's almost five-thirty in the morning," Kramer said. "What are you going to tell him?"

"*Malheur*, Peter, how should I know! I should have listened to you," Ben-David said heavily. "I'll call at eight, your time; he should be awake by then. Maybe he'll have cooled off, maybe he'll have had the night to consider the price of such a stupid move."

"I hope you're right, Baruch, but don't count on it."

"I'll call you after I speak to him," Ben-David said. Then, as an afterthought, he added, "I should have listened to you, but how did I know your boss was a *dingue*!"

At 8:27 A.M. Peter Kramer's phone rang. It was Ben-David.

"Well, Peter, I managed to buy some time. He agreed on a moratorium of the announcement of the problem. I convinced him that he must hold off doing anything until after our elections here in Israel. I didn't plead your case, I didn't want to add more fuel to the fire, but I did stress continuity for the treaty. I spoke very firmly to him, pointing out that if he insists on exposing you, he'll take me along with you because the opposition here would make political mincemeat out of me, and my party would be sure to lose the election, and with that the treaty would go up in smoke, considering that racist *salaud* they're running against me—he will never agree to peace with the Arabs. He finally agreed, granting two weeks, but he insisted that you have absolutely nothing to do with the treaty negotiations. He said he would insist on the parties meeting at Camp David, where he himself would be the chief negotiator between us and the Arabs.''

"Just like Carter, Sadat, and Begin," Kramer said.

"Just like Carter, Sadat, and Begin," Ben-David repeated.

"I think that's what it's all about, Baruch. He felt I was overshadowing him somehow, and that disturbs him. Now he can park me somewhere and wrap up the thing. That's all right, as long as he does it.''

Ben-David heard the glumness in Kramer's tone. "Listen, it buys us time, at least." He paused. "You know, Peter, you were right: he spoke very bitterly of you. The way he went on, I have to agree with you that there is something wrong there.''

There was a long pause in the talk, a talk that both men recognized as having to do with the mental condition of the most powerful man in the world.

Ben-David broke the silence. "The whole thing is so—"

Kramer finished the thought. "I know.''

Ben-David said, "Oh, I almost forgot. I told him that if you were suddenly out of the picture, the press would make something of it. He agreed. He wants you to attend the Foreign Ministers' Conference in Mexico City in a few days, as originally planned. You'll go, won't you?''

"Yes, if he asks me, I'll go." Kramer's tone was heavy, almost mournful.

"Peter, I hear your pain," Ben-David said. "I share it with you, my friend. I'm going to pray to God that He give me the solution to this problem. In fact, I'm going to demand it of Him, because I seldom ask anything of Him, and because it is right, and He will listen to me.''

THE WHITE HOUSE

NOON

The President buzzed his appointments secretary. "Cancel my next three appointments; I don't feel up to par. That's not for publication; just make excuses. Get Admiral Smith. Tell him I want to see him in my quarters as soon as he can get here. No, it's nothing, I'll be fine. Just get Smith."

Ten minutes later the President admitted Admiral Rufus K. Smith, USNR, to the sitting room of his sleeping chambers. Admiral Smith was his physician.

Smith opened his bag and took out a stethoscope. "I understand you're not feeling well, Mr. President," he said. "What seems to be the problem?"

"I don't know, Admiral," said Jensen. "I'm just a little shaky. See that?" he said, holding out a trembling hand. "I'm usually steady as the old rock."

Smith reached for his patient's arm, feeling the pulse. "Hm. Pulse is a little fast, Mr. President. Would you remove your shirt, please?"

As Jensen unbuttoned his shirt, Smith noticed his coloring; it was ashen. When he felt the pulse, he also noticed that the President's hand was clammy.

Smith listened to Jensen's heart and lungs and put the stethoscope on his carotids to listen for bruits, the tell tale sign of occluded arteries. Everything seemed normal, although his breathing was a bit shallow and labored and the respiration rate higher than usual for the athletic Jensen, whose signs and medical presentation were imprinted in Smith's brain.

"Have you been eating well, sir, and have you maintained the exercise regimen I prescribed for you?"

"I eat as well as I always have, although it's hard to keep an interest in food with this job, you know. I'm swimming twenty laps in the pool, and I jog a couple of miles."

"Yes, sir," Smith said, making mental notes. "What about your sleep? Are you sleeping well?"

Jensen shot a look at the doctor. "Why do you ask? I sleep just fine."

Smith looked at his patient a little more intently. He was being defensive about a routine question. Also, there was an apparent loss of appetite, else he wouldn't have said what he had about food. To the trained internist, the way a patient answered questions—the body language used—was as telling as instruments and tests. And Smith was a trained and highly competent internist.

"Your color is not as good as I've seen it, sir," Smith said, removing a blood-pressure cuff from his bag. "It may be nothing, of course, but it could be symptomatic of something that only further tests may reveal. And if you've not been sleeping well, that too could be another indication." He paused during the blood-pressure taking, which showed a slight elevation. As he put back the instruments, he said, "Mr. President, I know we just did a complete physical examination on you and you passed with flying colors. But still, it wouldn't hurt to run a few other tests. May I make an appointment at Bethesda as soon as possible?"

"The hospital? Oh, no—I can't." Jensen wrung his hands. Extreme anxiety, Smith diagnosed provisionally.

The complete physician now, and charged with the health maintenance of the nation's chief executive, Admiral Smith boldly asked, "Mr. President, is there something you haven't told me? You called me because you didn't feel 'up to par,' to use your words. As your physician, as one who knows you very well from a medical viewpoint, I see that you are not yourself, sir. You appear to be . . . anxious." *He appears to be like a volcano,* Smith emended silently, *a volcano about to erupt.*

"Anxious?" Jensen said, looking away as he buttoned his shirt. "Yes, I guess I'm anxious, Admiral. It's this damned peace treaty, on top of all my other problems—the problems of the country, I mean. But it's nothing a little rest, a little vacation from this place wouldn't cure. I'm not one for pills and all that, but . . . maybe you could give me a tranquilizer or some sleeping pills." Jensen licked his lips nervously. *Dry mouth—another sign of anxiety, acute anxiety,* Smith said to himself.

"Certainly, Mr. President. I'll give you some Valium, which will relax you and help you sleep. But frankly, sir, that would be only a Band-Aid solution. It would just mask the problem, and I think there *is* a problem. Just how long have you not been sleeping well, sir?"

Jensen, sitting now, ran his palms along his thighs. "I haven't had a good night's sleep in . . . I don't know . . . it seems like years."

"Do you know why?" Smith probed gently.

Jensen got up and started pacing, wringing his hands. He hesitated for a few moments, undecided, then blurted, "It's the dream! The goddamned dream!" Anguish was in his eyes.

Admiral Smith studied the President without comment. He wondered if he was now going too far. The shadowy world of psychiatry was not his forte, let alone delving into the psyche of the world's most significant patient. But he knew he must if he were to find the cause of his emotional problem. This was of prime importance to Admiral Rufus K. Smith, possessor of a vast portfolio of international stocks. He knew it was out of the question to call in a consultant—he would have to do it himself.

He took the irreversible step. "Would you like to talk about the dream, Mr. President?"

Jensen sat down again, stiffly holding the arms of his chair. He stared at the oval medallion in the ceiling and sighed deeply. He remained silent, but Smith could see the tremendous inner struggle that was at a bursting point.

Smith prodded gently, trying to break the psychic stranglehold. "Are the dreams about the peace treaty?"

"Yes . . . no . . . yes," Jensen said, still staring at the ceiling. "That is, one of the people involved in it is in the dream. I mean, he was in the dream last night." He looked at Smith suddenly. "Look, Admiral, everything I tell you is in the strictest confidence, isn't it? It stays right here, doesn't it?"

"Mr. President," Smith assured, "we have, you and I, a doctor-patient relationship, which in itself carries a sacred trust. Added to that, sir, you are the President of the United States, thereby making a violation of that trust tantamount to treason. Please have faith in me as your doctor, if not as your loyal friend and supporter." He put his hand into his coat pocket for his pipe and tobacco pouch, a gesture more of self-sedation than anything else, for Smith was feeling terrible rumblings in his own stomach, rumblings of fear. If word got out that Jensen was emotionally abnormal—and all the indications were that he was—it would lead to a personal disaster on the Zürich and London stock exchanges for Rufus K. Smith.

"All right, all right, Doctor." Jensen panted, closing his eyes tightly. "I have to tell someone! It's this dream I've had for a long time—my wife and I don't share a bedroom anymore because of it, it's so awful, and it's always the same . . . except last night it was different. I wake up panting and sweating. . . ."

"Take your time, sir," Smith said, puffing on his pipe. "What is the dream about?"

"There are four men—dead men, but somehow alive, if you know what I mean—and a tall man in white directs me to the four dead men who are lying on slabs in some sort of cellar or dungeon. It's a terrible place, all dank and ugly. Then I'm ordered to take the bodies to a car and drive them somewhere. Where, I never find out because at that point two little dogs, puppies with their tongues hanging out, run out in front of the car and I swerve to avoid hitting them, the little things." He sighed heavily. "Then the next thing I know, I'm on the ground looking up into the bright sky . . . and there's a fire down the way and—and the men are burning. . . . Their faces are—are *melting* . . . and I scream and try to run to them, but somehow I can't move my legs, and I can't—" He paused, squeezing his hands and looking out beyond the garden. "Then I wake up."

Smith's stomach relaxed somewhat. Everyone has nightmares, recurring terrible dreams, and perhaps the President was just overworked and tired. Perhaps a consultant mightn't be a bad idea after all, what with new drugs and therapy. "Do you know who these four men are, Mr. President?" he asked softly, relighting his pipe.

"The men? Yes. At first they seem to be fellows I played football with in college. Then, toward the end of the dream, they change. They become my tank crew in the war." He lowered his voice and mumbled something.

Smith leaned forward. "I'm sorry, I didn't hear that."

Jensen looked up as if intruded upon. "I said they died."

Smith studied his patient. He concluded that he must be treated with special delicateness, not only because of his position but because he seemed agitated and aggressive at times. "It must be an especially painful dream, Mr. President, but not at all uncommon among those who were in battle, such as yourself," Smith said soothingly. "The scars of the trauma of war are long in healing, especially in a sensitive person. These unhealed psychological scars sometimes flare up, manifesting themselves when one is under severe strain, as you must be with all your onerous responsibilities, such as the peace treaty, which you, yourself, mentioned."

Jensen looked askance, a look of sudden suspicion. "Did I mention the treaty? I don't remember mentioning the treaty."

Smith was taken aback by the almost-combative attitude. "Yes, sir, you did, and that's what—"

"Oh, yes. I remember now. I'm glad you brought it up, Admiral. Now, in the dream, things have changed. I mean, it isn't the same—the action is different." Jensen's tone was animated. "The same people are in it, but now someone else is in it, too. Now it's almost as if the dream is telling me—*telling me what to do!* I've been thinking about it all day, and I think it finally means something! This new face—it belongs to someone I know is my enemy, and my men and I set out to destroy him." He did not mention the fact that the four men died in his tank, nor did he mention the boys with the *Panzerfaust* whom he didn't kill.

Admiral Smith noted Jensen's lightning mood change, the look of resolve in his eyes replacing the fear and anguish of minutes earlier. He also noted the words *enemy* and *destroy*. Suddenly his stomach resumed its earlier protests. Fear was reestablishing itself in his gastric system. He also knew he was facing a situation far beyond his expertise, but with an inner sigh he probed further. "This face, sir, is it someone connected with the peace treaty?"

"Yes," Jensen said quickly, "the face belongs to a man named Bergdorf. He is my enemy," he added without passion.

"Bergdorf," Smith repeated. "Should I know that name?"

"You'd know the face. It belongs to Peter Kramer."

The stomach of Admiral Rufus Kingsley Smith, USNR, screamed in undisguised terror, tidal waves of acid gushing over its lining. "I'm afraid I don't understand."

"You will when I tell you," Jensen said.

Jensen's eyes were now hard, and his hands had stopped shaking. He was totally composed. Smith waited for Jensen to continue, now vitally interested in the dream and its concomitant effect, this fantasy about Kramer.

"Of course I've known all along that Peter Kramer was my enemy," Jensen continued casually. "But I couldn't prove it. Now he himself has given me the proof."

"Proof?" Smith asked, sitting on the edge of his chair.

"Yesterday he came into my office and told me he wasn't Peter Kramer, that his real name is Bergdorf, and that he is a wanted war criminal, a former SS officer."

"Great Scott, Mr. President!"

"Yes. When he said that, my first thought was the treaty, the danger a man like that, a Nazi, could bring to the peace treaty and the peace of the world. I immediately fired him, of course. He tried to make excuses, naturally, but I was so staggered, so angry and hurt, that I wouldn't listen to his alibis or whatever the liar had to say. I told him I would immediately turn him over to the French and West Germans, who are looking for him as a war criminal."

"This is incredible!" Smith said, wiping his brow and searching his pockets for a Maalox tablet. Immediately the fallacy in Jensen's reaction came to him: if he exposed Kramer, the treaty would collapse like a house of cards, and tensions between the warring parties would heighten—and there were the Soviets, sitting by, doing their share to kill the whole thing. There would be the possibility of global war! He remembered Peter Kramer; he seemed a nice enough fellow, certainly able, even brilliant. How could he be a Nazi war criminal? Jensen was indeed mad! "But Mr. President, if you expose him now, won't that cause major problems with the signing of the treaty? Especially since you're so close to making it a reality?"

"That's a possibility," Jensen agreed. "But I cannot compromise the integrity of the presidency, Admiral Smith. You forget—all of you forget, it seems—that it was I who structured the formula leading to a treaty. It was I who got the Jews and the Arabs together for peaceful dialogue. I don't need him, sir! I can jump right back into the fight and negotiate the damned thing myself! Just as Carter did, except that I'm a little more able than Carter was. I don't need Peter Kramer. He's the enemy, Admiral, and I've looked him in the eye. You can't have pity on them; you must be ruthless and strike first, or they will kill you! I know, believe me. If you drop the ball, you're dead!"

Smith found the antacid tablet, but he forgot to put it in his mouth. He just stared at his patient in impotent frustration. He was stunned into silence.

"You should know that Kramer called Ben-David and told him I fired him," Jensen said, now composed. "The prime minister called me this morning and asked me to hold up on my action on Kramer until after the elections in Israel, which are in two weeks. I agreed, but only on the condition that the Nazi stay away from the treaty. Ben-David assured me to that effect."

Smith couldn't wait to leave. He had an urgent call to make. "Mr. President," he smiled, "sometimes just talking things out can have a most salutary effect. Look, sir, your hands are steady now, and your breathing is normal." He put two fingers to Jensen's wrist. "Your pulse is steady, at a normal rate, and your hands are dry."

Simon Jensen held his hands out. "Yes, I see. But perhaps it is that I reached a decision and I am resolute in that decision." He lowered his voice, as if talking to himself, and added, "And now I know the enemy."

Admiral Smith left the White House as fast as his legs could carry him. He went to his club on Connecticut Avenue and to a phone booth in the lobby. He fumbled nervously in an address book and located a number. He placed a call, charging it to his credit card. The call was to a Dr. Heinz Langfeldt at the Züricher Anstalt, a Swiss bank.

WASHINGTON, D.C.

1:29 P.M.

The telephone in the booth of the Hollenbeck Club gave a sharp ring. Admiral Rufus Smith lifted the receiver before the full ring was completed.

"Heinz, I thought you weren't going to call me back," Smith said, his voice trembling. "What happened?"

"I'm sorry, Rufus, but I had some arrangements to make. And I didn't want to call you from my office. Now, calmly tell me what is happening."

"We have a catastrophic situation, Heinz! He's going to make a mess of things. I can't talk from here—we must meet immediately. We must do something!"

"It's that bad, is it? Can you come here? We can meet in Bad Gastein, as usual."

"That's out of the question now. He's not feeling well, and I should not be more than fifteen minutes away from him. You must come here, Heinz. Listen," Smith said, his voice changing from urgent to secretive, "I can tell you this much: He's fired Peter Kramer. He says he's a Nazi war criminal, and he's turning him over to the French in two weeks."

"Oh, dear God!" Langfeldt said. "I'll come at once. There's a night flight to Washington. Tell me where."

"I'll book a room for you at the Watergate. Call me from Dulles the minute you get in. We'll arrange to meet then." There was a pause of a few moments. Then Smith said, "For God's sake, come quickly!"

Smith left the steamy booth. He wiped his face as he stepped out into the fresh air. *How can I be loyal to a madman?* he asked himself silently. Then, aloud, he mumbled with conviction, "My country comes first!"

GEORGETOWN

8:00 A.M.

Admiral Rufus K. Smith looked in the mirror of his bathroom and saw that his eyes were bloodshot from lack of sleep. He normally applied eyedrops as part of his careful morning toilette. The daily trimming of his salt-and-pepper moustache was deferred that morning; time was important, and anyway his hands were a little shaky. He refocused his vision and dabbed lotion on his face, forgoing his usual primping.

He had always resembled Walter Pidgeon, he was told, even in his younger days, and he made a conscious effort to keep the resemblance intact by wearing his generous crop of hair much like the late actor's. His voice, too, had the same quality as his ideal's. That he was a handsome and imposing figure of a man, Smith knew well, and in his tailored naval uniforms he was even more attractive. There was little doubt that his mien and his melodious voice had been of great help to him in his career, especially when he had been voted president of the San Francisco chapter of the American Medical Association, which, together with his Navy Reserve commission, caught the eye of President-Elect Simon B. Jensen for the post of physician to the President, in spite of Smith's belonging to the other party.

He had never married—medicine was already his wife, he was fond of explaining—and when he moved to Georgetown, he installed a distant cousin as housekeeper. It was a mutually agreeable arrangement: she was flattered at taking care of her handsome and famous relative, and he was glad to have a woman in his house who took precise care of him, including occasional conjugal duties, depending on her employer's schedule and/or biological urges.

Although anxious about the previous day's events and his eleven o'clock meeting with Langfeldt at the Watergate, he managed to eat a light breakfast, even scanning his favorite dailies, *The Wall Street Journal* and *The Washington Post*.

Later, Smith settled back in a taxi, dressed in civilian clothes, wearing a homburg, looking like a movie star off a 1944 M-G-M set. He wondered what magic solution his Swiss friend would come up with for the crisis at hand.

He reflected on his association with Heinz Langfeldt. They had met years before, when Smith had gone to Vienna to look into some matters connected with a block of apartment houses he had picked up after the war for next to nothing. He was "taking the waters" at Bad Gastein in the Tyrolean Alps when he met Langfeldt in the steam baths. They formed a strong and successful friendship, Langfeldt providing vital financial information and Smith, later, furnishing choice inside facts from his confidential post in the White House, data that Langfeldt put to clever use from his offices in the Züricher Anstalt and in other vast dealings in the international world of finance.

Of course, Smith reassured himself as the taxi sped along the Potomac, he never gave Langfeldt anything that could be even in the slightest degree considered national security information. He would never do that, no matter how lucrative the partnership.

At precisely eleven o'clock Smith knocked on the door. It opened, framing the large bulk of Dr. Heinz Langfeldt.

Langfeldt smiled from behind a neatly trimmed beard. "Come in, come in, my dear Rufe. You're right on time."

"How have you been, Heinz?" Smith asked, handing Langfeldt his immaculate hat.

"Thank you, well. Please, sit down and join me in some breakfast. I'm having some excellent smoked salmon, and I took the liberty of ordering a portion for you, my friend."

"No, thanks. I've had breakfast. But I'll take a cup of coffee, if you don't mind."

Langfeldt poured coffee into a china cup and handed it to the nervous Smith. "It's that bad, old friend?" he said. "You're shaking from nerves. Tell me about it."

"He's mad, Heinz. In my view, the President is insane."

Langfeldt carefully spread cream cheese on a toasted bagel. "And how do you come to such a grave and ponderous conclusion?"

Smith related the prior day's awesome events. He was careful not to omit one word, one movement, one expression.

The Swiss economist wiped his lips and lit a Havana. He puffed the cigar into full bloom as he pondered what he had just heard. "I'm not a psychiatrist, Rufus," he said, pouring each more coffee, "but I don't have to be to reach the same conclusion as you. But first, you should know that Freiherr von Bergdorf, alias Peter Kramer, is not a Nazi, nor is he a war criminal. If anything, he is an unsung hero to Jews. Please believe me. It's a long and beautiful story, one that someday I'll tell you. But for now, his war record could not be more irrelevant. What *is* relevant, however, is the President's reaction to it and its far-reaching consequences." He twirled the cigar in his small mouth and blew smoke. "Which means, my dear Rufus, that we are at a crossroads of incalculable peril. We must act at once!"

Smith mopped his brow. "What can we do?"

Langfeldt was not ready to answer Smith's too-obvious question. He went on. "When I say *we*, Rufus, I mean that every man, woman, and child on the surface of this globe is faced with a most dangerous situation, a situation brought about by a man who is mentally unsound, who has his deranged finger on the button of the Doomsday arsenal! The collapse of the peace accord in the Middle East would be catastrophic in itself, and that will surely happen if he carries out his threat. But what that could lead to, even if he were normal—well, I don't have to draw you a picture."

"What can we do, Heinz?" Smith asked again.

Langfeldt's jowls twitched under his beard. He combed his mane of white hair with his fingers and looked hard at the President's doctor. "We must neutralize him, Rufus," he rasped. "We must neutralize him."

"The Presidential Incapacity Provision?" Smith said, frowning. "But how? You know how hard it is to get someone—*anyone*—declared insane in this country. But the President? They'd lock *me* up first!"

"I'm not talking of locking him up—I'm saying something else. And I think you know what I mean." Langfeldt stared at Smith.

"What? You mean—!" Smith couldn't say it.

"Precisely. You could do it, Dr. Smith. As his physician, you could find the way to do it. You would be—"

"That's impossible!" Smith broke in.

"—a hero in your own way, Rufus. It would be a brave thing to do. You'd be the savior of the world—just think!"

The Walter Pidgeonesque voice cracked. "How can you even suggest such a thing? I'm a healer, not a murderer!"

"The men who tried to kill Hitler weren't considered murderers," Langfeldt pressed. "They were trying to save their country! They were acting in the highest heroic principles, just as you would!"

Smith's face contorted in agony. "I'm no hero. How can you ask me to do that? No, I won't! I just won't, Heinz!"

Langfeldt leaned over the plate of salmon scraps. "Rufe, listen to me," he said gravely. "What we've got here is a full-blown paranoid-schizophrenic controlling the destiny of the planet, deciding from warped delusions, Rufe, if every person alive will continue to live." He picked up his butter knife and held it high. "He holds the nuclear Sword of Damocles in his deranged fingers, and it is quickly slipping from his grasp!" he said, crashing the knife on the table for effect.

Smith jumped from the unexpected blow. "Even if I wanted to, I couldn't. I don't . . . have it in me," he said, almost ashamed.

Langfeldt sighed audibly. He lifted himself gingerly out of the armchair and walked to the window. "In that case, Rufus, my friend, I won't press you further. I'll simply have to think of something else, won't I?" He relit his cigar with a wooden match fished out of his pocket, filling the room with the smell of sulphur and phosphorus. "The best way to light a good cigar is with a good wooden match, I always say."

Smith's face showed immediate relief. Incongruously, he even replied to the comment about the match. "Yes, those wooden matches are hard to come by nowadays." He mopped his face again, and in a statement meant only as a courtesy, he added, "Of course, you can count on my cooperation in whatever you decide."

Like Hemingway's old man of the sea, Langfeldt had eased up

on the fish line. Now he pulled it so taut that Smith was ready to be landed. "Under the circumstances, my dear Rufus, I expect your cooperation!"

"What—what do you mean? What cooperation?"

Langfeldt took three steps to where Smith sat. He put his hands on the armrests of the chair, hemming the admiral in. "I wish to be kept informed of the President's movements, *at all times*. I have only two weeks in which to develop a plan—not a very long time, is it? Will you do that, Rufus? That's all I ask of you," Langfeldt whispered.

Smith turned, avoiding Langfeldt's face and cigar breath. He felt reprieved, yet he knew he was inextricably involved. "If you insist on my complicity—"

Langfeldt drew back and shook his head sadly. "What words you use! *Complicity*." In his gravest voice he said, "Rufus, this globe spins ever so delicately on its political and financial axis. We must keep it spinning for our own sake and for the sake of our fellow men. We must not allow our personal feelings—our aversions—to restrain us from our duty to humanity. Your duty is clear."

Admiral Smith rose to leave. "All right. I will do as you ask. I can only hope God grants you the wisdom to do what is right—and that He forgives me."

Heinz Langfeldt rolled up a crisp dollar bill and sniffed the white powder he had bought from a cab driver. He breathed deeply and sighed. "Ah, what moral fools these Americans are," he said to himself in German, "and so impractical!"

Smith had two quick Manhattans at the hotel bar and left by a side door for the peace of his Georgetown house of red brick and white-framed windows and geraniums.

LONDON, BELGRAVIA SQUARE

THE PRESENT

His Highness, Prince Yazid ibn al-Muhallab drained the cognac in one gulp. He looked out the second-story window of his twelve-room flat and saw that the sun was brilliant on the clean sidewalks below, where Bentleys and Rolls-Royces pulled up to or away from the luxurious surroundings his minister had insisted on for him, the man in charge of investing the never-ending fund of petrodollars coming out of his country.

He checked his watch: time for one more before he left for his lunch meeting at the Grosvenor Club for Gentlemen with Johnson of Getty Oil. He downed another cognac and immediately felt better.

The door to his bedroom suite opened. It was Yussif, his bodyguard, looking somber and paranoid as usual. He wore his uniform, the black-and-white-striped *aba*. On his head was the *keffiyeh*, held in place by the twisted cords of the *agal*. Under all that, a sharp hooked nose dominated his strong Semitic face, on which grew tufts of black beard that tapered to a point. Two long-hilted daggers swooped to a curve under his sash, which he was ready to use in defense of his prince against all enemies. The black eyes under blacker eyebrows that shot withering glares at strangers were his bodyguard's most potent weapons, the prince had thought often; he knew the *jambiya* were powerless against the modern assassin. But he would not

say that to Yussif, as he would not understand and he would feel dis-
honored.

Yussif greeted the prince in Arabic: "Praised be Allah! Did you
sleep well, el Emir?"

"Allah be praised—yes, I slept well, Yussif," he lied.

The great nose of Yussif scanned the room; he sniffed and
homed in on the empty brandy glass. He verbalized nothing, but his
eyes were eloquent in his displeasure of his lord, who was some
twenty years Yussif's junior.

Prince Yazid held up a hand as a warning; he wanted no lectures
on vice or sin.

Yussif said nothing. *It's this dungheap of a land,* he protested
silently to himself. *By all that is holy, what are we doing here?*

A discreet knock opened the door. It was Mrs. Wheeler-Simms,
the prince's secretary, holding an envelope.

"Good morning, Your Highness. It's a cable."

It was from Langfeldt in Zürich. *Tomorrow* and *most urgent*
were the words in the message that made him sigh, hiding his immediate nervous anticipation.

"Please reserve space for Yussif and me on a flight to Zürich
for tomorrow morning, Wheeler-Simms. Then get us on a flight to
Riyadh the following day." He glanced at the empty snifter on the
table. "Also, please extend my regrets to your charming daughter
about the ballet at Covent Garden tomorrow, but you can see how
it is. The tickets, however, should not be wasted; please go in my
stead."

"Thank you, Your Highness. You are most kind," said Wheeler-
Simms. She looked efficient in her note-taking, but in truth she was
deeply disappointed. After months of subtle maneuvering, she had
finally worked it so that the prince would ask her beautiful—and un-
married—daughter out. That he wasn't interested in her daughter—
or any other woman, for that matter, as he was very much in love
with his wife—didn't seem to deter Wheeler-Simms. Time and her
daughter's ample charms would take care of that, she reckoned.

"One more thing, Wheeler-Simms. Call Johnson at Getty.
Make my excuses, et cetera, et cetera. Tell him I'll be in touch when
I return from Riyadh."

"Yes, sir. I'm sure he'll be understanding." *As much as I?*
wondered the secretary as she left the room.

Yussif was standing by, arms across his chest. "Leave me now, Yussif," ordered Yazid.

"I'll help you pack," he offered, hoping to keep him from sinning.

"No, I'll do it alone. Leave me!"

Yussif uncrossed his arms and stood his ground, but he knew he mustn't disobey. He would pray for his prince. "Yes, el Emir."

After Yussif left, Prince Yazid packed his robes and *keffiyeh*, which he would change into in Zürich. Then he carefully placed six bottles of cognac into a large bag and placed that underneath articles of clothing. He wasn't sure how long he would have to remain in Saudi Arabia; the thought of finding himself short was enough to evoke panic in him. He knew, of course, that there was some danger in being caught smuggling liquor into his homeland; it could mean the end of his career and even severe punishment, depending on the king's mood. But it was a chance he had to take. He couldn't think under what conditions he would not take the chance, so great was his need for it.

He stood in front of the bag, holding the last bottle and staring at it with a mixture of disgust and security. He looked for devils in the bottle, but all he could see was the pale amber fluid that kept the pain away. He felt himself perspiring lightly at the thought of being without his only friend. He put the bottle back into its carton and into the suitcase, completing the neat row, and wondered how long he would be in Riyadh. Then he smiled ironically in the knowledge that the answer to the question was simple: as long as the booze held out.

He licked his lips in guilt, thinking that this time, when he came back to London, he would definitely put the plan into operation, the plan he had formulated some time ago and kept putting off: to check into one of those superexclusive Swiss *Kuranstalts* where they could cure him of his bad friendship. They offered the height of discretion and privacy, and no questions were asked as long as one paid in advance for their excellent care. He would go through it all, he vowed—detoxification, withdrawal, substitution, psychotherapy, physiotherapy, megavitamins, special diet—the lot. He would check in as a Christian Lebanese—they wouldn't know the difference, or care. If only he could somehow find the time, scrounge up the opportunity—if only he would be left alone for a while! He screwed up his eyes and breathed deeply, and the pain hit, and he began to hyperventilate. Then he thought he heard voices. He did; it was the voice of Yussif, praying.

The pain! He walked to the bar and poured a glass of cognac. He looked at it hard in his hand. He grimaced and flung the glass against the wall as the voice of Yussif came to him. Then he quickly splashed another drink, spilling part of it. He poured it down his throat in one motion.

Then he thought of his beautiful wife, Princess al-Lat, whose name meant Daughter of Allah. Al-Lat, his Islamic conscience. Al-Lat, of the green eyes, of the questioning eyes. Al-Lat of the sad eyes.

BAD REICHENHALL

THE PRESENT

A blanket of fresh white snow from the early storm gently covered the slopes and rooftops of the Bavarian Alps spa. Karl-Ludwig Niesper breathed the crisp morning air deep into his lungs, then exhaled a cloud of steam. He looked around at the virgin landscape glistening brightly in the sun and speculated that the photographers would be out in force while the town was still picture-postcard pretty. Ordinarily, Niesper would have drunk in the sight, but he was burdened that morning, as he had been every morning for the past two years.

Karl-Ludwig Niesper was a powerful man. He was the managing director of the Bayerische Bodenkreditanstalt und Girozentrale of Munich, the parent company of a large group of West German mortgage banks financing several building projects in Eastern bloc nations. That was in public. In private, he was the sole conduit of the bank to very secret dealings with certain members of finance committees in those nations in which currency transactions were carried out. Large amounts of zlotys, forints, rubles, lei, and others from labor syndicates and other government agencies were safely laundered through Karl-Ludwig Niesper's contacts in Switzerland; he and the members of those committees made a great deal of money.

Karl-Ludwig Niesper was also a tough man, a fact attested to by those with whom he dealt—Russians, East Germans, Hungarians, and Czechs, among others. He knew, perhaps from his training in the Hitler-Jugend—that he could never give in to their demands, for to do so would be considered a sign of weakness, and then they would tread over him. He was hard, and they respected him for it, he knew.

He stood at the edge of the garden-park that led to the town promenade of shops and coffeehouses and noticed in admiration that the German snow-removal battalions had already cleared the paths and walks.

"Look, my dear," Niesper said to his burden, "already they have cleared the snow! Even at home they wouldn't be so quick."

His wife, Elsa, looked straight ahead from her wheelchair. "No, they wouldn't. Not with the Italians doing the work now."

She had said it in a flat, cheerless monotone, which had been her usual way of communicating since her accident.

"Well, we'll go now, my dear. We'll have a nice walk, then we'll have a nice breakfast at the *Konditorei*," he said, pushing the wheelchair with his paralyzed wife.

A red-cheeked woman walking her Shi'h Tsu greeted him warmly. "*Guten Morgen*, Herr Direktor . . . Frau Direktor."

In her cheerfulness, as she tried to avoid looking at Frau Niesper's blanketed and useless legs, the good woman had mixed in a touch of sympathy. Niesper knew that the look was intended for his wife, but he questioned in his mind if that was really so. After all, wasn't he the true victim in this tragedy? Wasn't it a look of condolence for him? Did she and the rest know that it was he who nursed her, who cleaned her after her bodily functions, who bathed and powdered her? Did they know she refused the skilled nursing that they could well afford? That she wanted him even to cook for her, to read to her until she dropped off to sleep? To dress her and push her wheelchair through the town every day, *every day*? Did they know that those daily excursions, subjecting them both to pitiful cluckings, were at her insistence? That they served only as active reminders of her plight, like a live nerve being jostled in agonizing acknowledgment of her paraplegia—and his own good health?

Niesper tipped his Tyrolean hat at yet another greeting.

Maybe not, he thought. Maybe they agreed with Elsa that if he had been home with her that day, as most husbands were, she wouldn't have been bored, and if she hadn't been bored, she wouldn't have drank, and if she hadn't drank, she wouldn't have driven, and if she hadn't driven . . . if, *if*, IF! His mind screamed the tiny word as he pushed the wheelchair and tipped his hat and smiled his greetings.

No, he thought . . . She was right, he thought. He should have been home, with her, where he belonged. From then on, he resolved, he would always be home. No matter what. It was she who was in the blasted chair—not him. It would be his privilege to push it.

"Herr Direktor! Herr Direktor!" It was Frau Huber, the housekeeper, and she was panting from running. "It's a telegram, Herr Direktor. I thought it might be important."

Karl-Ludwig Niesper read the cable, then showed it to his wife. It was from her brother, Heinz Langfeldt, directing Niesper to come to Zürich. "Most urgent," it said. She let the wire drop to the ground.

"You see I must go," he said, picking it up. "I'll return in a day or so." He looked sad, but he smiled inwardly in relief.

LONDON

THE PRESENT

Sir Anthony Duke sipped his port after the noonday meal. He listened politely and smiled at the appropriate times during the telling of a sexually oriented joke by Admiral Sir Edward Cunningham. Duke had heard the joke before, and he didn't like it. He found such jokes offensive. But because it was Sir Edward who was telling it, and Sir Edward was the chairman of one of the largest marine insuring companies in the world, Duke listened politely and smiled at the appropriate times.

A black-clad waitress, one of the old-timers of the Captain's Room at Lloyd's, shuffled in carrying a small tray with a message for Duke. It was a telephone summons, and he could take it in the booth by the door, she advised in a monotone.

It was Sir Anthony's administrative assistant, Freddie Tucker-Jones, calling from his employer's Moorgate office.

"Sorry to crash in, Sir Anthony," Freddie said in his clipped Mayfair accent, "but the wire's from Dr. L. He's asked that you be in Zürich tomorrow for a meeting at fifteen hundred hours."

"Does the old boy say what it's about, Freddie?"

"No, but he says it's most urgent, to use his words."

"Um . . . sounds ominous, doesn't it? Very well. Be a good chap and book me on a flight tomorrow, will you, Freddie? Sometime around noon should do it."

"Right. Uh, Sir Anthony . . . what about tonight? Is the party still on?"

"Good heavens, yes! Why shouldn't it be?"

"Ruddy good, sir! You won't be disappointed. I found a couple of lovely birds that are quite exotic. One's from New Zealand, the other, from Vietnam, I think. It would be a shame—"

"Not to worry, dear boy. Just bring your birds; we'll see how their feathers fly. And Freddie," Duke said confidentially, "I appreciate your efforts. There will be something extra in it for you, as usual."

Sir Anthony went back to the admiral and his jokes. He didn't want to displease his major client. At least he didn't have to see him often, he consoled himself. He got to London about once a month; his main residence was in Liechtenstein, where, in Vaduz, he owned a *bank privat*. Convenient things, those *banks privats*, where anonymity was what they sold; anonymous depositors were plentiful. That and his metals futures kept him busy. And very rich.

Final fittings at Guives & Hawkes for a half dozen suits, high tea with the Secretary of Marine and Merchant Shipping, and a concert at Royal Festival Hall finished a busy day for Sir Anthony.

The night, however, had just begun.

He sent his car and driver home, taking the underground to Russell Square. He turned into a small street near the British Museum, at that hour devoid of pedestrians. Nestled in between two bed-and-breakfast hotels stood a small warehouse. Duke unlocked the side door and turned on an overhead lamp. He went to a loading elevator and pressed B. The car lowered him to a dark hallway stacked with boxes. He opened a small door with another key. It led to a large room that looked like a gymnasium, but it wasn't, even though it contained barbells and other equipment, padded exercise tables, and full-length mirrors on three of the four walls.

With yet another key, Duke let himself into a small dressing room, complete with a modern bathroom. It was comfortably furnished and had a well-stocked bar. Stereo components were in a cabinet.

He closed the door to the suite, checked his watch, and poured a drink. He undressed his tall, lean body down to his underwear, and from a closet he took a shiny black one-piece outfit. It looked like a diver's wetsuit, but it was made of supple leather, and metal beads in oblong patterns were sewn into the fabric along the arms and thighs. He put on a hood of the same material. The ears were pointed, giving him a satanic look. Black suede shoes that looked like they could have belonged to a fifteenth-century harlequin completed the outfit. He took a long swallow of his drink and waited.

A few minutes later he heard the elevator clang into operation. His pulse quickened.

He turned out the lights in the dressing suite; a new light partially illuminated the room, coming through a two-way mirror on the wall. He could see the gym. Freddie came in with the two young women. One was blond and buxom with a rather plain face; the other was Oriental, slim and delicate, looking like an exotic flower. Freddie was talking, pointing, instructing. The women began to undress as Freddie went into the dressing room.

Duke whispered through excited breaths, "Good show, Freddie! Now turn on the tape, dear boy."

"Right," said Freddie, turning a switch that filled the rooms with contemporary rock music. "What'd I tell you? A charming pair of lovebirds, aren't they?"

"That they are, Freddie. You done ruddy good," Duke said in his best cockney.

The women were naked now, and they began fondling each other. The Oriental had long black hair, contrasting with the New Zealander's blond tresses. Her breasts were small, and she had full and round hips. The blonde had very large breasts. They caressed and stroked each other, laughing and squealing, as instructed by Freddie. This went on for several minutes and then the music stopped. Other music came on, this time the polyrhythms and blaring cacophonies of Stravinsky's *Rite of Spring*. The room was flooded with the thunder of tympanums and clanging percussion; trombones slid in their brassy wails, vying with the agitated beats of the snares. The effect was awesome to the confused women. Then a sudden silence in the score, and Duke, timing it precisely, leaped into the room looking like a shiny Lucifer, legs apart, white teeth exposed. Both women gasped audibly. Warmth flooded through Sir Anthony Duke when he saw the horrified faces and heard the gasps.

The music began again, this time with slow but accelerating groans of the contrabasses; a bassoon established the beginnings of a leitmotif, oboes and clarinets joined, reinforcing and abetting the devilish melody, and trumpets and French horns entered in threatening counterpoint. Duke grabbed the Oriental by her long hair and roughly pushed her facedown onto one of the padded tables. Quickly and expertly he tied her wrists and ankles to rings. In a flash she was spread-eagled. He shoved a cushion under her hips, raising her plump buttocks.

Satan now went to the blond.

She held up an arm. "Here, now, mite! You didn't say nothin' 'bout us getting bashed. You're gonna bash us, ain't you?"

Duke scowled at her, eyes and teeth flashing.

Freddie's voice came over the speakers. "Go along wi' 'im," he said in his native cockney, which always came through in times of excitement or stress, " 'e won't 'urt you, love. Jus' go along, and i' 'll be awright, I promise."

Duke smiled evilly and took the frightened woman by the hair, propelling her to another table, where he quickly tied her hands in back of her and her ankles apart, spreading her legs.

Sir Anthony went to a cabinet and withdrew a goose quill. He held it in front of him, then raised it toward the ceiling as if it were sacred. He started to sway to and fro to the beat of the music, then leaped like a ballet dancer around each girl. The feather darted, tickled. He spread the blond's labia and scratched with the feather . . . the Oriental's hole, too, opened and closed to the light strokes. They screamed in pain—or moaned in delight, it didn't matter to him. He danced more fervently, the smell of sweat and leather assailing his nostrils, exciting him.

He danced to the cabinet and took out a whip with long silk tassels at the end. He stood between the two women, swaying and grinning, and began to lash at them, across the buttocks of the Oriental and across the belly and breasts of the blond. They screamed and tugged at their bonds as thin red welts appeared on their skin.

The music was reaching its ear-splitting, monumental crescendo. Then the last, crashing, vibrant, profane bars of Stravinsky's warped genius thundered to a long, orgasmic close. Duke, holding the whip above his head in phallic reverence, shook and quivered violently in a climactic spasm. He crumpled to the floor in a panting, sweating, convulsive heap; only an echo remained of the magnificent clamor.

Freddie ran into the room, quickly releasing the women. Their eyes were wide more from amazement than from the slight stinging of the whip.

"Right, me lasses, you done bloody good. Get your duds on, and we'll have you out of 'ere in a jiff." He counted out some bills and put them on a table. " 'Ere's a hundred quid for each o' you for cab fare and a bi' left over for tea and cakes. Jus' 'it the bu'on on the lif' and you'll be on your way. That's the ticket, me darlings!"

The women folded the money into their purses and left hurriedly. Duke was already in the shower.

"They're gone now," Freddie yelled through the door.

"I heard you, Freddie," yelled back Sir Anthony Duke from within. The shower was suddenly quiet. "Fix us both a drink, will you?" The door opened. "Oh, and Freddie," he added, handing him the leather suit, sopping wet, "would you see that this thing gets laundered? It got mucked up a bit." He closed the door and went back into the bathroom.

Freddie Tucker-Jones held the suit at arm's length, a look of disgust on his handsome young face. "The whole thing's disgusting," he muttered under his breath as he put it into a plastic bag. "This hoppin' and leapin' about wi' whips and feathers . . . Bugger me if i' ain't bloody abnormal, the whole flamin' affair!" He looked at the bag. He would take it down to the French laundry. They bleedin' well knew what to do wi' it, the bleedin' French.

The next morning, feeling rested and revitalized, Sir Anthony Duke smiled ingratiatingly at the Swiss-Air flight attendant. He gave her his card. She smiled at the distinguished Englishman and thanked him. She was French-Swiss, he could tell, and quite lovely. She would call, he had no doubt.

He watched her from his aisle seat as she bent over in front of him. Her gabardine skirt, tight around her bottom, dissolved in Sir Anthony's imagination, and he saw a round mocha-colored orifice winking at him. Sir Anthony smiled and winked back.

RAMBOUILLET, NEAR PARIS

THE PRESENT

A crew of gardeners carefully clipped the sculpted hedges in the bright morning sun of late summer. Row after row of them, growing in symmetrical patterns, were the pride and joy of the mistress of the great manor house in which the family Durand lived. They had to be clipped like fine poodles, the gardeners were reminded, otherwise they would not be elegant. The word *elegant* was the standard by which the family Durand lived and breathed. Well, almost.

Georges Durand threw his head back and laughed boisterously, knowingly, at his son's story. He was having a breakfast of veal kidneys in Madeira; he skillfully kept them in his mouth as he roared with glee. "On the gearshift lever? You tangled your shorts on the—ha, ha!—on the gearshift lever?"

"Yes, Papi," the eighteen-year-old said as he cut into his omelette with his silver knife, holding it like a large pencil. "It was really embarrassing, because she started to laugh, then I started to laugh, then we were both laughing so hard that the whole conquest went *pphhtt!*—right out the window of that damned car!"

"Jean-Paul, you are truly a chip off the old block. You know, I must confess to you, the same thing happened to me, except that it was a thirty-six Chevrolet!" Durand burst out laughing again at the memory while he sopped up Madeira sauce with his baguette.

"No! Really, Papi? Then I don't feel so stupid after all," Jean-Paul said, smiling sheepishly. "Although I must admit, I thought I really had one for the books."

"Yes, it was 1939," Georges Durand said, going back to his memories. "Like you, Jean-Paul, I too was a young law student. Unlike the huge allowance I give you, my resources then were quite limited, to be sure. But it was then that I learned, my boy, that no matter how romantic the Bois de Boulogne can be, a clean, cheap hotel is a wise, shall we say, investment, under the circumstances." Durand looked at his son as he chewed kidneys and smiled lewdly at the same time.

"Really, Georges, have the decency to save your man-to-man talks for another time, when I'm not present." It was the voice of Madame Durand, sitting at the other end of the long table, having coffee and rolls, reading the morning paper. "Of course," she continued in the lull she had created, "I'm well aware that you two are pals, more than just father and son, and you enjoy sharing your little stories. But what you do outside this house would best be left there, where it belongs." She turned a page of her newspaper.

"I'm sorry, Mother. I didn't know you were listening."

"You didn't? Well, that tells one how much attention one receives around here, doesn't it?"

Durand spoke up. "That's all right, son. Your mother's remarks were directed at me." Turning to his wife, he said, "Really, my dear, you're so provincial! You don't even try to live in the twentieth century. Join the party; you may like it."

"I'll live as I choose, Georges, which is with my head held high," Madame Durand said calmly, still studying the newspaper. "I still have my dignity, despite your obvious indifference to it."

"Your dignity? I don't recall doing anything to offend your precious dignity," Durand said, now morose. "Ah, Anne-Marie, you certainly know how to put a damper on a man's day! I suggest we end this conversation before—"

Jean-Paul stood up, smiling, eyeing both his parents. "Uh, if you two lovely people will excuse me, I'm running a bit late." He kissed them both and left.

"You haven't offended my dignity?" Madame Durand pressed on. "Then what do you call your ongoing affair with that actress? Please understand one thing, Georges," she said, holding up a hand, indicating she wasn't through. "I do not spy on you, nor do I inspect your clothing—it would be beneath me to do so. But I do receive phone calls from my friends—*my* friends, Georges—which I find humiliating, to say the least. If you must bed down with her, please have the decency to do it discreetly. Do it as any respectable Frenchman who cheats on his wife does—in private."

Madame Durand rang a crystal bell. A servant dressed in morning clothes materialized. "More coffee, please."

"Anne-Marie, I have told you repeatedly that Desirée Montparnasse is simply a client, and as with most clients, I must, on occasion, entertain her," Durand said, veins bulging in anger. "It's expected of me, damn it all, and unless you want to pay our not insubstantial bills from your own income, I will conduct my business as I see fit. And I will not tolerate further discussions regarding Mademoiselle Montparnasse in this house!"

The servant waited, careful not to interrupt his employer, then handed him a tray with a telegram on it. Durand opened it in a peevish mood.

"Merde alors!" he cursed loudly. "I have to go to Zürich." *And of all days, tomorrow!* he said silently to himself. How was he going to explain this broken engagement to Desirée? Nothing short of a broken back would convince her that three broken engagements in ten days were necessary. *Damn! Damn! And look at Anne-Marie, sitting there with her newspaper, raising that skeptical eyebrow of hers. She thinks I'm going away with Desirée! How do you like that for bloody hell?* he thought ironically.

He got up from the table and pressed his cheek against his wife's and kissed the air. "If you'll excuse me, Anne-Marie, I must get to the office. I'll need to make some arrangements for my trip tomorrow," he said, mostly to himself.

Five minutes later Durand was crunching across the gravel path in front of the house, where the shining black and tobacco-brown Rolls-Royce waited for him. The liveried chauffeur held the door open.

"La place Churchill," Jules, Durand said, turning to make sure no one overheard the instructions.

Jules of course knew that his employer wanted to go to the bachelor apartment that he kept in the exclusive Neuilly district of Paris, where his neighbors were maharanis and sheikhs and wealthy film personages. Very wealthy, thank you. Durand's *garçonnière*, of course, faced the greenery of the Bois de Boulogne, which made it even more exclusive and expensive. He used it, according to his tax returns, to entertain clients; he also used it on occasion to house those who were in Paris on confidential matters, such as his main clients, the members of the Fratellanza—the Brotherhood—whose chief connection with Durand was the placement into the legitimate theater of business so-called operational profits, like the skimming of gaming funds, numbers rake-offs, vigorish from loan sharking, prostitution and pornography, and narcotics. But mostly he used the apartment as an encampment for "love in the afternoon" with, at the moment, the reigning queen of French cinema, Desirée Montparnasse, née Camille LaFleur, daughter of a neighborhood flower girl who now had a flourishing *boutique de fleuriste* on the Champs Élysées.

It was Desirée who had decorated Durand's *garçonnière* with her passion, oriental art. Persian carpets covered the polished wood floors; even the bathroom had Chinese rugs to keep the cold tile from Desirée's dainty feet. The salon was an attempt at nostalgia for the Twenties; there were gigantic and bulbous cushions throughout in place of chairs. French tapestries hung about, mingling with framed lead-glass contemporary representations of Art Deco, resulting in a cacophony of color that somewhat embarrassed the more artistically sensitive Durand. The red-gilt bedroom had a waterbed with a canopy held up by Ionic—or where they Doric? he wondered—columns. No doubt it was the most outrageous kitsch, although, he admitted, he did enjoy the waterbed—and in the togas furnished by Desirée, he did have a feeling of being Aristotle. Or was it Nero?

Well, whoever, Desirée Montparnasse, with her horrendous bad taste, knew how to fuck, he concluded. She had, he would argue, the most educated lips, tongue, and throat in France, and just in making that conclusion, Georges Durand became aroused in the back seat of his Rolls-Royce. And how else should he think of her but in bed? He couldn't recall one time when their activities had consisted of anything other than sex. No politics, religion, or even the weather entered into their conversations. Just fucking, and things connecting with fucking. Desirée had aptly referred to the apartment with that unique Parisian argot that said it so well: *baise-en-ville*, literally, a "fuck-in-town."

He wondered if she was serious about leaving him for Léon Clésinger.

Clésinger—that slimy little circumcised prick of a Jew, the self-anointed guru of café society and the pseudointellectual disciples of his pseudophilosophical bilge, Durand raged silently. He was converting her, using her name to promote his dismal and faddish muck. His new book was making the rounds of the *beau monde,* a piece of dreary hogwash with the presumptuous title, *La Philosophie s'insurger. What in hell was that supposed to mean, "Philosophy Revolts"! he asked himself. It was nothing more than the sick ravings of a superannuated hippie, designed to impress fools like Desirée.* Of course, the critics had praised it and were now touting it to the gullible public with terms like "deep and thought-provoking," "eclectic," and *"recherché." More like* réchauffé, he thought; a plate of warmed-over vomit! He knew the critics; if they didn't understand a work, they praised it for fear of being accused of being shallow.

Well, she could go with him and his matted jungle of beard, where surely she would find plenty of lice to pluck in her spare time—which will be abundant when her career goes down the toilet! It would serve her right, he judged in quickly accelerating anger and self-justification. To be thrown over for that little Hebrew and his fleas—no, damn it! He, Georges Durand, would be the one to drop *her!*

Come to think of it, it might not be a bad idea to end things with Desirée. For one thing, it would appease Anne-Marie; for another, word would get around in his circles: he would be "the man who threw over Desirée Montparnasse." They were green with envy as it was. It would certainly draw a few knowing—and admiring—winks from his confrères, wouldn't it? After all, Desirée was getting along in years, at least a little. What was she now, thirty? Well, that's not so old, but she was letting herself go. Her once-stupendous breasts were beginning to sag; the nipples were pointing down, he had noticed, and her thighs were not as creamy white as they had been before. Little blue veins were appearing more and more. Maybe that used condom Clésinger would find "character" in those varices and droopy *nichons. Let's face it, she's over the hill,* he ventured. Now, her young sister, Colette—there was something! That face . . . that body . . . that pout that made her mouth look like a ripe plum. *Another Bri-Bri,* he thought, licking his lips. Maybe there was another film career in the making. He would work on it, he decided, the idea exciting him in several ways.

The Rolls came to a stop in front of the *garçonnière,* bringing

Durand out of his reverie. He got out of the car and mentioned for the chauffeur to wait. He unlocked the heavy front door of the closed-circuit-television-monitored house. A small but fast elevator took him to the top floor and opened onto his apartment. The strong smell of incense still lingered from the last time he and Desirée had used the place. Wait! That was over ten days ago. She must have been there since then with Clésinger. Damn her!

Frowning, he opened the windows. He picked up the phone and told the concièrge to have the maid come up and change all the linens and thoroughly clean the place.

Next he unlocked a closet and knelt in front of a safe. He removed a briefcase, and still on his knees, he opened it with a key from his key ring.

Inside were packets of thousand-dollar bills and a sheaf of negotiable securities. A typed sheet on top of the money told him in code the breakdown, which totaled exactly ten million dollars. He snapped the case shut, not counting; it was always exact.

The money was still "warm"; it had just been dropped. It would be on deposit tomorrow, much earlier than usual, because of his going there at Langfeldt's request. His clients would be pleased, but then they were easy to please, he had learned over the years. As he rode down in the elevator, his smile faded as he thought the unthinkable—what it would be like to displease them.

His next stop was the offices of Durand and Duplessis in the Place Vendôme, to drop off the briefcase in the bank-size vault he kept there. Besides, he owed the junior partners and law clerks an appearance, for appearance's sake.

Within minutes the impressive car was going down the Avenue de la Grande Armée, ready to do elegant battle with the little Fiats and Citröens around the massive Étoile and its imposing tenant, the Arc de Triomphe, the beginning of the most famous and beautiful street in the world, the Avenue des Champs Élysées. Durand loved to ride down that street, which to him was the culmination of imaginative yet artistic city planning. He loved his Paris, and on days like this, with the sea of green treetops lining the boulevards, he felt like there was no other place—there should be no other place—in the world.

The Rolls made the turn around the great Place de la Concorde. A fleeting image invaded the memory of Georges Durand: as a young law student and a member of Colonel Rol's Communist forces, he had fought against German snipers in August 1944, during the liberation of his city. He hadn't thought of that for years, and now he had trouble swallowing; his eyes misted up in proud emotion.

The chauffeur expertly guided the smooth machine into Durand's parking slot. The handsome, debonair, impeccably dressed lawyer strode into the largest tax and investment firm in Paris and enjoyed the anticipation of the excitement his presence would cause.

After some conferring with employees, one last bit of business kept Durand at his oversize desk: a phone call to Desirée. He dialed the number of the studio in which she was shooting. Yes, it was urgent, he told the operator, and waited. Finally the star came on the line. He told her he couldn't see her as planned. An emergency meeting with his clients had come up, and he hoped she would understand.

"Really, Georges, this is too much! I'm not even angry anymore, just hurt that I mean so little to you after all we've gone through."

He heard silent tears drop on her end of the line.

"But you must believe me, Desirée," he purred. "I'm telling you the truth, as I did the other times." He did not sound too convincing because he didn't want to sound convincing. Nor did he offer to show her Langfeldt's cable.

"Then I'll tell you now what I wanted to tell you tomorrow. Georges, don't say no, because I think you owe it to me for our . . . friendship," she said, almost shrewlike. "I want you to lend me a million francs. I'll pay you from my next film."

"A million! That's a lot of money, my dear. Things are a little tight with me at present. I don't know. What do you need with so much money?" It was to subsidize her new friend Clésinger, he guessed.

"I have an opportunity to buy some property. I must have it, Georges. I'll pay back every centime! You can't deny me!"

Then it came to him. He'd lend her the money; it would be a good investment, with Colette as the collateral.

"Well, I'd have to cash in some bonds, and—well, my dear, I'll do what I can. I'm not promising, but I'll see. I'll call you when I get back in two or three days. Oh, by the way, you might bring your little sister—what's her name? Colette? Yes, bring Colette with you when we meet, would you?"

"Why should I?" she asked suspiciously.

"I know how close you two are. The least I can do is help her in any way I can. I mean, we really should start considering a film career for her too, don't you think? You know how good I am at these things, what with my experience and my contacts. Besides, those fellows over at Ciné-France owe me a ton of favors. You know how important it is to open the right doors at this stage of Colette's career, don't you?"

He let the words *Colette's career* echo in her ears for a moment. It had a good sound. Then he continued. "Think of how proud your good mother will be with *two* film stars in the family. It makes me think of Olivia de Havilland and Joan Fontaine, yes?"

A pause. Desirée was thinking. "Do you really think she has it, Georges? I mean, talent?"

"We'll soon find out, my dear, we'll soon find out."

MUNICH, HOTEL VIERJAHRESZEITEN

THE PRESENT

L.R. DeVries stood in the middle of his hotel room in his pants and sleeveless undershirt and fished in his pocket for a coin. He found a mark and flipped it to the bellman who had delivered Langfeldt's telegram. The bellmen bowed and thanked Herr DeVries for the small tip. After all, Herr DeVries was a longtime resident of this fine estabishment and deserved the highest respect. That he was a small tipper mattered not, for he was consistent. He always tipped in that way and to all.

"You're welcome, sonny," said DeVries, opening the cable and reading the instructions. He finished dressing, donning a heavily starched white Arrow shirt, dark lisle cotton socks, and black, square-toed Florsheim shoes made of smooth and shiny leather. A narrow tie of forgettable design went around his large neck; the ends rested on his rather prominent belly. He tucked in his shirt and buckled his belt under the belly, causing his pants to fall in a bunch on his shoe tops, giving him a perpetual baggy look.

He brushed down his ample crop of gray hair, which he would cover all that day whenever possible with a light gray Stetson set squarely on his head. He put on his coat, leaving it open, as was his habit, picked up his bulging briefcase, which was his office in Europe, and walked to the lobby for a visit with Max, the concièrge.

He would have to change his plans for visiting Remagen. Instead he needed reservations in Zürich.

With the exception of winters, L.R. DeVries now lived exclusively in Germany. He liked the orderly ways of the Germans, and because his business brought him to Europe several times a year, he had decided to move to Munich, which to him was the most German of German cities. It was centrally located, a stone's throw to Zürich, and convenient to the other places in Europe that his hobby took him to. Also, the Germans had excellent trains, and they ran on time. DeVries's hobby was visiting battle sites of the two world wars; the second was his prime concern. He was something of a romantic, as he had a seemingly inexhaustible list of places to visit and names to research—and venerate. At least once a month he placed flowers on the grave of his younger brother, buried in the American cemetery in Hamm, Luxembourg, who died in the Battle of the Bulge. While there, he placed a wreath on the tomb of General George S. Patton, another of his many private heroes. And the Swabian cathedral city of Ulm was yet one more place of hero worship for DeVries, notably at the gravesite of Erwin Rommel, where flowers were also strewn, and farther east, not too far from Linz, where the gray-green waters of the Austrian Danube flow, DeVries had visited more than once the tiny graveyard in back of the oldest church of Leonding, where rest the remains of an Austrian civil servant and his wife, Alois and Klara Hitler. That headstone, too, received its allotment of flowers from L.R. DeVries under the watchful eyes, he saw, of a Valkyrian woman in a loden cape who guarded against defacement of the grave of the parents of their mutual hero.

Now, what with Langfeldt's cable, he had to cancel a trip to Remagen to view the site of the Lundendorff bridge, which had dripped with the blood of both German and American soldiers in 1945. Now he would have to put his hobby aside while he took care of business.

L.R. (for LeRoy) liked to call himself a trouble-shooter rather than a representative for the several oil and gas companies with which he was associated. Through the Langfeldt group he had made his confrères a lot of money—tax-free money, which was the name of their game. They paid him well for his services and counsel, and although he was not a rich man—at least, not by Texas standards— he had tremendous financial power, mostly because the more he denied to his associates that he was "rich-rich," the more they believed the opposite. Like a fox, he used that belief to his advantage, keeping them guessing, speculating, wondering.

He had billions to play with, and yet his retainers and expenses were his only source of income. He didn't charge placement fees for the huge amounts invested in his clients' behalf, which gave concrete evidence that he didn't need it, which fed more fuel to the original notion. All that was fine with L.R., because it gave him power. And that power translated into political power in his home base of Texas—the Texas of oil and gas and depletion allowances, of oak boardrooms where bourbon and branch water and rib-eye steaks, pan fried, were served while decisions were made about cornering the silver market, or about how many millions would be plowed into a politician's campaign, or to fire the head coach at Texas A&M, or of the Houston Oilers.

It was L.R. who usually presided over those meetings, and his advice and counsel were considered gospel, especially when it came to deciding who, politically, was right for them, the big boys of the big state of Texas.

They still chuckled about Lyndon Johnson, a close friend of L.R. DeVries, and their subsequent battle over campaign contributions. L.R. had seen to it that Lyndon got a million dollars for his presidential campaign against John Kennedy in the Democratic primaries, then, later, another million in his fight against Barry Goldwater. That had been fine, until Lyndon found out that L.R. had given *two* million to the Goldwater election committee. The President had invited L.R. to a barbecue at his Perdenales ranch, where a scene had taken place between the two big Texans. Johnson had accused L.R. of disloyalty, and L.R. had accused LBJ of "jumpin' on the liberal bandwagon." The two old friends had had to be restrained from physically attacking each other. L.R. had left, but not before advising the President that he should make the most of the next four years in the White House, because his political career "wuzzn't worth a bucket o' warm spit!" It was a phrase that Lyndon Johnson would borrow from that scene time and time again, but more significant for L.R. DeVries, his power with the "good ol' boys" was at dizzying heights. His stock in the oil boardrooms jumped several points, and soon word got out to the grass roots, where he became somewhat of a folk hero in a Stetson.

L.R. DeVries set down his bulging briefcase on the counter in front of the concièrge of the Vierjahreszeiten Hotel. "Max," he said, screwing up his blue eyes, which were settled in wrinkled bags on a cherubic, smiling, baby face, "cancel my trip to Remagen and put me on a sleeper to Zürich [it came out Zerk] tonight. It seems I gotta earn m' keep."

BELLANO, ON THE SHORES OF LAKE COMO

THE PRESENT

Flora Berganza walked in purposeful strides directly to the dining room of the resort hotel. She wore a suit of black and white tweed and carried a briefcase, looking every bit the professional woman that she was. She carried a black sable coat over her other arm, since the September air in the Alps had an early chill. Honey-blond hair was severely pulled back into a thick chignon, and as she walked, she trailed a scent of Joy, which her pale skin handled well. She indicated a preference for a particular table by the window—the same table she had used the last time she had been at that hotel.

She ordered a light breakfast in a monotone, feeling ambivalent about being at that table with its memories of things past. She tried to enjoy the view of the lake and the fins of white sail here and there, but she realized she was making a conscious effort, and that annoyed her. She looked at her briefcase; it reminded her that she was in for an uncomfortable session with Langfeldt regarding some shares—a rather large block—of a South African mining concern that Monsignor Petroncelli wanted the Vatican to eliminate from its vast portfolio because of the possible bad public relations that the apartheid government could cause. Langfeldt had earlier strongly advised against it, based on what he predicted the stock would do. She knew he would fight again to retain it. She would try, once and for all, to resolve the issue on this trip, even though it was Langfeldt's show, according to the telegram she had received the day before. She knitted her brow when she remembered the phrase "most urgent" on the wire she had received that morning at her Milan apartment. She sighed and looked out the window again.

A waitress, clad in the traditional black uniform, served her orange juice, rolls, and coffee. She was young and pretty. Not beautiful, but earthy-pretty, with light northern Italian features, and she was somewhat tall with an athletic figure. Probably under twenty, Flora reckoned.

"Are you staying in the hotel?" the girl asked.

"No, I'm just passing through."

A pause. Flora looked hard at her, and the girl looked back. It was there, she knew. Whatever it is when one knows, when one says something with a look, when one sees the dilation of the pupils that respond positively, as Flora's expert eyes could see. Yes, it was there, the look.

"But I'm coming back through here again," she paused just long enough, "tomorrow or the next day. Will you be here?"

A look of pleasurable excitement came over the girl. "Yes," she answered, almost in a whisper. "I will be here all week until three, then I come back at six for the dinner shift."

"It would be nice if you were to serve me again. What is your name? I'll ask for you." Flora smiled with white, even teeth.

"Giannina. I was named after my father. His name is Gianni."

"A lovely name for a lovely girl. My name is Carla," said Flora.

The waitress gave a tiny curtsy. *"Fortunatissima, cara signora,"* she said in her most formal manners. "Now, I must serve the others, or I'll get into trouble."

"Yes, my little one, go. We'll talk some more when I come back through here."

"Spero che tornerá presto," the girl said, blushing at her boldness in asking her to come back soon.

"Sì, presto—glielo prometto," Flora smiled, teasing.

As the girl walked self-consciously away, Flora buttered a roll, and she abruptly felt the warmth of the moment leave. Her jaw muscles danced in anger as her thoughts darted to Alfredo Cardozo, president of Recursos de Fomento Pan Americano, a consortium of Latin

American banks. She took an angry bite of the roll, fighting the memory, but it overtook her as she lifted the coffee cup to her perfectly painted lips of pale orange. One eyebrow arched, and her nostrils flared wrathfully as the memory of that weekend invaded her being.

It had been balmy on Lake Como that evening—almost *föhn*-like—which made people do things they might later regret, she reasoned, which was probably the reason she had accepted his invitation. He thought he was so charming, so much God's gift to the women of the world, that she had thought of having a little fun with him, to tease him. The first and last man she had ever been with was in her days in law school. A fellow student, just a boy, really. It had been a terrible flop, the poor fellow coming within seconds of ending her virginity, which, in retrospect, she felt, had been the only benefit of the whole affair.

Then Alfredo Cardozo had made love to her. From the first look that evening, from the first touch, he was making love to her. As he ordered the martinis—perfect martinis, as per his meticulous instructions—as he lifted the glass to his lips, he made love to her. He buttered her bread, lemoned her oysters, sliced her filet, and in doing so he touched her ever so slightly with his fingers, and with his eyes, and with his breath, and he made love to her.

They had danced, she now remembered, and he had made love to her while he held her closely and brushed his lips against her cheek and her ears. He emanated a musky aroma, a combination of cedar and acrid, black tobacco and cologne, and the whole thing excited her senses . . . and soon she was intoxicated by what was becoming magical, and that magic was bringing about a new feeling, a new sexuality in her.

They danced for a long time, the quartet of Italian musicians sensing the romance unfolding, diminishing the tempo of their melodies as though joining in the lovemaking. Alfredo spoke to her of romantic things in romantic Italian, then said things to her in his native tongue that spoke of sex, which, though she didn't understand, she well comprehended—and she loved it. And on the floor in his room by the light of a wood fire, he released her large breasts from the constriction of her brassière, and he had gaped at the wonderment of what all along she had kept hidden, and he said, "My God!" and she responded, and when he caressed them and kissed them, she responded even more, and when he kissed her entire body and bit her buttocks and twirled her clitoris with his expert tongue, she had answered with loud moans and bucking upheavals of her aching pelvis against his unremitting face and when he had thrust a pillow under her convulsive hips and put the head of his large member against her opening and rotated it like a cudgel until she clamped his buttocks with her heels and pulled as hard as she could to alleviate the delicious pain and she cried and screamed at the different torment as the shaft sunk deep within her vibrator-abused pit and she loved the feeling of it and she who would not utter so much as the mildest oath in Italian screamed "Fuck me you bastard you prick you man!" and that was too much for him to bear—the bucking writhing twisting cold bitch-of-a-lesbian lawyer for the Holy See—it was like fucking a nun, a mother superior! And he exploded in her and the muscles of her vagina squeezed and milked him and he stayed hard in her and they fucked longer and longer until the senses peaked even higher than before and she screamed between clenched jaws and she bit him and pounded him and they reached the pinnacle simultaneously in an off-pitch duet of sobs . . . and moans . . . and whimpers . . . and groans . . . and the panting gradually became longer breaths . . . and then . . . there was quiet . . .

They rested in a tangled heap, their spent bodies glistening in front of the diminishing fire. Finally he got up and brought towels with which he gently dried her body. He then kissed her tenderly, holding her close to him, and she responded to the gentle intimacy and put her head on his shoulder and caressed his thighs and kissed his chest. Oh, she had felt so good, she remembered now as she poured more coffee from the pitcher. A woman in a man's arms. She had never felt like that before. And she felt his hairy thighs again, and his rough beard, and she liked the feeling.

They had relaxed in each other's arms. He lit two Delicados and gave her one, filling the room with the acrid smell of the black tobacco. Just like in the movies, she had thought as she inhaled the surprisingly mild smoke.

Suddenly, because if she didn't ask then, she never would, she looked at him in the flickering light and whispered the question she had never asked a man: *"M'ami?"*

He had smiled tenderly, she remembered, and looked at her for a long time. Then, he said, *"Sì, io t'amo!"*

She put her head back in the crook of his arm, kissing his dangling fingers, thinking that from then on every look, every touch, every kiss would be a new experience to her, because her life was now at a beginning, and the thought thrilled her. A new beginning, a renaissance of what should have been hers all along—the love of a man! She smiled inwardly, deciding in a love-induced impulse that he could do with her whatever he wanted. She would give up her powerful and financially rewarding connection with the Vatican if he wanted her to. It was only money, after all. And the power, well . . . she had proven to herself—and to them, the men of the "man's world"—that she was their equal, if not their superior. Now, she had thought, none of that mattered anymore. He had awakened her, thrilled her, made her feel! Her body and her heart were at last one. Oh! she thought, excited, she would even give him children! Yes! What an idea! She smiled. The heart of a loved woman was rejoicing!

He put on a robe and opened a bottle of a sparkling Italian moscato that he had in the minirefrigerator. They drank the bubbling wine that tasted, she remembered, like an elixir of love. Then they made love again; this time less furiously and much longer, with him having to fake orgasm, she knew, but for which she loved him even more.

In the morning, the replenished lovers displayed hidden talents in bed, performing imaginative and acrobatic feats that were mingled with happy laughter and more serious lustful moans.

With ravenous appetites, they ate a huge breakfast on the terrace overlooking the lake. Then they drove to Switzerland. In San Moritz, he bought her a large aquamarine pendant to match her eyes, and she gave him a gold lighter. They walked the terraced streets of the posh resort, hand in hand, window shopping, basking in their newfound joy.

She smiled as she remembered how he had pulled her into a chic boutique.

"You're getting rid of that potato sack of a blouse you've been wearing. Here, go try this on," he commanded, handing her a pale blue sweater.

She came out of the dressing room showing for the first time her fullness of body. And for the first time, she enjoyed it.

They had tea in a quaint *Teestube*. He stared at her unabashedly.

"What are you staring at?" she had asked him.

"I'm thinking how selfish you've been to have hidden such treasures from the world," he said, looking at her chest. "And I'm also thinking that I suddenly feel lewd and lecherous in their presence." He twirled an imaginary moustache and leered at her.

She blushed, smiling, feeling . . . feminine.

He stood up in the sparsely populated tearoom, which was next to a hotel. She saw the bulge at his crotch. She feigned a painful smile as he offered her his arm. "Madame," he said in his most formal manner, "may I offer you a bit of fucking?"

They spent an hour or so making hungry love; he, more and more excited by the conquest of such a previously unattainable and remarkably beautiful woman, and in doing so, making that conquest a crusade of sorts—a triumph of good over the evils of lesbianism—and she, seemingly trying to make up for long-lost love, the carnal pleasures, which were considerable, were secondary.

That night, back in Bellano, he showered in preparation for another idyllic evening of dinner and dancing and more love. She waited for him, sipping Campari, strolling though his rooms, lovingly touching his clothes, studying his cufflinks and his comb and hairbrush. She was happily wandering on clouds. Then she noticed his wallet, open on the dresser, and a picture in it. It was a snapshot of an attractive woman and two young girls. She looked at them curiously. Then she knew. The picture said "wife" . . . the picture said "family." She blinked, confused. *No*, she thought, *it's an illusion. Don't even look at it. Put the wallet down . . . it'll go away*, she remembered thinking. She sat down, took a long swallow of her drink, and looked toward the dresser—and the wallet.

She got up and looked again. The picture, of course, was still there, she recalled with no more bitterness. She sat down again.

He came out of the bathroom in a long terry-cloth robe that luxury hotels provide. He was drying his hair with a towel. He smiled at her and reached for a cigarette. He kissed her on the cheek, and she looked at him curiously, as if suddenly she was an intruder in a strange man's room.

"That's a strange look, *cara mia*. What have you been up to?" he had asked in that unique Bostonian-Spanish accent of his.

"Been up to?" she repeated, almost in a daze. "I've been up to nothing." Then she smiled, waiting to wake up from the bad dream. She asked, "May I show you something, Alfredo?"

He had looked at her inquisitively, wondering. "Yes, sure.

What will you show me, my darling?''

She picked up the wallet, removing the photo. "This."

"Ah," he said, smiling, "my family. My wife and my two girls. One is eighteen, the other, Marilúz, is twenty." He returned the picture to its place under the mica. "They're both very lovely, although this picture doesn't do them justice," he said casually, as if describing one of several cars he owned.

"Then you have a wife. I see." She said it calmly.

"I thought you knew. Look, when you didn't mention it, neither did I. I thought, under these most . . . extraordinary and beautiful circumstances, darling, that it would have been in bad taste."

"Yes, it would've," she said offhandedly, walking to the dresser and picking up the wallet. She looked at the picture again. "Mm, yes, you're right, Alfredo; they're both very lovely, especially this one," she said, pointing to Marilúz. "I'd like to meet her someday. I could teach her a thing or two," she smiled, returning the wallet to the dresser.

Alfredo's anger was immediate, but he controlled himself. "Look, Flora, you're angry with me, and hurt. And now you're trying to hurt me. But I forbid you to talk that way about my daughter. Leave my family out of this!"

Flora ignored his comment. She was thinking of the woman in the picture, his wife. She had a beautiful and kind face, and suddenly Flora felt a wave of sympathy toward her. She felt a strong love for this woman whom she had never seen but who was her sister in pain and humiliation.

She looked at him, eyes cold and steely. "You told me that you loved me."

"Yes, and I do love you, Flora." He took her by the shoulders and tried to kiss her.

She turned her face away. "What about your wife? Do you love her, too?" Her eyes bored into his for an answer.

"Yes, of course I do. She's my wife, for God's sake!"

Her eyes penetrated deeper into his. He looked away in discomfort.

"Look at me, Alfredo. Will you tell her about me? And when she asks if you love me, will you answer, 'Yes, of course I do. She's my mistress, for God's sake!'?"

"Oh, Flora, my darling! We'll work this out, I promise!"

The slap sent him reeling from the force.

"That wasn't from me, it was from your wife, who is probably decent and therefore too good for you."

"Flora! Listen to me!" He took a step toward her.

Her Guccied toe landed on his testicles, and he went down. "That was from me, you bastard!"

She unfastened the aquamarine pendant and dropped it onto the table. She picked up her coat and her purse, and as she got to the door, she turned. "I just hope I didn't scramble your brains!"

Now, a year later, Flora Berganza finished her coffee and left some money on the waitress's tray. She picked up her coat and her briefcase and, head held high, waved at the waitress, who smiled shyly and in anticipation, watching the elegant signora as she wrapped herself in the fur and climbed into her Mercedes.

Flora turned the ignition key and the car purred into action. She was ready to do battle with that fat prick Langfeldt.

As she drove to the Montafon Valley, not too far from Zürich, she put on a tape of Renata Tebaldi. The first aria was "Un bel di." As she listened, she thought of one last thing in connection with the Cardozo affair: her trip to London, and the hospital. She had checked in one day and had walked out the next, as if nothing had happened. That's all she would've needed, she reminded herself—a little snot-nosed brat hanging on her, tying her down. Of course she had done the right thing—the only thing, she told herself again, as she had done so many times before. Tebaldi was still telling her joyously how B. F. Pinkerton would return one fine day . . . to her and to her baby . . . his baby. She rammed a gloved finger at the tape-release bar, cutting off the sob story, and found some loud rock music. She took a tissue and wiped mascara from her cheeks.

MONTAFON VALLEY, WESTERN AUSTRIA

THE PRESENT

Flora Berganza's Mercedes convertible pulled up smoothly to the black asphalt apron of the chalet. The sun still shone brightly, reflecting silver and gold off some of the glaciers sloping down the mountains surrounding the valley. It was cold as she stepped out of the car, a snappy invigorating cold, and her lungs welcomed it. She threw her heavy fur coat over her shoulders and went quickly up the steps to the front door. She pulled on the rope, ringing the alpine cowbells, and she spotted the Ferrari. She pictured its owner, Alfredo Cardozo, standing by the fire inside, a cup of tea with rum in his hand; handsome, urbane, yet emotionally naive; passionate but impractical; tender, sweet, but with a cruel and unconscionable prick! *Oh, well,* she thought, *that was long past.*

Joachim Conti opened the door and spoke to her in effusive Italian. *"Signora avvocatessa! Benvenuta! Favorisca entrare. Ha fatto buon viaggio?"*

"Como sempre, un viaggio meraviglioso, Signor Conti. Ma tanto freddo!" she said, shivering. "Is everyone here already?" she said, turning to English. "Am I the last to arrive, as usual?"

Conti smiled noncommittally. "Come, signora, inside, by the fire. I'll bring you some tea with rum. It will warm you, I'm sure." As always, Conti was efficient without servility. He made a good secretary to Langfeldt.

233

Conti led Flora Berganza into a spacious, comfortable parlor furnished in rustic alpine chairs with large pillows. Parquet floors with oriental rugs added subdued color. A floor-to-ceiling window allowed a breathtaking view of the valley and the surrounding mountains. Two men were admiring the view; others were sitting in front of a massive stone fireplace, cups or glasses in their hands.

Conti announced the lawyer from the Vatican, and the men greeted her one by one, shaking or kissing her hand. One kissed her hand a trace longer than customary—Cardozo.

"Flora, as usual, you're looking marvelous," Cardozo said, smiling an uncomfortable smile.

"Thank you, Alfredo. I see you haven't changed much, either." Her words had an icy ring. "Except perhaps for the few pounds you've put on," she added. "How is your lovely wife and family?"

He nodded, understanding her bitterness. What had happened between them could not continue, not because of his marriage but because of what was in her, he thought. Yet here she was, trying to saddle him with the "other woman" guilt. "They are well, thank you," he said. "May I get you something? A tea, perhaps?"

"Thank you, no. Signor Conti is bringing me a cup." She walked to the fireplace, brushing back an imaginary lock of hair. She felt that she might have been a little unkind to him with her acerbic remarks—cruel, in fact—but hadn't he been cruel with her? She lit a cigarette, her eyes softening a moment from their annealed blue. Cruel for giving her that tiny but marvelous feeling of being a woman, a woman in love? And for what? So that Señor Macho could add her to his list of conquests, in the column headed "Beautiful Dykes I Have Fucked"! Ah, they're all alike, she said to herself as she gazed into the flickering flames.

On the other side of the room Sir Anthony Duke poured himself a whiskey. He spoke to his friend, Karl-Ludwig Niesper. "Then you don't know either, Karl-Ludwig? I thought, what with you being the old boy's brother-in-law and all that, you might have the *pukka-gen* on this meeting," he said in an exaggerated British public school accent.

"He tells me no more than the rest of you, Anthony," said Niesper almost sadly. "It's always been like that, you know. But whatever brings us here, I do not have a good feeling about it. Not good at all."

Duke pointed with his glass. "Well, whatever it is, we'll know soon enough. There's that lovely young thing, Conti, about to fetch his boss."

The two men watched Joachim Conti knock at a door and let himself into a room. Georges Durand, L. R. DeVries, and Prince Yazid ibn al-Muhallab also watched Conti, also in nervous anticipation. They too would soon learn the purpose of the extraordinary meeting called by Heinz Langfeldt, Swiss banker.

Joachim Conti watched his employer run a brush through his white hair and matching beard. "They're all here now," said Conti. "Shall I call them in?"

"One moment, Kimi," Langfeldt said, "one last piece of business." He went to a desk and unlocked a drawer. He removed a small glass vial and tapped some snow-white powder onto a silver plate, making two thin lines. With a gold razor blade he narrowed the lines expertly. He took a thin glass tube and placed the end on one of the white lines, bringing the outfit to his face. Langfeldt ceremoniously inserted the end of the pipet into his nostril and sniffed sharply. The powder disappeared. He repeated the process with the other nostril. He gave a short cough and looked at Conti. *"Willst du?"* he offered, holding the bottle of high-grade cocaine.

"Vielen Dank," Conti smiled gratefully, *"nicht jetzt."*

Langfeldt nodded. He sniffed deeply again. "You may let them in now, Kimi."

Joachim Conti stood in front of his employer. "One tiny moment, please." He removed a handkerchief from Langfeldt's breast pocket. "Stick out your tongue," he ordered. He moistened the tip of the linen with Langfeldt's saliva and blotted a few white specks from his dark blue lapel. Conti replaced the handkerchief with an affectionate pat. *"So. Alles in Ordnung!"*

When the Montafon participants entered the boardroom, the huge bulk of Heinz Langfeldt, Doctor of Economics, was already in its seat at the middle of the coffin-shaped table. He greeted each person without rising.

In front of every chair was a pad and pencil; silver-sleeved vacuum bottles of hot coffee and tea and pitchers of water were neatly lined up. In another room, a shredder would destroy all notes plus the next few sheets on the pads.

Anticipation hung heavy in the air as the conferees took their seats and looked at their director.

"I will share with you today," Langfeldt began, "information that has the most far-reaching ramifications not only for the financial world but for the political complexes that make up this globe as we know it.

"We at this table represent—and as such, control—large shares of the wealth of this world, therefore, in many regards, also its destiny. I doubt whether any of you will argue against the premise that we find ourselves in the singular position of being the financial conscience of this planet." Langfeldt looked around under bushy eyebrows. "As such, we have from time to time been forced to do certain things—free from government interference, praise be God!—to maintain within our abilities that certain balance, that ever-so-delicate economic and political balance needed in this, the most precarious of ages—the nuclear age."

Anxious feet shifted under the table; cups clattered as they were refilled; cigarettes were lit.

Having waited patiently for the nervous activity to cease, Langfeldt continued. "Of course, I need not remind you that we've had a hand, shall we say, in installing or maintaining certain governments, as well as doing our part in toppling others, at times through the singular talents of 'Joseph.' This latter activity we've done through covert means, sometimes quite illegal means, as you know. But then, some nations—the U.S., the U.K., Israel, and France, to name just a few, not to mention the USSR—operate within their own secret structures, much the same as we, except that they do it as a self-serving thing, sometimes without concern for even their closest allies.

"We, on the other hand, do our part in maintaining world balance. Key word, that, *balance*. Not status quo, for the world is not static, but progressive and dynamic—frighteningly so. But there is a measure of balance. The Soviets come up with a new delivery system or with more horrendous weapons that can destroy the world in an even quicker fashion; the Americans counter with their own in an effort to achieve parity. An interesting word, *parity*. We use it in the stock market, don't we? They, however, use it to describe the balance of destructive capability. And yet arms races produce arms-limitation treaties. Again, balance. Precarious, but nonetheless manageable. Remember what we, those of us here, had to do to force the U.S. to come off its gold reserves in order to balance the dollar internationally. We achieved parity once again, and the world went on, didn't it?''

Langfeldt paused to light a huge Havana. He peered at the now-impatient faces of his group.

"But you didn't come here for a lecture on geopolitics. I ask you to bear with me; it's just an old man's way of setting the tone and of reminding you of our raison d'être. Having done that—I hope—I must now tell you that we here are faced with the most challenging threat to this balance of which I spoke. But first I must again digress from the main issue. Oh, I know, I've dropped one shoe, and now I dangle the other. Please be patient. I must tell you a rather remarkable story so that you may know what it is we're dealing with, for without that knowledge, it will be difficult for you to reach a solution to the problem at hand—if there is a solution.''

Langfeldt puffed on the cigar, knotting his brow.

"This story—true in every aspect, I promise you—has its beginning in wartime Germany. SS-General Heydrich, of whom you have all heard, and Reichsleiter Martin Bormann, also not a stranger to you, formulated a plan in early nineteen forty-one in which they would perpetuate Hitler's Reich after Hitler had lost the war. A Fourth Reich, if you will. They were clever, these two, and astute enough to recognize that the war, even as early as forty-one, just before the invasion of Russia, was lost. The scheme—called Operation Nibelung—needed two vital elements for success: secrecy from the ambitious and self-serving Nazi hierarchy, and funds—a huge amount of funds. Heydrich came up with an untapped source of those funds—West European Jewry. The Eastern Jews had already been bled by the SS for the SS treasury, used for the German war effort. It was thus an unavailable source for Operation Nibelung. Ah, but the west, with the German deportation policies not yet in full force, was ripe for the plucking. Heydrich could pluck this source ruthlessly through his instruments, the SS security service and the Gestapo. But he needed help from someone in a high position, someone who could do this without raising too much suspicion. Enter the subject of our story, a young war hero decorated by Hitler himself, SS-General von Bergdorf.''

It had grown dark. Joachim Conti turned on some lamps.

"Through cajolery and outright lies," Langfeldt went on, "Heydrich installed Bergdorf in Paris as chief of the SD, the SS security service. Bergdorf soon learned what was really happening to Jews, and predictably the young and idealistic nobleman—he was a Freiherr, a baron—began rescuing Jews from deportation to Auschwitz and the like, naturally at great personal risk."

Duke interrupted. "Why do you say *predictably*, Heinz?"

"Heydrich knew enough of Bergdorf's background—family name, German honor, and all that—to cunningly predict his attitude regarding the treatment of Jews," Langfeldt said, frowning at Duke. After a moment's pause, he added, "I shouldn't like, Tony, your interruption to dilute what I just said, to shift the focus of my point, which is, Bergdorf rescued Jews. He was a true hero, something rare in any day and age. Not only did he have his position to lose, his rank, and even his family honor for treason, but his life."

"Sorry, Heinz," Duke said uneasily, "it's just—"

Langfeldt waved away the apology. "True, it was only a handful of Jews at the beginning," he said, "but Bergdorf had committed the unpardonable, which was what Heydrich had been waiting for. The trap was sprung. However, the evil Heydrich 'spared' Bergdorf's life by sending him back to Paris to continue his activities, but at a price. Just imagine! Well, the Jewish Underground in France was ecstatic with the chance of having Jews being able to buy their way to freedom, to life, unlike their eastern cousins. Then the money rolled in, not only from French Jews but from English and even American Jews who wanted to do their part. Later, Heydrich was assassinated, as you all know, but Bormann, in his powerful position as Hitler's secretary, continued Operation Nibelung with Bergdorf. When the war ended, Bormann fled to Argentina and Bergdorf to Spain, where I helped him assume a new identity. At that point—"

"You helped him?" Cardozo asked, frowning his surprise. "You were involved in this?"

Langfeldt smoothed off a crown of ash from his cigar into his ashtray. "Yes, I was involved," he said slowly, almost defiantly. "From the very beginning, in fact. And with Heydrich. It was through my banks that the accounts were opened to receive the funds that Bergdorf was entrusted to control. But let's not make judgments," he said with a touch of indignation. "We're none of us so sterling, are we? If we were, we wouldn't be in this room. Some other time I'll entertain a discussion of·that subject, Alfredo. Meanwhile, please allow me to continue my narrative."

An awkward silence followed. It was a rare show of truculence from Langfeldt.

"I'll try to shorten the story," he continued. "As I said, Bormann went to Argentina and Bergdorf to Spain. Time went by; the money in Zürich was growing, thanks to wise investments. Bormann attempted to contact Bergdorf, but the latter seemed to have disappeared from the face of the earth. Well, what really happened was that Bergdorf, of course, resolved not to turn over one franc of that money to Bormann. Instead, he and some Germans and Austrians, all driven by guilt, formed an alliance from which at least to attempt to make amends—atonement, if you will—for their collective share of responsibility for which their country was guilty. They used those funds to help finance Israeli operations such as Hagganah, the Shai, Mossad, Wiesenthal, and so on, to help bring to justice those who were directly responsible for the Holocaust."

Georges Durand shook his head. "A most bizarre tale, Heinz," he said. "Most bizarre indeed!"

To which L.R. DeVries added, "Yeah, an' ah can hardly wait for him to tie it up with why we're here!"

"I will, L.R.," Langfeldt promised, "just be a little more patient. In order to make the story shorter, let's move along to when our hero, Bergdorf, and his new wife go to America.

"They settle in a small New England community, blending with the countryside, and disappear from Bormann's view altogether. Under his new identity Bergdorf enrolls in a university, earning a Ph.D. in Middle Eastern studies, later becoming a member of the faculty. All the while, his activities with his group—of which I am a member, incidentally—continue.

"Many years go by. Aside from some prearranged advertisements from Bormann in the *Frankfurter Allgemeine Zeitung* during the first year or so, nothing more is heard from him. We assumed that Bormann considered Bergdorf dead, along with his hopes of getting to the treasure in Zürich."

"But Heinz," Duke said, "didn't the West Germans find Bormann's corpse in Berlin? How could—" Suddenly, Duke realized the incongruity of his question when he considered that Langfeldt had said that Bormann fled with Bergdorf and went to ground in Argentina. "Sorry," Duke said, reddening. "Of course the answer is obvious."

Langfeldt smiled kindly. "You've answered your own question, Tony," he said. "I'll continue. Later, Bergdorf published a paper on the Middle Eastern crisis. The paper got the attention of Secretary of State Hetherington, who invited Bergdorf to Washington. The secretary was impressed by Bergdorf's quick mind and asked him to consult with the so-called Middle Eastern experts. Well, one thing led to another, and soon after, he was named by President Jensen as his Middle Eastern consultant. The actual title was"—Langfeldt paused for effect, well aware of the bombshell he would create the instant he uttered the words that everyone at the table had been waiting with bated breath for—"Special Adviser to the President . . . for Middle Eastern Affairs."

Alfredo Cardozo blinked several times. "Wait—you don't mean—" The sentence hung in the air.

"Peter Kramer?" offered Langfeldt. "Precisely!"

"Well ah'll be a son of a bitch!" L.R. DeVries said.

"As I said before," Durand said, "a most bizarre tale!"

Flora Berganza smirked. "*Ironic* is a more apt word, an aspect of which is lost on all of you."

"I doubt that we are here to find meaningless labels for this situation, avvocatessa," an offended Anthony Duke said. "The point is, how does this affect us? For instance, is there someone else who knows Kramer's identity?" *Bloody lesbian,* he thought, *I never did like her.*

"Of course someone else knows, you fool!" Berganza said. "Why else would we be here now? Am I not right, Heinz?"

"I'm afraid that is so, my dear Flora," Langfeldt sniffed. "Kramer has been discovered. Ironically, it was one of those French Jews whom he helped escape Nazi Europe who did so—one Henri Varèse, known today as Baruch Ben-David, prime minister of Israel."

"*Mein Gott!*" swore Karl-Ludwig Niesper.

"No, my dear Karl-Ludwig," Langfeldt said, "Ben-David is not the problem. I'll get to that in a mintue. Kramer's discovery was one of those quirks of fate, really, the details of which you would find most interesting but of no consequence to these discussions.

Anyway, it happened. And when it did, they both recognized the need to inform President Jensen of this new and extraordinary development, in view of Kramer's involvement with the Arab-Israeli peace treaty. After all, Kramer is the architect, the moving force behind the treaty. The whole world knows that. But it wouldn't do for Ben-David to have this intelligence and not inform the President, would it? If Baruch Ben-David discovered Kramer, couldn't someone else? A rare chance after all these years, but still possible. And without a proper and believable cover story, the President would be embarrassed and the peace treaty in danger.

"However, the problem was not insurmountable," Langfeldt went on. "Kramer's identity could be kept secret until after the signing of the treaty with, if needed, some plausible explanation. But the pact would be history with its obvious benefits. Don't forget, history recognizes the end results, not the paths to them. Ben-David was certainly prepared to keep the great secret from even his most trusted colleagues in his government. Apart from having worked so hard for the treaty, which would mean peace at last for his troubled land, he and Kramer have established a strong friendship during the many months of negotiations. And over and above all that, he is deeply grateful to Kramer. Don't forget, he owes his life to him."

"Well, then, where's the bloody problem?" Duke demanded.

"The 'bloody problem,' as you put it, Tony, is in the White House," Langfeldt said, "in the form of President Simon Bolivar Jensen. You see, when Kramer informed him of his past, Jensen's reaction was extraordinary, to say the least. It was violent, that of an impetuous, impulsive man." Langfeldt paused to relight his cigar. All eyes were on him as he puffed blue clouds of smoke. "He went into a veritable rage, I understand. He felt betrayed. He swore that he would expose Kramer, that he would turn him in to the French and West German authorities. Remember, Bergdorf, as far as the French are concerned, was the SS-general who signed the deportation orders for Jews, thus making him a war criminal. Naturally, he's never been tried for that, but he is still on their wanted list. Anyway, getting back to Jensen, he fired Kramer on the spot, treaty or no treaty."

"But how do you explain such a reaction?" Durand asked.

"I'll get to that in a moment, Georges. Jensen told Ben-David on the phone that not only was his honor at stake but that of his presidency and that he was bound by constitutional oath to preserve that honor. Treaty or no, he could not swallow having a Nazi on his staff, he said. Ben-David must have realized that Jensen had taken leave of his senses and out of desperation in order to buy time to come up with something—anything!—he asked Jensen for a moratorium of two weeks, just long enough to assure his party's winning the election in Israel. This Jensen understood; he's a politician, after all. He agreed to the two weeks, and with that, Ben-David has assumed the heavy task of finding a way to save the situation—and perhaps the world.

"Now, to answer your question, Georges, as to Jensen's reaction in face of the consequences: Obviously the President is deranged. He's gone over the brink. He is a full-blown paranoid-schizophrenic. Strong words, I know, but my source is unimpeachable. It's none other than the personal physician to the President, Admiral Rufus K. Smith. It seems that after his meeting with Kramer, Jensen told Smith what had happened and what he was prepared to do. Mind you, this all came out in an emotional catharsis with his doctor. Then the reasons for his behavior emerged. According to Smith, they have to do with his wartime experiences. The details, which Smith related to me, are unimportant to this discussion but important insofar as the tortured mind and psyche of Simon Jensen are concerned, because these experiences have been transmogrified into a pathological hatred of Germans. And Peter Kramer is not only a German, but in Jensen's warped vision he is his rival, according to Smith. He has shown signs of jealousy of him because of Kramer's obvious success in the peace process. Whatever the psychological implications of all this, we must come up with a solution to the crisis it poses."

A dark and gloomy pall had descended on the boardroom. Each participant mulled over the devastating problem in his or her mind, each reluctant to bridge the gap of silence that had come up, for they all knew that a simple solution was not to be found. If it were, Langfeldt would have offered it. And he had not.

Cardozo was the first to speak. "To make sure we understand what is happening, let's bring this down to simple terms: As I see it, the Arab-Israeli accord is in danger of collapse because of the rash behavior of one man, President Jensen, who has threatened to expose Peter Kramer. Is the treaty so delicate that it wouldn't stand up under its own strength? After all, it means peace, doesn't it?"

Prince Yazid spoke for the first time. "No. If the treaty is not signed—if it does not go into force—the frail strings that now bind the Arab nations that have agreed to its terms will surely break. Khadaffi will seize the opportunity to create chaos among his Arab brothers, and the PLO will use the absence of a formal peace to go again on the rampage. Every fanatic of al Fatah will grant himself license to pick up a bomb and kill Jewish women and children just to prevent such a treaty in the future. I know my Arab brethren. Hussein wavers toward the strength of the moment, which by then would be the PLO." He looked at Cardozo. "No treaty is catastrophic."

Karl-Ludwig Niesper spoke up. "I should like to add my view on the subject. No doubt the Soviets will take advantage of the instability of the situation. Remember, the hard-liners in the Kremlin have never wanted détente between Israel and the Arab nations; it would reduce their influence in the Persian Gulf. This is especially alarming in view of the strong signal put out by the U.S. to the Soviets by deploying the Sixth Fleet in the Arabian Sea, which the USSR takes as an overt warning against any incursion in that area. As a result, Soviet subs of the Nevsky-two class are snorkeling around now with their nuclear warheads at the ready, just in case. I know this from reliable sources."

"By that, Herr Niesper, you mean your sources in the Politburo of the USSR?" asked a smiling Georges Durand.

"Whatever my sources, such a scenario could spell political disaster—and perhaps nuclear confrontation."

Another period of silence prevailed, each person knowing that whatever the solution to the crisis, it would have to be a radical one—the most radical yet for that radical-conservative organization.

Langfeldt sat like a Buddha, fingers entwined across his ample vest, waiting for an answer. It had never been easy in the past to decree an assassination if that was the only way, he mused. He continued to wait, hearing the breathing, the swallowing. He thought he could even hear the sweat erupting from pores.

Flora Berganza lifted her glass and drank mineral water. Suddenly, she brought the glass down onto the table with a crash. "All right! If somebody has to say it, then I will! He must die! Jensen must be killed!" Her eyes were cold and angry.

Langfeldt appeared relieved. "With those words, gentlemen, Avvocatessa Berganza has opened discussions on the subject. Does anyone have a different view as to how the problem can be solved?" He looked around at the faces.

L.R. DeVries said, "You want my two cents worth?"

"Yes, L.R.," Langfeldt said. "Although I will understand if you don't agree with the solution propounded."

"Ah agree with the little lady," DeVries drawled. "It don't seem to me like we got much choice. He's got to go."

Cardozo sprang up. "Is that the way you Texans always settle problems? 'He's got to go'?" It was an obvious reference to the Kennedy assassination.

"Now, ah told you, sonny, we never had nothin' to do with that, though ah gotta admit ah didn't shed no tears."

Langfeldt interposed. "Gentlemen, gentlemen, let's discuss ideas, not provoke controversy. Alfredo, if you have another suggestion, we'd like to hear it. Consider however, the time we have left—and the consequences."

"I think the whole thing is an abomination!" Cardozo shouted. "Again, we sit here deciding who lives or dies! It's un-Christian!" He shot an angry look at Flora Berganza, the financial representative of world Catholicism. She lit a cigarette, ignoring his glare.

"Of course it is, Alfredo," said Langfeldt soothingly. "Un-Christian and immoral. But I put it to you again—is there any other solution?"

Cardozo looked down at his pad. "No." Then he added quickly, "But surely there must be another way, there must be something. . . ." His pleading voice trailed away as he looked around for support. None came.

"My dear fellow," Langfeldt said with feeling, "if one of us could wave a magic wand that would cure the President's tortured mind, we would do it. But that's only in fairy tales, isn't it? And this is not the Brothers Grimm."

Georges Durand raised his pencil. "Dr. Langfeldt, one other factor, undiscussed but obvious, is that with a popular and charismatic U.S. President assassinated, the peace accord in the Middle East would be a fait accompli. That is, any party who may now be wavering would certainly agree to the pact, is that not so?"

"I quite agree," Langfeldt said, adding, "a martyred president who gave up his life for the cause of peace. He will get the Nobel Peace Prize!"

There was silence at the table as each mulled over the terrible irony of Langfeldt's words.

"Now," Langfeldt resumed, "may we vote on the motion? Namely: Faced with this crisis, do we retain the services of 'Joseph' to eliminate the President of the United States? May I have your votes, starting with Signora Berganza?"

Six firm yes votes were cast. One whispered "Yes . . ." from Cardozo was given.

Langfeldt said, "I'll make it unanimous. I will cable 'Joseph' immediately. I take it, as in the other instances when 'Joseph' was retained, you will leave the matter of the fee to my discretion? Very well." As an afterthought he added, "Of course, one must consider the magnitude of the assignment; the fee must be proportionate. On the other hand, the chances of him collecting the second half of the fee are in question, considering the risk to his person." His chest heaved a huge sigh as he realized he had brought the issue of a presidential killing down to practicalities.

With a mixture of emotion in which there was a touch of self-loathing, Langfeldt pulled hard on a desk drawer and withdrew a black velvet bag with a drawstring. "We'll now draw for the red marble," he said in bad humor. "Prince Yazid, please begin the drawing," he said, tossing the bag.

The Arab opened the bag just wide enough for his hand. He probed around the agate and velvet to see if it would be he who would make the actual arrangements with the assassin. Voting was one thing, but actually coming face to face with "Joseph," meeting him, looking into his killer's eyes, seeing the finger that would deal death—that was something else. He withdrew his fist and opened it, revealing a white marble. His face relaxed as he passed the bag ceremoniously to Georges Durand, international lawyer and investment adviser, whose offices in the Place Vendôme, Paris, received clients with names like Rico "Gin-Gin" Ginervino and Aldo "The Weasel" de Correggio. He drew a white marble.

Flora Berganza impatiently took the bag and quickly produced a white agate. She showed some disappointment.

Alfredo Cardozo, Harvard-educated Mexican economist, took a deep breath and reached into the bag. He knew what the rest of them knew—that he would draw the red marble.

A loud silence permeated the atmosphere. He looked at the marble, an ordinary one just like those he used to play with as a boy. Nothing special. Just red agate—the color of blood. He cleared his throat and smiled ironically. "Now I know how Pontius Pilate felt," he said.

All eyes were downcast except Flora Berganza's. They met his in an icy gaze, one eyebrow arched.

"Alfredo," Langfeldt said almost in a whisper, "if you feel you can't . . ." The question hung in the air.

"Just give me my instructions," Cardozo said. He stared at Flora Berganza, who dropped her eyes.

"Thank you, my friend," Langfeldt said, moved. "Please wait for me in Zürich at the usual place. I'll see you tonight; there's precious little time to lose. And now, all of you, thank you. We'll meet again, afterward. Now, if there are no further questions, I bid you farewell."

They all left. No good-byes, none of the usual handshakes. They just left.

"JOSEPH"

He pushed the Arabian the last few yards. He dismounted, walking the horse the rest of the way to the top of Mount Mars. It was hot in the afternoon sun of a Santa Ana, the weather phenomenon of high-pressure ridges that funneled winds through the canyons at increasing speeds, heating by compression as they neared the coast. The Santa Ana pushed the sea breeze back and scorched everything in its path.

Cline was thirsty as he trudged up the hill. He spotted a large oak; he would go on the few extra yards and take his water there in the shade, and the small self-denial would make the water taste sweeter and, somehow, wetter.

His mood that day was anxious, his reflexes taut, his mind alert to things beyond the bucolic tranquillity of the ranch. It was due to the telegram Fernando had brought from Cambria that morning while on his daily shopping trip. The wire directed Cline to go to New York and meet with a certain Dr. Cardozo. The wire was signed L for Langfeldt, his exclusive employer. Cline knew that it was to be an assignment.

He drank water and admired once more the magnificent view of the California coastline, where the rugged Santa Lucia range rolls and slopes to its end. Big Sur was fifty miles up the winding Cabrillo Highway to the north and San Luis Obispo, some sixty miles south.

His nearest neighbor was the ghost of William Randolph Hearst roaming his castle a few miles to the south. Cline looked down on the road; of the many cars that drove by, most of them were tourists in search of the overwhelming castle and its Spanish church altars, French tapestries, English armor, German medieval weaponry, and Italian tables covered with Irish linens and decorated with middle-American catsup flasks. He stared at the traffic, thinking how many thousand toured that abomination each year, coming within a few miles of his ranch without ever violating his privacy.

Cline scanned the coastline with powerful binoculars. It was a clear day, devoid of the usual haze, thanks to the Santa Ana. He could see the light tower on Cape San Martin, several miles to the north. The lighthouse reminded him of another much older one on the Adriatic coast near Dubrovnik, the ancient walled city in the Yugoslavian province of Dalmatia. It was there that he had last performed as ''Joseph'' for the Montafon Group. A slightly cooler wind caressed his moist skin. He drank more water, remembering the Dalmatian coast.

The weather had been hot that day too. An early summer sun beat down on him as he waited on the big rock for President Anthony Bashande of the new African nation, the Democratic People's Republic of Congo-M'Bala. Cline's position on the rock had been above the narrow, winding road leading to Dubrovnik, just a few miles away. He had buried the plastique device in the dirt of the little viewpoint off the road, a viewpoint just large enough to accommodate one large car. The place offered an incomparable view of the walled city, and Bashande's chauffeur would stop there. Cline knew they would stop there because he had studied his assignment, the people involved, and their idiosyncrasies.

He blotted beads of perspiration from his lip as he gazed at the shore and the pounding surf. He thought he could hear the haunting cries of the gulls, but he knew he was too far away for that and he heard them in his mind. He had heard the gulls that day near Dubrovnik as he waited for the African sightseer. Finally, a flash of sunlight had reflected in his eyes. A black Mercedes was negotiating a sharp turn in the road. They were coming. He took a tiny transmitter from his knapsack and flipped a toggle-switch to activate the electromagnet on the device.

A few seconds later a luxurious sedan glided to a stop at the precise spot. The magnetic device fastened itself to the undercarriage of the car like a hungry leech, the sound it made muffled by a thick envelope of foam rubber.

Four men in shirtsleeves emerged. Three of them, Africans in dark trousers, were stretching like bored panthers; the fourth, white, with pistol in a shoulder holster, strolled away lighting a cigarette. "Joseph" watched as the tourists pointed in awe at the view of Dubrovnik. After a while, the chauffeur–security policeman ground out his cigarette and indicated something with sign language, evoking laughter from the others. Apparently the men understood the mime and walked a few feet down the slope of the promontory. All three proceeded to irrigate one of the old cypruses conveniently growing there, seemingly for the relief of the traveler. "Jospeh" watched them shake and dance and zip up their trousers. He smiled, remembering a poem from an Army latrine wall that proclaimed: "No matter how hard you shake and dance, the last drop always falls down your pants." They got back into the Mercedes and backed out onto the highway in the direction of Dubrovnik. "Joseph" watched intently, timing, measuring. Then he pressed a button.

The explosion was no more than a dull thud.

The front of the big car bounced fifteen or twenty inches from the force of the explosion, enough to send it out of control, veering to the right against an embankment, then caroming violently across the narrow road. It smashed through the low rock guardrail and plunged almost straight down, more than three hundred feet onto the rocks below. He listened for what seemed an eternity for the impact. He even tried to discern a scream from some throat or another of the doomed quartet, but he heard nothing. Finally the sound of metal being crushed, and the occasional thin clinks of fragments bouncing on rock. Then only the sounds of the gulls, the haunting cries being carried by the wind.

"Joseph" climbed down the backside of the boulder and walked the few yards to his rented Porche 911-S parked off the road in a birch grove. Unhurriedly, he drove up the coast to Split, to blend in with the throngs of Western European tourists.

That evening, "Joseph" watched the televised report in the lobby of his luxury resort hotel. He didn't have to understand Serbo-Croatian to determine that the report of the incident, as it was given out by the militia, was being treated simply as a "tragic accident."

Cline stared at the horizon. By now, the rays of the afternoon sun were playing polychromatic scales on the ripples of sea, causing powerful kaleidoscopic effects. He closed his eyes to the almost hypnotic feeling and judged once again that the kill had been easy—but it had been difficult planning that had made it easy. That was why he was the best in what he did. He had been told once by Langfeldt that he had an intellectual approach to the business of killing. Cline agreed.

He had reasoned long ago that any living person, no matter how well protected, was vulnerable to attack by deadly force in one way or another. The trick was to do away with that individual in such a way that it wouldn't cost the operator his own life after the fact. An attack was possible by just about anyone who made the decision and then stuck to the framework of the plan long enough. It would be just a matter of time—and opportunity. It always came. But to do it and get away safely—that's what separated the professional from the zealot, the nut who was willing to trade his life for the target's. However, he reasoned further that if any given person was well enough protected, then the attack should be considered suicidal. Lee Harvey Oswald, if he was the lone assassin of John F. Kennedy—and Cline doubted it very strongly—had been lucky enough to get as far as he did, due to a totally incompetent Dallas Police Department. The real killers, Cline felt, had gotten cleanly away and were still functioning. Whether the operation went off as planned, he had no way of knowing, but what was certain was that they had done it—and got away. Cline agreed with Langfeldt that the Kennedy assassination had been planned by a group of extreme right-wingers, and performed by professionals who set Oswald up, deluding him with a well-executed but sham FBI- and CIA-rigged operation. But, as with all good operations, aside from the planners the world would never know.

Thus Cline concluded that thinking and deductive ability—the intellect—were the most important resources of the operator, or the "mechanic," as some called assassins-for-hire. Everything else was a tool, to be kept in the best of condition, of course—physical ability, equipment, disguises, and so on—but tools nonetheless.

"Joseph" had terminated six people in his career: four politicians, one financial "heavy," and one religious-political fanatic. In every case he had studied their complete backgrounds, including psychological profiles of the target and his top lieutenants. Thus he was able to anticipate, judge, and execute—a successful methodology.

Bashande was a case in point. Cline knew from studying reports of Africa watchers that Bashande, the newly elected president of a small African nation, was playing both ends—the West and the Soviets—against the middle. The West had helped him topple his old government in a coup; then, instead of remaining pro-West, he began putting out feelers to the Eastern Bloc nations, including Yugoslavia.

Assuming the alias of Joseph Slater from *The Daily Worker*, Cline interviewed key government officials in Belgrade, learning that President Tito's attitude toward Bashande was that he was an opportunistic upstart, long on ambition and short on Socialist ideology. When Bashande pushed for a state visit to Yugoslavia, Tito rolled out the pink, not red, carpet, treating Bashande's visit with polite coolness. He did, however, grant him VIP status, Cline learned, by assigning the African and his small party a car and driver, who would provide a brief tour of his country.

During his journalistic snooping, Cline learned of a series of photographs taken by Tito himself—he was a fair photographer. One of those photos was of Dubrovnik from a promontory on the highway from Titograd, one of the sites scheduled for Bashande's visit. Cline knew the place from former visits. He also knew that Tito would want Bashande and his party to get their view of Dubrovnik from exactly that viewpoint. Although he would not embrace the African's pushy visit, Tito would still be a gracious host.

And so it happened.

Paul Cline drained the last of the water from the canteen and noticed a bank of fog materializing offshore. The temperature had dropped several degrees, signaling the death of the Santa Ana. He looked at the setting sun, now a large wedge of cheddar, bulging at the sides as it flattened itself on the horizon of distorting haze. The sea was once again a dull gray-green. Soon the cool marine air would invade the warm land and there would be a sea of fog.

Cline whistled shrilly, bringing the grazing Arabian on the run. He mounted. The horse instinctively headed home.

A bright moon had risen in the still-light eastern skies, and his horse seemed to follow that moon as he deftly eluded the abundant chaparral and boulders. Cline had a final thought about the Yugoslavian operation: there had never been any references by the Tito government to the incident other than calling it an accident. Yet any trained investigator would have easily spotted the alien materials of the bomb. The very presence of the mysterious Joseph Slater would alone have been enough to launch some kind of investigation, in which a simple check with *The Daily Worker* would have prompted some interesting questions. But there had been no mention of either factor. Cline concluded that to have provided the M'Balese president with only token security in the form of one single guard, the chauffeur, would have been embarrassing to Tito. As it was, *Pravda* and *Isvestia* hinted strongly that the death of the "dynamic ray of hope for Africa" would not produce tears of sorrow in Comrade Tito. The result was the same, Cline reasoned—he had got the job done through his intellect.

A while later Cline was home, handing the horse over to Lorenzo for grooming and a supper of oats. He walked by Tomasa's kitchen, savoring the delicious aromas of her cooking. He showered to the music of a Bach Brandenburg concerto. He put on fresh denims and went to his study where Tomasa waited with a tall glass of iced *agua de tamarindo*, a fresh-tasting astringent ade made from root bulbs. The scent of Tomasa lingered in his nostrils as she left the room. It was a smell of clean skin and hair. He took a long swallow of the ade, thinking of her walk, the natural sway to her hips inherited from many generations of female ancestors who walked in that same gait and pace—head high, shoulders back and squared, hips swaying for balance while carrying the large water jugs on their heads, small feet stepping lightly, one in front of the other, in a straight line. These were the women of the Tarascan nation of the state of Michoacán in southwestern Mexico. Tomasa was full-blooded Tarascan.

He had looked at her in her *falda*, the floor-length skirt she always wore at home, and he imagined her legs under it. He had seen her legs only twice. Once when he picked her up at the airport in Los Angeles, she had been wearing a lady's suit and high heels. He had seen her legs then, and they were slim and well-shaped, with small ankles. The other time he had seen her legs was that day at the stream.

Her hips were small, rounded, tapering to a tiny waist. Her bosom—what he could see of it under her linen blouse—was small. Her skin was smooth and appeared to be completely hairless. It was velvety and the color of pale walnuts. Her long black hair was usually worn in a thick braid; sometimes she wore it loose, depending on her mood. The moods, he learned, were variable, the barometer was Cline's comings and goings.

Paul Cline had met Tomasa Juana Inéz de Jesús four years before while visiting a spa southwest of Mexico City. She was a chambermaid, and her brothers, Lorenzo and Fernando, were gardeners. Cline had been struck by her exotic beauty; almond-shaped black eyes of oriental quality; white, even teeth that broke easily into a fresh, almost childlike grin. One day she approached Cline for his help in finding her brother Lorenzo a job in the United States. Their combined wages at the hotel, she explained, were not enough to support their large family and to send two other brothers to college. They had lived on a small ranch all their lives, and yes, she had answered him, they knew and loved horses, and yes of course she knew how to cook and tend house. He hired all three of them for his newly acquired ranch near Cambria, California. Now, four years later, they were the only family he had—or wished to have.

Cline sipped his drink. He was hungry for Tomasa's fine cooking; he was even hungrier for her. But Tomasa was a *señorita*, her brothers had pointed out at the very beginning. As his Spanish improved, he learned what that meant: virgin. It wasn't just a polite form of address. It meant "untouched." *Señorita* meant that he, Señor Pablo, should know that and respect it. And he did.

Tomasa came back to the study. "*Señor Pablo*, your supper is on the table," she said in Spanish.

"*Gracias* Tomasa," he said. He spoke Spanish comfortably now, since taking crash courses, and learning, refining it from them.

He sat down to a bowl of *fidéo*, a thin soup of vermicelli with slices of banana floating in it. He sprinkled some sharp *salsa* in the soup, a sauce made from ingredients grown in Tomasa's garden: *tomatillo*, a green, acrid tomato; green chiles; and fresh cilantro. She brought to the table a large, colorful platter of butterflied beef tenderloin that she grilled over coals, accompanied by Spanish rice and bowls of *frijoles guizados*, pinto beans cooked with a pork bone in an earthen pot and simmered for hours to a creamy consistency. For bread, a wicker basket of steaming tortillas—corncakes just off the griddle. Tomasa made them herself, grinding the corn into meal on her *metate*, an ancient stone appliance used by her ancestors for hundreds of years before Columbus. She insisted on using the *metate*, along with the other invaluable kitchen tool, the *molcajete*, a stone mortar and pestle, disdaining the modern mixers and blenders provided by Cline.

That evening Tomasa wore her hair in a *chongo*, a huge bun of shiny black twists. That was her most severe hairdo, and it stated her bad mood eloquently; she knew Don Pablo would be leaving again.

The three men spoke in low voices at the table. Tomasa kept to herself, quietly picking at her rice. The brothers smiled at Cline in tacit acknowledgment of her mood.

Cline said to her, "I'll return in a few days. Shall I bring you something from my trip?"

"I have no needs," Tomasa whispered.

There was a long pause. Tamarindo water was drunk simultaneously.

"I'll bring you a shawl," Cline said.

Tomasa looked up at him self-consciously, then lowered her eyes. "As you wish," she said.

Fernando coughed, sending a signal to his brother. They both got up, bidding a good night.

Cline looked at Tomasa. He knew that what he was feeling was not lust anymore but a strong feeling for her as a woman, his woman. Maybe after this assignment, maybe then would be the time for long-range planning.

"Tomasa," he said to her tenderly, "soon . . . you and I . . ." The words remained unspoken.

Paul Cline got up and went to his room.

In the morning he drove to Los Angeles to catch a plane to New York. "Joseph" had a meeting with a certain Cardozo.

WASHINGTON, D.C.

THE PRESENT

Jimmy Ryan drank coffee in one of the rear booths of an all-night coffee shop. He drank it black, no sugar. He preferred it sweet, but he had been having it black, no sugar, since his days in the Marine Corps, when he noticed other guys having it that way. A movie in which John Wayne ordered his coffee black, no sugar, convinced him that that would be another step on his journey to being a he-man, the ultimate "macho."

He clamped a Lucky Strike—a short one, unfiltered—between his incisors and lit it, striking the match with his thumb along the emery strip without removing the paper match. He performed this exercise with one hand and did it expertly now, having paid the price of learning with several burns. He exhaled through his teeth in a wide grimace, which was part of the total ritual with which he smoked. He had consciously worked on these mannerisms as attention-getters; now they came automatically. He brought his cigarette to his lips, holding it between thumb and index finger, the remaining fingers held as if he were cupping the cigarette. It wouldn't do for Jimmy Ryan to hold his Lucky as most did, between their index and middle fingers; that would be doing it like a pansy.

Ryan looked around the almost-deserted coffee shop. No one had come in during the last half hour. Todd apparently wasn't going to show up. It wouldn't be the first time that Jimmy Ryan had been stood up by George Washington Todd, leader of the American Nationalist Socialist Party. *It's okay*, thought Ryan. *There must be a good reason.*

For Jimmy Ryan, Todd could do no wrong, especially since Todd had named him Gauleiter for Washington, D.C. It was an important position in the party and the most important position ever held by Jimmy Ryan, warehouseman. True, he was expected to do some unpleasant things, like recruiting, but as soon as the party became stronger, that would all change. And the party *would* grow as long as pinko Jew-lovers like Simon Jensen continued to run the country into the ground. Oh, how he hated Jensen! Especially since naming that nigger to the Supreme Court and putting that kike bastard in as secretary of labor! Well, you just wait, Mr. Jensen!

A waitress was replenishing the salt shakers across the aisle from him. She leaned over, showing her ample bottom.

"Hey, that's a mighty fine ass you got there, Consuela," Ryan said, grinning.

Consuela shot back an insult in Puerto Rican Spanish.

"Ah, come on," Ryan said, "don't get uptight. What if I said you got a *ugly* ass, would you like that better?"

Consuela softened a bit. "Look, Jimmy, you always treat me like a hooker or somethin'. I like you to treat me like a lady. Anyway," she laughed, "I know I got a nice ass!"

Jimmy Ryan laughed with her. Then in a more serious tone, he said, "Hey, Consuela, you know, I really like you. I always thought you was beautiful." He spoke in a soft Tennessee drawl. "I been meanin' to ask you . . . uh, well, I'm kinda shy, you know, an' uh . . ."

Consuela helped him. "You want to take me out, Jimmy?" It came out "Joo wanna take me out, Yeemee?"

"Yeah, I sure would, Consuela," he said shyly.

"Okay, Jimmy. I get off at two. I meet you here. But remember, you treat me like a lady, okay?"

Jimmy Ryan, who failed in most things he attempted, felt a slight swelling in his crotch and hoped he would not fail that night with Consuela. He was five feet seven, but all of a sudden he felt taller.

He picked her up at two promptly. There was a slight mist in the night air.

"Where you gonna take me, Jimmy?" she asked, bundling her coat.

"Uh, how 'bout a movie?"

"At this time? You crazy, Jimmy! Come on, we'll go to my place for a nice cup of cocoa. You like cocoa, Jimmy?"

Consuela García was known as a pushover by some. "You got round heels," her brother used to say of her. She liked to think of herself as a good woman who was always for the underdog, the orphans, the downtrodden, and occasionally the shy males. Her considerable physical endowments attracted many men; her fulminating temperament quickly discouraged anyone who didn't behave like a gentleman with her. In Jimmy Ryan she saw a shy little boy in need of a soft and motherly breast on which he could rest his Brylcreemed head.

"Take off your shoes, Jimmy," Consuela said. "Get comfy. I'll make us some nice hot cocoa. I like it made with milk and a little cinnamon—the old-fashioned way—don't you?"

"I ain't never had it that way, honey," Jimmy Ryan said, "but if you like it, I like it."

Jimmy Ryan removed his engineer's boots and sat on the Hollywood bed that served as Consuela's couch in the tiny studio apartment. He watched her prepare the cocoa. There was no question in his mind that he would bed down with her that night, but he knew he mustn't be overly aggressive. He hoped his last remark—the tone in which he had said it—wouldn't be taken with double meaning; such things could slam the door on any plans he might have. Oh, he could take her anyway—rape her, if he wanted to—but he didn't think he would have to. He perceived she was attracted to him because of his shyness. *Okay, let her think it,* he said to himself. But he knew different. Deep down he knew it was because of his inadequacies, his inner weakness. He fought the notion; it was a hard notion for him ever to admit. He would let her mother him, if that's what it took to get her into the sack.

He watched her as she bounced back into the living room with the steaming cups. She had a peculiar way of walking heavily that made her breasts and buttocks shimmy and jog. Like other males, Jimmy Ryan noticed—and squirmed a little. He wouldn't be caught dead mixin' with spics, but Consuela was different.

She sat next to him and tucked her shapely legs under her as she stirred her cocoa. "Tell me about you, Jimmy," she said, licking her spoon. "What kind of home you come from?"

He told her he was born and raised in a small farming town in western Tennessee, the youngest of three brothers and two sisters. He was the shortest of the three boys, which allowed for substantial protective mothering on his sisters' part. He had gone to church regularly, as did most folks from the Bible Belt, including his prematurely old mother. His poppa didn't, liking instead to sit on the porch drinking "a little red-eye and chawin' a plug" as he read the Sunday funnies.

His poppa, a big strapping man who liked to be called J.J., seemed to take pleasure in beating Jimmy "regular" every Sunday afternoon, when the red-eye bottle was empty. J.J. would sit around in his sleeveless undershirt and his Sears-bought pants, Jimmy Ryan remembered, and for no reason he would say to him, "Get your ass in the woodshed, sonny, 'cause it's time to make a man outta yew," and would calmly thrash him with a heavy belt until his "ass begged him to stop." It was routine; nobody ever even noticed, he said.

Jimmy Ryan told Conseula that maybe his poppa felt cheated in him being so little, compared to his brothers and his poppa, who were built like bears, he said with pride. The boys had their own bedroom while his poppa used to make him sleep with the "other" girls.

"Anyway," he said without bitterness, "I quit school and joined the Marines by forging my momma's name. That's when I was sixteen. Well, no question about it, the Marines made a man outta me, and you know, that proved my poppa right."

At Camp Pendleton, California, Jimmy Ryan "got in a fight with a nigger and stuck him with a knife. The nigger bled to death, but I proved it was self-defense, and all I got was six months' hard labor and a Special Circumstances discharge."

"Why did you stick the niggerboy, Jimmy?" Consuela asked softly, concerned. "Did you want to kill him?"

"Hell, I didn't wanna kill 'im. Hell, no. He was a uppity nigger," Jimmy Ryan explained. "Always comin' at me 'bout how short I was. He came at me with a knife and said somethin' real bad 'bout my mother. I just took the knife away from him and stuck 'im before he stuck me, that's all." He looked at her for a reaction.

He lied. Jimmy Ryan had been the aggressor. He had provoked

the fight. The black recruit had walked away calling him a honkey, and Jimmy Ryan had reacted violently with a knife he carried in his boot. *Can you imagine,* he had thought to himself as he stood watching the other man bleed to death from a stomach wound, *a nigger talkin' that way to a white man? Back home we'da lynched him sure!*

Consuela looked at him with pity. "People always treated you no good, huh, Jimmy?"

He looked down at the carpet. "I guess so," he said.

She took his hand. He played out the sympathy.

After a few moments, he looked at her. "Consuela, uh, I got this here real strong feelin' and, uh, do you mind if . . . if I kiss you?"

He was one of the downtrodden. "Okay," she said with alacrity.

He gave her a short kiss. Then he looked at her with innocence and kissed her longer. She responded. He moved his hand up her ribcage to her breast and stroked it lightly. Even though she didn't resist the caress, he broke the embrace suddenly. "I'm sorry, honey, I didn't mean it," he said, feigning self-disgust. "I guess I'm just used to being around cheap girls, you know, but you're real decent, not like most a the girls I know."

She was touched by his words and actions. She took his hand and held it. "That's nice, Jimmy. Most men I know are not so considerate, either."

The mist had now turned to rain. He decided to make his move. "Well, I better get goin'," he said, standing.

"Look," she said, "it's raining. You'll get wet."

"Aw, it's awright. I only live 'bout a mile from here. Anyway, I can get a cab," he said, looking out the window.

"You won't find a cab in this part of town, Jimmy, and you'll get robbed, prob'ly."

"Hell, Consuela, I can take care of myself!"

"No," she said firmly. "You stay here tonight."

"I don't wanna put you out none, honey. Besides," he said, pointing to the couch, "you only got that one couch, ain't you? Where will I sleep?"

She looked at him shyly. "It makes into a big bed. You can sleep with me." Then she added sternly, "But no hanky-panky, no monkey business, okay?" She laughed.

Jimmy Ryan laughed too, but mostly in relief. "Okay, honey, no monkey business!" he said, the familiar swelling in his crotch returning.

They undressed, she down to her bra and panties, he to his boxer shorts. They went to bed, turning out the light.

"How 'bout a kiss good night?" Jimmy Ryan asked.

"No, Jimmy. I tol' you, no hanky-panky." She turned away from him. "Goo'night."

He lay awake, feeling the warmth emanating from her body, and he smelled her perfume. He imagined what was going to happen, which gave him a large erection. *This is no chickenshit little hard-on,* he thought. *This is a monster!*

He waited. After several minutes he heard her breathe deeply, as though asleep. He made his first move. Rolling over, as though turning in his sleep, he put his arm around her bare belly, just the way he used to do it with his sisters back home. That action didn't elicit a response from Consuela; she appeared to be deeply asleep. He decided on a bolder course, with the idea that if she awakened and objected, he could always plead that he had been asleep. No great harm. On the other hand, if she were pretending to be asleep all along and that was her way of playing her "morality" game, he reasoned, well, then he could also play the game.

His hand inched up to the breast nearest him. He held it there for a while. Then he began to massage it. He could feel her heartbeat under his kneading fingers, a sure sign that she was playing the game. *Goddamn!* he said to himself, *just like my sister Cora Lee!*

Slowly, but not as slowly as before, he brought his hand around to her back and carefully unsnapped her brassière. She groaned in sleepy protest, making undistinguishable sounds, and turned on her back. Another sign! His fingers crept up her shoulder to her strap. He pulled it down, exposing her full breast. He fondled it for a few minutes, breathing laboredly. He made a tent of the top sheet and lowered his face against her ample bosom. *Jesus, what tits!* he said to himself as his lips touched the large orb. Her nipple became turgid— *Oh, yeah, she wants it!*—and his oral fondling became more intense. Still no sign of protest. Even though he was sure she was not only awake but intensely aware, enjoying, wanting, he still went through with the charade. Just in case, he reasoned. It would hurt him to be rejected—especially now.

His hand went down her smooth belly, under her panties. This would be the tip-off, he ventured. He massaged her pelvis for a while, but when he tried to introduce his finger into her vagina, she moaned and removed his hand with hers, placing it on her belly. It remained there for what seemed an eternity. His breathing was still labored, short puffs coming in shaky, washboard pants. *Goddamn,* he thought, *what if she's not playin'?* He panicked momentarily until he realized that his very stiff penis was hard against her thigh and she had made no move to separate herself from it. Once more infused with courage, his hand went back under her panties. That time she was quiet as his fingers found the entrance to her vagina. It was warm . . . and moist! *Hot damn!* he breathed, *she ain't playin'—she wants it!*

He massaged her clitoris, all pretenses aside now, probing deeply while sucking her nipple. She began moaning. That was the signal to remove her panties, which he did laboriously since she still was not openly cooperating. Finally he managed the naked legs open as he pushed his shorts down his legs, freeing them with his toes. His excitement was at a terrible peak as he got his feet tangled in the top sheet, which had been freed by the struggle, and his knees were banging against hers, but she still didn't move; it was going to be up to him. At last he mounted her, trying to guide his rock-hard penis into her passive body.

Still inert, Consuela didn't help. He jabbed between her legs, but he failed to find the opening. He poked more, but either he was too high or too low. His penis, having no directional or tactile discrimination, stabbed blindly, but that only brought him closer to his climax. The more he tried to control himself, the more he felt the surge of prostatic juices along the shaft of his mindless organ. With audible whines now, Jimmy Ryan prayed, "Oh, Lord, please don't do this to me!" But the Lord, if He was in control, as Jimmy Ryan thought He was, did do it to him. With a haunting, wailing "Aaaahhh!" he ejaculated copiously onto Consuela's pelvis and thighs.

He lay heavily on her and on his semen, not knowing what to do or what to think. He had blown it again, he said to himself.

Again! "Son of a bitch!" he mumbled, "I fuckin' blown it again! Fuck! Shit!"

Consuela came to life at last, whether out of pity for him or because she wanted to move his dead weight off her. She rolled him over, put her arms around his neck, and kissed him with tenderness, knowing what she had put him through. She got up and went to the bathroom. A minute later she came back with some wash towels and cleaned him.

"Jimmy," she said softly, caringly, "please don't feel so bad; these things happen. There will be other times, and you see how nice you make love to me. Please don't—"

He turned away. "Lemme alone," he whimpered.

Consuela looked at his pimply back in the light from the bathroom. She was deeply touched, and at the same time she was ashamed of herself for having put his machismo to the test by her "morality" game. She would give him another chance, she vowed. Hadn't it been her fault by not helping him get his *pinga* into her? she reasoned. *"Pobrecito mi Yeemee!"* she lamented to herself.

About an hour later she awoke to the sounds of soft sobs. She turned Jimmy Ryan around and began kissing him softly, then passionately, reaching down and taking his soft penis in her hand. She massaged it and stroked it, bringing some blood and life into it. Then she did something that she had in the past refrained from doing with others: she took his penis in her mouth. She was determined to let him have his second chance. Jimmy Ryan quickly hardened, and this time, she mounted him.

For the first time, he was aware of a new sexuality, a new virility. A second time around! He couldn't believe it. He had it in him all along, he said to himself, and it was only a matter of fucking the right woman! *Oh, thank you, Lord! That's what you were tryin' to tell me! It was there all along!* He bucked violently, letting out a whoop.

He rolled her over, getting out of her. "Look at this, baby!" He held his wet penis like a club, wagging it furiously in front of her wide eyes. "Not bad for a li'l sawed-off polecat like me, huh?" He grabbed her feet and lifted them high, spreading her legs. "Look out, honey, "I'm acomin' in!" He rammed with all his might.

"Jimmy!" Consuela said, "you hurtin' me. *¡Ay, pero mira qué bárbaro!"* she complained.

"Oh, yeah, it hurts, huh, baby?" he said, the excitement growing. "Well, I'm gonna hurt you more!"

"*Sí, precioso,* hurt me more—I love it!"

He thrust and pushed and twisted and jabbed. Ten minutes, fifteen minutes. Then he found he couldn't finish. Consuela, on the other hand, had had several orgasms and was begging him to let her rest. But to Jimmy Ryan, it was like riding a bucking bronco without fear of being thrown, so he kept pumping. Now convinced of his manhood, he wished he could finish; his back was starting to ache, and he was tired.

Then out of nowhere, he started to have fantastic and whimsical images of beating up his brothers and his father. Then of hitting his Führer, George Washington Todd, over the head with his clublike erection. His mind drifted to his most hated enemy. He imagined the handsome, blued-eyed face of Simon B. Jensen—traitor. Over the face was superimposed the cross hairs of the telescope of a high-powered rifle. Jimmy Ryan saw his own finger squeeze the trigger. No recoil, just the smooth exit of the steel projectile as it powered its way to the head of that man. He saw the actual impact in slow motion as it destroyed the head.

At that instant, Jimmy Ryan experienced the longest and most profound orgasm of his life.

WASHINGTON, D.C.

THE PRESENT

Peter Kramer walked into his office in the basement of the Executive Office Building and picked up his messages. One of them was from a Mr. Adam.

Kramer called in his secretary. "This message from Mr. Adam—what did he say?"

"Just what I wrote down, Mr. Kramer. That he would be in touch. When I asked him what was the nature of his business with you, he said it was personal. When I asked him when he would be calling back, he said just to say he would be in touch. He was very vague."

"What did he sound like? Young? Old? Any accent?"

"He had a German accent, I think. And he sounded like an older gentleman. Do you know him, sir?"

Kramer pursed his lips. "Know him? No, I don't think so," he said absently. "However, if he calls again, put the call through, please."

"Yes, sir."

Kramer sat back in his chair. "So," he said to himself, "he lives after all."

Two days later, Kramer was in Mexico City to attend the conference of Foreign Ministers of Developing Nations. There was a message for him from Mr. Adam.

MEXICO CITY

THE PRESENT

The mammoth stone face of Tlaloc, the god of rains, stood on his pedestal inside the great forest of Chapultepéc. Like a scowling sentry, he guarded that which was not there to guard anymore, and he seemed to know that the people no longer invoked him. Tlaloc, god of lightning and thunder, could be a wrathful god; but that day, that year, that period in his universe in which he still presided, the period called *nahuiquiauitl*, the Four-Rain, he felt benevolent. And he washed the air and the trees again, knowing that by the next sun the air and the trees and mankind would again be soiled.

And behind Tlaloc was the Cerro del Chapulín, the Sacred Hill of the Grasshopper, where the high priests of Tenochtitlán worshipped the Aztec deities in the days when the trees were green and healthy, and there was much *maís* and *chilli* and abundant *chocolatl* and *jitomatl* and *ahuacatl*. Those were good days, Tlaloc seemed to remember.

And then, Quetzalcóatl ordered many temples raised in his honor, and they came from afar to marvel at the bounty of the Tenochas, and their enemies feared them rightly.

And then others came. From across the Great Water others came, and they had golden hair and pale eyes, and the chiefs did not walk but rode upon great snorting, noble beasts. And they had sticks that made deadly fire and axes sharper and stronger than the obsidian axes of the Tenochas. And soon the great *teocallis* of the Lord Quetzalcóatl were destroyed, and new temples were built to honor the god of the Pale-Eyes. But the Pale-Eyes were poor, for they worshipped only one god, not like the rich Tenochas, who boasted of many gods. But that one god must have been very powerful, Tlaloc seemed to think, because he enslaved all the other gods and presided alone, and the Tenochas became poor.

And then the Tenochas and others became as one with the Pale-Eyes, and they too honored the powerful pagan god, and they gave many children to his service.

And then, still during the period of the Third Sun, a great chief of the Pale-Eyes came from across the Great Water, and a big *teocalli*—one almost as big as the Lord Quetzalcóatl's *teocalli*—was raised for him on the Cerro del Chapulín. And when this great chief learned that his temple was on the Sacred Hill of the Grasshopper, he feared offending the gods of Tenochtitlán, and he ordered a likeness of Chapulín to be placed in the court of honor of the big temple's garden.

And that was a good thing for the Tenochas who remained loyal to the true gods, for through Chapulín the spirits came forth and invoked the Lord Huitzilopochtli, the god of war, and the Lord Huehueteótl, the god of fire. And then, after these gods had done their terrible work, the Lord Quetzalcóatl would again preside in the Four-Sun.

Now, still during the third Sun, Tlaloc seemed to gaze on what was once the empire of the Aztecs, and he seemed to hear sounds coming from what were once the causeways and canals of the great city, sounds blaring in the soft night, sounds he did not understand or like.

"Chapulín," Tlaloc seemed to call to the Grasshopper on the Hill, "now that we have seen, do you invoke Huitzilopochtli and Huehueteótl?"

"No, Tlaloc."

"Then whom do you invoke, Chapulín?"

"I invoke Centéotl and Xochipilli," said the Grasshopper, wise counselor to the gods.

"But they are the gods of Maize and Flowers," protested Tlaloc. "It is time for the Four-Sun."

"Not yet. You must be patient."

"Then, what shall I do, Chapulín?"

"You must make rain, Tlaloc. Make rain."

Peter Kramer crossed the elegant Paséo de la Reforma, deftly avoiding the heavy traffic that polluted the air that Tlaloc had washed the night before. He knew his way around the center of the city from prior visits, and he chose to walk the mile or so from his hotel to the designated meeting place, the outer plaza of the Museum of Anthropology, under the brooding stone face of the rain god.

The gun, a snub-nosed .38, thumped heavily against his thigh from within the pocket of his raincoat. He put his hand in the pocket, holding the pistol, and he felt his fingers sweat against the steel. Kramer had "borrowed" the gun from Gerb, the big, affable security agent assigned to him on all his travels. Kramer had convinced Gerb that he wanted to be alone that evening, and it was only when Kramer had winked confidentially, intimating a romantic rendezvous, that Gerb had acceded.

Obviously, he thought to himself as he walked down the Reforma, he could not return the pistol afterward. He would have to dispose of it. A trash barrel would do; dropping it through a sewer grate where it would rust for years would do even better.

Killing Bormann—he knew it would not be easy. He had to think of it as destroying a dangerous animal. Still, it would not be easy. Even in the war he had not killed another man in cold blood. He had only commanded the tanks; he didn't know what it would be like actually to point a pistol at another and fire a bullet that would take his life. Yet he didn't know of another way. Since getting the messages from Mr. Adam, the code name only Bormann would use, he knew he must kill him, if indeed it was him, and the only way to find out was to see for himself.

He wished that Bormann had died somewhere along the line. His age alone, together with the rigors of evading his persuers, would seem to have dictated it. But Kramer had to face the reality that Bormann was probably alive—a deadly threat not only to him but to the peace treaty.

He came to the great circus of Diana the Huntress, where several broad avenues met for a moment. He crossed over toward the park entrance, watching in wonderment the raging torrent of cars involved in the perpetual sport of vehicular brinkmanship. He paused a few moments to catch his breath in the rarefied air and looked up at the splendidly sculpted bronze figure of Diana, poised naked, bowstring drawn back revealing muscular breasts, one knee atop a stone, her target waiting in perpetuity for her arrow. Kramer enjoyed the brief respite until he again felt the pistol in his pocket. Heavily, he headed to the meeting place.

Except for Tlaloc, the plaza was deserted. Kramer thought he could feel Bormann's presence—behind some shrub, perhaps; watching, waiting.

Kramer waited. As he did, he reflected on the terrible fact that twice, in the space of weeks, he had been reached by figures out of the past: first Baruch Ben-David and now Bormann, each instance presenting its own dangers. Why had he gotten involved to begin with? he demanded of himself for the thousandth time. He had been warned by Langfeldt that the risks were too great. It had been a calculated risk; so much time had gone by; he simply could not go through life playing the 'what if' game. And yet he wondered if Erika had been right when she had accused him of doing it out of a need to nurture his ego. Self-aggrandizement was the term she had so bitterly used. He had refuted her accusation by pointing out that had he remained simply an observer in another time, mightn't things be different today? She had wept and admitted she was being selfish. Afraid, but selfish. *"Ach, meine Erika,"* he whispered to himself in the language by which they made love, *"Ich liebe dich so!"*

A man in a raincoat approached. He wore a hat and a glint of light reflected off his eyeglasses. The man was shorter than he remembered Bormann being, and much thinner. He walked past Kramer, casting a casual glance. Kramer resumed his wait.

He wondered again if Erika's words had been the truth. Had it been a monumental ego excursion for him? A guarantee of historical immortality one way or another? Perhaps. But of one thing he was sure: he was the least qualified to make those judgments. Objectivity is lost in self-examination. Besides, he reminded himself, the wisdom of a decision rests on the events that are yet to happen and how those events sift through the sieve of probability, of chance. As it had been with Ben-David. The improbable.

A voice sounded behind Kramer, startling him out of his musings. He looked in the direction of the voice, which spoke Spanish.

It was the man in the raincoat. He was asking directions. Kramer smiled and shrugged ignorance.

The man asked, *"Bitte, Sprechen Sie Deutsch?"*

Kramer answered instinctively. *"Ja, natürlich."* He looked closer at the man. He wasn't sure. He didn't look like Bormann.

"Also, Sie sind Herr Krämer," the man said.

"Ja, ich bin Krämer." So, Bormann, it is *you.*

Kramer couldn't believe what he was seeing. An old man, to be sure; that was not surprising. But withered and sickly—*old* old—and shrunken from the bull-like body he remembered. Even his head looked shriveled under the hat. As his eyes searched into Kramer's from behind grotesquely thick lenses, Kramer saw the pale, wan visage of death.

The apparition spoke, still in German. "The years have been good to you, Freiherr von Bergdorf."

"I cannot say the same for you," Kramer said, realizing that the words came out too frank, too brutal. He immediately felt pity for him. "I'm sorry. I meant that obviously you are ill."

"There is no need to apologize for the truth," Bormann said, smiling. "Yes, I'm a candidate for the medical textbooks. I have diabetes, which has almost blinded me, and hardening of the arteries, which doesn't help the other. I don't drink anymore, but my liver—oh, well, who wants to hear all that! Shall we walk?" he asked, pointing in the direction of the vast and empty Chapultepéc Park.

They walked in silence next to a bridle path. Bormann spoke first. "I thought you were dead," he said, smiling.

Kramer dodged the lead. Instead he asked, "How did you find me, after all these years?"

"I wasn't sure until tonight," Bormann said, laughing nervously. "I had seen pictures of you in the papers and journals about your work with the peace treaty. I thought it could be you, but I wasn't sure, of course." He spoke casually, with no hint of complaint or demand of accountability. "Then," he continued, *"Time* magazine, or some other—I can't be sure—published a short biography of this Kramer along with a picture of his wife, Erika. It started to add up. I called you at your office in Washington, hoping to hear your voice, but you know what happened there. Anyway, now that we are here in this lovely park talking like old friends, now I'm sure."

"Excuse me, but how can it be that you recognized my wife?" Kramer said. "You never knew her. After my first wife, Trudi, died in an air raid, Erika and I were married in Spain after the war. How could you have known?"

"Ah, but I knew *of* her," Bormann said. "Our mutual friend, Heydrich, had a dossier on her—along with one on you, of course—and her photo was in it. I recognized her from that picture, and her name. I still have a memory, despite this sickly body."

"Heydrich had a dossier on Erika?" Kramer said, "But he died in forty-two. He didn't even know she existed."

"There's a bench," Bormann said. "Do you mind if we rest a bit? This altitude gets to me. You were saying, what? That Heydrich didn't know she existed?" He chuckled softly. "You knew Reini, my dear Bergdorf. He made it his business to know all. He even knew certain things about me that I still wonder today how he found out. Anyway, it seems that a dossier was compiled on you and your Erika by a certain SS-major of the Bistritz Gestapo office, with information provided by a member of your own household staff." He looked at Kramer for a reaction.

"My household staff?"

"Your butler, to be precise," Bormann said. "Curiously enough, an Irishman who was a Gestapo informer, conveniently living in your house."

"Halloran?" A name out of the past. Instead of feeling anger at the treachery, Kramer felt nostalgia for a moment. "What could Halloran possibly have reported to the Gestapo about Erika?"

"Heydrich showed me the report where Erika was supposed to have made some anti-Reich statements during a lavish dinner one evening at your home. According to the report, she was being critical of our Jewish policies."

"Oh, that. She was only trying to provoke her imbecile brother-in-law," Kramer said, suddenly defensive. There was something in the way Bormann had accused, something in the tone of his voice that inflected a threat—like in the old days. Kramer forgot for a moment that there was no more Gestapo to worry about, and his defensive reaction angered him. Then he added, "Besides, she was right in saying what she did, wouldn't you say so in retrospect?"

Bormann shrugged. "My dear Bergdorf, who am I to judge your wife after all these years? That's all in the past."

Damn it, Kramer thought, *that's not what I meant!* "I was not asking you to judge my wife. And its not in the past—it's history now. It's a part of German history loaded with shame, and they won't let us forget it!"

"You're right, Bergdorf," Bormann said with passion, "they won't let us forget. Like in the first war—they make us pay and pay. Not only bankrupting us, they make us pay with our national dignity, our sense of honor. And still it happens. Even after so many years, they still rub our noses in it!"

Kramer sighed in exasperation. "You misunderstand me again, Bormann. I meant to say that they should not let us forget, that we *should* bear the shame of our past. Our crimes against humanity must be remembered."

Bormann peered at Kramer. He smiled patronizingly. "My dear fellow, you've been rubbing elbows with the Zionists for too long. They've proselytized you, it seems, and now you're mouthing their platitudes. You know, Bergdorf, the whole thing is quite a bore!"

Why am I debating him? Kramer asked himself. *Kill him and be done with it!* But instead he asked, "Genocide is a bore? The Holocaust is a platitude?"

"Ah, yes, that word again. The favorite word of our Jewish friends."

"You know, Bormann, despite the time you've had to reflect, you seem to have absolutely no remorse."

Bormann shot him an angry look. "You're right. I have no remorse. The word is *regret*. Regret that we made mistakes that cost us the war. Regret that in losing the war Germany was put into the position of groveling before the world, beating its chest in contrition for having tried to make that world a better place."

"By killing Jews?" Kramer asked in disbelief.

"Back to the Jews? Very well," Bormann said, "let's deal with that question if you insist. Come, let's walk some more; I'll give you a new insight into history.

"Viewed in its proper perspective," he continued as they walked, "Germany's war against the Jews was just that, a war. True, there were some excesses that should not have taken place, but I'll get into that later. Still, it was a war, and they were the enemy."

"The enemy?" Kramer demanded. "Defenseless women and children? They were the enemy?"

"Ah, not so defenseless. Certainly, they had no conventional weapons. But through their subversion, through their economic stranglehold, they presented a formidable organized front. Don't forget, Bergdorf, that the Jew has always been an alien within the societies in which he assimilates himself—even in the Communist societies—and his allegiance has never been to the country that has given him a home. No, his allegiance is to Talmudic Law, a law that preaches the doctrines of the so-called chosen people, and to the Protocols of the Elders of Zion, which preaches the . . . the insidious political and economic domination of the world. So you see, my dear Bergdorf, we knew our enemy. *'Wer kennt den Jude, kennt den Teufel!'* " He quoted an anti-Semitic adage: "He who knows the Jew, knows the devil!"

"That's rubbish, Bormann. The contributions made by Jews to their countries—to mankind itself—are immeasurable," Kramer said. He realized that he was still arguing with him as in a debating society. *Kill him now!* he screamed to himself.

"Contributions to their countries?" Bormann chuckled. "How naive you show yourself to be! Einstein, a German Jew; Meitner and her nephew, Otto Frisch, Austrian Jews." He counted off the names on his fingers. "Von Neumann, Szilard, and Teller, Hungarian Jews; Fermi, an Italian married to a Jew, but really a Jew at heart. Do you know what this loyal group had in common?"

"Yes, of course," Kramer said, "'but—"

"Yes, of course,' Bormann mimicked. "They were responsible for nuclear weaponry, these loyal contributors to their countries! Yet not one of them remained in his own nation: they went to America, where they could make their loyal contribution to international Zionism!"

"Hold on, Bormann," Kramer said. "You conveniently didn't mention that each of those countries you referred to was part of the Axis, the anti-Semitic Axis. Those people left to escape persecution."

Bormann shook his head impatiently. "It is obvious that you're blind to many things," he said. "Please let me continue. In nineteen thirty-three, when Hitler was appointed chancellor and the National Socialists took control of the Reichstag, the Jewish tentacles were strangling our economy. The Jews had control of the press, the cinema, the professions, education, banking, finance, and international commerce, and they were well entrenched in national politics. Five hundred thousand German Jews—less than one percent of our population, just imagine!—were in control of more than twenty percent of our assets and a good part of the government! It was an unprecedented national disaster. Hitler simply had to take radical action, as he promised. This action resulted, of course, in the Nuremberg Laws of nineteen thirty-six—an answer to a do-or-die situation. There came, at last, some semblance of order in our institutions, and the Jew was left holding the dirty end of the stick for a change. Of course, many Jews chose to emigrate. Frankly, that was the idea behind Nuremberg—take back what the Jews stole, and they would leave Germany. We would be free of them, like being free of a plague. The plan worked until the outbreak of the war."

"You didn't mention *Kristallnacht* in your dissertation," Kramer said. "Or did you again conveniently forget?"

"Your interruptions are trying my patience, Bergdorf," Bormann said. "The so-called *Kristallnacht* was a single, isolated event; it took place on one night only. It was overemphasized by the Jewish international press, but it did little harm to Jews in Germany. A few broken windows, some books burned; some SA rowdies went on a binge, you might say. But now, in retrospect, I would say it was a byproduct of the people's celebration of being free at last of the Jewish stranglehold.

"From a propaganda viewpoint, it was damaging to the Reich. But please note that despite what the press played up, there were never any orders for *Kristallnacht* from the Reich Chancellery. It started as a result of one of Dr. Goebbels's inflammatory radio speeches, and it just got a little out of hand. Which brings me to my point, Bergdorf: Apart from the Nuremberg Laws, which were an emergency measure designed for national recovery, there was never any official policy directed at Jews. True, the Jew had been stripped of his German citizenship and prohibited from holding public office and the like, but he was allowed to exist."

"How generous!" Kramer said with contempt.

Bormann ignored the remark and went on. "Bergdorf, I don't expect you to believe it, but the Führer was not an anti-Semite. Yes, yes; I anticipate what you're going to say, but just listen for once. He wasn't anti-Semitic on a personal level. For your information, he was quite fond of his mother's doctor, who was Jewish. In fact, I remember once when he and I were walking in the woods at the Berghof, he told me, swearing me to secrecy, that of late he was having recurrent dreams about a girl with whom he had been in love—a Jewish girl, please note—when he was a young art student in Linz. His eyes filled with tears as he talked about her, Bergdorf, how her family, rich Linzer Jews, had refused to let her marry him because he was a struggling artist whose only sin was to be a victim of poverty. Although he didn't lash out at her parents or at Jews in general, it gave me food for thought. I concluded that that had been the turning point, that the rejection of him by the girl's parents made it possible for him to use Jews as convenient scapegoats and effective antagonists in his campaign to cement the leadership of the Reich.''

Kramer was finding Bormann's intimate portrait of his late mentor fascinating. He had never heard personal views of such an enigma. He let him go on.

"You know, Bergdorf, Hitler was strictly a political animal during that time. He was a very astute and assiduous student of human nature, especially of the German mentality, the *Volkgeist*.'' Bormann used a term liberally mentioned by Hitler during his speeches—*Volkgeist*, literally, "the spirit of the people." "He knew that everyone he addressed in the beer halls, and later in the packed stadiums, each one had his own 'good Jew,' be it his doctor, lawyer, grocer, or neighbor. But he also knew that, collectively, Jews were resented, even hated. Therefore, with unprecedented boldness, he campaigned on the Jewish issue, and he received almost unanimous support. We were, after all, in the midst of a devastating economic crisis, and he was convinced that international Jewry was to blame. He took that message to the people, and they gave him carte blanche to remedy the situation and get Germany back on her feet. Thus Nuremberg. Thus the genius of Adolf Hitler.

"Now, what is of interest in this," he continued, "is that no one said, 'Lock up the Jews.' You'll notice, Bergdorf, that the only concentration camp at that time was Dachau, and that was only for political dissenters and social criminals, not for Jews. Hitler did not say, 'Lock up the Jews.' He was too busy getting the country back on its feet, and the Jewish question seemed to be taking care of itself. It was not until the outbreak of war, when the Jews in the occupied territories became a problem, that he ordered that something be done. He called in Göring, as head of the Four-Year Plan, and laid the problem at his feet, saying, 'I want a solution to the Jewish problem.' He said it in that vague way of his, expecting one to read his mind, to find a final solution. Well, Göring passed the order along to Heydrich, and Heydrich interpreted Hitler's words in his own way. You know that fellow had an obsessive hatred of Jews; perhaps that's where the whole unfortunate business stemmed from. Anyway, the eager SS chaps went to work—Heydrich, Müller, Pohl, Eichmann, the lot. Working in total secrecy, they put the huge machinery of the autonomous SS in full gear. They recruited their own dedicated, hardworking loyalists to build the camps."

"And gas chambers," Kramer said softly, "don't forget the gas chambers . . . and the ovens."

"Well, yes; but that came later. At first they were using the prisoners as laborers for the war effort."

"Slave laborers, Bormann!"

"All right, slave laborers, if you wish! They certainly didn't have them on the payroll. It was war, and one used every resource possible. Later on, as I was saying, when the Jews were no longer a viable resource, they were"—Bormann searched for the word—"processed."

"What charming euphemisms you use," Kramer said with sarcasm. " 'Viable resource,' 'processed.' You mean killed, murdered . . . gassed. Exterminated!"

Bormann paused for a few moments. Then he added quickly, "But we in the party, in the chancellery, we didn't know about all that until much later. It was all the secret business of the SS."

"Oh, please, Herr Reichsleiter! You mean to tell me Hitler didn't know of the camps? Treblinka, Sobibor? The model camp at Auschwitz?"

"We didn't know, Bergdorf. Not then. Hitler was too busy running the war. He was thoroughly engrossed in the military conduct of the war after he took that job away from the generals. He didn't even have a moment to perform as a man with Fräulein Braun, you know. The only time he heard about Jews was during the Warsaw ghetto uprising, and that he treated as just another military operation by having it leveled to the ground. Oh, later on he learned of the camps, but that was toward the end. I remember one day a statistical report happened to reach his desk—it was from Auschwitz, when it was fully operational. The figure was for a ten-day period. I don't know how many thousands, but it was a very large amount. Well, Hitler was shocked, I tell you. I could see it in his eyes; the way he shook his head and asked, 'So many in ten days?' He was disturbed by the whole thing, I could see.''

"He was disturbed!" Kramer said. "Perhaps they should erect a monument to him in Tel Aviv for all his compassion!"

Bormann waved off the angry interruption and continued. "Hitler said to me, 'Bormann, history is going to judge me very harshly for the resolve I have shown in fighting this war that was forced on us, but I must be firm. Some of the measures we have taken may be extreme, but if it comes down to whether a Jew eats or a German soldier eats, there can be no doubt.' That's what he said, Bergdorf."

"Meaning what?"

"Meaning that he didn't know what the SS was doing with Jews—at least not until later, when it was too late. . . ." Bormann's words trailed off. He seemed to realize the folly of them. It would never have been too late to stop what was being done. He put up a hand as if warding off Kramer's rebuttal. "Wait! Wait! What I'm saying is that when he did find out, he accepted the responsibility. Genocide wasn't a policy of National Socialism. The killings occurred because the administrators were—were cursed by their German sense of duty and, in competing with one another, things got out of hand."

Kramer felt a deep loathing for the once-mighty master of intrigue and duplicity now reduced to making feeble attempts at justifying the most heinous crimes in the history of man. Suddenly he represented not just a dangerous beast that must be destroyed but an evil being that it would be a pleasure to kill. But he hesitated, needing even more passionate hatred to build up for the cold-blooded act of homicide. He knew it would come soon.

"It's remarkable how you can reduce it all to such simple and even mitigating terms, Bormann. Hitler didn't know, therefore he was blameless. Those who carried out the genocide were simply following their 'German sense of duty,' therefore were also blameless. Who then shall we blame? Don't tell me; I know—naturally, the Jews themselves! It was all their fault for just being there."

Bormann threw up his hands in frustration. "You keep twisting things around! Why don't you mention the atrocities of the other side? Like the firebombing of Dresden, where one hundred thousand civilians were roasted by the RAF? Or the Americans, when they dropped two, not just one, but two atomic bombs on Japan, also incinerating women and children? The Germans didn't have a patent on war crimes, Bergdorf. The British invented the concentration camps in the Boer wars, not the Germans. Don't interrupt, damn you! Tell me the Americans didn't have their own *Lebensraum* program? They slaughtered the Indians with the help of the U.S. cavalry, they decimated their crops, they made their buffalo herds extinct, they burned their villages and raped their women! They brought disease—smallpox and other plagues. Tell me that wasn't genocide, Bergdorf! But they were victors, weren't they, and it's the victors who write history."

"Not so anymore," Kramer said, holding the gun tightly in his pocket. "Out of the rubble now come the voices of the victims, Bormann. They are writing history now, for the first time, and the world has listened, and the world is saying 'Never again!' "

Bormann smirked. "Never again? What about My Lai and your Lieutenant Calley and your Captain Medina? They went on an orgy of killing Vietnamese women and children because they considered them—what's that interesting American word?—gooks, subhumans. All in the name of—what's that pat little phrase? Ah, yes, freedom, flag, and country."

"You make a point," Kramer conceded. "However, what you fail to see, Bormann, is that no system is perfect, and never shall be as long as the architect of the system is man, because man himself is imperfect. The vast difference in the cases you mentioned is that our system is highly vulnerable in a free and open society with a free press, a vulnerability tested and corrected by open dissent and free elections. Those cases you referred to were received with horror, as you well know, and the dissent of a free people proved to be the strongest deterrent for preventing its recurrence. All men have evil in them—and they are frequently motivated by that evil—but the good in men sooner or later rises to the front and dominates their will and their acts."

Bormann exploded. "Where do you get such bilge? It's the other way around, you fool! Man *profanes* whatever is good in him under the guise of liberalism and democratic precepts. He deludes himself with utopian drivel, thinking that all men are created equal. Well, they are not! Since the beginning of time only the fittest have survived, only the fittest have had the right to survive. It's through the patent failure of the democracies that we find ourselves struggling for survival, with food supplies dwindling and resources depleting, because *out there*"—Bormann pointed an angry finger—"is a danger far worse than hydrogen bombs. Out there is the real peril to this globe: the subhumans! Breeding others like themselves and multiplying like roaches, infesting the world like a plague. *Our* food they eat, *our* air they breathe, *our* space they occupy, *our* children they infect with their genes. The subhumans, Bergdorf, whose only contribution is to add to the census."

He was in a froth, hands flailing in the quiet air of Chapultepéc Park. "The Aryan race as we know it is on the brink of extinction, mongrelized by these vermin. And unless we do something about it now, we won't be able to stop the atavistic cycle we're in, and before long, we'll be swinging from the trees again." He grabbed Kramer by the arm. "We are at the eleventh hour, Bergdorf!"

Kramer had listened in near disbelief. Here was not a fugitive clinging to life through self-preservation, exiled by circumstance, running, eluding. No, this was deeply committed man. He was concerned about the world, as was Hitler about Germany, with the same extreme solutions to the problems. "And just what do you propose?" he asked.

"The answer to that is far too complex. Suffice it to say that there is a new feeling, a new *wave*," Bormann said, liking the phrase. "Yes, a new wave of young, dynamic, and clear-headed people; doers, activists involved not in choice phrases and rhetoric but in action. It's a new wave that is steeling itself for the upcoming battle against the usurpers of our Aryan culture. These are people who can see what is happening before their very eyes, thanks to electronics. They see Bolshevism raising its ugly head everywhere. They see Jewish Zionist Bolshevism taking over. They see Israel virtually controlling the foreign policy of the United States, like the tail wagging the dog. They see the inroad made by Jews in your adopted country, Bergdorf, in your President's cabinet, in the Congress, sitting on your Supreme Court—places of immense influence and power from which they can insinuate their doctrines of Zionism. It is these same Jews who want to see the extinction of the Aryan race so that they can rule with impunity. Well, this new vibrant surge," he said, pounding his fist into his palm, "is prepared to do battle now! This very moment. They, the young and strong, will do it. And I will guide them!"

"How?"

Bormann smiled. Suddenly he was trembling with self-induced excitement, caught up in his own anticipatory fervor. Suddenly his eyes were devoid of antagonism. "I see that you're becoming interested. It takes you back, doesn't it, to the days when you wore the SS runes. But this time it will be even more glorious because we'll do it not through force of arms but through force of will, through the power of the ballot—legally. We've already begun our fight by placing some important people in governments worldwide, either by election or by appointment. In the United States we've made some substantial inroads, and some of us sit in the Senate and in the House—some even chairing important committees. Soon others will be running for office with our financial help. Which brings me to the reason I'm here, Bergdorf: I want you to join us. I can give you undreamed-of power." He took Kramer's sleeve. "Join me, Bergdorf. But first you must turn over the money to me. You *do* have it, don't you? The money?" He smiled nervously, tugging on Kramer's sleeve.

"Yes, I have the money," Kramer said easily. It was what he had been waiting for—to tell him of the money. The money would bring things to their culmination.

"Ah, that's so good to hear you say! You know, all that I brought from Germany is gone now. I couldn't invest one cent for fear there would be a slip-up." He spoke in a conspiratorial voice. "I had to give money to so many of the others, and there was only so much to go around. The Peróns were so greedy; they took more than half of what came on the U-boats. Tell me, my dear Bergdorf, how much . . . how much is there?"

"I don't really know," Kramer said. "It changes every day. I made some smart moves with it, so it has grown quite a bit."

"Oh! Yes, Bergdorf, I knew you would do the right thing! This is what we need to make our plan work." He grabbed Kramer's lapels, speaking in fervent tones. "Come with me, Bergdorf, join me in this crusade! We can do it, you and I!"

Kramer pushed Bormann's hands off his coat. "I've been listening to you, Bormann, and you are twisted by hate."

Bormann's mouth sagged as he stared grotesquely, his eyes magnified by the thick lenses.

Kramer continued, "It would do no good to try to rebut your ravings because they are the ravings of a madman. The evil of which you were once a part is still dictating to you. Everything you stand for, everything you strive for, comes from hate and a warped concept of racial supremacy. Death and destruction are your standard bearers, and nihilism is your morality. You and your ideas are dead, Bormann, relics of a dark age in our lifetime, and if they are resurrected from time to time by stupid little men, we will know how to deal with them, beginning in our own new Germany, where decent people have lived all along and where courage, lost for twelve ugly years, has been recovered."

"What are you saying? Are you telling me—"

"Please don't interrupt," Kramer said softly, "I have more to say, and it's important that you listen. Not too long ago, the German chancellor got down on his knees at the monument in Dachau to ask forgiveness for what his country had done to its victims. That act may have revolted you. Well, I too have been on my knees, Bormann, for many years, but in a different way. That money—the millions by which you want to raise your corrupt phoenix once more—"

"It's mine!" Bormann screamed. "Give it back!"

"I *did* give it back—a good part of it, anyway—to its rightful owners, to the survivors. Much of it was used to track down some of your friends. It went to the Haganah, the Shai, Mossad. Sound familiar, Bormann?"

"You're lying!" Bormann hissed. "You want it for yourself, you swine! Traitor!"

Bormann reached into his coat pocket. He pulled out a small pistol and aimed at Kramer. It didn't fire; the safety was still on. Kramer grabbed the gun out of Bormann's hand and threw it a few feet away. Bormann lunged, striking at Kramer's face. Kramer put his longer arms around the former Reichsleiter and held him tightly. They struggled, arms around each other, as if dancing an absurd one-step.

"I'll kill you, you traitor!" Bormann said, panting, losing his eyeglasses in the close contact.

"I don't think so," Kramer said into Bormann's ear, "but if you should be so fortunate, I would, to borrow from your friend Eichmann, leap into the grave laughing in the knowledge that I was responsible for the *lives* of countless Jews"—he panted—"knowing . . . that for so many years . . . I have thwarted . . . your plans."

Bormann shrieked in anguished frustration. His legs caved in under him, and both men fell heavily in a heap. They lay on the pocked bridle path, panting, no words between them. Slowly, Kramer got to his feet and dusted his raincoat, looking down at the old man. He reached and took Bormann's arm, helping him to a nearby bench. He found the glasses and hat and handed them to him. Then he sat at the opposite end of the bench. Neither spoke. After a minute, Kramer looked over at Bormann, who sat breathing heavily. Then he remembered the gun Bormann had pulled. He staggered to the spot he had thrown it to and found it. It was an Italian Biretta. He put it in his pocket.

He looked at the crumpled form on the bench. The large hat and hunched-up coat all but obscured Bormann's face. His once-beefy fingers peered out from the sleeves, slightly curled and facing each other as they rested on the apron of his buttoned coat. He looked like a harmless old man lost in memories. Kramer wished he would present an immediate danger, wished that he would rise from the bench showing his fangs and claws so that it would be easier to kill him. But he knew he would have to kill him as he was—a panting, sick, defenseless . . . monster.

He felt the snub-nosed .38 in his pocket. He reminded himself that it was a double-action revolver. There was no need to cock the hammer when it came time. And yet his aim might be affected if he didn't cock the hammer.

He realized he was stalling. *Don't think; do it now,* he said inwardly.

He waited. He got another idea. Of course! He would use Bormann's Biretta, then simply throw it in the bushes to be found later with no consequence to him.

He stared down at Bormann. He fingered off the Biretta's safety lever. Wait! Was there a shell in the chamber? He slid back the breech halfway and saw a shell in the dim light. He pointed at Bormann's form. The chest or the head? *Make up your mind!* he said to himself.

But he just sits there, Kramer thought, *waiting for the bullet to come crashing into him!* "God damn you, why don't you say something?" He walked up to him. "Here, Bormann, your gun. Obviously you came prepared to use it on me. Well, here's your chance! Take it!" No answer.

"Bormann! Bormann?" He kicked him lightly on the leg. He didn't move.

"Bormann? Are you dead? Oh, please be dead!" He felt for a

pulse on the neck, and withdrew his hand in repugnance. It was the cold, fishy sweat of a fresh cadaver. He *was* dead. Martin Bormann was dead.

He stepped back and looked at the eyes, open but lifeless. Probably a heart attack after their macabre tango, he concluded.

He sat down to think. Should he hide the body? Why? The death was from natural causes. He would be found in the morning, the police would be called, then other agencies, and the press. At first, vague hints would come out as to the identity of the body, then confirmation, and then headlines in all the papers, with the attendant speculations.

The gun! He wiped it clean with a handkerchief and was replacing it in Bormann's pocket when he remembered the fingerprints that should be on it. He put the pistol in the dead man's hand, holding it with the handkerchief. He pressed the cooling fingers onto it and returned it to Bormann's coat pocket.

Kramer found a wallet in the breast pocket. There were several large Mexican peso notes, along with Paraguayan and Chilean currency. Several U.S. hundred-dollar bills were folded in another compartment. There was a Paraguayan passport in the name of one Martín Ricardo Hessler-Pérez with an address in Asunción. There was an exit visa on the passport, that of the international airport in Asunción, about two weeks prior. There were entry and exit visa stamps from Santiago, Chile, and Caracas, Venezuela, indicating that he had stayed only two days in each place. The next visa was that of the Benito Juárez international airport in Mexico City, ten days earlier. Ten days. What had he been doing in Mexico for ten days? The same thing he did in those other places, no doubt, Kramer thought— meeting with his disciples, the neo-Nazis, or old ones, or both. The new wave. The "new wave" and its Führer, Martín Ricardo Hessler-Pérez-Bormann, late of Asunción, Paraguay, late of the world.

Kramer wiped the wallet and passport and returned them to Bormann's pocket. Then he turned and walked away at a brisk pace. A light rain was starting to fall on the city again, and he closed his eyes and raised his face to it, needing its cool, cleansing, moisture. It was only then that the realization struck him that, by Bormann's natural death, he was relieved of the savage act of murder. But, he asked himself, would he have had the courage to kill him? "Yes!" he said aloud. "Yes!"

Then, as he came to the street, he looked at the people walking and driving by, examining their faces to see if, somehow, they knew, and if they knew, if things were different now. But things were the same; car horns blared, but no bells rang. There was no dancing in the streets in celebration of the death of the man who would enslave them because in his view they were subhuman.

And on his pedestal, the great stone god of rain seemed to say to the Grasshopper, "Chapulín, now that we have seen, do you invoke the Lord Huitzilopochtli, that he may bring *nahui-ollin* Four-Earthquake, so that the *tzitzimime* can kill all of mankind?"

"Not yet, Tlaloc," said the Grasshopper, "but soon, very soon."

MEXICO CITY

THE PRESENT

The lobby of Kramer's hotel was a sea of polyester and seersucker draped over the backs of American doctors on convention, enjoying the night life of the Mexican capital. Here and there small groups of gray- and blue-clad Japanese, Nikons and Minoltas hanging from their necks, clustered around their guides, who were going over the next day's activities and exhorting their clients in the wisdom of gastroenteritis prevention.

Kramer ducked into a crowded elevator and got off on the sixteenth floor. He let himself into his suite.

Enos Grba, the security agent, was asleep in front of the television set that was running the twenty-four-hour news programs from the U.S. on cable. Kramer went quietly to Grba's bedroom and returned the pistol to its shoulder holster in the drawer. He came out and turned off the television.

"Gerb, I'm back," Kramer said, shaking him gently. "I turned off the TV—you were snoring like a buzzsaw."

The big Serbian-American looked at his charge with wide eyes. "Oh, chief, it's you. I was getting worried. Glad to see you." He smiled knowingly. "Everything go okay?"

"Yes, everything went well. Were there any calls?"

"Nope, just your wife. She called just after you left. I told her you were at a meeting and that you'd call her."

"That's fine, Gerb. I'll call her now."

Kramer went to his bedroom. There was no mention of Grba's pistol being missing. He obviously hadn't noticed.

They spoke in German. Erika said she was still very nervous and worried about him. He told her there was nothing to worry about anymore.

"I was with B tonight, Erika, but don't—"

"What! B? You mean—"

He stopped her in midsentence. "Sh! Erika! You know who I mean. But don't worry, everything is well. He's dead, Erika."

"Dead? Did you—did you—"

"No, no. He died of a heart attack. I'll tell you about it when I get home. It's all right, I promise."

"But how did you see him?" she asked anxiously. "I mean, how did he find you? Was it a chance meeting on the street? Oh, I'm so confused! Tell me how it happened. How did—"

"Erika! We're on an open line. I can't go into it now. He called me in Washington a few days ago. He had seen a photo of me in the papers and insisted on seeing me here. I had no choice; I had to see him."

Erika's voice went even higher. "You arranged it with him? You knew days ago and you didn't tell me? How could you not tell me!"

"I didn't want to worry you, darling, as you're worrying now. And it was something I had to do alone." He sighed audibly. "You don't know how glad I am that he is no more."

"I too, darling," she said, relief in her voice. Then the thought suddenly occurred to her. "Are you all right? Were you hurt? Did he have anyone with him? Oh, Hans-Dieter, you could have been—"

"Erika, for God's sake! We're on an open line! No, I'm not hurt," he said affectionately. "I'm fine. Except for the knees on my pants getting dirty when . . . when I knelt to listen for a heartbeat. Anyhow, it's all over now, my dearest. Go back to sleep. I'll see you soon. I love you very much."

"I love you too, Hans-Dieter."

Peter Kramer lit a cigarette and looked out the window at the still-busy street below. A large bronze statue of Columbus parted the long ribbon of cars on the Paséo de la Reforma. Some of those cars, he knew, would continue west on the broad avenue and through the park. They would unknowingly pass the stiffening corpse of one of history's darkest individuals. More wicked even than his mentor, who at least was mad. But not so the disciple. He was truly the anti-Christ, the archfiend. If only he could point him out to them, the drivers on the Reforma. If only he could place a sign telling the world that there, on a bench in Chapultepéc Park, sat evil personified. Dead forever. The last of a blackness that came close to shrouding the earth with its malignity.

No, he corrected himself, not quite the last. He has deposited his spores somewhere, growing unnoticed, wicked and perverted . . . out there . . . nourished by the quintessence of hate. His "new wave."

They would insinuate themselves like ruinous vines into decent and open societies, eventually strangling the democratic principles of free thought and free choice. They would do that through the back door of the ultraright, thought Kramer, which by virtue of the Communist fear was firmly implanted in the current political scene. The veterans' organizations, the superpatriotic leagues, the churches, even. He thought of the Reverend Bobby Fauvus and his "Strength through Morality Congress," preaching a brand of fundamentalism based on intolerance, prejudice, and fear. And the others, who from the pulpit of their church-owned television stations held up the Bible and quoted chapter and verse, twisting the scriptures to their advantage, blatantly exhorting their electronic congregations to send money to them so that they might spread their gospel of demagoguery.

Moralists were convincing people that the Days of Wrath were upon them, and their rhetoric promised God's terrible swift sword if they did not see the light, if they did not urge their legislators to smite down those ungodly laws being proposed, such as the "wicked" Equal Rights Amendment and the anti-American, Communist-inspired Firearms Registration Act. These same preachers, Kramer remembered, were pushing hard for their own new sets of laws, laws that would make it a crime to be a homosexual or for a woman to have an abortion, no matter the cause or danger of her pregnancy, or for libraries to have on their shelves books that they, the conscience of the nation, considered pornographic.

He crushed out the cigarette. Wait a minute, he protested, aren't you getting a little paranoid? Isn't it possible that these so-called fundamentalists are simply that—people with archaic but sincere desires to get the country back on track by sound, conservative means, not necessarily with ulterior motives? After all, there is chaos in the nation today; crime is rampant, and violence and drugs are a way of life for many. There is little respect for law and order, and the world is caught in the throes of immorality and permissiveness. Respect for others, courtesy, civility, good manners—these things are in the past. What's so bad about patriotism and the recognition of a supreme being? These people are not unlike your own father, he argued, who was not an evil man.

Good points, he conceded, but simplistic. Good men like my father made a monster like Hitler possible, remember, honest, hard-working, God-fearing German burghers. Germany had been in trouble then, too. Soviet Socialists were taking over, there were riots in the streets, social morality was at an all-time low; permissiveness, homosexuality, and prostitution were flagrant. Unemployment, bread lines, inflation, depression—all the elements were there, remember? The same applies now. They may be sincere in what they preach, in what they do, but it is through those doors that the spores of Bormann's evil can flourish, he was convinced. Didn't he boast—just an hour ago, for God's sake!—that they would do it by the ballot, through the democratic process, through cleverly conceived campaigns? A rebirth of the old ideas, with the unwitting aid of the political right, quietly, unobtrusively, legally, lethally.

Peter Kramer walked with a sense of urgency to the closet and brought out his briefcase. He dropped it onto the bed and took off his tie and shirt. He propped himself up on the pillows and began studying a sheaf of papers. It was a list of congressional committees and their memberships. He began circling names, underlining others. He placed a call.

"It's all over, Heinz," he said to Langfeldt in Zürich. He had called Langfeldt before his trip advising him of the new developments. "He's dead. He had a heart attack right in front of me. It's over, thank God." He spoke in German.

"Are you sure?" Langfeldt said.

"He was as dead as mutton. I felt his pulse."

"All right, but do we still have to worry, Peter? Did he give any indication that there are others who know?"

"No. Even when things got ugly between us, he didn't use it.

As a threat, I mean, although he could have. I got the feeling that he was keeping it his little secret, even though it was clear that he was working with others.''

"Others? Do you have any idea who the others are?" Langfeldt asked, a touch of anxiety in his voice.

"Not specifically," Kramer said. "The new wave, he calls—he called it. Whoever they are, they're his followers. Perhaps he thought that if he shared the information of the Q-B thing with them, they might kidnap me and torture me to get to it, excluding him. I don't know—it's only a thought. You knew him better. What do you think?"

"The notion strikes me as plausible, Peter. If that's the case, we'll be all right from that end. Knowing him, he'd never tell a soul about Q-B."

Kramer said, "Heinz, there was another reason for my call. I know that both our lines are open, but it can't be helped. What I have to say cannot wait."

"Are you sure, Peter?" The ever-cautious Langfeldt was beginning to get nervous. "I can be there tomorrow if need be, you know."

"No, it can't wait, I tell you," Kramer said. "This . . . event tonight—I feel that there might be others, that my security may be—" He had trouble verbalizing the fears.

Langfeldt said it for him. "You fear for your life, Peter? Is that what you're trying to say?"

"Well—yes, I suppose. I don't like to make such a melodrama, but yes, I suppose that's what I mean. I don't know, of course; it's only a feeling, please understand. In any case, I would feel much better if we discussed now, not later, what should be done with the Q-B thing if—"

"Understood, Peter. All right, please go on; tell me what you have in mind."

Kramer sighed. "Heinz, this new wave business, it frightens me." He told Langfeldt of his conclusions, his feelings, his apprehensions—his fears.

After listening for several minutes, Langfeldt sighed too. "Peter, could it be that you're reading too much into the rantings of a fanatic? Could you be overreacting?"

"I asked myself those same questions. I don't think so. I have no doubt that the seeds are planted. And they will flourish. In fact, they're out there already. That government in Chile is not an accident. Look at Paraguay, and England, with those apostles of hate, the evangelists. And even in Germany, where they said it would never happen again, the resurgence of Nazism—it is swelling like a great wave, Heinz—a new wave.''

"All right. Do you have a plan?'' Langfeldt asked.

"Yes, but I need your help. I will send you a list of U.S. congressional committee members whom I suspect, according to their records, of being ultraright, which will make them either new wave or the unwitting tools of it. We must make use of Q-B to make sure they're not reelected. We must support their opponents by contributing heavily to their campaigns. We must do everything possible to hinder the election of the others. Right away. There isn't a moment to lose!''

The circumspect Swiss, the ever-careful banker who, in order to maintain the balance of economic and political power in the world, used assassination as one more device, said, "I must caution you here, Peter. If we go by your plan, we may sweep away the conservatives on both sides, and your congress will be overloaded with ultraliberals, which, in my view, is just as dangerous.''

"I fully agree,'' Kramer said readily. "That's why we must be clever. You must retain the services of a law firm in Washington that specializes in legislative analyses. Have them give you a running report on these people—on both sides of the aisle, of course. Just remember, however, that the liberals are easy; the whole country, the whole free world is alert to the Communist menace. But the others, the 'new wave,' they'll use the extreme right as a breeding swamp for their larvae. Heinz, we must reassess immediately our priorities for the Q-B thing. My God, what better way to use it!''

There was a long silence on the line. Then Langfeldt said, "You came to this decision after seeing him? After hearing what he had to say?''

Peter Kramer suddenly realized that it was he, and he alone, who had heard the last words of Martin Bormann. It was he who had this enormous burden thrust on his shoulders, and it was he who heard, through his executor, the factual and true last will and testament of Adolf Hitler.

"Heinz,'' Kramer said, "he told me just two hours ago that the world was on the verge of extinction because of the overabundance of inferior races, those that would breathe his air, eat his food, and take up his space. He told me that he and his followers were committed to finding a final solution. He intimated—perhaps even stated—that the only way to save the world for the Aryan race was through—'' Langfeldt heard him swallow hard, unable to say the word.

Langfeldt whispered the question. "Through genocide?"

Kramer whispered the answer. "Yes."

There was another long stretch of painful silence. Langfeldt broke it, asking, "You are convinced of this beyond a doubt?"

"Yes. Unequivocally, yes."

"Very well, then. I too am convinced. You have my full co-operation, Peter, and my promise that if anything should happen, I will see to it that your wishes are carried out."

"Thank you, Heinz."

NEW YORK CITY

THE PRESENT

The 747 jolted softly to a final halt. Paul Cline took his suitcase from the overhead luggage rack. He nodded a faint smile to the efficient TWA cabin crew and was quickly out of the chute leading to the curiously built TWA terminal at New York's Kennedy Airport. Some wags referred to the place as the "world's largest brassière." Some New York cabbies, not to be outdone, called it the Dolly Parton.

Cline squinted into the late afternoon sun as he looked for a cab. He found one, and the cabbie—whose name, according to the framed license on the back of his seat, was Bernard Spiegelman, and who, according to his accent, was from Brooklyn—talked a steady stream the entire trip to midtown Manhattan.

Of the many types of taxi drivers, Bernard Spiegelman fit the class of philosopher, sports expert, and political pundit. He jawed on about the treachery of the Dodgers for moving to the Coast, and about the "schmucks in Washington who're givin' away the country to the Russkies and the welfare bums," and about how "before the Ayrabs decided to shaft it to us, we could make a decent livin' *schlepping* a hack."

Cline found himself loathing Bernard Spiegelman. Not so much because of his obvious Jewishness—although that alone would have been reason enough for him—but because from the moment he entered the cab Cline felt an overpowering feeling of discomfort. At first it puzzled him; then a few miles later, he discovered the reason: Bernard Spiegelman—with the cigar stub in his perpetually moving mouth, the beefy, cheerful face, the almost-kinky black hair with gray curls on a large head supported by a bull's neck, the gravelly and loud voice so quick to laugh—reminded him of Abe Berman.

That was it, thought Cline. Berman. *The fucking Hebe!*

". . . now you take your coloreds. If they ain't dealin' dope, they're pimpin'. An' most of 'em on welfare, too."

Fucking Jew bastard!

". . . an' your PR's—you know, Porto Ricans—same thing. On the dole, robbing us poor workin' stiffs . . ."

Berman. Berman.

With a flair, the cab pulled up to the door of the Algonquin Hotel on Forty-fourth Street. "Okay, pal, the Algonquin. Remember what I told ya, an' watch out for them hookers; they'll steal your socks off. Uh, that'll be twenty-four eighty."

Cline looked at Bernard Spiegelman and smiled. He opened the cab door and pushed out his suitcase to the approaching doorman. Still smiling, he took out a large roll of bills and gave the doorman a ten, making sure that the cabbie saw the exorbitant tip. He then gave Bernard Spiegelman a twenty and a five-dollar bill, pausing with the roll in his hand. Cline grinned pleasantly at him and said, "Keep the change, Bernie, you've earned it." He walked away.

Bernard Spiegelman grinned back for a few seconds, then the unlit cigar butt dropped from his lips, his mouth remaining open in confusion. Cline was in the lobby and didn't hear his screams of outrage.

Paul Cline registered under one of his solid aliases. He told the room clerk to see to it that a dozen bottles of Vichy water were sent up to his room; then he followed the bellman to the elevator.

It was a sorry stunt he had pulled with the cabbie. It was just plain stupid to set himself up like that. What if there had been a scuffle with the kike and his wig had been knocked off? He'd have to be more careful in the future, he thought, embarrassed at his lack of control. Besides, he felt no real satisfaction.

Cline exchanged some bills for his key with the bellman. He left the door unlatched and flung off his coat and tie and walked to the bathroom. He removed his horn-rimmed glasses and peeled off the curly brown wig. He splashed cold water onto his face and massaged his scalp under the straight, blond hair, matted in perspiration from wearing the wig since that morning in California.

Abe Berman, he thought. Of all the cabbies in New York, he would have to get Abe Berman!

He walked back into his room, drying his face with the rough towel, and peered out the window at the street below. The room smelled musty and of the many coats of paint it wore. He wondered for a moment what it had been like the year of its birth, with necks of elegant ladies supporting opera-length strands of pearls and moustachioed gentlemen, looking like obese penguins in their white tie and tails, devouring schools of sole almondine and thick slabs of beef.

Abe Berman had hurt him deeply. Ah, the pain!

The buzzer interrupted his musings. He yelled at the door, immediately going back to the bathroom and closing it, while the room service waiter let himself in with the Vichy water. Cline told him to help himself to the bill he had left on the coffee table.

With the waiter gone, Cline poured the water into a glass and drank it in several long swallows. He opened a second bottle and took it and the glass to the bathroom along with his toiletries case. Undressing down to his socks, he took a small plastic bottle and sprinkled scouring powder on a moistened hand towel and scrubbed the oversize tub. He rinsed away the foam and brought out another bottle, this one containing a solution of carbolic acid for the final disinfection of the alien tub. He filled the tub with hot water, emptying a packet of bubble bath provided by the hotel.

He placed the bath mat on the tile floor and removed his socks, settling down in the the warm soapy cumuli, a glass of Vichy water in hand. Paul Cline began to relax for the first time since leaving the peace of his ranch.

He tried to imagine what Cardozo would look like. Probably a short, dumpy Mexican, smelling of Yardley aftershave. He wondered how good his English would be, then remembered that all of Langfeldt's international members spoke excellent English; it was their common language. He thought of Langfeldt, now his exclusive employer, and how generous he had always been in their fee-for-services arrangement, which included a retaining fee that was designed to keep "Joseph" exclusively his. Not only had the fees been large, but the subsequent investment advice given him by Langfeldt had provided Cline with more financial security than he had ever dreamed of.

He sipped more Vichy water, hoping its medicinal aspects would relieve some of his discomfort, although he knew that the discomfort would be gone only after the assignment was finished. It was always there—the cramping and gassiness in the lower gut—for two or three days prior to the job; then it disappeared a few hours before completion, when his entire system was under his rigid control.

His thoughts drifted to Bernard Spiegelman, then to Abe Berman. He didn't want to think about Abe Berman and struggled to make his mind a blank.

The clouds of froth had dissipated into scattered patches, revealing his submerged torso. He stared at the skinless glans-penis as it bobbed lightly on the water surface like a mindless cork. He held it in his fingers and examined a small wartlike growth at the end of the frenum. He knew it was not a wart but rather a node of scar tissue left after a sloppy circumcision, the work of, no doubt, an anxious and hurried *moel* in wartime Europe.

Cline wondered if preputial grafts were possible. If so, he wondered how many Aryan-looking Jews in Europe would have escaped the Holocaust; then he speculated that if such a graft were possible, would it un-Jew him. Never mind, he thought, I'm not a Jew.

Correction: According to Hitler, I am a Jew.

I used to be a Catholic, he reminded himself. Suddenly, his olfactory memory was flooded with the smoke of burning incense from the censer he used to present ceremoniously to Father Horvath when he was an altar boy. *"Confiteor Deo omnipotenti, beatae Mariae, semper virgini. . . ."* The Latin rang in his ears. Even if he had recited those words, had swayed that censer in the cathedral of Cologne in 1941, he would still be a Jew, attested by the fact of his parents' contribution to the German war effort in becoming soap.

Who gives a fuck? I don't.

He went through the ritual of replenishing the hot water, and he used the now-empty glass to ladle warmth onto his shoulders and chest.

Goddamn it! Out of a million cab drivers . . .

Oh, Abe, you miserable prick. You could've been the father I never had! Why? Why didn't you let me marry Sharon, Abe? It's funny, I'm not sure if I even loved her, but I did love you, Abe. It was you I wanted to be near.

Paul Cline's stomach growled in gastric spasms; he had finished the Vichy water. He decided against getting another bottle; he didn't want to give up the security of the warm tub. And too, the past was quickly coming back to him.

He lay back, now giving in completely to the thoughts. Soon he even enjoyed the reminiscences of those days in Chicago in the Fifties. His first job. He had been only seventeen when he got the job at Abe's Deli, and soon Abe was breaking him in as a counterman. He learned from Abe things such as slicing the pastrami for those enormous sandwiches and making sure the corn rye was sliced on the bias so as to have more of the crunchy crust. The pickles had to have just the right color for crispness and flavor or they went back to to Sam the Pickle Man. No, sir, Abe used to say, they had to be right! He used to make his own cole slaw in the kitchen in back. His own kreplachs too, just to make sure that everything was kosher. "Not kosher kosher, Paulie—you know, *kosher!* Clean and pure, like a Jewish momma makes at home."

Working at the deli and being around the Bermans—Abe, his wife, Esther, and their beautiful Sharon—had given him the first real sense of belonging. Outside the motherly arms of Franziska, Paul Cline was happy for the first time.

And then, the crusher.

Paul Cline, assassin, sighed with pain at the memories.

Flashes of black nights and rain and running, running. The lights of a farmhouse across muddy fields, a woman holding him, crying in fear, running somewhere, anywhere. . . . Pavel, she called him, saying to him don't worry, you'll be taken care of. The farmer Johannes and his sons, Karl and Johann, and Franziska, they will take care of you and hide you from the Gestapo . . .

Gestapo. He didn't know what that meant. The little boy thought it was a person, some ogre named Gestapo, and he was going to get him and eat him up. *Why does Gestapo want to eat me up, mamma? Because you're a Jew, but from now on, you are not a Jew anymore. Remember that, and the Gestapo will leave you alone. Remember that, Pavel!*

He sighed deeply. Other than the memories of Franziska, he

tried to block out from his mind the pain of life afterward, the bitter winters and hunger of the two years in devastated postwar Europe while the Cline family waited to emigrate to America. He tried not to think of the bitter fights with Karl and Johann because Franziska showed him more love than she did them. He tried to forget those years growing up in Cleveland and finally, the deepest pain of all, Franziska's illness from the deprivation of those starving times in Europe . . . and her death. He tried not to remember, but he could not forget.

Paul Cline's memory focused easily on the image of his mother Franziska; her warm bosom his head rested upon so many times, the rough hands that felt so soft when she cradled him and stroked his head, and that emanation from her that made him feel so safe and wanted. He didn't fight that memory; in fact he dwelled on it, the feelings missing in him for so long. Then, she was taken from him.

She was taken from him, and he was left with the cold and bitter disapproval of the others, his father and brothers.

A house laden with pain and emptiness. His father, after the funeral, somberly, slowly shuffled across the wooden floors, as if he were pulling his own plow, opened the china cabinet and took out the schnapps reserved for special occasions. He had taken a drink and stared balefully at him for a long time. Then the pent-up feelings were exposed in a quiet, low-toned, but crushing manner. "Paul," he had said in German, their common language, "you have deliberately deprived your brothers of their mother's love. I don't want you as my son any longer. You are not from my blood. A dirty little Jew is what you are."

The decision to leave had not been a difficult one for him, Paul Cline remembered as he studied his wrinkled fingers, feeling the ragged grooves from soaking so long. He would be a Jew, then. It was so simple to the seventeen-year-old.

The rewards of the decision were instant. Abe Berman had asked him as he applied for the busboy's job at the deli, "Cline, you say your name is, kid? It sounds Jewish. Are you a Jewish boy? Yeah? Okay, son, you got the job, and if you're smart, maybe one day I'll teach you the business."

Immediate warmth and friendliness and special interest were shown him by his new family, the Bermans. Other than from Franziska, he'd never known such affection. The Menorah Social Club of Temple Beth-Olam, his new friends and teachers. And Sharon.

He remembered the warm nights walking along the shore of the lake that summer after a movie or miniature golf . . . and Sharon. His first kiss, and his first erection born of actual touch and closeness and heady scents and tastes of Sharon's mouth and the feel of her body under the blouse.

He felt completely relaxed, and the cramping in his gut had ceased. The thoughts of Sharon caused an erection. He quickly shifted to other thoughts, maintaining even then, years later, her integrity.

Then the fateful night.

Balmy breezes, he recalled, were caressing his skin as he and Abe strolled down the quiet streets of West Rogers Park in north Chicago. They walked by the synagogue and around the side to the courtyard of the Menorah Center, and their shoes crunched under the sand and dirt of new construction.

"You know what that is, kid? That there is gonna be the Phillip A. Berman Hall. For the kids in the neighborhood. It's gonna be a recreation hall—you know, pool tables and chess and Ping-Pong, all that sorta thing. Keeps 'em busy and outta trouble." Abe's arm swept the air around him and he lanced his mouth with a cigar. He hooked his thumbs in his belt and rocked back and forth on his heels. "Costing me an arm and a leg, but I figure it's worth it. D'ya know who Phillip A. Berman was, kid?"

Paul had known from Sharon, but before he could answer yes, Abe said, "Phillip Abraham Berman was my son. That's right, was. He died in Israel in nineteen forty-seven fighting for statehood, except they called it Palestine then. Crazy kid, that Phil of mine," he had said, shaking his head as if relating a prank. "He wasn't yet seventeen when he quit school and joined the U.S. Army. Forged my name to the consent. The fuckin' army took him without bothering to check with me. Anyway, I squealed on him, and they kicked his ass out. Honorable discharge, of course. Well, he got so pissed off at me that him and some other boys from the neighborhood took off and went to Palestine to fight the Ayrabs. That's what he used to call 'em—Ayrabs." He chuckled, relighting his cigar.

"Sharon told me about Phil, Mr. Berman," Paul Cline remembered saying. But Abe was already too deep in the memory of his son to hear him.

"He was a real funny kid, Phil. He had a way with words, always making you laugh, you know. You could never stay mad at him 'cause he was a natural comedian. Always telling dirty jokes, really funny ones. Remind me to tell you some, you'll love 'em! I used to write 'em down; I got a notebook someplace. And the songs, boy what songs he used to bring home! I remember one song he used to sing to this hasher we had down at the deli. Bessie, her name was. Just between you and me," he confided, lowering his voice and shielding one side of his mouth with his hand, "I think she's the one who busted his cherry! Ha! Anyway, the song went something like this:

'Six lessons from Madame LaZonga, Will make your donga Six inches longa!' "

The afternoon rush was over on the streets below Cline's room at the Algonquin, and it created a quiet, interrupted occasionally by a car's horn. He slowly washed his chest and shoulders for the hundredth time, an affectionate smile on his lips as he pictured Abe, a cigar clamped between grinning teeth as he sang the bawdy song in his gravelly voice and did his version of the rhumba, lovingly imitating his dead son. They had both laughed hilariously. Then, as their laughter died down, Berman wiped tears of glee from his eyes and turned somber.

"The first day," he had said, "the very first fucking day he arrived in Palestine, an Arab patrol ambushed the truck Phil was riding in on his way to the induction base. Phil was killed instantly, they tell me. Never even got a chance to fire his gun. . . ." There had been a catch in his voice as it trailed off.

Abe Berman squatted by an open sandbag and picked up a handful of sand. Slowly he sifted the grains through his fingers. "Crazy kid," he said softly. "Just seventeen, and he went out and got himself killed by some faceless fanatic. An Ayrab, like he used to say." He sighed deeply and mumbled, more to himself, "It ain't fair!"

He looked up with an ironic grin. "You know, Paul, I was three

years in Europe fighting Hitler and his bunch. *Three fucking years!*"
he screamed in a whisper. "And the worst that happened to me was
a case of scabies on my balls."

"I'm really sorry, Mr. Berman. I know how—"

Abe stopped him in midsentence with a wave of his hamlike
hand. "No, that's all right, kid. C'mon, let's walk. I got something
else I gotta talk to you about."

A sudden stomach cramp hit Paul Cline. He experienced a tight-
ness in his chest at the same time. He was prepared to get out of the
tub, thinking, *Enough of this! Stop*. But the pains passed, and he settled down in the wet again, ready to receive the hurt.

"Paulie," Abe had said as they resumed their walk that night,
"what's with you and Sharon? I mean, you been seeing a lot of her
lately. How serious is it, son?"

Paul had been relieved at the question. His intentions with
Sharon were nothing but honorable, and he was glad to tell his boss
and future father-in-law about them.

"We like each other a lot, Mr. Berman," Paul had said without
hesitation. "I guess you could say we love each other. And some
day, I hope to marry her—with your permission, of course," he
added quickly. Almost in the same breath, he said, "I guess I know
what you're thinking, Mr. Berman. I mean, I figure you're thinking
I don't have much to offer her, like I don't have much money or an
education, if that's what you're thinking. I guess if I was in your
place I'd be thinking that, too. But we were talking, Sharon and me,
and I was thinking of going back to school and finishing up and going
to college. I could study, like maybe engineering, or I could be a vet,
'cause I like animals and horses, you know, and, well . . ." The
words had come out like a torrent until he ran out of them. Even so,
Berman hadn't seemed to be listening. He just walked alongside
Paul, looking down at the pavement as if absorbed by its cracks.

"So what do you think, Mr. Berman?"

Abe sighed a long, troubled sigh. "I wish I knew, kid."

"I—I don't understand, Mr. Berman," Paul said. "Is there
something wrong?"

Cline remembered Berman stopping in his tracks. Gently, he
took Paul by the arm and turned him so that they were facing each
other. "Paulie, you know I like you a lot," he said. "There's noth-

ing I'd like better than someday having you as a son-in-law. With Phil gone, you'd be like my own son. You believe that, don't you?"

Paul looked at Abe's troubled eyes and nodded, confused and afraid. He waited for the *but*.

"Now listen carefully," Abe Berman said in a subdued voice, uncharacteristically gentle, "I don't want you to make any plans about Sharon. Me and her mother want her to marry a Jewish boy."

Paul Cline got out of the tub and dried himself. He tied the towel around his slim waist and walked into the bedroom. He opened another bottle of Vichy water, and lay down on the bed. At the point of rejection, he had stopped listening that night in Chicago so many bitter years ago. And now he was doing the same thing. Except that it was the dark recesses of his memory that he was now refusing to listen to. Then what had never happened before happened. His mind told him, *Go on, you owe it to the boy. Go on*.

Okay. He took a deep breath and closed his eyes.

Again Paul felt relief when he heard Abe's objections. It was clear to him that Abe hadn't paid much attention when he had related his background. Paul laughed and said, "But Mr. Berman, I *am* Jewish! Don't you remember me telling you when I came to work for you I told you about my real parents and how the Nazis killed them? Because they were Jewish?"

Abe draped an arm around Paul's shoulder. "I know all that, son. I do remember all you told me. Your poor parents, may they rest in peace, along with so many of our people. May the God of Abraham remember them, too, the innocent ones."

"Then . . . you were just kidding me."

"Listen to me, son. This is really hard for me to explain. I didn't say you wasn't a Jew. I meant you ain't *Jewish*. I know, I know, but there's a difference. I'll try to explain it. You see, kid, being Jewish is a way of life, a state of mind, call it. It's being born Jewish, and dying Jewish, but what really counts is what's in between—*living* Jewish. Do you understand?

"Look," he continued, "when I was a kid I used to sit on my grandfather's lap, and he used to tell me stories about the old country, this little town in Russia where the Jews lived. It's probably gone now. Anyway, he used to tell me and my brothers the stories in Yiddish, because Yiddish was a language different from any language in the world, because it *had* to be, and it was one of the things that helped us survive in all those countries where the Jewish people had to go. Do you speak Yiddish, Paulie? No, I didn't think you did. Anyway, he used to tell us, me and my brothers, Jakie and Natie, about the pain and shame and disgrace, of the way it was in the ghettoes, and about the pogroms, and the way we were always treated. We were beaten up, and they would spit at us and burn our temples. For no reason, Paul. Just for being Jews. Like your dear parents, may they rest in peace. But you know what? We held together, somehow. And you know what held us together like cement? Our faith in our religion and in our traditions. We are Jews, and we lived like Jews. We had to, to survive. Even though I was lucky enough not to go through those times, I *lived* those times through my grandfather's words and tears, sitting in his lap. It's important to know these things, son. In fact, it's essential to being Jewish. You know, when I did my bar mitzvah, the—''

"Mr. Berman," Paul interrupted with anxious enthusiasm, "I've been studying for it, for my bar mitzvah, with Rabbi Fein! I've been going to *shul*. Sharon's so proud of me!''

"Yeah?" Berman said, smiling and patting him on the head. "How you doing with the Hebrew? It's tough, ain't it?''

"I'm learning it pretty good," Paul said. "And I'm enjoying it, too.''

"Yeah," Abe said, smiling, remembering. He sang in a soft, raspy wail, *"Baruch, atto Adonai . . ."* He shook his large head sadly. "Ai, Paulie, if that's all that it takes, but it isn't. Look, let me ask you: You said you're enjoying learning Hebrew? Yeah, well, let me tell you, I *hated* it. No, really, I hated it 'cause it was a chore like any other chore. Like homework, you know? But we had to do it. There was no getting around it because, Paulie, we're Jews, and that's the way it is. Now with you, you got options. We don't. So we learn it with our hearts, the Hebrew. You, you learn it with your head," he said, tapping Paul's forehead, "and maybe it's a *Yiddishe* head, God grant you, but it can't be in the heart, don't you see? A boy's bar mitzvah, Paulie, it's for the parents. The papa and the mama, to see their faces light up with pride, *Jewish* pride, 'cause that's one of the things that holds us together, our faith. It's the confirmation of all that's sacred to us. And sometimes, Paul, sometimes . . . that's all we got left.''

Paul walked, head down, his heart farther down. *I belong, but I don't belong. Just as it's always been. Who am I? What am I? Where do I come from? Where am I going?*

Abe Berman looked at him. ''I can see, I can feel the hurt in you. You're a good, beautiful young man who loves my daughter and who loves me, maybe 'cause we're Jews, I don't know. I don't even know if that's right or wrong. But what I do know is that if there's a question in my mind, then later there could be one in yours, and that would be wrong. Look, kid, what's wrong about the whole thing is that you're *tryin'* to be a Jew. That's—that's not right, somehow. Those things have to be natural, they have to come from—'' He threw his hands up in frustration. ''Goddamn it! I can see I'm losing you—you're hurt and you're closing your ears to me, and I don't know how to tell you any better than how I'm telling you now.''

Abe Berman stuffed his hands in his pockets. His anger was clearly visible; anger at himself for failing to say the right things to convince Paul of what was in his heart. ''I've never been a great one with words, Paul, but you gotta hear me. Look, I can tell you that it wouldn't be fair to me and Esther, that you wouldn't bring up a grandson like we was brought up, that we wouldn't have a grandson doing *his* bar mitzvah like our Phil, and it would be true. It would be like taking away from us our old-age benefits that we're entitled to, you know, like a grandson who sits on *my* lap—a *Jewish* grandson. Not some little boy who's half-Jewish, half-*goy* 'cause you wouldn't know these things, and you're trying too hard for it and you can't really make it. And the reason you can't make it is 'cause the others won't let you.

''I guess what I'm trying to tell you is that the lousy part about this whole thing, Paulie, is that you'd be buying a bagful of problems 'cause the *goyim* hate us, the coloreds, the spics—all of them hate us and you're asking for two strikes against you. But worse than that, Paulie—and this is really the hard part—the Jews themselves would give you the hardest time. Yeah, you look at me. Well, let me tell you, the Jews don't like converts. I know, I know, but you would be *like* a convert, and us Jews, we figure there must be something wrong with them to begin with, wanting to carry that burden around.

They're like curiosities, and they're never accepted—not deep down, anyway. And that would hurt you and my Sharon, and you don't want that kind of trouble. You'll have enough regular trouble in your life and you don't need all that shit.

"Look at you—blond, blue eyes, straight beautiful nose—you got *gentile* written all over you! You may not believe this, but ask any Jew if he had a chance to come back in another life, and he had a choice, it wouldn't be as a Jew. Sure, we're proud of what we are, 'cause we are what we are, but we figure, who needs it? Ask any *schwartzer* if he could be white—not just passing, but white—he'd jump at the chance 'cause this is a *goy*'s world. Look at how many Jews try to pass for gentile, changing their names and stuff like that. See, they know what it's like—and you don't.''

Abe Berman looked at Paul. "Aw, Paulie, don't look like that! I'm telling you all this, well, 'cause I love you like my son, and I don't want you and Sharon to be hurt." A few tortured steps later. "The funny thing is that you'd probably make a better son to me than my own Phil.''

They had arrived at Paul's rooming house. Paul started up the cement steps. "Will you be at the deli tomorrow, Paulie?" Berman asked anxiously.

Paul shook his head without turning. "I don't think so.''

Abe Berman kicked a tree in the parkway. "Goddamn it! You didn't understand anything I told you! Well, what I said to you made a lot of sense to me. Maybe I didn't say it too good, but by God, it made sense, Paul Cline, and one of these days you're gonna thank me!'' he yelled at Paul's back. "You're gonna remember what I said and thank me!''

The next morning Paul Klein took a Greyhound bus to Toledo and, changing his name from the German Klein to its Anglicized version, Cline, enlisted in the Army for paratrooper training. Years later, wearing the green beret of the Special Forces, the unique and powerful unit of the clean kill, he gave birth to "Joseph.''

Now, more years later, Paul Cline was on a bed in a Manhattan hotel, in the dark, a towel across his middle, tears welling up in his eyes, the first tears he had shed since tears of anger wet his cheeks in Chicago so long ago. And he was struck with the thought, the conviction, that the anger that had directed him with such cold passion had been all along mistaken. Abe Berman had rejected him, but now he realized that Abe had been right. A healthy kidney in another's body may be rejected because of the tiniest cellular anomaly, and it is rejected impersonally, even cruelly. But Abe, in his bearish but gentle wisdom, had done it out of love. Love for him, Paul Cline.

He got up and turned on the lights. He remembered the name of the taxi company and looked up the address in the phone book. He scribbled a note to Bernard Spiegelman: "Dear Bernie, I made a mistake." He signed it, "The guy with the twenty-cent tip." He put a hundred-dollar bill in the envelope. Then he dressed and walked to the Carnegie Delicatessen on Sixth Avenue and ordered a bowl of kreplach soup and a pastrami on rye, the bread cut on the bias.

NEW YORK CITY

THE PRESENT

Doctor of Economics Alfredo Cardozo walked by the profusion of potted palms that gave quiet elegance to the tea room of the Plaza Hotel. Casually he waved back at Ernest, the energetic, short, and balding mâitre d'hotel. Dressed as usual in a shiny-from-wear tuxedo, Ernest was supervising the preparations for lunch and would soon be smiling his toothy greetings at the regulars, the penthouse denizens in stone martens and foxes around their pearl-wreathed necks as they came for refuge from the human jungle of midtown Manhattan. Watercress ladyfinger sandwiches and endive salads would give validation to the chilled martinis and colorful Bloody Marys, while outside at the Fifth Avenue entrance of the grand hotel the stretch limousines formed their usual lines, two and three deep, regardless of the mounted policeman clopping by.

Cardozo stepped out into the flood of bright September sunlight. He was dressed in medium-gray English wool with chalk stripes, impeccably tailored to hide the slight paunch he carried on his six-foot frame. His shirt of Sea Island cotton gleamed in white. The only color he allowed his ensemble was a silk tie the shade of old Bordeaux, matching the hue of his cufflinks, pigeon blood star rubies. An admiring head or two turned as he checked the time—10 A.M.

He had time to window shop before his meeting with "Joseph."

He couldn't buy anything for Maruca, as he endearingly called his wife, María Eugenia, without having to lie to her about his trip to New York and its purpose. He stopped to admire a window display at the Steuben Glass boutique, where a cascade of Washington Delicious poured out of a huge crystal apple, filling the entire window with red. He gazed absently at the fruit, his thoughts going back to Zürich and the red marble. He resumed his walk quickly, forcing his mind to think of his wife.

Cardozo seldom lied to her anymore since he had put his life and marriage in order a few years back. Neither of them had mentioned the first few years of the marriage, when he used to play around with other women. She had forgiven him his affair with the British film star, even forgotten her humiliation in seeing the press photos of him and the actress, clad only in suntan lotion, on the veranda of a villa in Ischia, breakfasting in the sun.

He admired Maruca's courage; the way she had taken the outrage and indignity, the uncertainty and embarrassment. Of course, he had had to beg forgiveness with solemn vows of future good behavior, but the affair had helped put his life in order again, and he was an orderly man. Oh, naturally, there was a tacit understanding between them that there might be, on rare occasion, a straying from the narrow paths of fidelity, as long as he was discreet and as long as he left her her dignity and pride. *Casado, pero no capado*, went the saying, "married, but not castrated." *Castrated*—the word brought back his short but furious affair with Flora Berganza. He could still feel the toe of her shoe on his testicles.

The Berganza affair took his thoughts to Langfeldt, then to the reason he was in New York.

God, there must be another way! he said to himself. His thoughts of Maruca had lulled him, distracting him from his mission, and the distraction had allayed his anxiety over meeting with that "Joseph" person, that assassin! "God, there must be another way!" he repeated, this time aloud. He checked his double-faced watch, seeing the time in Zürich. He would call Langfeldt. He shook his head; no, there would be nothing to change the course of events now. He had drawn the red marble. He was committed. It was no longer up for discussion.

Damn it! He was an orderly man, and his world was in order, he thought as he walked to the last two blocks to the Americana Hotel, the meeting place. Goddamned Arabs! Goddamned Jews! Don't they care about order in this world of ours, of theirs?

He remembered, as a student at the University of Mexico, he had had some close friends—Jews and Arabs. The Jewish boys' families were in the garment business, and they made shirts and blouses and underwear; the Arab boys' families owned the textile mills that made the fabrics that were turned into shirts and blouses and underwear. They used to do business, the boys' fathers, and they used to shake hands on the price of the fabrics. They coexisted. Not that they went to each other's homes or weddings or bar mitzvahs, but they coexisted in a peculiar harmony that was hard to define, each respecting the other's identity, the other's culture. It had worked. Now someone had figured out a way for it to work in the land each claimed as their own. Maybe it wasn't a perfect way, but it was a way. But now there was a crazy man in the White House, a crazy man who for crazy reasons was trying to fuck up the works. And that must not be allowed to happen, reasoned Alfredo Cardozo, orderly man.

He walked into the Americana Hotel coffee shop with a clearer understanding of his purpose. Now he looked forward to meeting "Joseph."

He asked for a table against the wall; he could watch the comings and goings, as was his habit. He had a breakfast of ham and eggs. He pushed away the empty plates and settled back for another cup of coffee. As he started to look around for his waitress, a busboy walked up with a pot of fresh coffee.

"¿Más café, señor?"

Cardozo thought he detected a Mexican accent instead of the expected Puerto Rican Spanish. *"Gracias, sí,"* he said.

"Por nada, señor." Now Cardozo was sure. Puerto Ricans pronounced their word-ending *r*'s with an *l* sound. The busboy didn't. He studied the stocky Mexican, his coarse, black hair and high cheekbones, and he felt a little homesick hearing the familiar singsong of the Indians, of which the young man obviously was one.

The busboy came back with a cart to clear Cardozo's table. "What are you doing so far from home?" Cardozo said.

The busboy wiped the table, eyes shyly avoiding Cardozo's. *"Pos aquí nomás, patrón, jalando,"* he said in a combination of illiterate Indian-Spanish and citified vernacular. "Just working, boss."

Cardozo nursed his second cup of coffee, looking at his watch from time to time. "Joseph" was late. Maybe he wouldn't show. God, how he wished he wouldn't show! he thought for a moment, but he knew that "Joseph" would show and that he would have to wait, no matter what.

After a few minutes, the busboy came back with the coffee pot. Cardozo shook his head. Then the busboy asked in his Indian-Spanish, "Are you Dr. Cardozo?"

Cardozo looked at the Mexican quizzically, his smile fading.

"I have a message for you from Joseph," the busboy said. "He's not coming today, but—"

"What?" Cardozo said, confused. "What the hell is going on? Where is he?"

"—but that he would meet you here tomorrow at the same time."

Cardozo asked angrily, "Where the devil is he? Who are you? What the hell is going on here?"

"That's all I know, boss. With your permission . . ." The busboy walked away, disappearing through a service door.

As Cardozo stormed out of the hotel, the Mexican busboy changed his clothes in the locker room. Satisfied that he was alone, he removed the black wig, exposing the fine, blond hair of Paul Cline. He extracted the two small plastic rings from within his nose that had given the appropriate flair to his nostrils. He removed a set of dark brown scleral lenses that covered his blue eyes. Cold cream from his kit cleaned the brownish tint from his pale skin. In less than a minute Cline had transformed himself from a Tarascan Indian to a European.

Cline left through the alley, then blended into the noonday crowd on Sixth Avenue.

He walked toward the Metropolitan Museum of Art; there was an exhibition of Impressionist paintings on loan from the Hermitage that included a new Van Gogh, never before seen in the West. He had all day to indulge himself, he thought, as he strolled in the humid, monoxided air of the hot city.

There was an obstacle of people surrounding the Van Gogh. They fought with their elbows for at least a glimpse of the work, entitled "Storm off the Coast of Brittany," painted in the last year of the artist's life, when storms were thundering in his mind. Cline passed it up, instead comfortably viewing works by Russian classicists and neo-Impressionists, hitherto unknown to the West. The delicately applied hues of pink and ocher and subtle tans and grays of the Russian art made him think of his own art, which he would practice the next day in his bathroom at the Algonquin Hotel.

The next morning Alfredo Cardozo sat at the same table at the Americana. As he waited for "Joseph," he concentrated on the crossword puzzle in *The New York Times,* trying to distract his thoughts from the unknown factors of the "Joseph" situation, whatever they might be. The whole idea of "Joseph" was repellent to him, but like a spoonful of foul but necessary medicine, he tried to ignore it until the time came.

Cardozo heard a customer ask the hostess for the table next to his. *Damn! He looks like a fairy. That's all I need.*

The customer, rather tall and freakish, using a walking stick, sat down. Cardozo looked at him. He was probably an actor, he thought. Unemployed, by the looks of his clothes.

The man had removed his large Panama hat. Dark glasses partially hid bushy gray eyebrows and tired eyes. His seersucker suit had seen many a summer, and his yellowed, once-white shirt had a starched collar whose tips pointed slightly upward. The tie, broad and colorful, had a nineteen-forties knot, and his shoes were black and white wing-tips. He reeked of shaving lotion. His face, sporting a well-trimmed gray moustache, was handsomely chiseled for his probable seventy-plus years, thought Cardozo.

The man ordered orange juice, freshly squeezed, please, wheat toast, and tea with milk. As the waitress walked away, he looked nonchalantly at Cardozo's puzzle.

"A crossword buff, eh?" he said, smiling broadly. "I find the *Times* crosswords the most challenging, don't you?"

Cardozo sighed inwardly. "Yes, I do," he said. He returned to his puzzle, hoping the actor would leave him alone. "Joseph" was due any minute.

"Of course," the actor continued in the melodious voice of the thespian, undiscouraged by Cardozo's disinterest in him, "my favorites were always in *The Times* of London, which I used to do religiously every morning with my coffee when I lived there. Ah, that's when I was allowed to have coffee," he lamented. "My doctor won't let me drink it anymore. Anyway, as I was saying about *The Times* of London crosswords, the problem was in the British English, if you know what I mean. Their spelling is entirely different in many of our common words, you know. Yes, I'm sure you must. I can see by your mien and your—your bearing. You have a look of culture and education about you, sir, if you don't mind my saying."

Cardozo smiled patronizingly. "Thank you," he said without trying to encourage further instrusions.

The actor stretched his neck in the direction of the crossword. "Are you stuck? Perhaps I can help. I'm quite good, you know."

It was not in Cardozo's nature to be rude. "Well, now that you mention it," he said, "I need a four-letter word for 'pepper shrub,' second letter *a*."

"Try k-a-v-a," the actor said, raising his eyebrows, "but of course it could be spelled with *c* as easily. They're tricky, these composers!" He laughed softly.

Cardozo nodded, going back to the puzzle. *Damn it, where in hell is "Joseph"?*

"By the way," insisted the actor, "do I detect a slight accent in you, sir?"

"I'm from Mexico," Cardozo said dryly.

"Ah, Mexico! Beautiful place! Wonderful people, the Mexicans," the man said, ornamenting his tone. "I made a film there in the forties. Tampico—or was it Vera Cruz? I'm not sure which, but it was warm and tropical. Ah, the beautiful palms!" He made a swaying motion with his hands. "When the boat took us away, I vowed that I would return." He extended his liver-spotted hand. "By the way, my name is Victor Vanderbilt. Perhaps you've heard of me; I'm an actor."

Cardozo shook the actor's hand, which was dry and limp. "Alfredo Cardozo," he said. "I'm sorry; I was never much of a movie buff, Mr. Vanderbilt."

"Of course," said the actor. "Oh, well, never mind. It's been awhile since my face was on the screen. Perhaps it's for the best, what with the trash they call cinema today, wouldn't you think so, Mr. Cardozo? Cardozo—such a lovely name, so"—Vanderbilt searched for the word—"so *mellifluous*!"

"Thank you," Cardozo said with sincerity, "you're very gracious." No, he wasn't a fairy, he thought, just a lonely one-time actor living in the past. He looked at his watch. Where the devil was "Joseph"?

"Am I keeping you, Mr. Cardozo?" Vanderbilt said. "I'm not imposing myself, I hope. I wouldn't dream of it."

"No, not at all. I *am* meeting someone here. But he's a bit late, it seems."

"But of course," Vanderbilt said triumphantly, "you're waiting for 'Joseph'!"

Cardozo felt as if he had been hit in the stomach. He stared at the actor for a few seconds. "Listen, Mr. Vanderbilt, or whatever you name is, would you mind telling me just what in hell is going on?" He looked around the coffee shop and in a low voice demanded, "Where is he? Why does he send messengers? What kind of game is this?"

Vanderbilt looked at Cardozo in mock seriousness. "You are getting upset."

"Why shouldn't I be upset?" Cardozo said. "How dare you make a fool of me? First he sends me a busboy and makes me come back today. Now he sends me a chatterbox of a has-been actor who tells me not to be upset!"

"A has-been actor!" Vanderbilt repeated in an offended tone. "Why, my dear sir, I want you to know you're addressing a consummate actor."

"Stop it!" Cardozo fumed in a whisper. "You can tell your friend—"

"It's no use getting personal, you know," Vanderbilt said, lifting his teacup to his lips. "After all, he did come. Both times, in fact."

"What are you talking about, you old fool! I'm not—"

Vanderbilt interrupted: *"Pos aquí nomás, patrón, jalando."* It was the voice of the busboy.

Cardozo stared at the actor. Then the realization hit him. "You? You mean—the busboy—you? You're 'Joseph'?"

"Joseph" grinned. "Yes, that's my *nom de guerre*," he said, still in the tone and manner of Vanderbilt. "Well, what do you think, Dr. Cardozo? Do you yet maintain I'm a has-been actor?"

"I meant no offense, Mr. Vanderbilt," Cardozo said. He immediately caught himself and grinned abashedly. "I mean, Joseph. I— I don't even know what I'm saying. You're quite the expert. I'm impressed with your performance, to say the least." Then he added, "But why did you feel you had to do this, the charades, the disguises?"

The grin faded from "Joseph's" face. He removed his dark glasses and spoke in another voice, one completely different from Vanderbilt's. "Don't try to figure me out, Cardozo," he warned softly. "It's dangerous."

Cardozo stared at him, disconcerted by the menace in the eyes and tone of voice. "I'm not trying to figure you out. It's just that, under the circumstances, we should trust each other," he said.

"That's bullshit, Cardozo. Think about it. All you will ever learn about me is that I'm unpredictable. Now, let's get out of here and discuss the job."

A cab dropped them deep in Central Park, where they would be ignored. New York, despite its masses, was a private city where one would be ignored because there were too many faces not to; a bench in Central Park was just another part of that city.

"First off, how much did Langfeldt authorize you to pay me?" asked "Joseph."

Cardozo wasn't prepared for the immediacy of the question of fees. He swallowed and cleared his throat. "He said . . . five million."

"Pounds sterling," said "Joseph."

Cardozo cleared his throat again. "Dollars," he said with difficulty.

"No. I know the way Langfeldt deals. He told you to offer me half of what the group had budgeted, leaving room for negotiation. Let's save time by not haggling. I want five million pounds sterling."

What "Joseph" had said about Langfeldt was true; he had budgeted ten million dollars. Cardozo nodded. He felt intimidated by the assassin, and he wanted to end the business as soon as he could. "All right," he said, "half to be deposited in an account of your choice within forty-eight hours, the balance on completion of the assignment."

"Okay. tell Langfeldt the usual place of deposit. He knows where." The usual place was a numbered account in Guernsey, the Channel island. No names, no questions.

"It occurs to me," Cardozo said, "that you haven't asked who the subject of your assignment is to be."

"You mean who I'm to kill, Cardozo? Come on, spare me the melodramatic euphemisms of cheap spy stories."

All right, as you wish," Cardozo said dryly. "But you still haven't asked—"

"Joseph" interrupted. "I don't have to ask. I know. You want me to kill Simon Jensen."

"Ah, then Langfeldt told you. He said he wouldn't."

"He didn't tell me. I figured it out." "Joseph" looked at Cardozo. "I can see by the look on your face that you need some insight into this business. You see, political and religious leaders are commodities. They have a going price to kill, depending on their importance and on their security factors. The President of the United States and the Chairman of the Supreme Soviet are the only two who would merit such a large fee. The Russian doesn't have a two-party system of politics, therefore he doesn't concern himself with the security problems of open politicking as does Jensen with his constituency. I would not accept the job of killing Chairman Grigoriev, his security is too tight. And then there are other leaders whose security is such that no amount of money would tempt me. That leaves the American, whose security is, and always will be, loose. It's quite simple, Cardozo—it comes down to Simon Jensen. What's the time frame, if any?"

"It was fourteen days yesterday."

"Two weeks? Not very likely, without some help. Does Langfeldt have any inside help?"

"Yes. You're to get in touch with him for the details."

"All right."

Cardozo suddenly felt nauseated at the thought of what he was doing. It was real now—no more scenarios, no more dreams. It was happening.

"I must tell you why we're doing this, Joseph. We—"

"Joseph" held up a hand. "Hold it, Cardozo. I'm not interested. My fee is all I care about." He motioned with his head. "If you walk down that lane, you can find a cab. Tell Langfeldt I'll be in touch."

WASHINGTON, D.C.

TUESDAY

"Joseph" drove the van slowly down the street. The embassy was on the left. He looked to his right, studying the buildings and their positions. A three-story apartment house was located slightly off-line of the embassy's front door. That one gave him an angle, a broader scope than being right on top of it. He turned right at the corner, saw the service alley, and followed it, slowing at the building's rear, where he noticed a heavy door that opened, he gauged, with the tenants' latchkeys. Next to the door was the gate to the garage, opened by remote control units, most likely. Okay, he thought. He drove back to the street, parking a few doors behind. He turned off the engine and looked at his watch—7:50 A.M. The day man would be arriving soon. He sat back and waited.

At two minutes before eight a man in a blue-gray uniform with a newspaper under his arm sauntered down the sidewalk and up the stoop of the apartment building. Less than a minute later another man in an identical uniform left, carrying a lunch pail. After ten minutes, "Joseph" went to the front door of the building. He wore an ill-fitting blue suit and an old fedora. Heavy glasses rested on his large nose, and bushy gray hair stuck out from under the hat. He looked like a man in his sixties. He too carried a newspaper folded under his arm. He rang the buzzer. Another buzzer opened the door. He walked in, feet shuffling in a tired, aching gait. He put the newspaper down on the counter.

"Mornin'," he said to the doorman. "Name's Henry. Frank L. Henry. I'm a private dick." He pulled out a business card with the same name and an address in Kansas City, Missouri. The card was dogeared and soiled. The doorman looked at it, handing it back with some aversion, which was the intended reaction.

"You're a long ways from home, pal," the doorman said, grimacing at the midwestern twang. "What can I do for you?"

"Yep, a long ways," the detective said, "but with the jets nowadays, its okay. I got Andy Jackson in my pocket sez you can help me out," he said easily. "I'm on a divorce case and I'm followin' a lead. What do you say?"

"Hey, pal, I don't know," the doorman said, shaking his head gravely. "I'd like to help you out, but it wouldn't look right, you know what I mean? These here people trust me," he said with too much sincerity.

"Okay," the detective said, "I ain't working for Rockyfeller, but I guess my client'll okay two Jacksons." He reached in his pocket and pulled out some folded currency.

"Tell you what, pal: make it five-oh and we'll talk. Guy's gotta make a livin,' you know what I mean?"

"Gotcha. If it's worth forty, it's worth fifty, I always say." He put two twenties and a ten on the counter.

The bills flew into the doorman's pocket. "Whattaya wanna know, pal?"

"Well, like I said, I got this here lead," the detective continued. "Some dolly, 'bout twenty-eight, maybe thirty, blond, fine figure, dresses pretty good. Drops by coupla times a week to see some fella. Stays a spell, then vamooses, alone. I wanna know who she comes to visit. That's about it."

The doorman looked up to the skylight, his mouth screwed up in concentration. "A young dame? Naw, not here, pal. Least not on *my* shift. Sure you got the right place?"

"Well, that's the lead I got. I figure you got only four tenants here, 'cording to your register outside. You figure any of 'em going for some dolly for a coupla hours play?" he drawled.

The doorman massaged his chin. "Well, let's see. First off you got the Bakers on the first floor. She don't go out much, and if he screws around, he don't bring 'em here. Naw, that lets *him* out. Then there's the old guy on two, Mr. Ripley, but he's too old. If he ever got it up again, it'd be one for Ripley!" He laughed with glee. "Get it, pal? One for Ripley?"

The detective stared. Then he smiled. "That's pretty good," he said, eyes opaque. "Now, what about the other floors? Who you got there?"

The doorman turned serious again. "Let's see. On three you got the Grands. Nice-lookin' couple, but they're always together, like two peas in a pod, you know what I mean? Always traveling. Matter-afack, just now they're on a cruise somewhere or other. Won't be back till next month sometime."

The private investigator had heard all he needed to hear.

"Now, on four," the doorman went on, "you got the two broads that work over at the Pentagon. One of 'em's a bulldyke—I know that for a fack—and the other, well, you know. That leaves them out, don't it?"

The old man nodded. "Don't look like any of 'em fit the bill. Looks like I got a bum steer, don't it?"

"Yeah, I think you did, pal. Sorry 'bout that," the doorman said, putting his hand in the pocket where he had stuffed the fifty dollars.

The man turned to leave. "Yep, a bum steer. Ain't the first time," he said as he shuffled out.

The doorman watched him with sympathy. He picked up his newspaper and turned to the sports page. *Poor old fart,* he thought, *his corns must be killing him.* "What a way to make a living," he mumbled to himself, licking his thumb as he turned the pages.

The private dick disappeared into the back of the parked van. A few minutes later "Joseph" climbed into the driver's seat and gunned the van into life. He headed for his motel on New York Avenue in the northeast section of the city. It was a busy street that led to the Baltimore turnpike with many tourists coming and going. No one noticed him or his van with Maryland plates, rented with false papers.

He parked in front of his room on the ground floor and checked his watch. It was not yet 9:00 A.M.—still plenty of time to have breakfast at the motel's coffee shop and get back to the room and wait for the call. Eleven A.M. sharp, the voice had said; then, again at 11:00 P.M., if needed, if there had been any changes in the President's schedule.

The voice had been Admiral Smith's, as prearranged with Langfeldt. He had called the day before with the information that Jensen would be seeing the Israeli prime minister at his embassy the following day. It was a meeting called by Ben-David at the last minute, and because it was a Jewish holiday, Ben-David had asked that it be held at the embassy. Jensen had agreed. There had been no notification of aides, no announcement to the media; just a quick private session between the two leaders. The only thing Smith wasn't sure of was the time. He was to let "Joseph" know by 11:00 A.M.

At precisely eleven the phone rang. "Tomorrow," the same voice said, "tomorrow at 1:00 P.M.—same place. No idea how long it will last, nor will I expect to know." The voice was shaky, unsure. "Wait!" the voice said in a panic. "Don't hang up! Isn't there—isn't there . . . *another way?*"

The assassin snarled into the phone. "Shut up! Just call tonight if you have to. Otherwise don't say another word." He slammed down the receiver. He noticed some perspiration on it. That wasn't par for his course, and it disturbed him.

He splashed cold water onto his face. Then he looked in the yellow pages for a rifle range. He found one nearby and memorized its address. He took a rectangular case out of the closet and examined the lock and tiny seal he had put on it. They were intact. He got in the van and drove to Maryland and the rifle range.

Halfway there "Joseph" parked the van in a deserted picnic area. He put on a baseball cap with the Coors logo on it and dark goggle-type glasses. Out of a kit he found a bushy moustache that he pressed on his lip. He opened the rectangular case and assembled a custom-made Belgian 5.56-millimeter rifle made by one of the foremost gunsmiths in Europe and precision-sighted at a hundred meters. He would test once more its accuracy at plus-or-minus ten meters.

At the rifle range he fired six shots, all hitting an area of impact no larger than three inches in diameter—more than enough to cause a mortal wound to the head of the President or, for that matter, anywhere within the "bottle" of his body—the torso, from his hips to neck. From prior use, "Joseph" knew well the devastating, explosive force of the special little bullets, not much larger than a common .22.

Satisfied with the accuracy of the sniper weapon, he returned to the motel and changed into comfortable tweeds for a tour of the National Gallery of Art. The Mellon Foundation had acquired some long-sought Post-impressionist paintings, and they were on loan to the museum. He walked a few blocks and flagged a cab.

The assassin returned to his room at ten-thirty that evening, time enough for a phone call from the White House. He didn't know—nor did he care to know—to whom the voice belonged. That was Langfeldt's business. All he knew was that the owner of the voice had been close to panic before. He wondered what kind of blackmail Langfeldt was using on him. He made a solution of water and ammonia in the sink and put half a towel in it. He knew that the blackmail, in whatever its form, was effective. Langfeldt was always sure of what he did. He wiped down every place in the room that could have fingerprints on it, and when he finished he put on surgical gloves. He would wear the gloves until he left the room for good the following morning.

He looked around, satisfied with his thoroughness. He glanced at his watch: 11:06. No phone call.

It was on. The point of no return.

WEDNESDAY, 6:30 A.M.

"Joseph" awoke the next morning to the shrill alarm of his wrist-watch. He was alert immediately. He did a few minutes of rigorous exercise, then took a cold shower. He began honing his mind, ready-ing it for the assignment, by remembering the details of the paintings he had studied the day before. A piece of the disturbing dream he had had flickered through his mind, the image of Franziska. He blinked it away. Then another face intruded, the face of Abe Berman. The dream began to take form, but he willed it away. Something was wrong—his sweaty hands last night, and now this. He turned off the shower and dried himself and the inside of the glass stall. Puzzled, he walked naked to the bedroom and sat on the floor. He did a series of yoga exercises, and after twenty minutes of concentration the faces disappeared. He was ready.

He put everything in the van and left by a side entrance heading for Massachusetts Avenue.

He arrived at 7:35, certain that the night doorman would be awake by then. He had to take care of the door before the day man arrived at eight. He studied a plastic identity plate with his picture on it, wearing the wig and moustache he had had on the previous morn-ing. Across the plate in bold letters, it said THE BELL SYSTEM, super-imposed over Bell's logo. He clipped the plate to his shirt pocket and, tool box in hand, headed for the door of the apartment house across from the Israeli embassy. He buzzed.

The doorman buzzed the door open and "Joseph" stepped in.

"Hi," he said cheerfully. "Telephone company."

The doorman yawned. "You guys up so early?"

"Oh, I don't mind," the repairman said. "Already did one place up the street. I gotta look at your terminals; annual inspection. Shouldn't take but a couple of minutes."

"Yeah? Awright. Down the stairs, on the far wall."

"Thanks. Won't be but a sec."

"Joseph" jaunted down the stairs into the garage. He spotted the locked telephone equipment panel and ignored it, looking around for the outside door. He saw it and started over. Then he heard the *clunk* of the elevator. He froze, listening. It wasn't stopping in the lobby; it was coming down to the garage.

He moved quickly, hiding behind a support column with empty parking spaces. The door opened and two women, one plain and efficient-looking, the other young and pretty, came out.

"You know what I mean, damn it!" the plain one was saying. "He was hitting on you, and you know it! Or did you like it?" she whined. "Honestly, Jo," the other one said, sometimes you make me feel so cheap." She got in the passenger side of a Plymouth, slamming its door.

The doorman had been right—the two who worked at the Pentagon were having a lover's quarrel. He winced at the sound of screeching, angry tires.

He went quickly to the outside door and opened it, looking for any device that might trigger an alarm. There was none. He took a roll of strong, transparent packaging tape and placed three strips over the spring latch. He tested it twice and watched the door close automatically each time with its pneumatic closer. The tape held well. He went back to the lobby.

"Everything checks out okay," he said to the doorman.

"Okay, buddy," the doorman said as he folded his dogeared newspaper. "Say hello to Ma Bell for me." Then, with the thought hitting him, the doorman reopened the paper and turned to the financial section to check on how his few shares of AT&T were doing.

WEDNESDAY, 7:30 A.M.

Jimmy Ryan came down the rickety stairs of his rooming house. The odor of sauerkraut announced that it was Wednesday, the day his landlady, Mrs. Movius, faithfully prepared the kraut and *Wurst* dish. She always began cooking it early in the morning, and by midafternoon the whole place smelled to him of rotten cabbage. Still, he was glad she was busy; he didn't want to meet her that day. He was behind in his rent again.

He walked down the stairs carefully, trying to avoid a particular riser that creaked loudly, sending Mrs. Movius a sure signal. He miscounted the steps and hit the informer hard, bringing the landlady out like a shot.

"Mr. Ryan, pliss," the old lady said, drying her hands on her *dirndl*-type apron, "I must esk you for tzuh rent. You are four weeks behindt now, undt I heff my bills to pay."

"Uh, I'm sorry, Mrs. Movius," Jimmy Ryan said. "Look, I get paid today. I'll get you your money, don't you worry none." *Jesus Christ! Everybody's carpin' at me!* Jimmy Ryan said to himself.

"I vood appreciate it, Mr. Ryan," the landlady said. "Undt pliss, don't fall behindt no more. If you do, I heff to esk you to liff." She looked at him sadly, but there was conviction in her eyes.

Shit, Jimmy Ryan thought. *Nobody's faithful anymore.* He recalled when he used to come home from demonstrations or meetings, wearing his army surplus suntans with a Sam Browne belt, pants tucked into his engineer's boots, and on his sleeve a swastika armband—an obscure relic from the violent past, a past Jimmy Ryan was trying to give rebirth to. But Mrs. Movius didn't notice anymore.

He had rented the room from her on the strength of her pure German background. He had hoped to gain her friendship and confidence in him and for what he stood. He didn't understand that she wanted no part of what Jimmy Ryan thought was noble.

One night, coming home from a dress rehearsal at party headquarters, Jimmy Ryan had knocked on the German widow's door in full uniform, including a white U.S. Army helmet liner emblazoned with the symbol she had learned to fear so long ago. She had gasped inwardly as he stood in front of her, feet planted apart, thumbs hooked on his Sam Browne belt, eyes proud and serious, a tight smile on his lips. Mrs. Movius had looked at him sadly, then advised, "You must be careful in ziss uniform, Mr. Ryan. Ve are in America now, undt not in tzuh oldt dayss in Chermany."

From then on she had ignored his endeavors, as she had ignored the endeavors of other zealous young men in brown shirts and jackboots and ski kepis and swastika armbands in her hometown of Königsberg in East Prussia. She had clucked with quiet disapproval then, as she did now.

Jimmy Ryan clocked in. He was twenty minutes late, which was not unusual. He walked by the foreman's cage office and waved a greeting. "Hi, Charlie. Uh, sorry I'm late; had a meetin' last night."

"That's okay," the foreman said. "Hey, Jim, got a sec?"

Jimmy Ryan noticed that the usually cheery foreman was acting nervous and hesitant. "Yeah, sure, Charlie. What's up?"

"Sit down, Jimbo. Get the weight off your feet," Charlie said, his lips smiling but his eyes serious. "Uh, look, Jimbo, it's not my idea, but . . . well, Marv? over at the front office? he said I should let you go." Charlie shuffled some papers on his desk, avoiding Jimmy Ryan's eyes.

Jimmy Ryan's eyes narrowed. "You cannin' me, Charlie?"

"Jimmy, they say business is slow, real slow, an' they can't afford to keep you on." Charlie looked pained. "They said to tell you that you ain't bein' fired, just laid off. Tell 'em that when you look for another job. Laid off 'cause the business was bad, you know? We'll give you a good ref'rence, Jimmy.''

Jimmy Ryan was confused and angry. He pulled out a Lucky Strike and lit it, clenching the cigarette between his teeth. "That's some crocka shit in the mornin'," he said to the end of the Lucky.

"Yeah," Charlie said with sympathy, "a real crocka shit. By the way, Jim, here's your pay envelope. It's got two weeks extra in it. Sev'rance pay.''

"Tell Marv he can shove it up his ass.''

"Aw, come on, Jim," Charlie whined, "don't make things rougher on yourself. Take it. You can use it." He pushed the envelope at him. "C'mon," he urged softly, "take it.''

Jimmy Ryan ground out the cigarette on the floor. He took the envelope and stuffed it into the breast pocket of his denim jacket. "Well, fuck, I was lookin' for a job when I found this one, wasn't I?"

Before Jimmy Ryan was halfway out the warehouse, he noticed Al, the supervisor, talking to a young black man. The young man was in work clothes and seemed to be paying close attention to Al's instructions.

Jimmy Ryan returned to Charlie's cage. His voice was soft, but his eyes were slits of hate. "That nigger over there with Al, Charlie—is he takin' my job?"

"Well, it ain't exactly like that, Jimmy," Charlie said in conciliatory tones. "See, the front office, they—"

Jimmy Ryan screamed, "You mean that nigger's takin' my job away from me?"

"Chrissake, Jim, hold it down, will ya? I tol' you the front office got a lotta heat from the gov'ment. We store a lotta their files down here, you know. An' they said we wasn't keeping up with the affirmative action shit, ya know? They tol' us we gotta hire more of 'em, the niggers an' the other minorities, or they gonna take the business someplace else. You gotta un'erstand, Jimmy," he pleaded.

"Yeah, I un'erstand, Charlie," Jimmy Ryan said, breathing hard, containing his fury. "You bet I un'erstand. The niggers are takin' over, Charlie. An' you guys are goin' along. Us white people, we ain't got no more rights, Charlie, 'cause the niggers an' the Commies are takin' over America, Charlie. Yeah, I un'erstand awright, Charlie. You know what?" he asked between clenched teeth.

Charlie looked at him wide-eyed. "What, Jimmy?"

"Fuck you, Charlie. That's what."

Jimmy Ryan turned and left. As he reached the loading dock, he balled up his fist, extending his middle finger, and swept the warehouse with the fist, shouting at the top of his lungs, veins popping out of his neck, tears of rage in his eyes. "Fuck all of yooz! *Fuck you!*" He grabbed his crotch and bent his knees, pumping his pelvis at the gaping audience. *"Eat this, you cocksuckers!"*

After cashing his check, Jimmy Ryan went to the first bar he could find and proceeded to get drunk. Soon he was wallowing in self-pity, an activity not difficult for Jimmy Ryan under ordinary circumstances. But now he had some legitimate laments with which to add tears to the beer he was using as a chaser for his jiggers of rye. Added to his troubles, the night before, George Washington Todd, the National Führer, had berated him for his lethargic efforts at recruitment. The party was going broke for lack of dues and contributions, he had said, and he threatened to demote him from D.C. Gauleiter to a plain storm trooper. Jimmy Ryan had protested. What could he do—stop people on the streets and ask them if they wanted to join the American Nazi Party? "Shit, nine outta ten people in D.C. are niggers, anyway!"

He threw down another shot. "Then there's ol' lady Movius," he mumbled to himself. "Pleess, Mr. Ryan, tzuh rent, or you moof out," he mimicked under his thickening breath. "Moneymoneymoney! That's all they think about. Never give a guy a chance, fuckin' traitors!"

A fellow drinker at the bar thought Jimmy Ryan was talking to him. "Whatcha say, buddy? Din't catch that."

Jimmy Ryan looked at him with drunken eyes, mean drunken eyes. "Fuck you too, mac. Mine your own fuckin' bi'ness."

A short while later Jimmy Ryan was thrown out bodily by the club-wielding saloonkeeper. The humiliation was now complete. He staggered down the street, blotting his cut lip on his sleeve and spitting out a bloodied tooth. He bent over to pick it up. "Fuck it," he decided, and walked to his rooming house.

He was beyond plain anger—his rage was all-encompassing, a fury he had never before felt. It wasn't directed at the bartender, or even at the guy who had beat him up—it was focused on Secretary of Labor Ira Strauss, the Commie-hebe, who was seeing to it that good, honest, hard-workin' white people were bein' turned into second-class citizens, their jobs taken from them and given to the niggers! But most of all, the rage was toward the President of the United States, Simon Jensen, the Commie-Jew-lovin', nigger-ass-lickin' traitor to his own!

Would he go on welfare now that he had lost his job? He couldn't—he *wouldn't*—do that like the rest of 'em. It sickened him to think of sitting at the desk of some smart-ass jigaboo, puttin' him down with questions 'bout how come he wasn't workin'. Some uppity coon lookin' down on him like he was so much trash! Shit, he'd never do that! Of course, he couldn't go home neither, havin' to face Poppa, who said he'd be a failure, a bust! He'd rather die first.

That's it. He'd die, but die like a man! He wasn't gonna blow his brains out with a .45. No sir, he'd take somebody with him. Maybe some important jig—or a big Jew, even. Yeah, he'd go out in a blaze of glory, then all of 'em—George Washington Todd and his poppa, all of 'em—they'd remember Jimmy Ryan, they'd know who Jimmy Ryan was. The whole fuckin' world would know who Jimmy Ryan was!

He flung open the screen door to his rooming house, stopping at Mrs. Movius's apartment first to slip some money under her door. (Let no man say that Jimmy Ryan left this world owing one penny!) He ran up the stairs to his room and opened the bottom drawer of his dresser, flinging socks and underwear to the floor. Then he found it. He looked at it with affection, as at an old friend who made no demands of him. It was still as clean and shiny as it had been when he stole it from the Marine Corps armory. It was packed with stubby, copper-nosed, .45-caliber bullets. With a savage motion, he slid one into the chamber.

WEDNESDAY, 7:50 A.M.

"Joseph" waited in the van. At 7:55 the day man sauntered down the street and into the building. A few seconds later, the night man left, also sauntering. He wondered what there was about the job that made them walk as if they had been delivering mail all day in tight shoes. He waited another ten minutes, then started the van and drove to an unattended parking lot, putting money in a numbered slot that bought all-day parking. He took his kit and walked back to the rear of the building. He opened the service door, removed the tape across the latch, and quietly closed it. He walked up the fire stairs to the third floor.

He rang the bell, making sure that the Grands had not cut short their trip. He waited. Nothing. The first lock was difficult under his pick but finally opened. The second lock easily gave in to a plastic card. The door opened to the musty odor of unoccupancy.

He looked over the entire apartment. It was large—five rooms, two baths. Pictures of middle-aged people, pleasing and obviously well off, were displayed about the tastefully furnished place. Photos of young people sat on the mantel.

He studied all the windows. The living room offered the best view of the front of the embassy, a hundred or so yards below and across. He placed an easy chair at an angle to the window, giving him a perfect view of the comings and goings. Then "Joseph" took off his leather driving gloves and opened the kit. He slipped on the surgical gloves and removed the parts of the long gun. He assembled it and fed it a clip of the little bullets of certain death. He operated the bolt, sliding one into the breech, flipped off the safety, and put it down near him on the floor. A look at his watch told him it would be a long wait.

The assassin went to the kitchen. The refrigerator was empty except for some Jell-O and a couple of bruised apples. In the freezer he found some frozen orange juice, which he made. It went down well; he hadn't had breakfast. As his stomach rumbled its thanks for the nutrients, he scanned the spotless kitchen. An image of himself as a youngster, squeezing oranges on a press at Abe's Deli in Chicago, flashed through his mind. "Don't give 'em that canned *shmuey*," Abe would say. "Give 'em fresh and they'll come back!" He poured another glass, and the image changed to Tomasa squeezing oranges for breakfast. He washed the glass while feeling a powerful urge to be with her at that moment—and with Abe.

He found some instant coffee in a cupboard. He put water in a kettle and heated it, thinking of the strange turn of his mental processes—Abe and Tomasa just now, and his mother, Franziska, yesterday (or was it that morning?). In the past, "Joseph" had never mused about anything or anyone. Only those involved in the job. Paul Cline did, but never "Joseph." What was happening?

He ate a mealy apple, chewing it in quiet pique at the intrusion into his normally detached cerebration.

He sat down on the kitchen floor and did ten minutes of yoga exercises, successfully cleansing his mind. Still, a slight hangover remained of the sentimental contamination, affecting his overall mood.

He washed and dried the cup, putting everything back the way it had been. He wasn't concerned that they would find traces of the President's assassin there; certainly they would. And the doormen would quickly give their stories to the Secret Service. No, he was just being considerate of the Grands. They looked like nice people.

He found some issues of *Time* magazine, and he sat down in the easy chair by the window and began reading and doing what was a matter of routine in his job—waiting.

ARLINGTON, VIRGINIA

WEDNESDAY, 10:00 A.M.

Erika Kramer parked at the curb in front of their modest house. She lifted out a bag of groceries and walked slowly around to the back porch. She was walking more slowly of late, minimizing it with the explanation that she was not as young as she used to be. But she lied. It was because of the pain.

She put the groceries away methodically, keeping her thoughts restricted to the work at hand. She would deal with the other problems later, after she felt better and could think more clearly.

Quietly she opened the door to their bedroom. Peter was still asleep. She knew that he had been up all night, and she knew the reason why. She had heard the conversation with Baruch, and it was clear that her husband did not wish to share his pain with her. She understood, for it was the same reasoning that made her keep her pain from him.

She brewed some camomile tea that would alleviate the hurt. Despite her medical training, she still reverted to the homeopathic remedies of her youth.

She took the cup of tea to the small garden. A cool hint of early autumn was in the air, and she sat in the warming sun to think. She had much to think about, to ponder—and so little of it to share with him.

She sipped the tea. Its fragrance distracted her from the scheduled topic of consideration to the scenes of her youth. Snatches of images, vivid in color, came to her as she tasted her childhood through the camomile. Lilacs in bloom . . . orange and purple fields of saffron swaying in the mountain breezes . . . chestnut trees proudly self-adorned for the cold. Then other aromas—the leather and soap and freshness of the young Vikings who came and left . . . and blond Vikings who returned with their smells of blood and pus and mud . . . and death.

She shivered in the sunshine as she remembered the cold of the mountain . . . the hard-packed ice of the roads, the carriages drawn by skeletal horses snorting great sprays of steam. She sipped the tea once more, knowing that the effort to forget was futile, and she gave in to the unique sound of tanks churning up the streets, spewing cobblestones like missles, with their treads . . . guttural curses of dark Germans, no longer blond Vikings, as their Panzers spun and weaved on the ice like sailors on a drunken binge.

Then, as much as she tried not to, she remembered other Germans—or were they Austrians? It didn't matter—who also cursed . . . but at her. High-born whore, they called her. Those too had smells about them. One in particular. She still smelled his breath of tobacco and liquor. She told him, she recalled with disgust, that he smelled of death. Years later, as he stood in the dock in Jerusalem to answer for his crimes, she would know why he smelled of death.

The pain hit and ran. Lately it was coming more often.

She sighed, resisting the temptation to relive the horror of that dawn in Budapest. She tried to make herself think of the problems at hand—the crisis with Jensen and Peter. She closed her eyes, trying to blank out the memories, but they crept back inexorably, unrelenting and pitiless.

Another smell invaded her memory, fetid air made by humans on their way to slaughter. She again heard the wail of a bearded Jew, resignedly crying out the prayers for the dead. Then she heard the sound made by that Jew's head as it split open under the blow of the SS rifle butt. She heard the awful silence, broken only by the scraping sounds made by the dying man's legs and arms as they quivered against the cement in death's spasm.

A spasm of a different sort struck her abdomen. She grabbed at her belly, the teacup falling to the grass. The pain and the retrieval of the unbroken cup brought her back to the reality of the present and the consultation with Temkin.

She worked with Joel Temkin at the National Institutes of Health at the Bethesda Center: she as a research scientist, he as chief investigator of a government-sponsored cancer research program. They were close friends and they shared a deep mutual professional respect. It was Temkin whom she saw in his private office when the symptoms first appeared. That morning he discussed his findings with her. He used terms with which she was familiar, terms like leukocyte count, Pel-Ebstein fever, hemohistioblasts, lymphadonopathy, and splenomegaly, all adding up to what she originally suspected—acute lymphoma, or the more benign term, Hodgkin's disease. It somehow sounded better. Less formidable. Less deadly.

She had sat at Temkin's desk taking notes, trying to appear dispassionate, as if she were sitting at a lecture and an anonymous patient were being presented to the tumor board. She had written down the drugs of choice, the toxins she now would look at differently—Vincristine, Carbazine, and Prednisone. Temkin had been infuriated by her stoical attitude. "God in heaven!" he had sworn to her in the German they always spoke, "how can you be so passive? Cry, shout at me, show your outrage at this obscenity!"

"Your outrage is enough for both of us, Joel," she had said, smiling. "Besides, I've had a full life. It so easily might not have been."

Erika rinsed out the teacup in the kitchen sink. She went to Peter's bed and gently sat on it. She studied his sleeping features and ran her fingers through his thinning hair. *If only his problems were as simple as mine,* she thought to herself.

She bent over and kissed him lightly, deciding to let him sleep longer. Yes, it had been a full life.

WEDNESDAY, 12:18 P.M.

Shit, it makes me wanna puke! That's what Jimmy Ryan was thinking as he looked in disgust at the two women on the screen. He felt cheated for paying five dollars to watch them kiss and fondle each other, sighing in feigned passion. With no interest in the activities of the movie, he gazed around the dark theater that smelled of popcorn soaked in Lysol. He saw solitary forms scattered throughout, eyes glued to the grainy screen, an occasional glow of a cigarette. Lonely forms seeking their only relationships with the opposite sex. He studied one form in particular: it had a garment of some kind over its lap and the garment was moving vigorously up and down, its owner hypnotized by the mock celluloid passion. *Scumbag!* thought Jimmy Ryan. He looked in the opposite direction; one of the forms across the aisle didn't bother covering his lap. He pumped leisurely, oblivious to his audience. "Aw, shit!" Jimmy Ryan said aloud to no one. He wanted to leave that place of sticky seats and stickier floors, of disinfectants and food and fuck knows what else. But he had paid his money. At last a male appeared in the plotless movie, a grinning dwarf with a monstrous organ adding to the humanoid obscenity of his person. Jimmy Ryan sat back, suddenly fascinated, as the monstrosity performed. He took out the .45 from his belt and placed it against his crotch, barrel up. The women on the screen moaned and hollered in genuine passion and pain, and Jimmy Ryan lovingly stroked the barrel of the gun.

WEDNESDAY, 12:55 P.M.

"V' chotveynu b' seyfer hachayim . . ." "Inscribe us in the Book of Life . . . oh God of Life . . ."

Baruch Ben-David, political Jew, listened with newfound intensity as the rabbi intoned the ancient Hebrew.

". . . for this is the closing of the Gate . . . in which the fate of all nations is sealed. . . ."

The fate of all nations. And what was that fate? wondered Baruch Ben-David. What had been inscribed by wise men so long ago that he, the latter-day leader of Jews, could act on so that the Book of Life would not close to the children of Abraham? Where would he find the wisdom? he demanded.

". . . and may it please You, oh Lord, to inscribe for a good life the names of us, Your Children, who are in Your covenant."

What say you now, wise men of old, to the leaders of those nations, nations of states united, unions of republics of the people, nations so great and powerful that they may bring asunder the Holy Covenant, thus forever sealing the Book of Life? he wanted to know.

An aide interrupted the pleadings of Baruch Ben-David. "Prime Minister," he said, "The President has arrived."

"I will see him in the ambassador's office," Ben-David said.

WEDNESDAY, 12:58 P.M.

"Joseph" sat up quickly. A white Chevrolet was pulling up to the embassy. Four men got out of the car and took up positions a few feet away from the entrance. "Joseph" put the rifle with the silencer up to his shoulder. None of it would be visible from below; he was pointing it through the open casement window, the muzzle inside the room. He sighted a Secret Service agent through the telescope. He couldn't miss his target.

Another car pulled up directly in front of the embassy. No police on motorcycles, no sirens, no flags indicating the car of the President of the United States, no limousine. Just a normal-size Cadillac with dark glass. *His "low-profile" car*, he thought to himself. The door was opened by one of the agents, and the head of Simon Jensen appeared in the cross hairs. "Joseph" moved his finger on the trigger. He hesitated for a second, not more; Jensen was looking to his right, his head turned slightly so that "Joseph" could see only a portion of it. He wanted to make sure he had the right target. The President moved quickly to the door of the embassy, an agent walking behind him. "Joseph's" hesitation cost him his chance. The split second needed for the shot was gone. He would have to wait for Jensen to come out. This time he would be quicker. He had to be.

He sat down, a wave of chagrin and disappointment hitting him hard. Another time he would have gotten off the shot with no problem. Yes, he wanted to make sure, but there had been plenty of time. What had gone wrong?

Suddenly he was angered by his question to himself. Damn it! He didn't know what, if anything, had gone wrong. If he had fired at the wrong man, or missed—what then? He simply hadn't had a clean shot. The next time he'd be ready. As always, he'd be ready.

His surgical glove–encased fingers caressed the rifle across his lap. And he waited.

EMBASSY OF THE STATE OF ISRAEL

WEDNESDAY, 1:00 P.M.

"I'm very grateful you could come, Mr. President," Baruch Ben-David said. He motioned to a chair in the ambassador's office, reserved for the occasion. "I assure you I would have come to you if it were not for Yom Kippur, our most solemn of holy days. It is only under extreme circumstances that I travel, let alone conduct business during this time, Mr. President."

"You've come thousands of miles to see me, Mr. Prime Minister," Simon Jensen said. "Certainly I can come a few blocks to see you. Although if it's about this Kramer business . . ." Jensen shook his head and compressed his lips, letting the sentence hang.

"That is exactly and exclusively why I'm here," Ben-David said with some force. "You should know that from the very beginning. I'm going to try to change your posture, your judgment regarding Peter Kramer."

"Thank you for your candor," Jensen said. "I'm willing to listen, but my mind is made up."

The Israeli gazed at his counterpart for a few moments. Then he said, "Mr. President, the friendship you have shown the State of Israel is too valuable, too genuine, for there to be an atmosphere of rigidity between us in these troubled times. I have come a long way, at a most inappropriate time, God knows, to present my case regarding Peter Kramer. The least I expect from you is an open mind. I have evidence to present on Peter's behalf. I present it not so much with the idea that you and he should, as you Americans say, kiss and make up. No, that is between you and him. But you should not allow this affair to influence in any way the outcome of the peace accord in which we, the government of Israel, place such vital significance. Forgive my bluntness, but these things need to be said."

He stood up and said to the seated Jensen in a grave tone, "If after reviewing the evidence, Mr. President, you are still of the same mind, then I will accept your position, and I will set out to find other ways to meet Israel's commitment to peace. What ways? At this point, I confess I do not know, and I can only hope that God gives me the wisdom to find them."

Simon Jensen's jaw muscles danced in mild chagrin. He had just been accused of putting his personal feelings above world peace. "Very well, Mr. Prime Minister, I'll listen."

Ben-David sat down across from Jensen. "I feel tension between us. Perhaps it would help if we called each other by our first names, as before." He smiled disarmingly.

Jensen returned the smile. "Yes, Baruch, I would like that," he said.

Ben-David nodded, grateful for the more relaxed atmosphere. "Si," he began, "what we have here is a situation that really doesn't have to exist. You accuse Peter of perfidy, of dishonesty. That simply is not the case, and I will prove it to you—"

"He lied to me, Baruch," Jensen interrupted. "How can you or anyone else justify lying to me, especially about something with such potentially damaging consequences?"

"Precisely my point, Si. The consequences don't have to be damaging. It's in your hands whether they are or not. First off, Peter did not have to tell you about his past, but he did. Second, his lie, if that's what you insist on calling it, was only a lie of omission. He withheld telling you—telling all of us—certain things, things that in his eyes would have threatened his security and that of his wife. Any of us would have done that; it's the instinct for self-preservation. But there is far more to it than just trying to save his skin, and that's the irony of the whole thing, Si. But I'm getting ahead of this remarkable story."

Ben-David stood up and walked to the ambassador's desk. He picked up a large manila envelope. "In here," he said, tapping the envelope, "you will find the motives, the reasons for his, shall we say, lack of candor. This is a detailed intelligence report gathered by Mossad on Hans-Dieter, Freiherr von Bergdorf, alias Peter Kramer, and his activities during and after the war in Europe. In here, you will find memoranda to Prime Minister Ben-Gurion and to me. You will also see my own memoranda to the file involving my personal experience with this file, with this man. I know these things to be facts because I was there. I am one of those who can shed light on this affair, and it is light that we are after. You know, Si, Francis Bacon said, 'If a man will begin with certainties, he shall end in doubts.' Read this file, Si. You will see that it ends in truth!"

Jensen gazed intently at Ben-David, his eyes hard, his jaw set squarely, his mouth a slit of obstinance. "You want me to read that file?" Jensen finally asked.

"Yes, Si. All of it. And very carefully, please." He smiled. "You owe me at least that much, remember, making me come all the way to Washington on Yom Kippur. I will leave you alone. When you finish, just press that buzzer on the desk. I'll be waiting."

"Just a minute, Baruch," Jensen said, the corners of his mouth drawn down. "I don't know what's in that envelope, but I sure as hell know one thing: the man can't be trusted. His kind can never be trusted. I know that for a fact, damn it! Look, I went to war against the likes of Freiherr whatever. I saw what those butchers did. I saw what they did to your own people, Baruch, with my own eyes I saw!"

"Si, listen to me," Ben-David said softly. "Peter is not one of those. Trust me."

"Christ almighty! Trust you? I trusted him! He slickered me, and he's slickering you, don't you see? Don't you know what he's after? I'll tell you—he wants Jack Hetherington's job, he wants to be secretary of state, and he's using us, you and me, and the peace accord to get what he really wants, the Nobel Peace Prize!"

"Si, you don't really believe that!"

"The hell I don't! But he'll get it only over my dead body!" Jensen was on his feet now, his fist in the air. "Over my dead body!"

Ben-David's mouth dropped open. "Si, calm down! These are nothing but fantasies. Get hold of yourself, man. You're the President of the United States!"

"Yes. That's right," Jensen said. "I'm the—" He shook his fist at Ben-David. "What right do you have talking to me that way?"

Ben-David exploded. "The right I have given myself as a friend and admirer of Simon Bolivar Jensen, a great and courageous president of this great country, not the petulant and obdurate person who stands in front of me making fists!"

Jensen listened to the booming words, and his eyes grew wide. Slowly his fists relaxed as he realized the truth in the statement. He sat down, looking out the window, and bit his lip in thought.

"Read the file, Si," Ben-David gently prodded. "I'll leave you now. If you need anything, just use the buzzer." He turned to leave, and as an afterthought he said, "Read it, my friend, and let's put this behind us. Then we can go forward, you and I, to do what we have to do."

Simon Jensen heard the door close. He was alone. The early afternoon sunlight streamed through the windows, casting deep shadows into the large room, and he suddenly felt desperately lonely. Not since the day after the inauguration, when he found himself in the Oval Office for the first time, did he feel so alone. He felt the same butterflies in his abdomen as he did that cold January day after all the noise and hoopla of the inauguration had turned into a deathly silence. He studied the tiny specks of dust dancing in the shaft of sunlight and felt the same desperation.

He looked askance at the file on the desk as if it were something lurid, something menacing. He didn't want to know what was in it; he was satisfied with his own assessment of Peter Kramer. Sometimes you have to go with your gut feel, he said to himself, rather than with the so-called facts, the irrefutable evidence. Hadn't he gone with his gut feel so many times before? How else had he achieved his goals? That Kramer was the face in the dream, he had no doubt. That he was the enemy, he had no doubt either. The dream was his gut feel.

He took a deep breath and opened the flap on the heavy envelope, withdrawing a thick folder. "Let's just see how wrong I am," he said aloud.

Simon Jensen turned the first page of the half-inch-thick folder.

The pages were attached by a two-part fastener so that each page could be easily flipped upward. The top sheet was printed in Hebrew characters and in parentheses said, "English Language Version." At the bottom of the sheet was typed, "Approved—sub-Director, Head Office," over which was scrawled the signature of Eliahu Allon. In the middle of the page was:

BERGDORF, Hans-Dieter von

aka

KRAMER, Peter

Jensen flipped to the first item, which was titled "Summary of Military Record," in which Bergdorf's activitites were related, from his enlistment in the Waffen-SS in Klausenburg, Siebenbürgen, his training at the SS cadet school in Bad Tölz, to combat in Poland, France, and Yugoslavia as a Panzer regimental commander in *Das Reich* division. Jensen was forced to imagine Bergdorf-Kramer sitting in a tank turret, wiping away his earlier impression of Kramer skiing down the slopes of the Swiss Alps. Kramer had been a tank commander, the same as he, Jensen grudgingly conceded. *(So what? Lots of guys were.)* He read of Bergdorf's wounds, and the Knight's Cross, personally presented by Hitler. *(I was decorated by Patton, who was ten times the man Hitler was!)* Still, he read on, now with more than just mild curiosity.

The next dealt with Bergdorf's post in Paris as chief of the *Sicherheitsdienst-Frankreich*. In parentheses it said, "SS security service, or SD-France," and that he was the representative of SS-General Heydrich. *(Heydrich—yeah,* hangman *Heydrich, they called him. He was assassinated in Poland or Czechoslovakia or someplace like that. Now why would a hero-soldier like Bergdorf tie in with a guy like that?)* No explanation was offered, but a footnote noted that the Reichssicherheitshauptamt, the Reich Head Security Office of which Heydrich was chief, was the ruling body of the SD, the Gestapo, and other police agencies, all responsible in one way or another for the arrest and deportation of Jews and other "undesirables" for special handling in the concentration and extermination camps. The footnote ended with an ominous statistic—over 90,000 Jews were processed by the SD-France for deportation.

Jensen stopped reading. He spread his hands over the papers, controlling an overwhelming impulse to rip them to shreds. *(Fucking Nazi butcher! And he wants the Peace Prize!)* He closed his eyes and saw Bergdorf-Kramer's face in the dream . . . wearing black . . . and a death's head on his brow.

He poured a glass of water from a pitcher on the desk and drank thirstily. His eyes went to the file. He was anxious now to get back to it. He turned to the next page.

It was a letter in French. *(Damn!)* Then he saw a rubber stamp imprint: "Translation Attached." Before turning to the translation, he studied the letter, on French government stationery. *"Ministère des affaires étrangères,"* the letterhead said. He knew enough French to know that it came from the French Foreign Ministry. There was an illegible signature, but the typed signature was that of Baron Guy de Belfort, and below that it said, *"Sub-ministre."* It was dated 1951. He turned to the translation. It was a letter addressed to Ariel Kahan, First Secretary, Embassy of Israel.

> In response to your query of the 15th last, please be informed that I was well acquainted with Freiherr H.-D. von Bergdorf during the German occupation of France, 1940/44. I met General Bergdorf shortly after he arrived in Paris, May 1941, and at that time we formed a fast and sincere friendship born of mutual respect and common family traditions.
>
> I was active in the Resistance and, particularly, in the Organisation Juive de Combat, a clandestine branch of the Union Général des Israélites de France, the UGIF, in which our activities centered around efforts to rescue French and other Jews necessary as a professional nucleus destined for the postwar formation of the State of Israel. General Bergdorf, in his position as a high SS and police official, joined in the effort to rescue Jews by establishing a pipeline of escape out of German-occupied Europe, during which time more than 2,000 Jews were freed from the clutches of the Gestapo, all at the risk of General Bergdorf's life.
>
> While it is true that thousands of other Jews were deported during General Bergdorf's tenure, one must be fully aware that he was the nominal head of the German security apparatus and, as such, responsible for the implementation of German policy as regards Jews and perforce signed such orders. In that same vein, if the question is raised as to why he did not refuse to carry out those hideous orders, the answer is clear: If he had not remained in his position, it would not have been possible for him to continue his

sub rosa activities on behalf of Jews. One should note further that it would have been impossible in any case for one person, with the exception of Hitler himself, to have done more, considering the severity of the situation.

If you have need for further information, I offer my fullest cooperation.

"Jesus!" Jensen said, and quickly turned to the next page of the file.

He looked at a document entitled, "Deposition of M. le Baron Guy de Belfort (Translated from the French)." Present were A. Kahan and M. Rubin of the Embassy M-3 Section. The deponant insisted on giving sworn testimony.

The five-page deposition described in detail Hans-Dieter von Bergdorf's efforts to rescue French Jews. It ended with Belfort's impassioned admonition: "If you find that Baron von Bergdorf is still alive, please treat him well. He is a hero to our people. One of these days France herself will honor the memory of this gentle and noble man."

The President of the United States held his head in his hands as he read the words that contradicted his own beliefs. He shifted in his seat. Something was wrong here, he thought. He couldn't be that far off base about the man. *Look at the dream, for God's sake! Dreams don't lie. A hero, the Frenchman had called him. Well, maybe Bergdorf had put one over on him, too. The old fellow seemed rather naive, the way he talked, and it would be easy to fool him, making him think one thing when all along he and Heydrich were ripping off the Jews. Then Heydrich buys it, leaving Bergdorf with the loot. Sure, that's it! Dreams don't lie.* He turned the page.

The President perused a series of memoranda on the Q-B investigation by Mossad, including the suppositions, speculations, conjectures. There was also the analysis by Isser Harel regarding the Nazi treasures and their probable dispositions. Then the Bergdorf connection. He examined the cold and tedious reports. As had Mossad, he too put the pieces together.

He reread the items dealing with the Q-B group. A temporary lapse in his gut feel made him conclude, with the objectivity of his brain, that Bergdorf-Kramer was indeed Q-B. But that objectivity soon crumbled under his visceral convictions. It was only supposition, speculation. As was noted in the memoranda, there was no hard evidence.

Then a remarkable item: "Transcript of Recording of Telephone Conversation—Prime Minister and Isser Harel" dated less than two weeks ago. It was stamped "Confidential—Need to Know Only" and below that, "File Original—No Copies Made." When Jensen finished reading, a wave of extreme discomfort hit him, and he felt a painful lump in his throat as he reread the telling words of David Ben-Gurion: "a friend of the Jews."

Simon Jensen cleared his throat a few times and, with difficulty, swallowed some water. He turned the page.

It was a memo to the file signed by Baruch Ben-David. It told of that day in Drancy, outside Paris, in 1942, of the marshaling yard for Jews on their way to Auschwitz, Sobibor, Maidanek, Treblinka—and of the German officer who had saved him and others from the SS ovens. It was terse, laconic. No explanations were offered, no opinions or even adjectives described the feeling of what happened that night. Only the events were related. And the name of the officer—SS-Brigadeführer von Bergdorf.

An intricate geometric design of shadows from the window panes now fell across the ambassador's desk. Idly Jensen studied the sharp angles of light and shade as he absorbed the meaning of each piece of material in the file. But when it came time to analyze those meanings, he threw up the stone wall between him and the truth, as if afraid to contradict prejudice.

He sighed deeply with a hint of guilt, but he quickly put the guilt away. He read another memorandum, also from Ben-David.

I met with Ambassador Kramer of the U.S. Peace Accord Delegation. The meeting took place yesterday at the Dead Sea near Sodom. During our conference I informed Ambassador Kramer that I recognized him to be Major-General von Bergdorf, attached to the security forces of the German Schutzstaffeln during the occupation of France, 1940/44. Kramer admitted this to be factual. It was ascertained at this time that no one else in an official capacity, or connected with the peace accord negotiations, was aware of these facts. Because of the sensitive nature of Ambassador Kramer's position as regards the peace accord, and because of the political implications that could result should this information fall into the hands of the enemies of peace, we both agreed that President Jensen should be made privy to this intelligence forthwith by Ambassador Kramer.

Subsequent to this conference, and subsequent to further study of this file, I contacted Ambassador Kramer in regard to the unanswered question contained in the file, namely the Q-B question. Ambassador Kramer admitted to me that he is, in fact, connected with this group. It is obvious to me that he is the principal member and founder of the group known as Q-B.

Oh God, Peter. Then it wasn't you in the dream!

The next page was yet another memorandum to the file, this one from deputy chief of intelligence Eliahu Allon.

> The Prime Minister discussed this matter with me, and we agree that the identity of Ambassador Kramer is that of former SS-General Hans-Dieter von Bergdorf. We are in further accord that he is the principal member of the group known as Q-B, a.k.a. "Kube" Group. After further discussion we both agree that the Q-B funds originated with SS-General Reinhard Heydrich in 1941; then, subsequent to Heydrich's death in 1942, the beneficiary of those funds was to be Martin Bormann. According to Mossad information Bormann is still alive; last known address, San Carlos de Bariloche, Rio Negro Province, Argentina. We are further in accord that the Q-B Group, under Kramer, has had control of the Bormann Swiss account. As this appears to be conclusive, the PM and I agree that, under these new circumstances, i.e., Kramer's great visibility, there now exists a possible peril to him from Bormann and/or his forces, thereby placing the peace accord in danger, a situation unacceptable to Israel. Recent reliable information to the PM is that Kramer is traveling to Mexico City imminently. Therefore I have taken steps to provide covert security to his person.

"Oh God! Oh God!" cried Simon Jensen.

The next page was a report from Mossad agent Zvi Asher, dated just a few days earlier. Jensen's hands trembled in anticipation of what would come next in this most fearful and perplexing story. He began to build horrible images, frightful scenarios. He suddenly realized that he feared for Kramer's life. Those Nazi butchers were after Peter! He read:

> Picked up subject Kramer at Benito Juarez Airport, Mexico City. Subject accompanied by US State Dept. security agent. Kramer and agent checked in at Fiesta Palace Hotel, then went to Foreign Ministry in Government Square until 1910 hrs. Kramer returned to hotel with agent and remained there until 2100 hrs. Left hotel alone, walked to the entrance of Museum of Anthropology in

Chapultepec Park. At 2145 hrs Kramer joined by unidentified man, 65–75 yrs., approx. 180 lbs., approx. 5.5 ft. They did not shake hands. They walked into park, talking. They continued in this way for approx. two hours during which time very little could be heard or learned from our vantage point in the bush alongside the path they took, this despite some shouting. The man was seen to draw a pistol and aim it at Kramer. Mossad agent Ezra Nahmias, on assignment with me, drew his weapon to fire at the man when Kramer took the man's pistol and discarded it 10–12 ft. away. They struggled for approx. 20–30 seconds, both falling to the ground. Kramer helped the man to his feet and sat him on a bench. Kramer stood in front of the man for a few minutes, talking to him. Kramer then retrieved the discarded pistol and dropped it in the man's lap, at which time Kramer drew a pistol from his raincoat pocket and pointed it at the man, who appeared not to move. Kramer did not fire; he spoke a few words, then approached the man, who still did not exhibit signs of life. Kramer was seen to go through the man's pockets and examine what appeared to be a wallet. Kramer returned the material to the man's pocket. He wiped a pistol with a handkerchief and placed it in the man's outer pocket. Then subject Kramer left, with agent Nahmias following him to his hotel. I stayed behind and approached the man on the bench. I made a cursory examination, concluding he was dead. Since there was no gunshot or visible wounds, I concluded that he had died of natural causes, probably due to the exertion of the physical struggle earlier.

I photographed the body with a Minox camera w/flash, and I impressed the dead man's fingerprints on the enclosed mica for possible identification.

Kramer is in Washington, DC, as of this date under protective surveillance by agents Nahmias and myself, with backup of agents Naor and Kedem of the DC section. End.

"Thank God!" Simon Jensen said with tears in his eyes.

The next items were two envelopes stapled firmly to the back of the heavy manila file folder. The first one contained a transparent sheet of celluloid inside a plastic bag. A pithy notation from some technician at Mossad headquarters said simply, "We have no comparison prints." The next envelope held several glossy three-by-five prints of a dead man, eyes slightly open, staring dully into eternity. A large scar that caved in part of the forehead showed clearly on the shiny photos.

The last item was a short newspaper clipping glued on a sheet of paper. The banner showed it to be a small, back-page news item from *Excelsior,* a Mexico City daily. A translation attached said that the body of a German with a Paraguayan passport was found that morning in Chapultepéc Park. The judicial police concluded, lacking evidence to the contrary, that he had died of natural causes. Confidential sources in the police say the man was in reality Martin Bormann, fugitive war criminal, intimate of Adolf Hitler, Nazi leader.

The President of the United States closed the folder. He felt depleted. He drank some water. He looked at the large blue and white flag with the six-pointed star of King David and pondered the many questions the file had evoked.

He sat in the room for a long while, alone with his thoughts, his feelings, and his reappraised judgments.

Finally he rang the buzzer on the desk, feeling a desperate need to talk to his friend, the Prime Minister of Israel. A few minutes later Baruch Ben-David came in.

Ben-David immediately felt the mood in the still room. It was different from the one he had felt when he had left the President several hours earlier.

"Simon," he said quietly, reflecting the eerie repression of the chamber, "you have read the file."

"Yes, Baruch, I read it. Thank God you made me read it. If I had acted the way I had intended, I think I would have resigned the presidency, because I would have destroyed it and the peace treaty, thanks to my damned egomania. I see that now." He spoke calmly, evenly.

"Really, Simon," Ben-David said, "that's going a little far, I think. What's important is that—"

Jensen interrupted. "What's important is that I had lost my grip on things, and worse, on reality. That is an impossible position for a world leader to be in, you'll agree."

"All of us, sometime or other, lose their grip," Ben-David said softly. "It's natural, under the stress of our jobs."

"No," Jensen said, "I don't mean that. There's something else. There's something that is gripping me," he made a fist and twisted it for emphasis, "that's got hold of me. Something . . ." He paused, looking at Ben-David. "Look, Baruch, let's for a few minutes forget who we are, that we are world leaders. Let me talk to you man to man."

Ben-David saw the controlled tension in his counterpart and

tried to alleviate it. "Friend to friend, Simon," he said. "Count on it."

Jensen nodded. "I have a recurring dream, a nightmare really, and it stems from a wartime incident. Aside from my doctor, who could offer nothing other than a few medical platitudes, I've never told a soul." He related the dream and the incident in Ruhmannsfelden in detail.

Afterward, both men sat quietly, assessing the tale, and Jensen said, "You don't have to be Freud to see the relationship of the incident to the dream, a nightmare that is punishing me for having fumbled the ball."

"Ah, guilt," Ben-David said. "The most unproductive and useless activity ever invented by man."

"I shouldn't feel guilty for killing my men?"

Ben-David shook his head sadly. "You didn't kill them, Simon," he said. "You acted on instinct, a good and decent instinct. Your act had to do with humaneness, with charity and compassion. You were looking at children over the sights of your machine gun, two young lads, for God's sake! At that moment, in view of the unnecessary carnage in the brewery moments before—your baptism of killing—your instinct was *preservation* of life, all life, even at the cost of your own. Or didn't you ever think of that? A man who instinctively takes a life instead of saving one doesn't know the meaning of the gift of life!" he said with intensity. "Look at Peter with that monster in Mexico. If anyone deserved to be killed it was that man. And yet Peter found it abhorrent to his sense of humanity to pull the trigger. Although it is certain that he would have done it—considering all that was at stake—God spared him the awful task."

Jensen looked at Ben-David with troubled eyes. "I think . . . I think when I read that . . . I mean, Peter is not a coward, and yet he couldn't kill him in cold blood." He stumbled for words. "I realized that maybe I'm not—that maybe the dream has been wrong all along." He shook his head. "I don't know. I guess what I'm trying to say is, I think now I can work it out. I just wanted to hear *you* say it, Baruch, what I think—what I now feel."

Baruch Ben-David reached out his hand to Simon Jensen. The President took the hand with both of his, gratitude in his eyes. "You are a courageous man, Simon. You've always been a great leader of a great country. Now you'll be even greater."

346

"I should like to talk with Peter now," Jensen said.

"Before you do," Ben-David said, "there's something you should know, something that Peter told me earlier. There's this new situation that he learned from Bormann. Something called 'the new wave.'" Ben-David told the President what he knew.

"Peter has made copious notes on it," Ben-David said. "The notes are in the safe in his office. He wanted me to tell you all of this, not knowing how you would respond to that," he said, pointing to the file. "He also wants you to know that he has committed the Q-B fund, which is substantial, to fighting this new menace. He judges that the fewer who know about it, the more effective the fight against them will be."

The President nodded. A look of determination was in his face, the Jensen look of leadership. "I will not allow this to happen, Baruch. I will use all the power at my command to stop them. This I promise."

Ben-David put his finger on the buzzer and rang twice.

"Peter is here, just outside this room." He smiled warmly. "I thought you might want to see him."

Peter Kramer walked in, apprehension in his face. He looked back and forth from one man to the other, trying to read their mood.

President Jensen met him in the middle of the room. He held out his hand. "Peter, you must find it in your heart to forgive me."

"There is nothing to forgive, Mr. President."

WEDNESDAY, 3:28 P.M.

A tall young black whizzed smoothly down the sidewalk and bumped Jimmy Ryan's shoulder.

"Watch where the fuck you're going, man," Jimmy Ryan said to the youth's back. The young man, clad in shorts and knee socks, was carrying a large radio on his shoulder, deftly zooming down the sidewalk, enjoying his music and the near-collisions. Jimmy Ryan had held his ground, and they had bumped.

The tall skater did an artful swivel, stopping a few feet in front of Jimmy Ryan, American National Socialist. "Say what, mother-fucker?" he said.

Rock and soul music blared from storefronts and other "ghetto blasters," producing a cacophony in Jimmy Ryan's ears, adding to his murderous wrath. He undid the two buttons on his denim jacket, exposing the evil-looking butt of the .45 on his belt. His eyes, slits of undisguised hate, bored holes into the other's. "Nigger, take your black ass outta here, or you're a dead nigger." His voice was low and filled with menace.

The black's eyes widened. "Be cool, man. I'm gone!" He skated away, wiser than his few years and alive. Jimmy Ryan's eyes told him that "the little dude was in a killing mood!"

Jimmy Ryan smoothed his hair and walked on aimlessly up Fifteenth Street. He was angry, a pent-up geyser of rage looking—*need-ing*—to spew forth the pellets of hate he carried in the clip of the automatic. He had decided earlier that it would be his last day on earth and that he would go out in a blaze of glory. He thought of the young skater; he was glad he had kept his temper. Killing an uppity nigger ain't a blaze of glory, he reasoned.

He turned on K Street and stopped in his tracks, noticing the traditional emblem of the pawnbroker, the three orbs. He walked slowly to the window of The Windsor Loan and Jewelry Co., M. Teitelbaum, Prop. "Buy, Sell or Trade—No Item Too Small or Big—We Loan the Most!"

He stared at the window of the pawn shop. Fuckin' hebe stole my radio an' my twenty-two. Said he had a hunderd radios back there, 'nough to open his own radio shop. Five bucks for the radio and ten for the rifle. Take it or leave it, misteh. Being flat broke, he took it. Later, Jimmy saw the radio—*his* radio!—in the window with a price tag on it. "Special Buy! $24.95." Five times what he had given him, the scumbag kike. *They're all like that,* he thought as he looked at the cluttered window. Diamond rings under bright spot-lights, and the watches and bracelets whose cries from their former owners Jimmy Ryan could hear, victims of the Shylocks, demanding to be avenged. Toasters and coffee makers, record players and ra-dios. "Bargain!" "Reduced to Clear!" "Discount!" Then he re-membered the tattoo on Teitelbaum's arm. *One that got away!* he thought. He flipped off the safety on the .45 and pulled back the hammer. *Oh, if only I was wearin' my uniform so that he could see who's gonna do it to him,* he thought with passion. *I'll tell 'im any-way, just before I blast his Jew-face away.*

His flood of hate was too great, too promising, to question whether killing a Jewish pawnbroker would be the sought-after "blaze of glory." He went into the shop, mumbling under his breath, " 'Vengeance is mine,' sayeth the Lord."

"What d'ya say, mac?" the man in the cage said. "I din't hear ya." It wasn't Teitelbaum in the cage. The guy looked like a white man; he din't look like no Jew, he thought. He smiled at the man. "I said I'm lookin' for Mr. Teitelbaum. I wanna see him, please." He looked around. *Prob'ly in back,* Jimmy Ryan thought. Tough shit for this guy—gonna have to die with the hebe.

"He ain't here, mac. He don't work the holiday. Jewish people never work on Yum Kipper, din'tcha know? Come back tomorrow."

Jimmy Ryan hid his disappointment. "Oh, yeah. I forgot," he said. Then his eye caught sight of a copy of the B'nai B'rith *Messenger* on the desk inside the cage. "Well, I'll be back some other time," he said pleasantly, and left.

That's it, he thought as he walked out. *The B'nai B'rith, or some other Jew outfit. Take a few with me that way.* His mind began to race in logical sequence: *A synagogue, maybe—or the embassy! The fuckin' Izz-real Embassy! Oh shit! I can take a whole bunch of 'em, Izz-real Jew hebes! There's my blaze a'glory!*

Jimmy Ryan, trembling with exquisite intensity and feverish excitement, turned and walked hurriedly up Sixteenth Street. He and his Colt .45 automatic turned left on Massachusetts Avenue, only a few blocks from the Embassy of the State of Israel.

WEDNESDAY, 5:24 P.M.

Jimmy Ryan strolled by the embassy again. It was the third time he had strolled by it, convinced by the presence of the swarm of security men and the official-looking but unmarked cars that some high-ranking Jew was in there. Whoever it was had to come out eventually, and he had visions of firing at the Jewish face. He could see the bullets leaving the barrel of his gun, spinning through the air, striking the unknown face, hurting, ripping, destroying it for the cause of the white Christian race.

He stopped at the corner and lit a cigarette. He envisioned the newspaper accounts all over the country—all over the world!—of Jimmy Ryan, white, Christian, American, making his place in the sun. The thought excited him to a feverish peak. He waited.

Eight minutes later, Jimmy Ryan pushed through the small crowd outside the embassy. He knew someone—someone big—was coming out. He hoped it was the ambassador. He didn't know who the Israeli ambassador was, nor did he care. Whoever he was, he would be big enough to insure Jimmy Ryan his moment of glory.

A group of men came out and stood on the sidewalk, just a few yards from where Jimmy Ryan stood. One of the group waved as the crowd began to cheer. *Oh, Lord! It's Jensen! It's that Jew-lovin' motherfuckin' nigger-lovin' traitor to his people and race! Shit, Lord, You are good to me! You're makin' this happen for me, Lord!*

A Secret Service man stopped him and others from getting closer. But Jimmy Ryan was close enough.

He reached into his jacket for the .45, cocked and safety off.

"Hey, Simon Jensen!" he hollered. *I want to see your eyes, traitor!* he thought. Simon Jensen turned, the smile still on his face. Jimmy Ryan drew and fired.

As the bullet left the muzzle, Jimmy Ryan saw that it wasn't Jensen's face. It was some other guy's, and at the same time he heard pops and felt hot stinging in his side and shoulder. Jimmy Ryan fired again, but the last sting made him fire high and miss everything. His body was dancing funny, then he felt his head explode, and after that he didn't feel anything.

Excerpted from the account of Ephraim Yuval, Commercial Officer, Israeli Embassy, Washington, D.C.:

"The Prime Minister, President Jensen, and Ambassador Kramer were standing in the garden of the embassy and they were smiling and joking, all in a pleasant mood. It was sundown and Yom Kippur was at an end and everyone seemed very happy. Ambassador Kramer said something like, 'It's first and goal on the five,' and they all laughed. President Jensen said he had to get back to the White House and offered a lift to Ambassador Kramer. The three of them went to the door of the embassy, where the President's car was parked. A small crowd noticed the President, and they waved, and he waved. Everybody smiled. All except this little man in a denim jacket. He didn't smile; he just looked at the group standing by the cars. His face had the look of someone who had just hit the jackpot and could not believe his luck."

WEDNESDAY, 5:32 P.M.

"Joseph" leaped from his chair at the sight of the activity below. His gaze froze on the embassy door; his pulse quickened, and his mouth became dry. He lifted the rifle and sighted through its telescope. Within seconds the head of Simon Jensen was in the cross hairs. He looked at the features of the smiling President—handsome, bronzed, healthy. He put his Latex-enclosed finger on the trigger and squeezed. Nothing happened. He checked the safety—it was off. He squeezed again. The trigger was frozen. He took a deep breath and felt beads of sweat running down his brow. The President stood there still, waiting for the bullet, waiting to be blown apart. He waved and smiled.

Then the President looked to his right; "Joseph" thought he heard a shrill voice shouting, "Hey, Simon Jensen!" and at the same moment another man stepped to the President's right, arms extended as if to ward off a blow. A shot rang out, and the man staggered back simultaneously, his fall knocking down the president. The man's white shirt produced a red blotch, and his face showed confusion. "Joseph" turned the rifle to his left and saw through the scope a man holding a gun. Immediately a volley of *pops* sounded; the man swayed and fired again. "Joseph" had the man's head in his scope. The trigger unfroze, and he fired one shot at the head. *Pphtt!* The head jerked; white and red matter erupted from it, and he dropped heavily to the ground. Now, screams from the spectators on the street. They began running in all directions, some of them falling to the ground. Others rushed to the slumped body, and men in dark glasses formed a cordon around the President and the man who had been shot in the chest. Other men, guns and Uzi submachine guns drawn, were running here and there, searching, barking orders. "Joseph" stood in the window, entranced. Twice the men in dark glasses looked directly at him, then looked away.

"Joseph" sat in the chair, just listening, not looking anymore. He heard residual sounds of eyewitness reactions, shouts of authority taking over, distant sirens drawing close. He thought of his escape plan. What plan? He didn't have a plan! The food he had eaten started to rebel, looking for escape from his furious stomach. He ran to the bathroom and vomited. With the rubber gloves still on, he soaked a washcloth in cold water and put it to his face. He looked at his reflection in the mirror; it wasn't clear whose face looked back, "Joseph" or Paul Cline. He stared at it and knew that there was no escape plan because he never intended to kill the President. Cline-"Joseph" wondered if the rebellion had happened earlier in the shower, when he saw his mother's image—or Abe Berman's beefy face—or when Tomasa's features had flown by his inner eye. No, Paul Cline corrected, it happened before—in New York at the Algonquin, the night he made his peace with Abe Berman. It had begun then.

It was "Joseph" who had gone through all the preparations, but it was Paul Cline's paralyzed finger on the trigger. It was Paul Cline whose hands perspired after talking to the voice from the White House. It was Paul Cline whose forehead erupted with rivulets of sweat as he sighted the President in the cross hairs. But it was the last spark of the existence of "Joseph" who had fired the shot that destroyed the assassin below.

Paul Cline looked back at the eyes in the mirror, and he knew. He had known for a long time that it would eventually happen, but he hadn't known when. Now he knew. "Good-bye, Joseph," he said to the eyes.

WEDNESDAY, 5:50 P.M.

The paramedic ripped open Peter Kramer's bloodsoaked shirt. He applied a pressure bandage to the wound, trying to stem the flow of blood. He feared the heart was pierced. Kramer's face was ashen; the other paramedic was trying unsuccessfully to get a blood pressure reading. A large-gauge needle was pushed into a vein in the wrist, and a plastic bottle of saline solution was connected. The saline in itself was useless, but the vein would be ready for immediate transfusion and other drugs.

The two men lifted Kramer onto a stretcher, leaving a large pool of his blood on the sidewalk. They secured the stretcher into the ambulance.

Simon Jensen had been kneeling alongside Kramer, holding his hand until asked by the paramedics to please get out of the way. He stood back, looking disheveled and shaken. The lapel of his suit jacket had been ripped by a Secret service agent trying to get him into the presidential armored car immediately after the shooting, but Jensen had insisted on staying by Kramer. Now, as he watched the paramedics work, a wall of agents and police surrounded him, shielding him completely. When he saw that Kramer was being taken away, Jensen broke through the cordon and got into the back of the ambulance. The chief of the detail motioned for the others to follow, and he himself got into the ambulance, making a crowd.

"You'll make it, Peter!" Jensen said in desperation. "Just hang in there until we reach the hospital."

The paramedic hooked Kramer up to a cardiac monitor, then felt for his pulse and a blood pressure reading; the pressure was too low for a cuff to register it. He whispered into a microphone, "I've got a BP of seventy by palpation only, pulse thready. Heart rate one forty, respiration thirty and shallow. Patient ashy and diaphoretic. Saline IV going. Over." A crackly voice came back: "Okay. Change to Plasmanate full speed. Start second IV and observe shock precautions. Over." The paramedic said, "Negative on the IV—veins are collapsed. Switching to Plasmanate. Over and out."

The paramedic looked over his shoulder at Kramer. His expression was blank. He caught the President's frantic eye and looked away.

Kramer opened his eyes. He coughed silently, and blood spilled from his lips down his chin. Simon Jensen gently blotted the blood with a bandage provided by the paramedic. "You will make it, Peter. Just . . . just hang on," the President whispered.

Kramer reached with his hand and found Jensen's. "Simon . . . the 'new wave' . . . you must . . . stop them!" he said.

"I promise. Don't talk now. Just hang on!" Jensen fought back tears of frustration, sorrow, and anger. *That bullet was meant for me,* he thought. *Peter saved my life.* He looked at the gray face again. *Don't die, Peter!* he prayed silently. *Please, dear God, don't let him die!*

WEDNESDAY, 6:08 P.M.

They wait. Surgeons, neurologists, cardiologists, the rest. Like members of a relay team waiting for the slap of the baton in their hands, poised, ready to jump, they wait. The cardiopulmonary machine is primed with blood in case a bypass of the heart and lungs is necessary. The ambulance arrives, the injured body is wheeled in at an urgent speed, plastic bags of intravenous fluids are pendent from their hooks in the charged atmosphere of a trauma center. X-rays of the wounded chest are taken, and just as quickly a Swan-Ganz catheter is inserted in the carotid vein and skilled fingers weave it into a heart chamber for vital intracardiac pressures. Simultaneously, a Foley catheter is threaded into the bladder to measure urinary output, a clue to nonfunctioning kidneys—a sign of shock. Yet more plastic invades the injured body; this time an endotracheal tube hooked up to a breathing machine is pushed through the mouth. A cardiac-assist pump hums into life, helping the lacerated body maintain its blood circulation.

Under shadowless lamps a thoracic surgeon barks the question, "What are the ABG's?" The arterial blood gases show that the oxygen in the blood is very low and the patient is in acidosis. Sodium bicarbonate is shot into the intravenous tube. The cardiologist asks about blood pressure; he is told that it barely registers in the arterial line, this despite the Dopamine given earlier. The neurologist monitoring brain and brain-related functions has hooked up an electroencephalograph. It will be the ultimate authority of life or death. He informs the frantically working surgical and medical teams that the pupils are still responsive to stimuli, an encouraging sign.

The injured body is sliced open by the quick scalpel of the thoracic surgeon. The hole in the lung is deftly sutured while the sounds of instruments clattering metallically bounce off the tile walls, jarring some already taut nerves. Then, the more reasonable quiet of the soft murmurs of those repairing, pumping, watching, monitoring.

The lung is pushed aside, the pericardium is patched of its wound caused by a .45-caliber slug. Then the heart itself is sewn up tight, and it beats its thanks.

They've been working feverishly, racing time, the enemy. They are not cognizant that the injured body is that of an ambassador, a most important person; it could be the body of the President himself—or that of a derelict from Skid Row. Only after they have saved the body's life—or lost it—will they become aware of the identity of the hapless being, but it would not have mattered in any case, in any way.

WEDNESDAY, 6:45 P.M.

Erika Kramer answered the insistent ringing of the doorbell. The large frame of Baruch Ben-David stood there.

"Baruch! Oh, how wonderful! When did—" Erika froze as the look on Ben-David's face told her that something terrible had happened, and it had happened to her husband. "What's wrong, Baruch? Something's happened to Peter."

Ben-David walked in. "He's been shot, Erika. He's at the hospital now. They're—"

"Is he dead?" she asked, stopping him in midsentence, her large eyes growing larger, her knuckles to her mouth.

"No, the doctors are attending him now, Erika. He's at Mercy Hospital." Ben-David lowered his head. "He took a bullet in the chest," he said softly.

Erika said, "I see. And what do they say? How bad is it?" She tried to keep control of herself, but tears were appearing in her eyes.

"Not good, I'm afraid."

She walked around the room, looking at the floor as if debating a question. "How did it happen? And why?"

"We don't know yet, Erika. It appears that it was an assassination attempt on the President. What is sure, however, is that Peter saved the President's life. He—"

Erika interrupted. "What do you mean, Baruch?" she asked with a slight shake of her head, as though not believing.

"Peter stepped in front of the gunman as he fired. He took the bullet meant for Simon Jensen."

Erika stared wide-eyed at the Israeli. Then she gave a short, bitter laugh. "How typically German!" She put her hand to her heart and recited in mock solemnity: *"Ich schwöre dir, mein Führer, Treue und Tapferkeit . . . und auch mein Leben!* We never change, do we, Baruch?" She laughed again, a long, acerbic laugh, morbid and cynical in its anguish. "How ironic!"

Ben-David frowned at the emphasis she had placed on the last words of the Führer-oath: *"und auch mein Leben,"* "and even my life." He immediately saw the irony. The oath of loyalty to Hitler— to the death—an oath violated by her husband years ago, violated out of humanity. And now . . .

He took her by the shoulders. "Erika, I understand your bitterness. But you should know that this afternoon the President and I had a long talk. Simon Jensen is a changed man. He's not—"

Erika pulled back from him in undisguised anger. "How can you understand?" She spat the words. "How can you ask me to accept this? He's going to die, I know it!" she screamed. "They've taken him from me, Baruch! They've taken him from me!" She clutched her stomach and sat on a couch. "Oh God oh God! Why couldn't he leave things as they were? What did he have to prove?"

Ben-David sat next to her and put his hand on her arm. "My dear Erika, please listen to me. You must see it my way, for it is the only way to find the courage, the only way to bear this tragedy. I know it is the only way I myself can bear it."

But she wasn't listening. Her face became dark, and she stopped weeping. "I hate him, Baruch," she said in grim and somber tones. "I hate my husband for what he did. I told him, I warned him not to get involved in the treaty, because our lives would change and because it wasn't safe. But no, he *needed* to beat his chest for what the others did. Mea culpa," she said, striking her chest with her fist, "mea culpa! He had to atone for *them!* He appointed himself a—a martyr for Germany!" She grit her teeth. "I hate him for what he did to me . . . to us . . . to our lives! Can you understand?"

Ben-David let her have the badly needed catharsis, a small price to exact for her loss. He stroked her head. "I understand," he said:

She wiped her eyes. "He had taken an oath to a madman before, and now, he—he puts the oath into effect for another madman!"

Ben-David seized the opportunity. "That's just it, Erika, he's not a madman. Simon Jensen was disturbed, I know. But now, thanks to Peter, he has—how can I put it?—he has emerged a far better man. He's changed. Listen to me, dear Erika, you must know these things, you must hear these thing while the wound in your heart still bleeds. Simon Jensen is going to be a great leader, and the world will benefit from him, I promise you. Peter is gravely wounded; if he dies"—Ben-David's voice fought the tears—"if he dies, he will have given up his life for the only man on this earth who can make the difference between peace and global conflict. You must see it this way, Erika, because it's the truth, and because if you don't, it will have had no meaning. You must let this magnificent truth carry you through what you have to face!"

She stood up and walked around the room. Ben-David's words echoed in her head, her heart. She smiled through the tears at him. "Please, dear Baruch," she said, "put your arms around me. I need to be held."

He embraced her, feeling the bitterness leave her. "I love him so much," she murmured.

"I know, I know," he said, desperately trusting his own words.

The embassy car took them to Mercy Hospital. Erika spotted the little chapel near the entrance. "I'll wait here," she said.

WEDNESDAY, 8:57 P.M.

The two men waited in the office of the administrator of Mercy Hospital. They waited for news from the trauma center. A tray of food lay untouched on a coffee table.

Simon Jensen turned to his friend. "You should eat something, Baruch. Don't forget, you've been fasting. You'll end up a patient here yourself if you don't eat."

Ben-David shook his head, more in despair than in refusal. "Who can eat at a time like this? What kind of madness is taking over the world, Simon?"

The grief-laden remark was meant rhetorically, but Jensen responded to it. "I've been doing a lot of thinking, Baruch. I doubt if this tragedy came about as a result of this 'new wave' business you related to me. The gunman has been identified as a member of the American Nazis, according to papers found on him. I seriously doubt that it was any kind of conspiracy on their part. They don't operate that way. I'm sure the fellow was just a crazy who went off on his own, just as all the other kooks in history who were ready to give up their lives in exchange for some sort of warped glory. Unfortunately, there are more of them out there, the kamikazes, and as long as there are free societies they will be there because the laws of free societies are there to protect even them, until it's too late to stop them. But what really worries me is this 'new wave' thing. If what Peter said is true—and I have no reason to doubt him—that is the real menace. A menace because of the way in which they operate, covertly yet legally, on a philosophy of which the ingrained prejudices and fears we all have in us are reached and manipulated by insidious means. We must be alert to them, Baruch, and be prepared to act swiftly and, I hope, with the help of other nations.''

Ben-David nodded. ''Yes, Simon. Once the peace treaty is a reality, we must give it our top priority.''

''Count on it, Baruch.''

Michael Lieppman, thoracic surgeon, peered into the chest of Peter Kramer. He saw he was breathing, but with assistance. His heart was beating regularly, but it too was being helped by the machine. Everything pointed to irreversible shock—the death sentence. He looked at Charles Morrell, the cardiologist. ''Charlie,'' he said, ''I think we've gone as far as we can. What's your feeling?''

''I think we've gone beyond that, Mike,'' Morrell said. ''We could've quit an hour ago and it wouldn't have made any difference.''

Raj Prasad, anesthesiologist, looked up from his stool. ''Not to mention irreversible brain damage,'' he said.

Lieppman glanced at Stuart Mann, neurologist. ''What do you think, Stu?''

''The pupils are fixed and dialated,'' Mann said, ''and the EEG shows a flat line, consistent with brain death. Sorry. You fellows really worked on this one.''

Lieppman sighed and pulled down his mask. ''Okay. We gave it our best shot.''

Morrell looked at the big clock on the wall. ''Let's see. The patient expired officially at . . . twenty-one hundred hours?'' He looked at Lieppman for confirmation.

''I guess so,'' said Michael Lieppman, M.D.

WEDNESDAY, 9:08 P.M.

There was a soft knock on the door of the administrator's office. Simon Jensen moved to the door and opened it. A man wearing the wrinkled green surgeon's scrub suit stood there. Etched on his tired face was the outline of the surgical mask he had worn for several hours. Another scrub-suited man was with him.

"Excuse me, Mr. President. I'm Dr. Lieppman, and this is Dr. Morrell." His voice sounded dry and routine, offering no clue of elation or regret.

"Is he going to make it?" Jensen asked the obvious, without acknowledging the introductions.

"I think we should talk with the wife, Mr. President. Is she here with you?" Lieppman asked.

"The hell with protocol, Doctor," Jensen said angrily, "we've been waiting for more than three hours!"

"Yes, sir. I'm sorry," the surgeon said. "Ah, Mr. President, I'm sorry to inform you that Ambassador Kramer expired. We did everything possible, I assure you."

Jensen ran his fingers through his hair. He looked at Ben-David, who closed his eyes and bowed his head. The muscles in Jensen's jaw danced in silent fury. He wanted to shout, to cry to the heavens his feeling of sorrow and infamy. But he merely whispered, "I see."

Baruch Ben-David lifted his tired body out of his chair. "Dr. Lieppman," he said, "I am Baruch Ben-David, a friend of the family. Let me take you to Dr. Kramer, the ambassador's wife. She's in the chapel. May I join you when you tell her? I think she'll need a friend with her."

"Of course, Mr. Prime Minister," Lieppman said.

"I would like to come, too, Baruch," Jensen said softly.

As they walked down the silent hall, Baruch Ben-David said to no one, "How can humanity replace such a man?"

". . . und in Diene Hände übergebe ich Dir, mein Gott, die Selle von Hans-Dieter."

Lieppman, who was fluent in German, heard her pray to her God for someone's soul, not his recovery. He peered into the serene chapel and realized that she knew he was already dead, this Hans-Dieter for whom she prayed, and who apparently was her husband. He dared intrude into the intimacy of her plea. "Frau Doktor Krämer?" he inquired.

Erika Kramer turned her head slowly, looking over her shoulder. "Ja, bitte? Oh, you are the doctor," she said, switching to English. "You have come to tell me." She got up from her knees very slowly. At that moment the only thing she was thinking of was her prayer: ". . . and in Thy hand I give to Thee, my God, the soul of Hans-Dieter."

"May we speak out here, doctor?" Lieppman spoke quietly, as if not wanting to disturb what sanctity there could be in a small room of stained glass and prayers and tears.

Erika came out to the lobby. She saw the President and nodded politely. Then she held her chin high and looked at the physicians in their wrinkled clothing and somber faces. She took out from her small fist a piece of paper, unfolded it, and showed it to Lieppman.

"This is the precise time in which my husband's noble spirit left his body, doctor," she said evenly. "I know you did everything possible, even after his death, which was over an hour ago. For that, you have my heartfelt thanks."

The two physicians looked at the time written on the paper. They looked at each other. Lieppman nodded, and Morrell said, "That appears to be correct."

"Believe me, doctor, it is," Erika said. "When two hearts are as one for so long, it is clear to one when the other stops beating. Please allow me to spare you any further words, as they are unnecessary." She turned to Jensen. "Now, with your permission, Mr. President, Baruch, I will take my leave."

She started down the hall. Jensen hesitated, then went after her. Ben-David followed. "Erika, please," Jensen said, unsure of himself. "I—I want you to know . . ." He paused, searching for the words as she stared at him. "I want you to know that I'm here—alive—because of Peter. The bullet—it was meant for me. He stepped in front—"

"Obviously, Mr. President, he felt that your life was more important than his," she said without emotion.

Jensen looked down at the floor. "I can't be the judge of that," he said. He looked up at her. "You know, Erika, Peter and I had something of a rift in our relations. That was repaired today. We mended our fences. He helped me a great deal, much more than you'll ever know." He fought back tears but his voice betrayed his feelings. "We were going to do so much together—great things."

"It's possible, then," she said, "that my husband left those great things to you, Mr. President. The peace treaty was his greatest dream; the 'new wave,' of which he undoubtedly spoke to you, was his greatest fear. I know that if he died with the knowledge that those things were left in your powerful hands, then he died a happy man."

"I gave him my solemn promise, Erika," Simon Jensen said with force.

Ben-David added solemnly, "I did too, Erika."

Erika looked at them and nodded. "Well, good-bye then." She blinked several times, her head still erect. Then tears came to her eyes. Jensen held out a hand as if to steady her, to offer his sympathy, to share her pain.

But she stepped back from his gesture. "Don't misunderstand these tears, Mr. President," she said with a trace of a smile, a proud smile. "They are tears not of sorrow but of joy. My husband died as he lived—courageously and unselfishly. The knowledge that I will soon be with him, God willing, brings on these tears of happiness." She smiled without rancor and left.

TRANSYLVANIA

ONE MONTH LATER

Erika Schuler von Bergdorf looked out the window of the castle. The morning sun was the cool yellow of a looming early winter in the mountains. A sudden breeze toyed with the gold and purple leaves on the courtyard cobblestones below. Birch and ash trees stood guard over what was once Schloss Falkenhorst. It was now the Hotél Populár România, a favorite among the elite of the Rumanian proletariat.

She had signed the register the night before, using her full name, Erika, Baronin von Bergdorf, even though she knew that it would mean nothing to anyone but her. She was addressed as Frau Bergdorf.

Erika reserved a small suite for "an indefinite period," paying a month's rent in advance, delighting the management. She hoped a month would be long enough. The pain was worsening day by day. She had plenty of narcotics with which to dull the pain. But not, she hoped, the memories.

She dressed and took a pill, hoping it would enable her to keep her breakfast down during the climb.

She picked up the flight bag containing the box and went down to the almost-deserted dining room. The snows came early in the Carpathians, she remembered, and few tourists came during the cold. That pleased her; she would not have to engage in small talk with curious or bored travelers, and she would have the place practically to herself, to explore, to seek and perhaps find a little corner of her youth in the time she had left. She admonished herself not to be too sentimental about the changes, the missing articles, the carpets, the tapestries that could fill a museum . . . the vanished loved ones . . . the vanished loves.

She sighed deeply and smiled at the girl who brought the standard fare of boiled egg, rolls, and coffee.

She finished breakfast and picked up the bag. As she left, she peeked into the vast living room. The huge Bechstein was still there! A faded Manila mantle graced its lid, an incongruous souvenir from the past. She lifted the cover and touched the yellowed ivory. An old friend. A lump formed in her throat. An old friend, a mute witness to *his* fingers . . . to *his* love that night, aeons ago.

She walked along the gravel paths—she saw that some roses were still there—and out a side gate on her way up the mountain, the Falkenberg.

She followed a path overgrown with weeds that were once flowers, slowly up the incline, pausing to catch her breath as the pain dug at her. The willowy trees whispered their greetings, and she felt better. She tired easily. She sat down on a patch of grass with the bag in her lap and reached into her jacket, pulling out a bottle of capsules. She swallowed one and lay back.

As she rested she heard the sound of the cold wind, and she thought of the funeral—his body in an open casket under the rotunda of the Capitol. A hero's funeral, with honor guards, as the President had insisted. The Requiem Mass at the cathedral. She hadn't wanted it, but Jensen had insisted on that, too. The ride in the presidential limousine with him, telling her that the Arab-Israeli peace treaty was now a reality. President Jensen had informed her before she left for Europe that he had worked out the ways of dealing with the "new wave." He had changed, she knew, and it was Hans-Dieter who somehow was responsible for the change, she further knew.

She struggled up with the bag, making the top of Falkenberg on her next try. She looked around, panting for breath. So much of the forest was gone to the more practical Communist uses for the trees. So much had changed. But somewhere, out there—beyond the forest—a little bit was left of that life she knew and loved. Now she would be sure if it.

She opened the bag and removed the wooden box. Inside was another box, one made of aluminum. She handled it carefully, lovingly, as if unwrapping a child from its blanket. She removed the cover and turned it upside down on the grassless mountaintop. The wind that was perpetual on the heights seemed to stop for a few moments, as if inspecting the voyager. Then, in an impetuous gust, it carried the ashes away, sailing, rushing toward other mountains, other hills, to settle sometime—it didn't know when—in the soft peace of the valleys and the dales, over the land that gave birth to him. She watched her husband's last journey in fascination and took a deep breath, suddenly without pain.

Hans-Dieter, Freiherr von Bergdorf, was home.

EPILOGUE

In Jerusalem there is a gentle wooded slope on Mount Herzel, that place where soldiers sleep, not far from Yad Vashem, that place where Jewish martyrs are remembered. On that slope there stands a slab of granite with words carved in gold on its black surface. The words pronounce for all humanity to hear:

Baron Hans-Dieter v. Bergdorf
Known to the World as Peter Kramer
Nobel Laureate—Peace
"And inscribe his name, O Lord,
in the Book of Life,
for he is a Righteous Gentile
and a Friend of Man."

MORE SUSPENSE/THRILLERS FROM BART

☐ 017-8 CODENAME: NEEDLEPOINT by Robert Marsh $3.95
                                          Canada $4.95
☐ 022-4 THE FINAL FOUR by Roy H. Parker $3.95
Canada $4.95
☐ 014-3 THE JOSHUA FACTOR by Donald D. Clayton $3.95
                                          Canada $4.95
☐ 011-9 PROPHET OF TERROR by G. Lee Tippin $3.95
                                          Canada $4.95
☐ 005-4 THE VOICE by Colm Connolly $3.50
                                          Canada $4.50
☐ 047-X THE HONOR O PETER KRAMER by Augusto $3.95
         Ferrera   Canada $4.95

Buy them at your local bookstore or use this handy coupon:
Clip and mail this page with your order

BART BOOKS
Dept. MO
155 E. 34th Street, 12E
New York, NY 10016

Please send me the book(s) I have checked above. I am enclosing
$_____ (please add $1.00 for the first book and 50¢ for each
additional book to cover postage and handling). Send check or money
order only—no cash or C.O.D.'s.

Mr./Mrs./Ms _____
Address _____
City _____ State/Zip _____
Please allow six weeks for delivery. Prices subject to change without
notice.

MORE SCIENCE FICTION FROM BART

☐ 008-9 BLACK IN TIME by John Jakes $2.95
                                              Canada $3.95
☐ 003-8 MENTION MY NAME IN ATLANTIS by $2.95
          John Jakes   Canada $3.95
☐ 012-7 THE WORLD JONES MADE by Philip K. Dick $2.95
                                              Canada $3.95
☐ 016-X BART SCIENCE FICTION TRIPLET #1 by $3.50
          Isaac Asimov, Gregory Benford,   Canada $4.50
          Poul Anderson
☐ 032-1 BRING THE JUBILEE by Ward Moore $3.50
                                              Canada $3.95
☐ 037-2 DRAGONS OF LIGHT edited by Orson $3.95
          Scott Card   Canada $4.95
☐ 033-X DRAGONS OF DARKNESS edited by Orson $3.95
          Scott Card   Canada $4.95
☐ 046-1 THE DEVIL IS DEAD by R.A. Lafferty $3.50
                                              Canada $4.50
☐ 048-8 FOURTH MANSIONS by R.A. Lafferty $3.50
                                              Canada $4.50
☐ 057-7 MISSING MAN by Katherine MacLean $3.50
                                              Canada $4.50

Buy them at your local bookstore or use this handy coupon:
Clip and mail this page with your order

BART BOOKS
Dept. MO
155 E. 34th Street, 12E
New York, NY 10016

Please send me the book(s) I have checked above. I am enclosing
$_____ (please add $1.00 for the first book and 50¢ for each
additional book to cover postage and handling). Send check or money
order only—no cash or C.O.D.'s.

Mr./Mrs./Ms _____
Address _____
City _____ State/Zip _____
Please allow six weeks for delivery. Prices subject to change without
notice.